Camp Club Girls
Kate

4-in-1 Mystery Collection

Camp Club Girls
Kate

Janice Thompson

BARBOUR BOOKS
An Imprint of Barbour Publishing, Inc.

Published by Barbour Books, an imprint of Barbour Publishing, Inc.,
1810 Barbour Drive, Uhrichsville, Ohio 44683, www.barbourbooks.com

Our mission is to inspire the world with the life-changing message of the Bible.

Member of the
Evangelical Christian
Publishers Association

Printed in the United States of America.
06411 0219 BP

Camp Club Girls:
Kate's Philadelphia Frenzy

Calling All Supersleuths!

Cr-r-rack! The Philadelphia Phillies baseball player hit the ball with his bat and the noise split the air in the stadium. The dirty white orb soared over the field at lightning speed, heading right for the stands. Kate Oliver watched it, her heart thumping wildly as it sailed in her direction.

All around her the fans hollered, "Catch it, catch it!" at the top of their lungs.

Catch it?

"Oh no! You don't understand! I don't know *anything* about baseball!" Kate murmured. The girl in front of her ducked, and Kate stuck her hand up in the air, knowing she couldn't possibly catch a baseball, especially not one moving this fast! She started sweating as it flew closer, closer, closer!

With a *ka-thump*, it smacked against her open palm. "Owie!" Man, did it hurt! She looked down at the ball, shocked. Shaking like a leaf, Kate whispered, "I did it! I really did it! I caught the ball!"

All around her the fans cheered. The players on the field clapped their hands as they looked her way. Kate stood up, held the ball in the air, and bowed as the stadium roared, "Go, Kate! Go, Kate! Go, Kate!"

Then—quite suddenly—she woke up.

"What a dream!" Kate said with a groan. "I couldn't catch a baseball if someone paid me a million dollars!"

She trembled as she thought about the ball flying toward her. Why would she dream about baseball when she'd never even been to a game before?

From the corner of the room she heard a strange *ka-thunk, ka-thunk, ka-thunk.* Odd. The same sound as in the dream. Kate squinted her eyes in the summer morning light to see Biscuit, her dog, playing with a baseball. He rolled it with his nose across the hardwood floor until it hit the wall. Then he grabbed it in his mouth and began to chew on it. A few seconds later, he rolled it across the floor till it hit the wall once again. *Ka-thunk!*

"Oh no!" Kate jumped out of bed and grabbed the gooey, chewed-up ball. "Not the ball Andrew's dad signed for me!"

Biscuit whimpered and tucked his tail between his legs. "Go ahead and apologize, you nutty dog!" Kate said. "It won't do you any good. This ball is worth a lot of money!" She held up the slobbery ball and sighed as she saw the chew marks. "Well, it *was* worth a lot of money."

Clutching the ball, she suddenly realized why she must've dreamed about baseball. *Oh, that's right! I have a mystery to solve. . .a very important one!* But she couldn't do it alone. No, she needed help from one of the Camp Club Girls!

Kate put on her glasses then tapped a button on the phone beside her bed and said, "Sydney."

The phone automatically dialed the number and Kate heard it ring. "Answer the phone, Sydney! C'mon, answer. . .please!" she coaxed.

"H–hello?"

"Sydney!" Kate squealed. "This is Kate. I'm *so* glad you're awake."

"Awake?" Sydney sounded groggy. She groaned and said, "Kate, it's seven in the morning. . .on a *Saturday*. I'm *not* awake yet. Can you call back later?"

"No, please don't hang up! I need you," Kate said. "It's really important."

The tone of Sydney's voice changed. "What's happened? Are you hurt? Is it one of the other girls? Who's in trouble? What's happened?"

Kate couldn't help but laugh. "Nothing's happened to me or any of the other Camp Club Girls. We're all fine. But something's going on here in Philly—something really big—and I need your help. I sent you an email a couple of days ago, but you didn't answer. Didn't you get it?"

"I've been at sports camp, remember?" Sydney said. "I sent you a text message last week."

"Oh yeah. I forgot. Sorry." Kate started to explain why she called, but just then Biscuit came to the edge of the bed and started whimpering. *Ar-ooo! Ar-ooo!*

Kate groaned. "Hang on, Sydney. Biscuit won't stop crying till I put him on the bed. He's so spoiled."

"Okay." Sydney yawned loudly. "But you're the one who spoils him. You always have. . .ever since that first day when we found him at camp."

"I know, I know. I can't help myself." Kate reached down and lifted Biscuit—The Wonder Dog—onto the bed, and he gave her face a couple of slobbery kisses. "Eew, stinky breath! Gross!"

Not that she really minded. She'd loved him from that first day when the Camp Club Girls found him on the golf course. Slobbery kisses or not! Chewed-up baseballs or not!

He gave her one more kiss and almost knocked off her glasses. She pushed them back up with her index finger and turned to the dog using her sternest voice. "Down, boy!" He rolled over onto his back, ready for a tummy rub. "No, silly. I'll do that later, if you let me talk on the phone!"

He finally curled up at her side and she went back to talking to Sydney. "Are you still there?"

"Yes, but what were you saying?" Sydney asked with another yawn. " 'Cause if this can wait, I want to go back to sleep. I'm tired. They really worked us out at sports camp. We ran four miles every morning and played team sports for the rest of the day. Every muscle in my body hurts."

"I'm sorry, but please don't hang up yet." Kate didn't mean to sound so firm, but she couldn't help it. "That's why I'm calling you, because you're the biggest sports nut in the Camp Club Girls."

"Hey, are you calling me *big*?" Sydney pretended to sound offended.

"No, silly."

"You're calling me a *nut*?"

"No." Kate laughed. "I meant sports *fan*. I need a friend who knows something about baseball."

"Well, why didn't you say so? I *love* baseball." Sydney, now sounding completely awake, began to talk about some of her favorite players and some of her all-time favorite games. None of it made a lick of sense to Kate, who cared nothing about baseball or any other sport.

Kate didn't want to interrupt her, but she had no choice. "Sydney, I'm sure those people are all great, but I need to tell you about something big that's happening here in Philadelphia."

"What?"

"Do you know Tony Smith? The Phillies shortstop?"

"Are you kidding? Of course!" Sydney squealed. "Who doesn't? Do you know how many awards that guy has won? He's a great player. There's such a cool story about how he came to play for the Phillies. He's a free agent, you know. I read all about it online a few months ago."

"Yes, but have you read anything in the past couple days?" Kate asked. " 'Cause now people on the web are posting stories, saying he's not happy playing for the Phillies. They're calling him all sorts of names and saying he wants to play for another team."

"No way." Sydney gasped. "That's too bad. I thought he liked Philadelphia. I guess I need to catch up on my reading."

"No, that's just it. He *does* like it here." Kate sighed. "Look, I don't really know that much about baseball. Or basketball. Or football. Or any kind of sports, really. But Tony's son, Andrew, is my friend. He says the stories aren't true, that someone started rumors just to hurt his dad."

"Are you serious?" Sydney's voice grew more excited. "Wait. . .you know the son of a pro baseball player? Can you get his father's autograph? Tell him you have a friend in DC who wants a signed poster. If he says no, tell him I ran track and field in the Junior Olympics. That should do it. He can autograph it to Sydney Lincoln, the future Olympian."

"Slow down, slow down!" Kate laughed. "We can talk about autographs later. You're not letting me finish the story. Andrew says someone's out to get his dad by putting lies on the web. They're making Tony look really bad. Some of the players and fans are mad at him over something that's not even true. So Andrew asked me to help him figure out who's trying to frame his dad, but I need your help."

"Sydney Lincoln, baseball fan, at your service. Just tell me what to do."

Kate giggled. "Well, you can pray, of course. But there's something else too. Can you come to Philly and stay with me for a couple weeks till we get to the bottom of this? We've got to stop whoever is setting up Mr. Smith."

"Wait, what do you mean? Come to your house? Like, a vacation?"

"Sure, why not? You'll be here for my birthday. It's on the Fourth of July, you know."

"Oh, that's right! I remember. And right in the middle of baseball season. Talk about perfect timing!"

"Better than you think! Andrew and his dad gave me tickets for the Tuesday night game. We're going to sit just behind the dugout."

"No way!"

"Yep." Kate grew more excited as she spoke. "My mom will call your mother today to ask her if you can come. You can take the train from DC."

"To Philadelphia? Woo-hoo!" Sydney squealed. "Ooh! Puh-*leeze* pray my mom says yes. I want to come so much! Can you imagine how exciting this is going to be? Two supersleuths working together. . .again!" After a moment's pause, she asked, "Have you let the other Camp Club Girls know yet?"

"No. We'll email them," Kate responded. "But I need you on-site, Sydney, because you know about baseball. I really don't know anything. To me, those guys in uniform just look like they're running around. The whole thing is kind of, well, boring."

Sydney laughed. "There's more to it than running in circles—and it's not boring—but you can count on me to help you figure things out. And by the end of this, you'll know a lot about baseball, I promise. Maybe I'll even turn you into a fan!"

"Now that would really be something!" Just then Kate heard a knock on her door. She hollered, "Come in!" then whispered, "Hang on a minute, Sydney."

Her mother popped her head in the door. "G'morning, sunshine! Is that Sydney? Did you ask her if she wants to come visit?"

Kate nodded and smiled. "Yes!"

"Great! I'll call her mother after breakfast and see if she'll bring her to Philly on tomorrow's train. How does that sound?"

"Delicious!" Kate shouted. A wonderful aroma filled the room. Kate closed her eyes and drew in a deep breath. "Ooh, speaking of delicious, is that bacon I smell cooking downstairs?"

"Yes. I'm making pancakes and scrambled eggs too." Her mom winked. "Come down as soon as you're done with your call." She closed the door.

"Mmm." Kate turned her attention back to Sydney. "Sydney, I've gotta go. Breakfast calls. But talk to your mom quick, before my mother calls her, okay? That way she's prepared. We want her to have time to think about it. Oh, and Sydney?"

"Yes?"

"Thanks. I *really* need you."

"Aw, you're welcome." Sydney giggled. "Just pray my mom says yes, okay?"

"Okay. I'm praying." Kate hung up the phone and bowed her head to pray. If she ever needed help from above. . .it was now!

Gadgets and Gizmos

After praying, Kate bounded down the stairs with Biscuit on her heels. He yapped, yapped, yapped the whole way! What a silly little dog!

She stopped to look in the large round mirror that hung on the stairway wall. Her shoulder-length blond hair needed to be combed, and her glasses were smudged and crooked again. Oh well. No one cared, right? She couldn't be a supersleuth and have perfect hair at the same time, could she? Oh, but if only she could do something about those freckles!

As soon as she got to the bottom floor, Kate ran smack-dab into Robby, the robovac. As always, Biscuit started barking at the funny little vacuum cleaner that kept the floor clean.

Ruff, ruff! Ruff, ruff! Biscuit took several steps backward but never stopped barking.

"Stop it, Biscuit! I've told you a hundred times. . .Robby won't hurt you."

"That's right," her mother called out from the kitchen. "And besides, Robby's doing us a favor, picking up all of the dog hair that Biscuit sheds."

The dog reached out his paw and tried to tap the vacuum cleaner. It turned around and went the other way. Kate giggled. "See? You'll never be friends if you keep hurting his feelings!"

She went into the kitchen and practically drooled when she saw the yummy food. Bacon sizzled on the stove and a skillet filled with fluffy yellow eggs looked delicious. To the side of the stove she saw a big stack of pancakes. And the table was set with their nicest dishes, the ones mom only used on very special occasions. *Something big must be happening.* Kate the supersleuth would find out what it was. . .pronto!

"Mom, what's up?"

"Your dad got a patent for one of his projects," her mother said with a smile. "Remember that robotic security system he's been working on in the basement?"

"SWAT-bot?" Kate's eyes widened. "The little robot with the police uniform? Really? That's so cool!"

"Yes, so we're celebrating in style." Her mom lowered her voice. "Be sure to tell him how proud you are, okay, honey?"

"Oh, I am proud!" Kate wanted to be just like her dad when she grew up.

"Good girl." Her mother smiled. "After breakfast I'll call Sydney's mom. I know how much you need your friend's help right now."

"I really do, Mom. She knows everything there is to know about baseball. And I think she and Andrew will be good friends."

"Andrew's a great kid," her mother said. "And I'm so happy the Smiths have been coming to church. I've enjoyed getting to know his mom."

"And Andrew loves it too," Kate said. "But he's been so upset over this thing with his dad that I'm afraid he'll stop coming. Some of the kids in our class at church are saying mean things. They think his dad's a traitor to the team, and Andrew's really upset. That's why I want to help him."

"That's my girl," Kate's dad said, entering the room. "Always helping others."

Kate rushed to her father and hugged him. "G'morning, Dad!"

"Good morning, pumpkin. What's this about Andrew's feelings getting hurt?"

"People are spreading untrue stories about his dad," she explained.

"Ah. So the rumor mill is at work?"

"Rumor mill?" Kate asked. "What's that?"

"Oh, it's just an expression," he explained. "When lots of people are talking about someone behind his back, it's called a rumor mill."

"The Bible is pretty clear about gossiping," Kate's mother said as she put the food on the table. "The Lord doesn't like it. . .at all! People get hurt once the rumor mill gets going, just like Andrew and his dad. And his mom too."

Kate sighed. "I want to help make them feel better."

"That's my girl." Her father kissed her on the forehead and then looked around. "Where's Dex?"

"I thought I heard him moving around in his room earlier." Kate's mother looked around.

"I'll bet he's still asleep," Kate said. Her little brother often slept in late on Saturdays.

"No, I'm not."

They all turned as they heard his voice. Dexter entered the room in his pajamas with his hair sticking up all over his head. Kate couldn't help but laugh at the funny blond spikes. He looked like a martian.

Dex sat down and their father prayed over the food. Kate loved to hear her father pray. It always made her feel so good inside.

As they all ate yummy warm pancakes drizzled with maple syrup, he started talking about SWAT-bot.

"I'm so excited about the new patent," Kate's dad said with a grin. "This will open so many doors for my inventions. And SWAT-bot will be featured in a prominent scientific magazine too. That's quite an honor."

"I'm so proud of you, Dad," Kate said when he finished. "This is the neatest thing that's happened to our family in ages!"

"It is pretty cool," he admitted.

"Will you be on the news?" she asked.

"Oh, I don't think so, honey. Getting a patent isn't like being a big sports star or something."

"Well, it should be!" She paused and then said, "Andrew's dad is famous, and now my dad is too!" She stuffed more pancakes into her mouth, adding a quiet, "Mmm!"

Her father laughed. "Well, I don't know about being famous. I'd just as soon *not* be! There's a lot of pressure on people like Tony Smith to perform well. Not a lot of people even know what I do, so if I make a mistake, people are less likely to notice."

"Speaking of sports, is it still okay if Sydney and I go to the game with Andrew and his mom on Tuesday night?" Kate asked.

"I think so," her mother said. "I'll talk to Andrew's mother and make sure she's comfortable taking two preteen girls. If she's fine with it, I'm fine with it."

"Cool! Andrew's whole family is going to love Sydney. She knows everything about baseball. I know nothing." Kate couldn't help but sigh. "But maybe I'll learn something while I'm there."

"I suppose I should have taught you more about sports," her father said, shaking his head. "Maybe I should've taken you to a few Phillies games or watched football with you on television. I've just always been more interested in technology. Sorry, kiddo."

"Who needs sports anyway?" Kate giggled. "Seriously, I love the gadgets and gizmos you bring home from work, Dad. You know how crazy I am about electronics. And I don't miss being involved in sports at all. . .honest."

She grinned and took another bite of food.

"Me either, Dad," Dexter agreed, wrinkling his nose. "I'd rather help you build things. Who needs baseballs and footballs and stuff?"

"Well, the apple doesn't fall far from the tree, does it?" Their father winked.

Kate looked at him curiously. *Apple? Tree?*

"He means you kids are just like he is," her mother said. "Like father, like daughter." Dexter frowned and their mother added, "And like father, like son!"

Kate laughed and asked her mother for another pancake. With so much work to do, she needed food to keep up her strength! Besides, the pancakes were terrific!

After breakfast, Kate pleaded, "Can you call Sydney's mom and ask if she can come? Now? Now, Mom?"

"All right, all right." Her mother rose from the table and grabbed her cell phone. "What's the number, again?"

Sydney jotted down her friend's telephone number on a napkin.

"Here you go, Mom. And please, please, please do your best convincing job! I really hope her mom says yes!"

Dexter headed off to play with a tiny electronic car, and minutes later, Kate's mother was talking with Sydney's mom on the phone. Kate could tell that Mrs. Lincoln liked the idea by the smile on her mom's face.

Kate hated to interrupt, but she had to know! "Can she come?" she whispered.

Her mother nodded and winked at her.

Kate squealed. "Tell her 'Thank you! Thank you!' " She jumped up and down; then she waited until her mother and Mrs. Lincoln worked out the details. After they ended the call, she asked, "When is Sydney coming?"

"Tomorrow afternoon. We'll pick her up at four o'clock at the train station. Now, before she gets here, you need to get upstairs and pick up that messy room, young lady. You can't have a guest with all of that clutter everywhere."

"Okay."

Kate went running up the stairs with Biscuit following behind. She looked at her messy room and sighed. "Where should I start?" She didn't mean to be a slob, but with so many things to keep up with, how could she be tidy?

Kate spent a few minutes tidying up. Then she got distracted, looking at the hope chest at the foot of her bed. It had belonged to her grandmother, and Kate stored her gadgets and gizmos in it. Her dad had carved the words KATE'S GADGETS into the lid. She ran her finger along the words and smiled. How fun to have a special place to keep all of her goodies!

She opened the lid and glanced inside, smiling when she saw the familiar items. Kate picked up the tiny black digital recorder, checking to make sure the batteries were good. She snapped it on and recorded a few words, then said, "Perfect!"

Next she found her teensy-tiny digital camera. She checked the memory card to make sure she had plenty of room for more pictures. Looked like she was in good shape there too! "Great!"

Kate picked up something that looked like an ink pen. It was really a text reader. You could run it along words in a book and it would record them. She tested it by running it along the words in her Bible. Right away it recorded one of her favorite verses, Philippians 4:13: *I can do all things through Christ which strengtheneth me.* "Cool."

Thanks, Lord! I really needed that reminder. You're the One in charge of this case anyway, and I know You already have all the answers!

Next Kate reached for her cell phone. It would certainly come in handy over the next couple of weeks.

So would the next gadget she pulled out. Kate stared at the smartwatch her father had given her just a few days earlier. She could hardly believe it was possible to check her email or browse the web on this smartwatch, but she had already tried it out and knew it worked! How exciting!

Finally, Kate pulled out a pair of mirrored sunglasses, smiling as she put them on. "Yep. You really can see what's going on behind you when you're wearing these. Cool."

She spent the next half hour organizing the chest. Once she had everything in place, she closed the lid tightly, thinking about all of the treasures her dad had given her over the past few years. They would all come in handy after Sydney arrived and they got to work. In the meantime, she needed to get to work cleaning! One of her favorite Camp Club Girls would be here soon. What exciting adventures were ahead!

Inspector Gadet

"Hurry, hurry, hurry!" Kate bounced up and down, waiting for Sydney's train to arrive from DC. She glanced at the clock: 4:05. "They're late, Mom!"

"Only by a couple of minutes," her mother said. "Be patient, Kate!"

"But we have work to do!"

Minutes later, Kate heard a familiar voice. She looked up as Sydney rushed her way. Dozens of dark braids bounced around Sydney's head as she ran. Man! Was she ever fast!

Kate let out a squeal. "Oh, you're taller than last time!"

"Yes. I've grown two inches this year," Sydney announced, brushing a braid out of her face. She flashed a broad smile and her white teeth looked even whiter against her beautiful dark skin. "What about you?"

Kate sighed and slumped her shoulders. "No. Sometimes I wonder if I'm ever going to grow."

"It'll happen." Sydney laughed. "And if it makes you feel any better, your freckles have grown since the last time I saw you."

Kate groaned. "They're always like this in the summertime. Wish they would just disappear!" She frowned just thinking about it. Why couldn't she be normal. . .like the other Camp Club Girls? Why did she have to be so. . .different?

"Aw, I think you look great!" Sydney said, interrupting her thoughts.

"Thanks." Maybe different wasn't so bad after all.

Just then a beautiful woman who looked a lot like Sydney rounded the corner, gasping for breath. "Sydney, you're too fast for me! I can't keep up!"

"Sorry, Mom!" Sydney giggled. "I've been running track for so long, I sometimes forget others aren't as fast."

"You must be Mrs. Lincoln!" Kate rushed to the woman and surprised her with a big hug. "Thank you, thank you for letting Sydney come! I'm so excited!"

"Well, you're welcome. And. . .I can tell you're excited!"

"When do you have to catch the train back to DC?" Kate's mother asked Mrs. Lincoln. "Do you have time to come to our house for dinner?"

"No, I'm afraid I have to get right back. The train returns in twenty minutes, in fact. But that's really for the best. I have to be at work in the morning."

"We're so grateful you've brought Sydney to stay with us," Kate's mother said. "We'll be in touch. And you have my number if you need anything."

"Thank you so much for inviting her. I'm sure she's going to have the time of her life!"

"I always have fun with Kate!" Sydney said.

Sydney and her mother said their goodbyes, and then Mrs. Lincoln headed off on her way to catch the train back to DC.

The girls talked all the way back to the house. In fact, they arrived home in no time at all. Kate's mother fixed big, thick, juicy cheeseburgers and crispy fries for dinner—Kate's favorite. She ate not just one cheeseburger, but two. And she loaded up on fries, even asking for seconds.

"You sure can pack away a lot of food for such a tiny thing," Sydney said with a smile.

Kate shrugged. "I love burgers and fries."

"I'm trying to eat healthier," Sydney explained. "Especially since I'm involved in so many sports. Got to stay in tip-top shape."

"Hmm." Kate didn't comment. Maybe some people were meant to be in tip-top shape and others were not.

Biscuit began to whimper at her feet. She tore off a teensy-tiny piece of her hamburger and slipped it under the table.

"I saw that," her mother said. "Biscuit doesn't need table scraps. He has his own food."

"I know. Sorry," Kate said.

"Remember that first day we found Biscuit. . .at camp?" Sydney asked.

"How could I forget? He was so hungry—and so scraggly looking." Kate sighed. "I guess that's why I spoil him now. He had such a hard life before coming to live here."

"There's no harm in a little spoiling," her mother said with a wink. "Just not too much. Oh, and by the way, would you like to know what we're having for dessert?" When the girls nodded, she said, "Ice cream sundaes."

"Woo-hoo!" Kate added an extra scoop of ice cream to hers and poured on extra syrup. Then she put a huge dollop of whipped cream on top. It tasted like heaven! When she finished, she thought about asking for another sundae but decided not to. The girls would have plenty of time to eat later. Right now, they had a case to solve!

After dessert, Andrew stopped by. He took one look at Sydney and grinned with that crooked grin of his and said, "Wow, you're taller than I am."

"Yeah, maybe a little." Sydney shrugged. "But how old are you?" She gave him a curious look. "I'll bet I'm older."

"I'm eleven." He looked a little embarrassed.

"Well, I'm thirteen," Sydney explained. "So that explains it. But I am tall, even for my age." She sighed. "To be honest, I don't like being the tallest in my class. When I was younger I always had to stand in the back row in class pictures. I just wanted to be the little shrimp in the class like Kate here."

"Hey!" Kate pretended to be upset. "I'm no shrimp. Why do you keep talking about how short I am?"

"You're not short," her mother called out from the kitchen. "You're petite. Like me. That's a good thing."

"Yeah, I'm petite. That's a good thing," Kate repeated.

They all laughed, but inside she wondered if she would ever grow.

Andrew turned to Sydney with his arms crossed at his chest. "So Kate tells me you're a baseball fan. Have you ever played?"

"Yep. Played softball last year. And I'm a golf fan, and a football fan, and a track and field fan." Sydney grinned. "I love sports. Can you tell?"

"I can. And I love sports too. Usually." A worried look came into Andrew's eyes. "Did Kate tell you about what's going on with my dad? All the terrible things people are saying?"

"Yes, and that really stinks! I think your dad is a great player, and he obviously loves his team. So we need to get busy trying to figure out who's trying to frame him."

"Yeah, but I don't know how we're going to do that. I don't even know where to start. I've never solved a crime before. Or cracked a case. Or whatever you call it."

"Just leave it to the Camp Club Girls!" Sydney said. "We're supersleuths."

"Supersleuths?" Andrew looked confused.

"Sure." Kate giggled. "Like Nancy Drew."

"Nancy *who*?" he asked, his brow wrinkling in confusion.

"Nancy *Drew*. . .oh, never mind." Kate slapped herself on the forehead. "You just have to trust us. We've solved a mystery or two before this one. That's why I called Sydney for her help."

"You're in good hands, in other words," Sydney said with a smile. She turned to Kate with a sparkle in her eye. "Kate, did you ever show Andrew all of your crime-solving gadgets?"

"Ooh! Good idea," Kate said.

"I've heard her talk about them, but I've never seen them," Andrew said.

"My dad teaches robotics at Penn State, and he's always bringing home the coolest stuff," Kate explained. "You wouldn't believe it. And here's the best part—there's always something new coming out, so I get his old stuff. Only, it's not old to me. It's really neat. And I've learned so much. I'm going to start inventing things like my dad. . .soon. We're already working on a top secret project."

She clamped her hand over her mouth, realizing she'd said too much. It wouldn't be top secret if she told people.

"Trust me when I say she's got *so* many amazing electronics," Sydney said. "When we were at camp, she showed us things we'd never seen before."

"Oh, I have a lot more stuff since Discovery Lake Camp," Kate explained. "So hang on. I'll be right back." She ran upstairs and grabbed several items out of her gadget chest. *Ooh, Andrew's going to love all of this!*

She came back downstairs a few minutes later, nearly dropping the armload of stuff. She could hardly wait to show them her gadgets.

"Wow." Andrew looked at her arms with wide eyes. "That's a lot!"

"My dad is always bringing home more. You think this is a lot—one day I'll take you down to his workroom in the basement and show you all the good stuff. It's like an electronics store down there, only better." She described several of the neatest things her dad had worked on. By the time she finished, Andrew and Sydney were staring at her with their mouths open.

"Your dad is amazing!" Sydney said.

"You are too." Andrew still looked surprised by all of the things in her arms.

She put the items on the dining room table and they gathered around. One by one, she told Andrew about her goodies.

"This is a great digital recorder. It's different from most of the ones you can buy in stores because it's so tiny. And here's a pen that actually records text."

"Records text?" Andrew looked shocked.

"Yes. Watch." She ran it along the headline in the newspaper and it recorded the words TROUBLE IN THE PHILLIES CAMP.

"Hmm. Maybe we'd better save that one for later." She paused, examining the pile of electronics.

She reached for the slim, shiny smartphone. "I ended up with dad's cell phone when he got his new one. It has a GPS navigational system on it. And it's got a 12-megapixel camera and can take amazing videos. Best of all, the cell phone is linked to our family's laptop, so I can send and receive files. Everything is connected. It's way better than anything else out on the market right now. My dad showed me how to do all of that. And wait till you see this watch." She pulled it out and Sydney and Andrew looked at it with curious expressions.

"I can't believe you're only eleven." Sydney shook her head. "You're just so. . .smart! You could be a professor or something. Or a scientist, even. Have you ever thought about that?"

"Sure, I think about it all the time," she said. "But you really don't need to build my ego! My little brother, Dexter, is almost nine and he already knows how to do most of this too." Kate shrugged as she thought about it. "I guess our parents just taught us lots of different stuff from other kids. We're kind of like that family in *Honey, I Shrunk the Kids*. Only, of course, our dad never shrunk us or anything like that. But he does have some cool inventions, just like the man in the movie."

"Well, I think your whole family is cool." Sydney picked up the cell phone and tossed it from one hand to another, like a baseball. After a couple of nervous looks from Kate, she put it back down. "I know!" Sydney squealed. "I'm going to start calling you Inspector Gadget because of all these gadgets and gizmos you own. I can't wait to tell the other girls."

"Inspector Gadget?" Kate laughed. "That's a good one."

"It fits you," Andrew said, looking at the digital recorder.

"Look at this," Kate said, holding up a tiny penlike device. "It's a translator, shaped like an ink pen."

"A translator?" Sydney asked. "What would you need that for?"

"Well, say you're in a situation where you find a clue, but it's written in a different language," Kate explained. "All you do is run the pen along the words, and then it translates the words into English so you can understand them."

"Wow, I guess that might come in handy," Sydney said.

"I came up with this one myself," she said, holding up a dog collar.

"Just looks like a regular collar," Sydney said. "Is it Biscuit's?"

"Yes," Kate explained, "but it's not an ordinary collar. It has a tiny built-in microphone that transmits to this receiver." She held up the tiny black receiver and smiled. "So let's say I send Biscuit over to a suspect and I want to hear something he or she is saying. I can hear every word through the microphone."

"That's pretty impressive," Andrew said. "So you girls use Biscuit to help you solve your cases too?"

"Sometimes," Kate said. "Like that first mystery we solved at Discovery Lake Camp. He was a big help to us back then!"

"What else do you have?" Sydney asked, leaning down to look at the items.

"Hmm." Kate glanced at each one, finally pulling out a tiny metal clip. "This is a money clip one of my dad's students came up with."

"A money clip?" Andrew asked. "I think my dad has one of those. It just holds the dollar bills together so they don't get lost, right?"

"That's not all this one does," Kate said. "This one actually keeps track of how much money it's holding. It scans the bills. So let's say you reach for your wad of cash, wondering if you have enough to pay for a $25 item at the mall. This money clip will flash $27. Or $32. Or $40. Or whatever. You don't have to pull out the money and count it."

"That would save a lot of time, I guess," Andrew said. "And it wouldn't attract people's attention like standing there flashing money would."

"Yep, that's the idea behind most of these gadgets, actually," Kate said. "They just make life a little easier. And they're nifty."

"Nifty?" Sydney and Andrew spoke the word at the same time.

"Cool," Kate explained.

She pulled out a funny-looking pair of shoes. "These are different. One of my dad's students from last semester came up with these shoes with springs in the soles. They help people with joint pain in their knees and ankles. The springs relieve some of the tension as the person walks. Cool, huh?" She put on the shoes and began to walk with a spring in her step. . .literally. "They also make you run faster," she added.

"Ooh, I'd like to have a pair of those," Sydney said. "I run track, you know. Those shoes would make me lightning fast!"

"No doubt!" Kate pulled off the shoes and handed them to her friend. "Try them on. They're too big for me anyway."

Sydney slipped them on her feet. "Ooh, they're perfect! Just like in *Cinderella*."

"If the shoe fits. . . ," Andrew said with a grin.

"Keep them," Kate said with the wave of a hand. "My dad won't care. We have plenty more. And they will make you super-duper fast!"

"Wow!" Sydney stared at her feet. "Thank you so much. I can't wait to run in them!" She looked around at all the gadgets then back at Kate. "I'm amazed by you! I never met anyone who knew so much about. . ." Sydney looked around. "About stuff."

Kate laughed. "Thanks, but it would really help me out a lot right now if I knew more about baseball, not electronics!"

Sydney stood and began to bounce up and down on her springy shoes. With a huge smile, she slung her arm over Kate's shoulder. "Aw, just leave the baseball stuff to me. I'll leave the technical stuff to you. We're gonna make a great team, short stuff!" Sydney said with a chuckle. "Just you wait and see!"

"Well, let's get going, then!" Kate said, feeling her excitement grow. "Let's solve this case!"

CHAPTER 4

The Rumor Box

Kate grew more excited by the minute! The "Who Framed the Phillies Shortstop?" mystery had finally begun! Oh, she could hardly wait to get going!

"So where should we start?" Andrew asked, looking confused. "What do you two supersleuths think? Do you even think it's possible to track down the person who's framing my dad?"

Kate nodded. "Of course! And we'll start by going online and trying to find the source of the rumors. See who started all this stuff about your dad. Maybe getting that information will lead us to another clue, and then another, and then another! Before long, we'll have the case solved!"

"I wish I was as sure as you are." Andrew sighed.

"Well, keep praying," Kate encouraged him. "God already knows who did this, after all. If we pray for wisdom, He will give it to us. That's what the Bible says. So pray for wisdom! That's what we need to figure this out."

"Are you ready to start?" Sydney asked.

"You kids are welcome to use the internet," Kate's mother said, entering the room. "Just don't stay on too long and only use the webcam if I'm close by. You can never be too careful, you know."

"Thanks, Mom." Kate went to the computer. "Andrew, where did you find that one article that upset you so much?" she asked. "I hate to ask you to look at it again, but it's important for us to find that website."

He gave her a blog address and she typed it in. When the web page came up, she scrolled down until she saw the article about his father.

"Look right there," Andrew said. His brow wrinkled and Kate could tell he was upset.

They all leaned toward the monitor and Sydney read aloud: "Phillies fans got a wake-up call today when Tony Smith announced his unhappiness with playing for the team. According to Smith, 'I could have done better than these losers. And I plan to. . .next season when I move to a different town.' "

Sydney gasped. "That's horrible. And it really makes it sound like he said that."

"If I didn't *know* that it was a lie, I'd totally believe it," Kate said. "It sounds so real."

"But he *didn't* say it," Andrew insisted. "And it's not even true. My dad loves playing for the Phillies. Honest! And he loves living in Philadelphia. You should hear him talk about the historic district. And the Franklin Institute. And the Liberty Bell. He thinks this is the best place we've ever lived, and I agree!"

"We're going to get to the bottom of this, Andrew," Sydney promised. "So don't worry about what others are saying." She paused a moment then added, "Maybe that's a lesson God is trying to teach us. Maybe we're supposed to learn how to ignore it when others are talking about us, saying things we don't like. When the rumors get going, we just need to trust God. . .and not worry."

Kate scrolled down a bit more. "Look, here's another article," she said. "They took a picture of your dad looking mad and wrote a bunch of stuff about how he doesn't get along with his teammates. They make him sound like he's a real. . ." She paused then whispered, "Jerk."

"That's not true either." Andrew stood up and began to pace. "My dad is a great guy. And he's so nice to everyone. I don't know why anyone would say that."

"Oh, I know. I know." Kate nodded, hoping to reassure him.

"Man, but he looks really mad," Sydney observed. "I wonder why."

"I don't know." Andrew leaned down near the monitor and looked closely. "Hey, wait a minute! Look at that picture. Something about it doesn't seem right." He pointed. "The bottom part of the face doesn't even look like my dad's. Not at all. The chin is different." Andrew leaned in even closer. "This is *too* weird."

"Hang on a sec." Kate downloaded the photo and enlarged it until it filled the screen. "Ooh! Very sneaky. Check this out! This photo has been altered. It's only visible when the picture is enlarged like this, but you can see that the bottom half of the face is from one photo and the top from another." She stared at it in disbelief. How very strange that someone would take the time to do something like this. But why?

"Well, those are definitely my dad's eyes," Andrew said. "And his nose. So the top half is his face, but not the rest." Andrew made a fist and for a second Kate saw the anger in his eyes. "Why would someone do this to my dad? They would go so far as to forge a photograph? And misquote him? It's not right."

Sydney began to pace the room. "There's something more going on here than we know about. This isn't *just* about someone who doesn't like your dad. There's some reason why they want to see him gone from the team. Some bigger reason."

Andrew's eyes grew wide. "W—what are you thinking?"

"I'm not sure. Jealousy, maybe? Who knows? But someone with computer skills has gone out of his—or her—way to do this. We're dealing with someone very good at altering photographs."

"One of the other players, do you think?" Andrew suggested.

Kate shook her head. "That doesn't make any sense. Why would they do that? Besides, we'd better not assume it's one of the players. My dad says that's how the rumor mill gets started."

"Rumor mill?" Sydney and Andrew said at the same time.

"Gossiping," she explained. "Didn't you guys ever watch that VeggieTales episode when you were kids?"

"'Larry Boy and the Rumor Weed'?" Andrew's eyes widened. "Sure did! I have it memorized!" He burst into the theme song from the show and before long the girls were laughing.

"Well, it's kind of like that," Kate explained. "There's power in our words. Good and bad. So when we speak bad things over people— especially things that aren't true—it can really hurt. That's why it's so important not to gossip."

Sydney nodded. "And besides, there are enough rumors flying around already, so we have to be extra careful. We don't want to start any more. If we're not careful, we could end up blaming the wrong person. Imagine how bad that would be!"

"True, true." Andrew nodded.

"I have an idea!" Kate reached for a tissue from the box on the coffee table. "We need to start a rumor box."

"A rumor box?" Sydney gave her a curious look. "What's that?"

"Well, every time we hear a rumor, we'll stick it in the box and wait. If it's true, we'll pull it out of the box. And if it's not, we'll leave it in the box to remind us that it was just a rumor. That way we've protected someone who was innocent. So either way we win! And so does the person being talked about."

"Great idea," Sydney said. "Let's start by putting those rumors about Tony's teammates in there."

Kate ran into the garage and came back with a shoe box. "What about this? Do you think it will do?"

"Perfect!" Sydney said.

They wrapped the box in some old Mickey Mouse birthday paper and cut a hole in the top. Then Kate wrote on a piece of paper: *"Rumor— Andrew's father doesn't like playing for the Phillies."*

She folded up the paper and put it in the box. "There. We know *that* one's really a rumor, so it's in the box for good."

"Ooh! I have another one!" Sydney said. She grabbed a piece of paper and wrote, *"Kate Oliver is the smartest girl in the world!"* Then she grinned and said, "I made up that rumor myself. Hope it doesn't hurt your feelings, Kate."

"Hurt my feelings?" Kate laughed. "Not at all. And you can put it in the box, but I promise you, it's not true! There are a million zillion people smarter than me!"

"I haven't met any of them yet," Andrew said with a smile. His expression changed right away. "So now what do we do?" he asked, looking confused. "Just finding that blog site doesn't really tell us anything. How will we ever know who created it, or why they said all that stuff about my dad?"

"Hmm." Kate paused to think. "We have to figure out who owns these blogs and who's making these posts. And then we have to pay special attention at the games to look for anything—or anyone—suspicious."

"That's right," Andrew agreed. "There's really only one way to know for sure what's going on at a Phillies game. We need to go to one. So are you girls on for Tuesday night?"

"Am I ever!" Sydney let out a whoop. "This is gonna be the greatest game in the history of mankind. We can do a little crime solving and game watching all at the same time. Talk about a winning combination."

Kate wasn't sure it sounded like so much fun. "I still can't figure out why everyone loves baseball so much." She groaned. "Just a bunch of guys running around a court to score points."

"Court?" Sydney snickered. "You mean *field*?"

"And they're not points, Kate," Andrew said. "They're runs."

"Court, field. Points, runs." She shrugged. "What's the difference?"

Sydney laughed as she looked at Andrew. "Man, oh man! Do we ever have our work cut out for us! Not only do we have to solve a mystery; we have to teach our friend here a little something about baseball."

"Hey now, don't you worry about me," Kate said, giving them a stern look. "If I can figure out how to use a smartwatch, surely I can figure out a little something about a game like baseball. How hard can it be, after all?"

Sydney smiled. "Well, c'mon, then! What are we waiting for! Let's give this girl a crash course in baseball, Andrew."

Sydney began to search online for a baseball site. She finally found one titled EVERYTHING YOU EVER WANTED TO KNOW ABOUT BASEBALL BUT WERE AFRAID TO ASK. "Perfect!" she said, rubbing her hands together. "Now, let's get cracking! We've got a lot to learn, and only two days to learn it."

Kate groaned. In spite of Sydney and Andrew's excitement, she didn't really want to learn a lot about baseball. What was the point?

On the other hand, she did have a mystery to solve. Maybe. . .just maybe. . .she could learn a few things about baseball by Tuesday night. Then she and Sydney could crack this case wide open!

CHAPTER 5

Take Me Out to the Ballgame

On Tuesday evening, Kate arrived at Citizens Bank Park—the stadium where the Phillies played—with Sydney, Andrew, and Andrew's mom. The whole place seemed alive with excitement. Everywhere she looked, people rushed around with smiles on their faces.

Once inside, she looked up at the stadium, amazed at its enormous size! She'd never been inside such a huge place, especially one filled with so many people!

"Wow, this place is so large!" she said. "And it's so high tech!" Her eyes shifted this way and that, trying to take in everything at once, but it was too much.

"I can't believe you've never been here," Mrs. Smith said with a smile. "It's like a second home to us, now that my husband plays for the Phillies."

"I'm just not a big sports fan," Kate admitted. "But maybe it'll grow on me." She couldn't help but think that spending time in this stadium could make a fan out of just about anybody!

"Oh, I guarantee you'll fall in love with the Fightin' Phils in no time!" Mrs. Smith said, nodding. "We all have."

Kate thought about that a moment. Obviously the whole Smith family loved the Phillies. How could anyone say they didn't? Yes, all of this was surely just a big misunderstanding. And she would get to the bottom of it!

Sydney moved faster than everyone else, as always. Kate trudged along behind her, almost getting lost in the mob. She'd never seen so many people together in one place before. And most of them wore Phillies colors: red, white, and blue. She looked down at her orange shirt and pondered the fact that she looked different from everyone else in the crowd. Usually that didn't bother her. Kate never kept up with fashions, anyway. But tonight it suddenly seemed important to blend in.

Hmm. I'll have to do better next time.

Her glasses slipped down her nose and she pushed them back up with a sigh.

They worked their way through the hustle and bustle of the crowd, and then Mrs. Smith led them to their seats about ten rows behind the dugout. "What do you think of these, girls?"

"Oh, they're amazing, Mrs. Smith!" Sydney said. "I can't thank you enough. I can practically hear the players talking from here. And we're so close to the field! Oh, it makes me want to put on my new springy shoes and run out there!"

"Thanks again for inviting us." Kate looked around the stadium in awe. "This place is so cool. Look at all of those scoreboards. And the video screens! This is an electronic wonderland!" *Better than Disney World*, she decided.

Sydney just laughed. "You are so funny, Kate. This is a sports arena, not an electronics store! Enjoy the game!"

"Okay, I'll try." Kate shrugged and settled into her seat. She looked at the little area Mrs. Smith had called the dugout. Interesting. Small. Just big enough to fit the players inside. Kate wondered if they liked being in there. She started to ask Andrew but decided not to. He might make fun of her. Still, it might help solve the case to know what went on in the dugout. Maybe she could ask him about all of that later.

Mrs. Smith went to the concession stand to buy some sodas. Kate had never paid much attention to baseball before. Oh, sure. . .she'd seen a little when flipping channels on the television. And she had tried—really tried—to pay attention to the things that Sydney and Andrew had taught her the other night on the baseball website. But sitting here—listening to the roar of the crowd—was totally different. She could almost feel the energy in the air. And the voices of the crowd. . .wow! She'd never heard so many people talking together at the same time. It was hard to focus for sure.

She looked around at all of the people. Several ate hot dogs or popcorn. Yummy smells filled the air and made her tummy rumble. Mom had fixed an early dinner, but she could hardly stand to smell such great smells and not want more. In the distance, she saw a boy with nachos in his hand. *Yum!* She practically drooled just thinking about them. *Ooh! Look at that little girl over there.* She was nibbling on cotton candy. Where could Kate find some of that?

Just then, several children walked out onto the field. Even from Kate's seat close to the field, they looked pretty small. But why were they on the field? Surely they weren't baseball players. If so, then she really didn't know anything about this sport!

"Ooh, this should be good." Andrew jabbed her with an elbow. "The children's choir from a local school is singing the national anthem. I wonder if they're any good."

"Ah." So *that* explained it! Kate stood with the rest of the crowd and tried to imagine what it must feel like to be out there—looking at so many people. Were the children nervous? Would the players be nervous when the game began? Mr. Smith probably would be, since so many people were upset with him. Andrew said it had affected his game. That wasn't a good sign.

The voices of the children rose in beautiful harmony as they sang, "Oh, say, can you see, by the dawn's early light. . ."

As they continued, Kate pulled out her micro-sized digital camera. She zoomed in on them, looking at each child through the lens. In the middle of the first row, a little girl—shorter than all the others—sang with all of her heart. She had a face full of freckles. Kate liked her right away.

After the children sang, the audience members sat down. The ground below filled with men in uniforms. Several of them spread out and stood on little mats. They wore gloves on their left hands. Well, all but a couple, who wore them on their right hands. One guy stood in the middle of the grass with a ball in his hand and threw it at another guy with a bat. That guy hit it with a loud *smack* and the crowd roared. The ball flew through the air. . .way, way, way off in the distance.

The whole thing was captured on a giant screen that was raised above the outfield of the stadium. For a minute, Kate thought about the men working in the video room. . .wherever that was. What a cool job that would be!

"Wow, did you see that?" Sydney turned toward Kate with excitement in her eyes. "Jackson practically knocked it out of the park!"

"Oh, that's too bad," Kate said, frowning.

"No, that's *good*!" Andrew explained.

"So that's our guy?" Kate asked, pointing down to the field. "Right? The one in the white uniform running around the place mats?"

"Those are bases, Kate. Bases." Mrs. Smith gave her a funny look.

"Ah. Okay." She paused a moment then said, "Well, if he hit it out of the park, why are they making him run around all of those bases?"

Sydney turned to Kate, a stunned look on her face. "No. He has to get home!"

Andrew shook his head. "Just watch the game, Kate!"

She kept watching, but it just didn't make any sense. The little man in the white uniform circled the field below. Some of the men were jumping up and down, shouting. One was even throwing a ball at him. When he finished running, the crowd went wild, celebrating. Sydney, Andrew, and his mother all jumped up from their seats and started shouting.

"Did you see that?" Kate asked as they sat down again.

"What?" Sydney turned to look at her.

"That man. . .the one in the cool blue outfit with the number 14. He tried to hit our guy. He could have hurt him."

"Tried to throw him out, you mean," Sydney said with a nod.

"Out of the *game*?" Kate tried again.

"No." Sydney looked at Kate with a strange expression on her face. "Just *out*."

"Is that good?" Kate asked.

"Good?" Andrew stared at her like she had two heads. "Kate. . .Jackson just hit a homer!"

"A homer? *That's* good, right?" Kate shouted, hoping to be heard above the crowd.

It worked. The man in front of her turned around and stared.

"Oops." She smiled at him and shrugged.

"It's *very* good," Andrew whispered. "The Phillies are going to win this game if they keep playing like this. But can we talk about this later?"

"Sure." Kate sat quietly for a moment while the others watched the game. She reached into her bag and pulled out her tiny digital camera. Zooming in on the field, she snapped a couple of pictures of Andrew's dad as a ball whizzed across the field. He caught it and the crowd went crazy.

"Your husband is such a great player, Mrs. Smith," Sydney said.

"Thank you, honey. We think so."

After a few minutes, Kate couldn't resist talking. "So what's *he* doing?" she asked, pointing to the guy with the black shirt on the field below.

"That's the ump," Sydney responded. "He's officiating."

Kate gasped. Pushing up her glasses with her finger, she opened the camera once again and zoomed in on the ump for a closer look.

"What does that mean?" she asked.

"He's making the call," Sydney replied.

"Who's he calling?" Kate asked, snapping a photo.

"No, he's calling the shots," Andrew explained.

Sydney said, "Don't you remember anything we talked about the other night?"

"A little." Kate sighed. Loudly.

Kate looked around through her camera lens. When she tired of looking at faces in the crowd, she sat twiddling her thumbs, watching numbers light up the electronic board above.

"What does that mean?" she asked, pointing up at them.

Sydney groaned again. "Kate, I'm hungry. Would you please go and get me a hot dog and a drink?" She pulled some money out of her pocket and handed it over.

"Sure!" Kate answered, pleased to have something else to do, especially since it involved food. She looked up at the many, many people in the stadium. "Might take me awhile, though. Hope you don't mind."

"Oh, I don't mind. Take your time." Sydney turned back to the game.

"I'll come with you, Kate," Mrs. Smith said.

"Okay." As they left their seats, Kate noticed a man a few rows down standing with a camera in his hand, snapping pictures. Even from this distance, she could tell it was an expensive camera. *Wow. He must be a real fan.*

Something about the man caused a little shiver to run down her spine. What was it she had told Sydney and Andrew again? *"The Bible says if you pray for wisdom, God will give it to you!"*

At once, she began to pray. If she ever needed wisdom, it was now!

A Face in the Crowd

Kate walked up, up, up the steps, through the maze of cheering fans, as she headed toward the concession stand. Mrs. Smith walked just behind her. All the way, Kate listened to the noise from the crowd. They finally located the snack area. The cashier was watching the game on the screen as Kate paid for Sydney's hot dog and soda. He yelped as the crowd in the stadium shouted in one loud voice.

"Struck him out!" the cashier hollered.

"Wow. I hope it didn't hurt!" Kate said, growing worried. Sounded pretty painful.

Mrs. Smith and the cashier each gave her a funny look. "No, honey," she explained. "He didn't actually *hit* him. Just. . .struck him out."

Kate just shrugged. With people saying so many confusing things, she was really starting to understand just how easily rumors could get started.

With food in hand, she followed Mrs. Smith back into the stadium. Kate managed to trip across nearly every toe in the row as she squeezed back down the crowded aisle toward Sydney and Andrew. They were both seated with their eyes glued to the field. Neither looked up as she sat down.

"Here you go," Kate said as she tried to hand Sydney the hot dog.

"Thanks, I'm not hungry," Sydney responded, eyes glued to the field.

"But I thought you said. . . Oh, never mind." Kate opened the hot dog wrapper and ate it herself. Just as she finished it, music began to play.

"Time for the seventh-inning stretch," Sydney said, standing.

"Seventh-inning stretch? Oh, okay." Kate stretched and let out a yawn. "There. That feels better. This game is making me sleepy anyway."

Andrew rolled his eyes and then laughed. "You're a hoot, Kate Oliver. You know that?"

The game started again. As it continued, Kate tried to pay attention. She really tried. But the whole thing was just so. . .boring. Why did baseball move so slowly? These guys seemed to take forever to get from one place mat to the next. Why didn't they just go all the way at once?

Oh well. There were more exciting things to do, right? She used the zooming feature on her micro-camera to watch the people in the crowd. She wasn't sure what she was looking for. Her gaze stopped on that suspicious-looking man with the camera about three rows below. He wasn't taking pictures anymore. No, this time he had something very small in his hand.

"What is that?" She zoomed in a little better to see. Looked like an MP3 player of some sort. Why would someone bring a music player to a game? Seemed a little odd. Unless he was bored like her, of course. But he looked like someone who cared a lot about the game.

Hmm. Kate sure couldn't tell much from behind him, but something about the man made her uncomfortable.

Just then, the crowd shrieked and the man dropped whatever he was holding. He slipped out of his seat and reached to grab it. A look of relief passed over his face as soon as he held it in his hand again.

"Whatever it is must be pretty important," Kate whispered. She made a mental note to bring her smartwatch next time she came to the game. It would sure come in handy for looking things up—like that MP3 player, for instance. "I wonder what brand it is," she whispered.

"Did you say something?" Sydney looked at her curiously.

"Oh, nothing important." She shrugged and tried to tuck away her curiosity to pay attention to her friend.

"Look," Sydney said, jumping with glee. "It's Tony Smith's turn at bat." She clapped her hands together with a nervous look on her face. "Oh, I hope he hits a homer!"

Kate zoomed in to get a good look, even taking a couple of pictures for good measure. When Tony's first swing missed the ball, the crowd reacted with a loud boo. "Why are they so mean?" Kate asked. It hardly seemed fair. The whole crowd seemed to be against him. Why would they turn on one of their own players like that?

"Maybe he'll hit the next one," Sydney said. "He's a shortstop, but he's also a great hitter. Usually." She began to bite her nails, looking more nervous by the second.

"Shortstop?" Kate looked at her curiously. "I heard you say that before. But what does it mean? What's a shortstop?"

Sydney answered but never took her eyes off of Tony. "A shortstop is the guy who stands between second and third base. Out there," she said, pointing to the field. "That's a really important defensive position in baseball. More balls go to the shortstop than anyone else."

"Wow. So he must be good."

"Yep! He's great!" Sydney said.

Unfortunately, Tony took a swing at the next ball and missed it too.

Sydney groaned, but the crowd's reaction was even worse. This time they got really upset. A fan behind them yelled something mean about Mr. Smith, and Kate turned to give him a "Shame on you" look. He didn't even notice.

"I'm telling you. . .Tony is the best," Sydney insisted. "That's what's so confusing about all of this."

"I think he's just nervous because of the way people are shouting at him," Andrew explained. "My dad hardly ever misses."

Thankfully, the third time the ball came right for the center of Mr. Smith's bat. Kate found herself chanting, "Hit it! Hit it!" along with Sydney.

"You can do it, Dad," Andrew said. "C'mon!"

As if he heard his son, Tony Smith cracked the bat against the ball and it shot off into space. Well, not space, exactly, but way across the court. Or was it *field*?

"He did it! He did it! He did it!" Sydney yelled. She let out a loud yelp and Kate put her fingers in her ears.

As the crowd began to cheer, Tony ran to first base, then second, where he stopped for a split second. His gaze darted to the right, then to the left. Finally he took off running again, making it to third, just in the nick of time before the guy on the base caught the ball in his glove.

"Safe!" a loud voice shouted.

"Wow! That's so cool!" For the first time, Kate felt excited about the game! Maybe sports weren't all bad, after all. Maybe she just hadn't given them a real chance before.

Andrew looked at her with a smile on his face. "Now we're talking!"

"Great hit," Sydney agreed with a huge smile on her face.

The next batter hit the ball the wrong way, and it came flying into the stands near Kate and the others. She squealed as it flew over her head. The announcer hollered, "Foul!"

"Man!" Kate started shaking. "I didn't know baseball was such a dangerous game! And what's all this stuff about a foul ball? What does that mean?"

"It means the ball went the wrong way," Sydney explained.

The camera zoomed in on a man above them, who caught the foul ball. He had a big smile on his face. Kate wasn't so sure what he was happy about. She wouldn't be smiling if someone hit her with a ball that went the wrong way, especially one flying so fast! Still, everyone else seemed to think it was wonderful.

The cheering died down and the game started up once again. Minutes later, the crowd began to cheer. Their shouts filled the stadium from top to bottom, side to side. Kate could hardly hear herself think, the noise was so loud!

"We're going to win this one!" Andrew shouted above the roar of the people around them. "Put another one in the win column for the Fightin' Phils!"

Sure enough, the Phillies won the game. The people all around Kate began to celebrate wildly. She'd never heard such excitement. Crazy, how people could get so worked up over a game.

Well, all but one person. She glanced down at the man she'd been watching all evening. He sure didn't look happy the Phillies had won. . .but why? Wasn't he a fan?

Hmm. Very interesting.

After a minute or two of thinking about that, Kate joined in the frenzy, shouting and cheering. "If you can't beat 'em, join 'em!" she said, then giggled.

"Let's go down to the dugout and say hi to my dad," Andrew said. He led the way through the crowd down the stairs. Kate followed him. She stopped cold when she saw the man in the red shirt up close. He tucked something into his pocket then turned her way with a cold stare.

"What's your problem, kid?" he asked.

"I, um. . .nothing." She tried to dart past him, but the camera in her hand fell to the cement. She grabbed the phone and ran to the dugout, ready to be away from the creepy fellow! Something about him gave her cold chills all over. *Brr!*

When they reached the dugout, she watched the other players congratulating each other. However, she noticed no one said much to Tony Smith. Kate had to wonder about that. *Why are they ignoring him? He played well too.*

Were they really *that* upset with him? She watched awhile longer, noticing people from the stands asking for autographs. They went up to all of the players except Tony. The sad expression on his face almost made Kate cry.

Why are they treating him this way? Can't they see that he loves this team. . .that he's giving 100 percent? Don't they care that he played well? That he's working overtime to be the best he can be?

Suddenly she felt very, very sorry for Mr. Smith. Just then he looked her way and smiled. "Hey, Kate. Thanks for coming."

"You're welcome, Mr. Smith," she said, feeling her spirits lift. "It was a great game. You were terrific." She gave him her biggest possible smile.

"Thanks." He looked embarrassed. "But please call me Tony. That's all I am. Just Tony."

"Tony the Tiger!" Andrew said with a smile. "That's what most of his fans call him."

Mr. Smith shrugged. "Well, some of the fans, anyway. Not everyone."

"Tony the Tiger! I *love* it!" Sydney shoved her way ahead of Kate, her black braids bobbing up and down as she headed straight to Mr. Smith. "You're the best shortstop ever, Mr. Smith. Can I please have your autograph? I'll treasure it forever and ever!"

"Well, of course." He took the program from Sydney and signed it with a smile. "I'm honored." After handing it back to her, he looked at all of them with a twinkle in his eye. "Now, who wants some ice cream? My treat."

"Really, Dad?" Andrew asked. "You have time for that?"

"Sure." His dad nodded. "I've been too distracted with practice lately. Need a nice outing with family and friends."

Sydney's eyes grew wide. "Wow!" She looked like she might faint. "I'm really going out to have ice cream with a sports star. Can you believe it? This is one of the coolest things that's ever happened to me!"

"I'm no star." Mr. Smith gave them a sheepish look.

"Well, sure you are! And I can't wait to tell my friends back home about this." Sydney chattered on about how cool it was, but Kate was distracted, staring at her camera. Somehow, when it had fallen to the floor, it had taken a picture of the man. She could barely make out his face because of the strange angle, but something about it just scared her. A chill ran up her spine and goose bumps covered her arms. She wondered why looking at him made her feel so nervous.

She shook off her fear as she whispered a prayer. No point in worrying about someone she didn't even know, right? Besides, there would be plenty of time to think about that later. Right now, she had some ice cream to eat!

CHAPTER 7

A Brilliant Beyond Brilliant Idea

The morning after the ballgame, Kate woke up bright and early with a great idea. She rolled over in the bed and stared at Sydney, who slept like a rock. "C'mon, wake up," she whispered. "I need to talk to you. Wake up, wake up, wake up!"

Sydney opened sleepy eyes. "I'm awake now." She groaned. "What time is it, anyway?"

"Seven thirty," Kate said, glancing at the clock. "I know it's early, but this is really important!"

"Ugh." Sydney put the pillow over her face and groaned again. "What is it about you and mornings? Don't you ever sleep in? It's summer, remember?"

"Don't you like to get up in the mornings and run?" Kate asked.

"Yes, but not this early!"

"It's just. . .we have too much work to do, and I've had a brilliant beyond brilliant idea." Kate giggled with excitement. "I think you're gonna love it!"

That seemed to get Sydney's attention. She pulled the pillow back and stared at Kate with a curious look on her face. "Oh?"

"We need to start a new blog site," Kate explained.

"A blog? You mean, like a web page?"

"Sort of. Blogs are a little different from websites. A blog is really more like an online journal. Kind of like a diary, almost. It's the same basic idea as a web page, but we would update it every day and write cool articles and stories and stuff." Kate bounced up and down, thinking about the possibilities. It all made perfect sense.

"So why do we need this blog site, again?" Sydney asked with a yawn. She swung her legs over the side of the bed and stood up.

"Well, think about it. If we start a Phillies blog and write great stories and articles about Tony Smith, maybe the person who's trying to frame him will *see* our site and leave comments."

"Probably not *good* comments," Sydney said, shivering. "It might get kind of ugly." She began to do stretches, leaning to the right, then the left, then right and left again.

"Doesn't matter." Kate pushed back the covers and scrambled out of the bed to stand next to her. For fun, she did a couple of stretches too. "We don't have to worry about what he or she says. We just want that person to post so we can track him—or her—down through the web. There are ways to do that. I think I can figure it out if I take my time."

"So how do we do it? Build the blog, I mean." Sydney looked like she wasn't sure about all this. She spread out her arms and began to do jumping jacks.

Kate decided to join her. "B–building the b–blog won't be the p–problem!" Kate huffed and puffed as she jumped up and down. "I've b–built websites before." She stopped jumping and bent over, panting. After a minute, she rose up and stared at Sydney, who continued doing jumping jacks. "I did our school's website."

"Of course!" Sydney dropped down to the ground and began to do sit-ups. "I'm sure it'll be great, if you're making it!"

"Should be easy." Kate pushed up her glasses. "But this Phillies site will be a little different because I don't know much about the team. I guess it would help to know a little something about them. How much can you tell me, Sydney?"

"Quite a bit," her friend said, bobbing up and down on the floor. "But since I'm not from Philly, it might help to have Andrew help us."

"Or. . .the Camp Club Girls!" Kate rose from the bed and began to pace the room. "While we're concentrating on the problem, they can help us."

"What? We'll ask them to go ahead and do the research we need?" Sydney said. She rolled over onto her stomach and started doing push-ups. "Wait, I thought I wasn't the only one who was out of town this week. . . ."

"Yes," Kate said. "I think nearly all of them are out of town. I think Elizabeth is home but helping out at her church's VBS, so I don't think she's available much either. So we may not have our normal contact with the rest of the girls, but we can try to talk to them at night, I guess."

"Sounds like a plan." Now Sydney was huffing and puffing. Still, she never lost count as she pushed up, down, up, down.

"Probably someone will be able to help us learn more about the Phillies. Then we'll have some good stuff to put in our blog. The girls will find all the statistics and quotes we need to put together great stories and articles. In the meantime, let's go downstairs and eat breakfast; then we'll get busy on that blog site."

"Okay, just twenty more!"

Sydney finished her exercise routine; then they raced down the stairs, almost tripping over Dexter, who played with his electronic car on the bottom step. "Hey, watch where you're going!" he cried out. "You could've stepped on my car."

"Sorry, Dex," Kate said. "We have work to do. But first things first!"

They went into the kitchen and fixed bowls of cereal. Kate filled her bowl to the top, but Sydney carefully measured out a small portion.

"This stuff has a lot of sugar in it," she said. "So I'll just cut back a little on how much I eat."

"Okay. Whatever." Kate shoveled in big spoonfuls of the crunchy stuff, talking with her mouth full. "This will be great, Sydney. I love being a detective, don't you? Like Nancy Drew, even!" She took another bite then added, "Oh, and guess what? Maybe after we figure out who's doing this to Tony Smith, we'll be on the news. We could be famous."

"Supersleuths forever!" Sydney shouted.

"Supersleuths forever!" Kate echoed with a giggle.

Sydney sipped her orange juice and her eyebrows shot up. "Hey! Maybe the newspaper will want to write an article on my sports connection. I've played softball, you know. And I'm going to be in the Olympics someday." She began to talk about all of the things she hoped to do before she turned twenty, but Kate had a hard time keeping up. Her thoughts were on the blog they were going to start after breakfast.

"True, true." Kate took another big bite of the sweet cereal and then paused to think about that. "This is so exciting! Supersleuths of America, unite!"

"Go, Inspector Gadget!" Sydney hollered. "We're going to be famous!"

Kate laughed and finished eating. As she rinsed out her cereal bowl, her mother entered the kitchen.

"You girls are up early. I'd planned to make French toast. Looks like I'm too late."

"French toast?" Kate's mouth began to water. "Yum! I'm not full. What about you, Sydney?"

"Well. . ." Sydney didn't look so sure.

"Aw, come on! My mom makes the best French toast in Pennsylvania," Kate said. "Don't you have room for at least one piece? Or two? I could eat a dozen!"

"I don't know how you do it," Kate's mother said. "You must have a hollow leg."

"A hollow leg?" Kate stared down at her legs. "What do you mean?"

Her mother laughed. "That's just something my mom used to say. It means I can't figure out where you're putting all of that food you eat! Your stomach surely isn't big enough, so you must have a hollow leg it goes into."

"Oh, I don't know." Kate shrugged. "I'm just always hungry. But maybe I'm about to go through a growing spell or something." She laughed. "Maybe by next week I'll be six feet tall!"

"Now, *that* would be a story for the papers!" Sydney said, snickering.

Kate looked at her friend and sighed. Sydney was so great at eating only healthy foods. And she was so tall and muscular. So athletic. Maybe that was the way to grow taller—to eat only healthy foods and to exercise a lot. Oh well. Not everyone had to have muscles, right?

Dexter joined them at the table. He put his battery-operated car on top of the wooden table and pressed a button on the remote control. It raced across the table and over the edge, into Kate's lap.

"Better watch out, Dex," she cautioned. "If you keep running over me with this car of yours, I'm going to confiscate it."

"Confiscate?" He looked at her curiously. "What's *confiscate*?"

"It means she's going to take it and keep it," Sydney explained. "You'll never see it again."

Dexter's eyes widened. "No way!" He snatched the car and put it on the counter nearby, then watched it as he ate.

They enjoyed some warm, yummy French toast. Kate ate until she was very full.

Biscuit came to the side of the table and whined. Kate tore off a tiny piece of the French toast and slipped it to him, hoping no one would notice. He gobbled it up and cried for more.

"Shh," Kate whispered. "You'll get me in trouble!"

"I heard that," her mom said. "Don't you feed that dog any more table scraps, Kate Oliver. He's going to end up chubby."

"Chubby? Biscuit?" She looked at him and shrugged. Maybe he had put on a couple of pounds since coming to live with her, but surely a few nibbles of people food couldn't hurt him.

After eating, Kate decided it was time to work on their new Phillies blog site. She signed onto the web then went to her favorite blogging site and clicked the START A NEW BLOG button. Over the next half hour, she and Sydney put together a cool-looking site filled with the Phillies colors—red, white, and blue. With her friend's help, Kate added some basic information about the ball team.

"I'll fill in the side panels with information later," Kate explained, "but this is enough for now." She paused a moment then added, "But now we need to write something really cool about Tony Smith. . .something to convince fans he's a great guy!"

"Well, you heard all that stuff he said the other night when we were eating ice cream—how he loves playing baseball." Sydney nodded. "How he's played since he was a kid. I'm sure he wouldn't mind if we used some of the things he said."

"Great idea!" Kate quickly wrote the title to a new article: "Tony Smith— a Player Phillies Fans Can Trust."

"This article should do it," Katie said. "I'll bet that person who's been writing the bad things about Tony is watching the web to see what others say. So this article we write will be like putting out bait. I'll bet he writes some sort of comment." She paused a moment. "But we need a lot more information about Tony. Good stuff."

"We need actual quotes," Sydney said with a sparkle in her eye. "More specific stuff than what he shared after the game. Stuff about the team, and about how much he loves his teammates and his coaches. And Philadelphia! We really need to play up the Philadelphia connection. This is the City of Brotherly Love, you know."

"Yes, I know." Kate grinned. "I've lived here all my life, remember?"

"Oh yeah." Sydney gave her a sheepish look. "So do you think Tony will give us an interview? We could be, like. . .reporters!" Sydney smiled. "I always thought it'd be fun to be a sports reporter, and now I get to be, thanks to this website!"

"*Blog* site," Kate corrected her. "And I don't know if he'll give us an interview or not. Maybe we could call Andrew and ask."

Just then the phone rang. Kate looked down at the caller ID, noticing Andrew's number. She stared back up at her friend, stunned.

"Wow!" Kate and Sydney looked at each other.

"It's like a miracle," Kate whispered. "God was listening to us."

"He's *always* listening to us!" Sydney echoed. "But that's extra super cool."

Kate picked up the phone and started talking fast. "Hey, Andrew. I'm so glad you called. We were just talking about you. Sydney and I are starting a blog site and we need your help. Do you think your dad will give us an interview? We really need to get some great quotes to put in our first article."

"Probably, but there's something happening right now, Kate. Turn on the radio."

"The radio?" she asked. "What station?"

He told her, and Kate turned it on right away. She heard a man's voice saying, "Ladies and gentlemen, I guess this confirms the rumors we've been hearing about Tony Smith's thoughts on playing for the Phillies. You heard it in his own words."

"Heard *what* in his own words?" Kate said. She turned her attention back to the phone. "What was it, Andrew? Your dad was on the radio?"

"No." Andrew sounded more upset by the minute. "That's just it. He *wasn't* on the radio. He never gave an interview, I mean. But it *was* his voice. How did they do that?"

"Wait. You're saying they found someone with a voice like his who pretended to be him?"

"No, that's the crazy part. It really was my dad's voice. We all heard it, and even my mom said so. We know his voice. My dad is so upset right now."

"Of course, but. . ." Kate exhaled loudly. "It just doesn't make any sense. First people start rumors about him, and now his voice is on the radio, telling people the rumors are true?"

"Yes. But it doesn't make any sense."

"No kidding." She sat on the edge of the bed. "Andrew, we're going to get to the bottom of this, I promise. Someone taped your dad's voice without his knowing it."

"But how? And when? He hasn't given any interviews in weeks, not since all the rumors started. Coach Mullins told him not to. Said the reporters would twist his words. So he's stayed away from reporters. He's already really upset. You know he's been working with that charity for kids with muscular dystrophy, right?"

"Of course!" Kate knew all about it. The top secret project she and her father had been working on was a special robot to help kids with muscular problems. She hadn't told a soul yet, not even Sydney or the other Camp Club Girls. First they had to work out some of the kinks. There was no point in getting people excited about something that might not even work.

"My dad's worried that the people at the Muscular Dystrophy Foundation won't trust him now," Andrew said, sounding sad.

"Why would he think that?" Kate asked.

"Because it's already happening. Have you seen that bank commercial my dad is in?"

"Sure, I see it all the time. I love the part where your dad says, 'A penny saved is a penny earned.' That's a Ben Franklin quote, you know."

"Yeah, I know. But you won't hear my dad saying that anymore. The president of the bank just called and said they're not running the commercial anymore. They're taking it off the air because they think my dad is bad for business."

"Oh Andrew! I'm so sorry. But I'll be praying, I promise. And we're going to do everything we can to fix this. With God's help, I mean." Kate paused a minute. "When is the next game?"

"Saturday afternoon."

"Can you get tickets?"

"We have season tickets. Four seats. So that's not a problem."

"Good ones?" she asked. "Close to the dugout?"

"Well, sure. Same seats as last time. We always sit in the same place. But what are you thinking?"

"I'm thinking I'd better learn a lot more about the team before I go. In the meantime, just stay calm. Oh, and write down everything you know about the Phillies for our blog, okay? And it would be great if you could get a couple of quotes from your dad, telling how much he loves the team. We'll use those in our articles."

"O—okay." He sighed.

"I'm so sorry about all of this, Andrew. But don't worry. God has this under control. I know we can trust Him."

"I know. It's just hard."

"Well, let's pray about it, then." Kate began to pray out loud over the phone, something she'd never done before. It made her feel really good to pray for Andrew, and by the time they hung up, she could tell he felt a little better.

Afterward, Kate put the phone down on the desk and looked at Sydney with a dramatic sigh.

"What happened?" Sydney asked, her brow wrinkling in concern. "Sounds bad."

"Yes, it is. What a mess! Someone is really working hard to make Mr. Smith look bad. And it's working. The bank just canceled a commercial he's in. And Andrew's afraid it's going to get even worse—that the people at the Muscular Dystrophy Foundation will drop him as a spokesman too."

"This is just so sad."

"Yes," Kate agreed. "We need to find out how someone taped Tony's voice without his knowing. That's the only way we'll ever get to the bottom of this."

Sydney began to pace the room. "Man! Do you think it was a reporter? Maybe someone snuck in the locker room or something? Or. . ." Her face lit up. "Maybe someone tapped his phone. What do you think?"

"I don't know, but I'm going to get to the bottom of this," Kate said.

"Let's send an email to the other Camp Club Girls. We need their help. This is too much for the two of us to handle on our own."

"Good idea," Sydney said.

Kate sat down at the computer. She began to write an email to the Camp Club Girls.

Dear Bailey, Alex, Elizabeth, and McKenzie:
    Please meet me in the Camp Club Girls chat room tonight at 7:00 eastern time. A mystery awaits! Sydney and I need you. . .ASAP!

As she clicked the SEND button, Kate leaned back in her chair and smiled. "There! That should do it! If anyone can get to the bottom of this mystery, the Camp Club Girls can!"

CHAPTER 8

Camp Club Girls. . .Unite!

Kate and Sydney spent the rest of the day at the pool, swimming with Dexter. It was nice to enjoy some fun time. Kate thought about the first time she met Sydney and the other Camp Club Girls at Discovery Lake Camp. What fun they'd had, solving their first case and getting to know each other. Now they were all great friends. And on days like today, swimming with Sydney, Kate could almost forget the Phillies and all of the problems Andrew and his dad were going through.

Almost.

After a few minutes of fun, Sydney announced, "I need to swim one hundred laps. Hope you don't mind, but I want to make the swim team this year and I need to work on my speed and strength."

Kate shrugged. "Okay. No problem." She went to the shallow end and sat on the steps. Two women her mother's age sat on the steps next to her. She couldn't help but hear their conversation.

"They need to kick that Tony Smith off the team," a woman in a black bathing suit said. She fanned herself with her hand and rolled her eyes. "Seriously, he needs to find someplace else to go!"

The other woman—dressed in a green suit—reached for a diet soda and took a sip. She shook her head and said, "He's hurting the morale of the other players. His attitude is terrible! And lately he hasn't even played well!"

"Excuse me. . . ," Kate started to say.

The woman looked her way. "Yes?" the lady in the black suit said. "Can we help you?"

"Oh. . .never mind."

Kate wanted to explain that it was all a big mistake—that Tony actually loved the Phillies—but decided not to. It would be better to prove them wrong than to tell them they were wrong. And she would do that—with the help of her friends.

The afternoon ended too quickly. Kate's mom and dad took the girls out to eat at an all-you-can-eat pizza buffet that evening.

"I love, love, love this place!" Kate said as they entered. She stopped inside the door and drew in a deep breath. "Do you smell that? Do you? It's the most wonderful smell in the world. Smell the garlic? Smell the pizza crust baking? Smell the pepperoni and sausage? Oh, I think that's the best smell ever!"

"You're funny! You know that?" Sydney laughed. "Just smells like pizza to me. But look at that salad bar! They have great veggies. I'm going to love this place."

"Veggies?" This was one of Kate's favorite places to eat, but she'd never noticed the vegetables before. Oh well. She grabbed a plate and got in line. She loaded up on the good stuff. . .three pieces of sausage pizza, one slice of pepperoni, a bowl of spaghetti and meatballs, and two slices of dessert pizza.

Sydney grabbed a bowl and filled it with salad, loading it with bright orange carrot sticks, round red tomatoes, and lots of green cucumbers. Afterward, she took a tiny slice of cheese pizza.

Kate looked at her, stunned. "That's all you're eating?"

"Sure." Sydney shrugged. "Why?"

"Oh, no reason." Kate tried not to feel bad about all of the food she ate as they shared the meal together, but she had to wonder if she was the only one who loved pizza. She even made a second trip back to the buffet for two more slices of pepperoni. Her mother looked at her and said, "Hollow leg!" Kate just laughed.

They arrived home at ten minutes until seven.

"Don't forget to feed Biscuit," Kate's mom said. "And take him outside for a few minutes."

Kate filled Biscuit's bowl with food and watched as he chomped it down. "Slow down, boy! You'll end up weighing a ton! You won't be a very good crime solver if you're too chubby to chase the bad guys!"

Biscuit never even looked up from his food. He just kept eating and eating.

Afterward, Kate took him outside. Sydney went with her. They stood in the backyard talking about the case while Biscuit roamed the yard and chased a squirrel. From inside the house, Kate heard the grandfather clock chime seven times.

"Oh! We're supposed to be online to meet the other girls!"

They raced back inside, where Kate signed onto the internet. She giggled as she entered the chat room. Bailey—the youngest in their group—was already there.

Bailey: *Hey, Freckles! Whazup? U said it was important!*
Kate: *Wait till the others sign on. I'll tell u everything, I promise.*
      Something is happening and we need ur help!
Bailey: *Okie dokie.*

"Who is it?" Sydney asked, settling into the chair next to Kate.

"Bailey." Kate pointed at the screen. "She's the first one to sign on."

"Of course!" Sydney laughed. "Bailey might be the youngest, but she's always ready to roll!"

A few seconds later, Alex signed into the chat room. Kate smiled when she saw her name. Alex knew everything there was to know about solving tough cases. Surely she would be able to help!

Next Elizabeth Anderson signed on. Elizabeth was fourteen—older than any of the others. She always knew just what to do. Kate had enjoyed getting to know Elizabeth at camp. She was so mature, and loaded with godly wisdom!

At five minutes after seven, McKenzie joined them. McKenzie was thirteen and never gave up on a case, even a really tough one like this. Kate could hardly wait to share the news.

McKenzie: *What's up?*

Kate quickly filled them in on the story, sharing everything about Tony Smith and his problems with the team. Afterward, she typed, *We need all of you!*

Elizabeth: *We're here! Whatever u need, just tell us!*
Kate: *Sydney and I have assignments for you. How do u feel about*
      that?
McKenzie: *Gr8!*
Bailey: *Cool! Assign away, oh Chief.*

Kate smiled as she typed.

Kate: *McKenzie, you're a deep thinker. And you're so smart! We*
      need you to think of all the reasons why someone would
      want to do this to Mr. Smith.

McKenzie: *I'll put on my thinking cap.*

Kate: *Alex, you're so encouraging! We want you to put together a
team of kids to write letters of encouragement to Mr.
Smith. Those letters will lift his spirits, and he really
needs that right now.*

Alexis: *Sounds like fun.*

Kate: *Elizabeth, you're such a prayer warrior. I would feel better if
I knew lots of people were praying! Could you help with
that? Put together a prayer team, maybe?*

Elizabeth: *I'd be happy to! I'll ask lots of people to pray at certain
times of day.*

Bailey: *What about me? What can I do?*

Kate: *Keep posting comments to our new Phillies blog. Write some
great things about Tony Smith. Let people know what
a terrific guy he is. It would be great if all of you could
do that. . .and ask your friends and family members to
post their comments too. The more, the better! Just ask
them to say nice things only. Okay?*

Kate quickly gave them the link to the new site and they all agreed to
help.

Kate: *We also need someone to do some research on the Phillies
and their history. We also need good stuff on Tony Smith,
like how much he's helped kids with muscular
dystrophy. . .that sort of thing. Internet searches may be
enough, but it may also mean a trip to the library.
Anyone game?*

Bailey: *I can do that too. I'll dig out Phillies info, Philly Queen
Mystery Solver! My fam is going to Chicago this weekend,
so I'll look at one of the big libraries there.*

Alexis: *And I can help by finding out stuff about Tony Smith.*

As they ended the chat, Kate turned to Sydney.

"What do you think?" she asked. "What else can we do? It will be a
few days before Bailey gives us information. And it'll take awhile for the
rest of the Camp Club Girls to get going too. What can we do. . .right here,
right now?"

"Hmm." Sydney wrinkled her nose as she thought about it. "I suppose
we should find some local people who Tony Smith has helped in some

way. Get some personal interviews of lives he's touched."

"Great idea!" Kate agreed. "And when we're done with that, let's figure out the best possible way to get people to notice our new blog site."

"How do we do that?" Sydney asked.

"It's not as hard as you think. Just takes time." With the wave of a hand, Kate explained, "I can announce the site to all of my friends here in Philadelphia and ask them to send the link to their friends, and their friends' friends, and so on. Before long, people all over the country will know! Also, I'll go to some of the other Phillies blog sites—the ones saying the bad stuff about Mr. Smith—and leave comments with a link to our site. That'll get 'em there, I'm sure!"

"I'll do the same thing," Sydney agreed. "I know lots of people who love sports. As soon as our blog site is up and going full speed, I'll send the link. Before long, we'll have the best Phillies site on the internet!"

Kate couldn't help but laugh. "It's funny, isn't it? A few days ago I knew nothing about baseball. And now I'm writing about it. Go figure!"

"It's all for a worthy cause," Sydney said with a nod. "And besides, you'll fall in love with baseball, I promise. It's such a great sport. And with players like Tony Smith, what's not to love?"

Kate shrugged. She still wasn't so sure about the whole baseball thing. But maybe next Saturday's game would be the true test. Perhaps there she could solve a mystery—and at the same time fall in love with the game of baseball!

CHAPTER 9

Supersleuths on the Job!

On Saturday afternoon, Kate and Sydney went back to the stadium for another Phillies game with Mrs. Smith and Andrew. Kate deliberately wore a red-white-and-blue T-shirt and a pair of jeans. She wanted to fit in with the other fans this time—not stick out like a sore thumb in a bright orange shirt! Besides, this whole sports thing was beginning to rub off on her. Sort of, anyway. She was actually starting to get excited about baseball! And solving the case, of course. She could hardly wait to do that! Whoever was framing Tony Smith would soon be caught if she had anything to do with it.

They entered the stadium to the strains of "Take Me Out to the Ballgame." Hearing the song made happiness rise in Kate's heart. How exciting!

Sydney's face was practically shining with joy. "I love, love, love coming here!" she said with a squeal. "But you're going to have to keep an eye on me, Kate, 'cause I'm gonna get caught up in the game and forget we're supposed to be crime solving! You know how I am! I might be a supersleuth, but I'm also a sports fan!"

"Of course! But I won't let that happen. Inspector Gadget is on the job!" Kate giggled. "I've got my dad's super-high-strength binoculars, and I brought my tiny digital camera again, just in case I see anything strange. Plus—and this is really cool—I've got my smartwatch. I'm ready no matter what comes our way!"

"I still can't believe you can read web pages on a watch," Andrew said, shaking his head.

"What are we looking for exactly, though?" Sydney asked.

"Well, maybe a nosy reporter hanging out around the locker room," Kate explained. "Or one of the players in the dugout acting suspicious. Anything, really."

"Before the game starts, let's pray, okay?" Sydney said. " 'Cause I know we need God's help with this. It's too big for us to solve by ourselves."

"Sure!" Kate agreed.

Once they settled into their seats, Kate bowed her head and Sydney said a quick prayer. Even though it was super loud in the stadium, Kate felt sure God still heard them loud and clear!

After praying, Andrew headed to the dugout to say hello to his father. Kate watched him wind his way through the many, many fans to get to the small dugout area. What would it feel like, to have a sports hero for a father? Especially now with people saying so many mean things about him?

Kate could sort of imagine what it felt like to have a famous father. Her dad was going to be famous when SWAT-bot hit the stores! Not that he needed to be famous to impress her. She already thought he was the very best dad in the world.

Minutes later, Andrew returned to his seat looking sad. "I told my dad to have fun," he said, taking his seat. "He said it's getting harder with each game, but I just reminded him that he loves the sport. And I told him about that Bible verse we learned at church last week."

"Which one? I don't remember." Kate gave him a curious look.

"You know—that one that says blessed are you when men persecute you and say bad things against you?"

"Oh yeah!" Kate remembered. "Well, that one certainly applies, doesn't it!"

"Well, my dad is being falsely accused. And with all of these rumors flying around, he's really being persecuted by others. So he *must* be mighty blessed."

"That's a great way to look at it," Kate agreed.

"He should just relax and have a great game," Sydney said, wrinkling her nose. "He can't control what other people are thinking, anyway."

"Yeah, but I still wish they wouldn't think bad things about him or *say* bad things about him. I know it hurts his feelings. . .and mine too!" Andrew sighed. Kate felt bad for him.

"I guess God is teaching us all a lesson about spreading rumors, isn't He?" she said. "Maybe that's the point of all of this—to show us just how wrong it is to talk about people behind their backs, especially when it's not true!"

"I'll be a lot more careful about who I talk about, that's for sure," Sydney said. "I'll think before I speak even if I don't know the person."

"Me too," Andrew agreed.

"No more talking about people behind their backs!" Kate announced in her strongest voice.

"Speaking of not talking about people behind their backs. . ." The woman in front of them had turned around with a stern look. "Would you kids mind being a little quieter during this game? Last time one of you was shouting in my ear through the whole game." She looked at Sydney, who put her hand over her mouth.

"Oops! Sorry," Sydney said. "But I'm such a big fan! I can hardly control myself. Especially when Tony Smith is on the field."

At the mention of Tony's name, the woman rolled her eyes and mumbled some not-so-nice things. She turned back around to face the field.

"Never mind all that," Kate whispered to Andrew. "She'll be a fan of your dad's again too after we solve this case."

Several rows down, something caught Kate's eye. She watched as a man in his late twenties stood and pulled something out of his pocket. *Hmm.* Something about him seemed strange. He turned her way for a moment and she caught a glimpse of his face and noticed his Phillies shirt. Grabbing Sydney's arm, she said, "Oh, there's that man again. The one in the picture." Kate pointed at him.

"Is he here with someone else?" Sydney asked. "Or is he alone again?"

"Looks like he's alone. That's kind of weird, isn't it? Don't people usually come to games with friends or family members?"

"Usually," Sydney agreed.

The man sat down, but Kate kept watching him. A shiver ran down her spine every time she saw the stranger, but she wasn't sure why.

"Looks like there's a family to his right and a young couple on his left. But he's sitting in the same seat as before." She watched him through the binoculars. "He has an MP3 player in his hand again. Something's attached to it." Kate watched him through the binoculars, and then had another brilliant beyond brilliant idea. "See that empty seat in the row in front of him? The one next to the older man with the white hair?"

Andrew looked beyond all of the people seated in front of them until he could clearly see. Then he nodded. "Oh yeah. I see it now. What about it?"

"It's been empty all this time. I don't think anyone is using that seat. So I'm going to go sit in front of our suspect to see what I can see."

"Our *suspect*?" Sydney and Andrew said at the same time.

"What makes that man a suspect?" Andrew asked. "He hasn't even done anything suspicious!"

"Oh, it's just a gut feeling," Kate said, feeling that little shiver again. "I know in my brain that he's up to no good." How she knew, she couldn't say.

"Wow." Andrew shook his head. "I guess I have a lot to learn about solving mysteries. I just thought he was an ordinary fan."

"He probably is." Sydney laughed. "But Kate will figure it out, one way or the other."

"That's why I'm going down there to sit," Kate explained. "If I sit in front of him, I'll hear everything he says. I don't want to falsely accuse him, after all. There are enough rumors flying around."

"Good point." Sydney nodded.

"I brought the perfect thing for looking at things in the row behind me. . . ." Kate reached into her gadget bag and pulled out her large pair of sunglasses.

Andrew looked at her like she was crazy. "Sunglasses? In the stadium?"

"Oh, they're not just sunglasses," she explained. "They've got side mirrors. See right here?" Kate pointed to the tiny mirrors. "When I put these on, I can see what's happening behind me."

"No way." His mouth gaped.

She nodded and handed them to him. He put them on and then whispered, "Hey, the lady behind me is eating nachos. Do you think she'll share? They look great!"

Kate laughed. "You'll have to ask her. Meanwhile, I'm going to go down there. Well, if your mom says it's okay." She turned to Mrs. Smith, explaining her plan. "I promise to stay right there."

"Just be careful, honey. Don't do or say anything to that man if you can help it."

"Oh, trust me. I'm a supersleuth! I won't give myself away." *I hope!*

Kate wiggled through the crowded row of people until she reached the stairs. Then she climbed down one, two, three, four rows. She looked beyond all of the people in that row till she saw the empty seat. Then she whispered a prayer that God would help her with this plan.

Feeling more courageous than before, she eased herself beyond the screaming fans. Just then, one of the players hit a home run. Perfect! With all of the standing and cheering, no one even noticed that she slipped into the seat. She sat and quickly pulled the glasses from her bag. Thankfully, they fit over her regular glasses. As she pressed them into place, she had a clear view of the man behind her. She grabbed her digital recorder and began to whisper into it.

"Male suspect, late twenties. Wearing a Phillies T-shirt. Holding an MP3 player, brand unknown. Has a suspicious look on his face. His gaze keeps shifting. He's not watching the game at all. Must be here for other reasons. Keeps looking at the ground."

Just as she said "looking at the ground," the elderly man with the white hair in the seat next to her gave her a strange look. "Do you mind if I ask what you're doing, kid? You're making me nervous. Who are you talking to?"

"Oh, I, um. . ." She shrugged. "I'm just taking notes."

"About the game?" His already-wrinkled forehead wrinkled even more. "What are you, a reporter or something? You're a little young to be working for one of the papers. And you're certainly not a TV reporter."

"Well. . ." Kate pulled off the glasses and looked into his eyes. Actually, now that she was writing articles for the blog site about the team, she could *almost* be considered a reporter, right? Still, she didn't feel right saying so. But what could she do to keep the man from asking so many questions?

She pointed at her digital recorder. "I'm just working on a project for a friend. I'm not a real reporter, but I am taking notes. It's a *top secret* project." Kate shrugged and smiled at him, hoping he wouldn't ask anything else.

"Well, would you mind working on it in someone else's seat?" He crossed his arms at his chest and gave her a stern look. "My wife is running late, but when she gets here, she'll want her seat. She'll be mad if I give it to a pip-squeak like you."

What is it with everyone thinking I'm so small? Kate wanted to say, but didn't. Instead, she sighed and muttered, "I'm sorry I bothered you. I'll move."

She started to stand, but all of a sudden the man's mean look faded and a crooked smile took its place. He gave her a sympathetic nod. "Aw, never mind, kid. It'll be awhile before Margaret gets here. She's visiting with the grandkids. So just sit there until she does. And take good notes—for whatever it is you're working on. I'll just sit here and pretend you're some big-name reporter doing a story on the local news or something. You've intrigued me with that top secret stuff."

"Oh, thank you!" Kate could hardly keep from squealing. "Thanks *so* much." She looked down at the field, noticing Tony as he caught a ball in his glove. "My friend thanks you."

"Mm-hmm." He turned his attention back to the game, but Kate had other things to do. She focused on the mirrors in her glasses and watched in awe as the man behind her punched the buttons on the MP3 player in his hand.

"It's definitely attached to something," she whispered into the digital recorder. "But what? And why?" After a few more minutes of glancing downward, she realized it was a cord of some sort. And it ran all the way down below the seats.

"No way!" He was surely up to something! But in order to know for sure, she'd have to take a closer look.

Kate pulled out her digital camera. How could she take a picture of his MP3 player without him knowing it? And yet she must! She'd never be able to look up that particular model on the internet unless she got a closer look.

An idea occurred to her quite suddenly. She turned around and looked up three rows to where Sydney sat with Mrs. Smith and Andrew. With a bright smile on her face, she stood to her feet and gave them a big wave, as if she were greeting old friends she hadn't seen in years. The man with the MP3 player looked at her curiously but didn't say anything. Thankfully, Andrew and Sydney waved back, though Mrs. Smith looked a little confused.

Kate lifted her cell phone and pretended to take a picture of them. Just for effect, she hollered out, "Say cheese, Sydney!" then snapped a shot—not of Sydney, but of that *very* interesting-looking MP3 player in the man's hand.

She caught another shot of the man's face. Then she took a picture of Sydney and Andrew, just for fun. The man leaned forward and for the first time Kate could clearly see the cord that ran from the MP3 player underneath the seats. His earphones? *Hmm.* She'd never seen a cord that long for earphones. *Something very suspicious is going on! But what? And why?*

Just then, the man leaned in her direction and his cap came tumbling off. *Yikes!* Kate used the opportunity to reach down to the ground and snatch it. As she did, she took a good look at the cord. She gasped as she realized it led all the way to the dugout! No, the cord certainly wasn't for earphones. But what in the world was this fellow up to? Why would an ordinary fan do something like this? Goose bumps covered her arms.

"Hey, kid. What are you doing?" an angry voice rang out.

She turned to look at the man in the Phillies shirt, her heart thump-thumping in her chest. "I, um. . ." She held up the cap and smiled innocently. "I thought you might want your cap back. You dropped it." She handed it to him with another big smile.

"Oh." He shoved it on his head and glared at her. "Well, thanks. Now pay attention to the game. You're making me nervous."

She wanted to say, *"No, you're making me nervous,"* but didn't. No point in making him suspicious.

Kate had just started to breathe a relieved sigh when a shrill voice startled her.

"Excuse me!" Kate looked up to find the owner of the seat staring at her. The older woman had white curls, thin lips, and a mean look on her face. "I think you've got my seat, little lady. Scoot on out of it and go back where you belong."

"Yes, I, well. . ." She swallowed hard then nodded her head. "Your husband said I could. . . Oh, never mind. You're right. So sorry. Have a nice day." As she scooted past the older couple, she hollered out, "Go, Phillies!" then darted back to her seat.

Sydney grabbed her hand as she took her real seat once again. "Oh, I saw the whole thing through the binoculars! Good save! I'm so proud of you. But I was a nervous wreck, Kate. I was praying the whole time."

"Thanks." Kate sighed. "I needed it, trust me. Oh, but, Sydney, I got a couple of great photos. I want to look up the MP3 player on the internet. I think I know what he's doing with it, but I want to be sure."

"You go, Inspector Gadget!" Sydney giggled. "So what are you thinking? Is it a regular MP3 player that just plays music, or one that you can record with?"

"I'm not sure. I think it does both." She opened the phone and looked at the picture a little more closely. "I'll figure this out; don't worry."

She reached over to turn on her smartwatch. Unfortunately, she couldn't connect with the Wi-Fi.

"They must not have wireless access here," she said with a sigh. "I'll have to wait and check it out on our computer at home."

"Aw, don't worry!" Sydney said. "You'll figure it out. I know you will."

"Yeah, but my birthday is Wednesday, and I want to get this case behind me before then," Kate explained. "I don't want to be thinking about solving this mystery on my big day! I want to have fun."

"Oh, we will. . .even if we're still on the case," Sydney said.

"Did I tell you where we're going?" Kate asked. When Sydney shook her head, she continued. "My parents are taking us to the coolest '50s-style soda shop for burgers, fries, and ice cream. Oh, it's the best place in town. The waiters and waitresses are dressed up in '50s costumes and they sing and dance every hour on the hour. We're going to have a blast—but only if I'm not thinking about who's trying to frame Tony Smith. So I don't want to waste even a minute!"

The crowd roared and Sydney rose to her feet, hollering at the top of her lungs. "Woo-hoo! We're not wasting any time at all, Kate. Don't you see? We're at a baseball game in one of the coolest stadiums in the world. Put away those gadgets and enjoy the game. There will be plenty of time for crime solving later!"

With a smile, Kate decided to do just that! She put away her gizmos and turned her attention to the game.

Clues, Clues, and More Clues!

On Monday morning, Kate received a call from Bailey.

"I have a lot of information for your blog site, Kate," Bailey said gleefully. "Hope you're ready for this. I've been working extra hard!"

"Am I ever!" Kate said. "And thanks! Let me get to the computer so I can write all of this down!" She dashed downstairs with Sydney on her heels. Opening a blank screen, she said, "Go ahead, Bailey. I'm ready!"

"Great. Well, let's get started. I wrote down a lot of notes since I went to the library. Hmm, let's see. . ." She paused a moment. "I'll start with this information. The team was founded over a hundred years ago."

"Wow. A hundred years? I didn't even know there was baseball that long ago," Kate said. She couldn't imagine it!

"There was!" Bailey responded. "And Philadelphia had a team! But did you know they weren't always called the Phillies? They were originally called the Quakers."

"Wow. The Quakers? That's interesting. What else?"

"The Phillies are a major league team," Bailey explained, never missing a beat.

"That's good?" Kate asked.

"Yes, Mystery Queen," Bailey said. "They're professionals. And they're also members of the eastern division of the National League."

Kate didn't know what that meant exactly, but typed it anyway. Maybe Sydney could fill her in later. "What else?"

"The Phillies won the World Series championship in 1980," Bailey continued. "Against Kansas City. They had a video clip of that at the library."

"Wow, a world championship," Kate responded, scribbling down the information. "That's good, right?"

"Yes, my baseball-deprived friend. That's good." Bailey laughed. "They also won the National League East Division in 2007. And in 2008 they

60

changed their uniforms." She went on to explain lots of other things about the team, and before long Kate had tons of information to add to the blog site. Oh, she could hardly wait! It would be the coolest Phillies site ever! One that hundreds—no, *thousands*—of people would want to visit!

Wow! Kate could hardly believe it! She quickly scribbled down the things Bailey told her. *Oh, I hope I'm not missing anything!* She'd never typed so quickly.

"Oh Bailey, terrific!" Kate said as they finished. "Thank you, big-time! And. . .go Phillies!" For the first time, she really meant those words. It felt good to finally be a fan!

She ended the call with a giggle. Then Sydney called Alex, getting even more information! Afterwards, they signed online and Kate plugged in the information, making the site the best it could be. After that, she tweaked the colors a bit and then wrote an upbeat article about Tony Smith, telling what a great player he was and how much he loved the team. She read through it three times just to make sure it was good. For fun, she even uploaded a couple of cool pictures she'd taken with her camera at that first game, pictures of Tony catching a ball. That should get people interested in the site and in Tony! And it should prove that he was still a great player, despite what people thought about him.

Sydney sat at Kate's side as she worked, offering suggestions and making comments. Finally, Kate added the finishing touches. She sat back in her chair and looked at the blog site one last time. "So what do you think, Sydney?" she asked, staring at it in awe. Her heart thump-thumped with excitement.

"I think it's a-*ma*-zing." Her friend grinned. "I think *you're* amazing. You're not just good with gadgets. You're good with just about everything. This is the coolest blog site I've ever seen, and Phillies fans are going to love it! And I'm pretty sure people from all over the country are going to visit this site and post comments."

Kate practically beamed with joy. It felt good to hear such kind words from her friend. "Hopefully we'll catch whoever is doing this to Mr. Smith, then," she said.

Sydney's expression changed, and for a moment Kate could see the anxiety in her eyes. "Just be prepared, Kate. In order to catch the bad guys, we'll probably have to read some not-so-nice stuff about Tony. Mean stuff, even."

"Yeah, I know." Kate sighed. "But it'll be worth it to find out who's doing this." As she looked at the photos on the site, she remembered something. "Oh, I forgot to upload that one picture I took of that guy's MP3 player. I've got it on my camera, right here."

She grabbed her tiny digital camera once again and transferred the photo of the MP3 player onto the computer so she could enlarge it for a closer look. "All I need is the brand name and the model number. Then I'll be able to track it down. Surely the company that makes them has a website. I'm gonna figure this out."

It didn't take long to figure out the MP3 player was called the Audio Wizard by a company called Tekkno-Elekktronix.

"Hmm. Never heard of this brand or model," Kate said. "Just goes to show you I don't know about every gadget! I'll bet my dad's never even heard of this one! Must be new on the market or he would've told me."

"Well, let's find their website," Sydney said. "That would be the best way to get information."

"Probably." After a few minutes of browsing the web, Kate located the Tekkno-Elekktronix site with a picture of that same MP3 player. She read all of the information on it then looked over at Sydney, stunned.

"This is different from any other audio players I've ever seen," she said, staring at the site. "It's got all sorts of cool capabilities. See this cable?" she pointed at a long black cord in the picture.

Sydney nodded. "What about it?"

"Well, I'm pretty sure it's the same one the man at the game was using. I thought maybe it was an earphone cable at first, but that's not it at all. Look at the end of the cable." She grew more animated with each word. "That's a tiny microphone."

"No way." Sydney leaned closer and gasped. "Oh, you're right! Looks like a clip-on one. Is that what the guy at the game was using? A microphone?"

"Yes." Kate bounced up and down in her seat. "That has to be it! Sydney! I'm really, really sure I know how Mr. Smith's voice ended up on the radio. That man at the stadium has been recording Tony's conversations in the dugout, then using them as voice-overs and pretend interviews for blog sites and radio interviews."

"But that doesn't make sense. Tony wouldn't be saying anything about being unhappy with the team in the dugout." Sydney gave a little shrug. "Just the opposite, in fact. I'm sure when he's with the other players, he's saying nice things."

"Oh, I know. But words can be twisted, you know. Even good words. And before long, rumors can fly. Let me show you how I think he did it." Kate closed out the website and opened a software program on the computer. "Check out this software my dad installed. I think you're going to find this interesting."

Sydney shrugged. "What about it?"

"It has voice-editing capabilities."

"Oh?" Sydney still looked confused.

"Yeah, let's try it out. Why don't you say something into the computer's microphone and I'll record you."

Sydney leaned into the little microphone and said, "Okay." After pausing for a minute, she said, "I miss all of my friends from Discovery Lake Camp. Remember when we first met Bailey? A little girl with big ideas! And Alex. . .she knows everything there is to know about Nancy Drew. Good thing we asked her to help us with this case. And Elizabeth. . ." Sydney sighed. "I sure miss Elizabeth, don't you? I don't know anyone who knows as much about the Bible as she does. And I miss McKenzie. She's so smart. She always knows just what to do. I didn't really like all of the food. Some of it was pretty bad too. But the people were fun."

Kate recorded every word and then played it back. "Okay, sounds great. Now let me try something." She worked with the recording for a few minutes, cutting out some of the words. Then she played it back.

"I sure don't miss my friends at Discovery Lake Camp. And I don't like Bailey. Elizabeth was pretty bad too."

"Whoa." Sydney looked at her, stunned. "Well, that's my voice, all right. But that's not what I said at all."

"Exactly." Kate nodded. "I just took the things you did say and rearranged them to come up with this version."

"Scary!" Sydney's eyes widened. "Very scary!"

"Yes, and I'd be willing to bet that's exactly what the guy at the game did after he recorded Tony Smith's voice. He altered it; then he started the rumors with twisted-up words."

"You're probably right. But it makes me wonder what Tony really said."

"Probably something completely innocent. You can see how easy it is to twist words."

"Yes, I can." Sydney had a worried look on her face. "But why?"

"Good question." Kate shook her head. "If he's a Phillies fan, why would he want to sabotage one of their players?"

"Hmm." Sydney began to pace. "Maybe a news station is paying him to get a juicy story to increase their ratings. You know? Like what happened to Alexis at that nature center with the dinosaurs. The case we called 'Alexis and the Sacramento Surprise.' Maybe he's a reporter or something, just out for a story!"

"Maybe." Kate sighed. "But that angle doesn't make a lot of sense. They have too many big stories right now, anyway. Can you think of anything else?"

Sydney's eyes widened. "Ooh! Maybe he's mad because Tony's a shortstop."

"But why?"

"I dunno." Sydney shrugged. "Maybe our bad guy played shortstop in high school and hoped to get drafted to the pros someday. Could be *he* wanted to play for the Phillies, even. You never know. There are probably a lot of bitter wannabe players out there who never got their shot at the pros."

"Maybe." Kate stood and began to pace the room. "Or. . .maybe he's not a Phillies fan at all. Maybe he's a spy for another team. Maybe he's there to bring down the Phillies' morale so they'll lose their games. What do you think of that? Makes perfect sense to me. If you can turn team members against each other, they won't play as well. Before long, they'll start losing games."

"Well, I know I don't perform as well when my spirits are low," Sydney said. "So that makes sense."

"Exactly. So maybe this person is really just trying to get everyone worked up. . .over nothing!"

"I don't know. Maybe." Sydney shrugged. "But one thing is for sure— we're making progress! Before you know it this crime will be solved!"

"Hopefully in time for my birthday," Kate added with a wink. "It's on Wednesday, you know." She wanted to get this case behind them!

"Of course I know!" Sydney laughed. "You've only told me 150 times. You were born on the Fourth of July!"

"My mom says I'm a Yankee Doodle Dandy," Kate said with a grin. "And I love the fact that everyone sets off fireworks on my big day. It's a reminder that God thinks I'm special."

"You *are* special, Kate." Sydney flashed a smile. "But not just on the Fourth of July. You're special every day of the year. I'm so glad God made us friends!"

"Camp Club Girls forever!" Kate shouted.

"Forever and ever!" Sydney echoed.

Just then, Dexter rushed by and shouted, "Boys rule, girls drool!"

Kate laughed. "It's the other way around, silly. Girls rule, *boys* drool."

"Oh." He grabbed his robotic car and put it down on the floor, making it spin in circles. Biscuit, who was trailing along behind the girls, began to bark and run in circles behind the car. Pretty soon he gave up and dropped onto the floor panting.

Kate laughed. "Silly dog. When will you ever learn?"

In some ways, watching Biscuit chase that car was a little like solving a case. If you weren't careful, before long you were just going in circles, getting nowhere. And it could wear you out too!

Dexter scooped up the car in his hand and headed off into the other room. "I told you. . .boys are the best. I can always fool Biscuit. Some crime solver he is! And you girls think you're the best, but boys really are!" He walked off, muttering something about how girls weren't as smart as boys.

"He doesn't know how great the Camp Club Girls are, or he wouldn't be saying that," Sydney said, turning Kate's way. "But we'll forgive him. He's just a kid."

"Hey, I'm no kid!" Dex's voice rang out from the next room. "I'm almost nine! That's practically a teenager."

Both of the girls laughed.

"I can hardly remember what life was like when I was nine," Sydney said with a wink. "That was years ago!"

"And now that I'm almost twelve, nine seems *forever* ago!" Kate added. "A million jillion years, even."

Thinking of turning twelve reminded her of her birthday party. Thinking of her birthday party reminded her that they had to solve the case in just two days! Thinking about solving the case in such a short amount of time reminded her that they really, really needed to get to work.

"C'mon, Sydney!" she said, grabbing her friend's hand. "Let's send another email to the Camp Club Girls! We need them now more than ever!"

SWAT-bot to the Rescue!

The following morning, Kate received a call from Andrew. He sounded out of breath and very upset. In fact, she could hardly understand his words.

"K–Kate! Something terrible has happened!"

For a second, she thought he might start to cry. Kate sat straight up in the bed, clutching the phone to her ear as she asked, "What? What happened, Andrew? Tell me!"

"S–someone tried to b–break into our house last night. Our alarm went off. Thank goodness the person took off. Nothing was stolen, so that's good. But it was awful!"

"Ooh!" Kate shivered just thinking about it. "How scary! Did you wake up? Did you see him? What did he look like? Did the police come? Is your dad upset? What about your mom? How is she doing? Do we need to come over and help? Should I wake up my parents? What can I do?"

"Slow down, slow down. . . ." Andrew groaned. "You always move too fast for me, Kate. I can never keep up."

"Sorry." She drew in a deep breath and waited a second. "But I'm just so upset, Andrew! This is awful!"

Just then, Sydney woke up and popped up in the bed. "What happened?" she asked, rubbing her eyes. "Something with Andrew?"

Kate nodded. She put her hand over the phone and whispered, "Yes. Someone tried to break into the Smiths' house last night. A burglar! Isn't that awful?"

Sydney's eyes grew wider and wider. "Did he steal anything?"

"No." Kate shook her head. "And everyone's safe." She turned her attention back to her friend on the phone. "Andrew, I'm going to talk to my dad. Remember I told you about SWAT-bot—the little security robot he created? The one that just got patented?"

"Sure. But what does that have to do with anything?"

"Hang on and I'll explain. See, my dad is working on a second one. . .a more advanced version. I'll bet he will loan it to you if I ask. Would you like me to ask?"

"Would I! I'd feel so much safer if I knew SWAT-bot was on the job." Andrew sounded relieved, and Kate was happy to help. She felt sure her father would agree.

"Here's the really cool part," Kate said. "If anyone tries to break in again, SWAT-bot will call the police right away. He's programmed to do that. He'll recognize who belongs in the house and who doesn't. My dad can explain how all of that works. But here's the neatest thing of all—I know you won't believe this! He'll also take pictures and video without the person knowing. That's something ordinary alarm systems don't do. He also records voices and turns them into digital files that can be played back later. So if a crime is committed, he's a witness!"

"But what if the bad guys just steal him? He's really small, right? If they do that, the police won't know what to do or who took him."

"Wrong!" Kate said with glee. "If the burglar steals SWAT-bot, his GPS tracking device will lead the police right to the criminals and they won't even know they're being followed! Isn't that the coolest thing? He's a surefire security-bot!" She started to say how proud she was of her dad for inventing it, but Andrew interrupted her.

"That's cooler than all of your other devices put together." He paused. "Just let me know what your dad says, okay? I'm going to tell my parents right now. And thanks, Kate. I don't know what we'd do without you. I really mean that."

"Oh, I'm happy to help!"

As she finished, Sydney looked at her curiously. "We're getting closer to figuring this out, aren't we? I can feel it! We'll solve this case in no time."

"With God's help." Kate paused a moment and said, "So I guess we'd better ask Him for His help, because I sure can't do this on my own!" She took Sydney's hands in hers and they bowed their heads.

"Lord, it's me, Kate Oliver. Again. I know You know who I am because the Bible says You even know how many hairs are on my head. That's a lot more than I know, Lord."

Sydney chuckled but didn't say anything.

"Anyway, Lord, we really need Your help right now!" Kate continued. "We're on a big case and we don't have answers. But You do! We ask You to protect the Smith family and lift their spirits. And help us find whoever is doing this so everyone can see how great and mighty You are. In Jesus' name. . ."

"Amen!" She and Sydney shouted together.

Kate swung her legs over the side of the bed. "We have work to do, Sydney! I'd be willing to bet that would-be burglar is somehow connected to that guy at the stadium, but we have to prove it! I'm putting SWAT-bot to work!"

"Let's do it!"

Minutes later, Kate and Sydney bounded down the stairs. As always, she nearly tripped over her brother, who played with his electronic cars. "Dex, watch what you're doing! Playing with your cars on the stairs is dangerous."

He scooted over to let them go by, mumbling, "Boys rule, girls drool."

Kate just rolled her eyes. She ran into the kitchen, where her father was at the breakfast table reading the paper. He looked up as she came racing in.

"Dad, I need to borrow the newer, more advanced SWAT-bot. Is he ready to help solve a crime?"

"Solve a crime?" He put the paper down and gave her a curious look. "What are you talking about, honey? Why do you need SWAT-bot again?"

She quickly told him what had happened at Andrew's house and her father flew into action. He went down into the basement and came up with the security robot in his hands. "I'm not quite done tweaking him, so his photo abilities might be limited. But I think the video recorder works. And I checked the GPS tracking device yesterday, so it's working fine."

Kate patted the little robot on the head. "Work hard, SWAT-bot, and maybe you'll be famous someday! You'll get your picture in the paper!"

"Do you want me to drive you girls to the Smiths' house?" Kate's dad asked.

"Yes, please!" Kate jumped up and down, ready to roll!

Sydney grinned. "I'm gonna get to see Tony Smith's house? How cool is that! But do we have time for me to run first? I haven't exercised in days and I'm starting to feel flabby."

"Flabby?" Kate looked at her and laughed. "You're all muscle."

"It'll take me a few minutes to get ready," Kate's father said. "So go for a run, Sydney. But be back as soon as you can."

About ten minutes later, with Sydney a little out of breath, everyone climbed into the family van and Kate's dad drove them to the Smiths' beautiful two-story home with blue shutters. She had only been to Andrew's house a couple of times before, but never with Sydney. Her friend seemed overjoyed at the idea of going to a pro ballplayer's house.

When they arrived, Mr. and Mrs. Smith were still talking to the police.

Mrs. Smith even had tears in her eyes. And Tony's fists were clenched, like he was angry. But who could blame them? Kate would be upset if someone broke into her house too!

They invited Kate, her dad, and Sydney inside and then continued talking to the officer, who took notes of everything they said. He left after a few minutes, promising to do all he could to help. Kate wondered what it would be like to be a police officer. Surely his crime-solving abilities were even better than those of the Camp Club Girls!

As soon as the policeman left, Kate's dad went back out to the van and brought SWAT-bot into the house. "I want to loan you a new security device," he explained. "I think he's going to come in handy."

"*He*?" Tony's eyes grew wide. "Is this a robot? I've never seen any thing like this little guy before. I've heard about them, of course, but never-seen one."

"He's not on the market yet," Kate's dad explained. "But hopefully he will be before long. This is SWAT-bot, and he'll help protect your home."

"Wow." Tony stared at the little robot. "That's pretty amazing. Is it complicated to use?"

"It's not as difficult as it looks," Kate's dad explained. "In fact, he's pretty simple to operate. And you can check on your house no matter where you are. Just call this number"—he handed him a piece of paper with a number on it—"and SWAT-bot will report any suspicious activities."

"That's the coolest thing I've ever heard," Tony said with a nod. "And a lot better than our current security system."

"That's why my dad got a patent for SWAT-bot," Kate said, beaming with pride. "He's going to be super famous."

"Hardly." Her dad laughed. "And I have no interest in being famous, for that matter. But if he helps keep people safe, then I'm a happy camper."

Hearing the words "happy camper" made Kate think of the Camp Club Girls. She would send them an email to update them on the case, especially the part about Andrew's house getting broken into. Surely Elizabeth would put her prayer warriors to work! And McKenzie would probably be full of great ideas. So would the other girls.

Kate's dad continued showing Tony how to use the little security robot and said, "If you have any questions, you can always call me."

"I can't thank you enough." Tony walked with them to the door, but Kate could tell Sydney didn't want to leave. She paused at the door of the library—the room nearest the front of the house—with her mouth hanging open.

"Oh my goodness!" She pointed at the awards and plaques on the wall, turning in a slow circle to see them all. "Is all of this yours, Mr. Smith?"

"Yes." He nodded but looked a little embarrassed. "But I told you girls to call me Tony. Everyone does."

"Okay. Tony." Sydney looked at him and beamed. "C–can I look at some of these?"

"Of course." He flipped on the light in the library and led the way inside.

Kate stared at the walls filled with framed certificates, plaques, and awards. She'd never seen so many things of honor in one place before! Why, Mr. Smith must be a real superstar. Even her dad looked impressed, and he didn't care much about sports!

Tony led them around the room and showed them all of his awards. He explained each one. Sydney's eyes looked like they might just pop out of her head!

"This just makes me want to play ball!" she said. "Oh, I wish I could get out on that field and hit a homer for the Phillies!"

Kate giggled, watching her friend. What fun this must be for a sports nut like Sydney! This was probably almost as exciting to her as solving a case! At least, it seemed that way.

As he finished up the tour, Mr. Smith reached for a baseball and tossed it into the air. "I have quite a few of these signed baseballs if you girls want one." His expression grew sad. "Not many fans are asking for them these days." He set it on the desk with a sigh.

"Are you kidding? I'll take one!" Sydney practically jumped up and down. "Thank you, Mr. Smith. . .er, Tony. This is the best gift I've ever received."

"No problem! Happy to do it."

Kate was so thrilled for her friend. If anyone deserved a special gift, it was Sydney. Meeting Mr. Smith face-to-face was probably one of the coolest things that could've happened to her. And to get a signed baseball made it even better!

Tony led them back into the big foyer, and Kate could tell they were about to leave. She looked up at Mr. Smith, wanting to take care of one more piece of business. "Oh, while I'm here, is there some way to find out the name and maybe even the address of someone who has season tickets to the Phillies games?"

"Hmm." Tony's brow wrinkled. "Well, I might be able to contact a friend of mine who works up at the box office. But why?"

"Well. . ." She hesitated to tell him, afraid he might think she was crazy. "I, um. . ."

"Go ahead and tell me, Kate," he said, looking concerned. "Maybe I can help you if I know more."

"Okay." She exhaled loudly. "I saw a man at the stadium. . .and I can't be sure, but I think maybe he's the same man who tried to break into your house."

"What?" Tony looked tense. "What makes you say that?"

Kate quickly explained about the man at the stadium and his suspicious actions. When she told Tony about the MP3 player and the cord attached to it, he looked stunned.

"Are you saying someone's been recording my voice without my knowledge?"

"Maybe," Kate said. "At least, that's what I suspect. And I think he's been working hard to make you look bad, taking your words and twisting them up to make it sound like you don't like the team."

"Whoa!" Tony said. "That's scary."

"Yes, but it makes perfect sense," Kate's father said. "He must've edited your words and used them against you."

"That's awful," Mrs. Smith said, fanning herself. "Who would do such a terrible thing. . .and why?" For a minute, she looked like she might cry again. Kate almost felt like crying herself!

"That's what I'm trying to figure out," she explained. "And you have nothing to worry about! Sydney and I are on the case! And the rest of the Camp Club Girls are helping us!" She told them all about McKenzie, Alex, Elizabeth, and Bailey. Mr. and Mrs. Smith looked very impressed.

"Well, with so many supersleuths on the job, I'm sure we'll catch this bad guy in no time," Tony said. "And in the meantime, I'll contact my friend at the stadium box office. Maybe he'll tell me who sits in that seat—especially if he knows it's related to the break-in of my home. I'll have to share anything I learn with the police, of course."

"Of course!" she agreed.

Mr. Smith said goodbye to Kate's dad and waved to both of the girls as they walked toward the car. "I can't thank you enough!" he hollered from the front door. "And when you catch the person who's doing this, I'll treat you to something really special! Just wait and see!"

"Something special?" Sydney gasped then whispered to Kate, "What do you think he means?" After a second of staring into space, she squealed, "Oh! Maybe he'll give us a tour of the stadium!"

"Or maybe he'll ask us to sing the national anthem before a big game." Kate giggled. "That would be hysterical. Have you ever heard me sing before?"

Sydney laughed. "Yeah. I remember hearing you at camp. You weren't so bad."

"I wasn't so *good* either." Kate giggled again. "But that's okay. Whatever Mr. Smith has in mind will be awesome. But first"—she looked back toward his house as he closed the door—"first we have to solve this case!"

CHAPTER 12

Blogging for Clues

When Kate and Sydney arrived back home, they decided it was time to check out their new blog site to see if anyone had visited or left comments. Kate was thrilled to see that several of the Camp Club Girls and their friends had posted enthusiastic notes about Tony Smith. She glanced over the first few, impressed by how much the girls seemed to know about the Phillies.

Am I the only one who knows nothing about baseball? Hmm.

She would really have to do something about that. Maybe by the end of all this, she'd be the biggest Phillies fan ever!

"Hey, Sydney," Kate said, waving her hand. "Come on over and check this out."

Sydney drew near and whistled as Kate scrolled down, down, down, showing her the comments on their site. "Wow! Go, Camp Club Girls!"

"Looks like they got their friends and even some of their family members to post too." Kate scrolled down through all of the comments, smiling as she read most of them. However, she soon stumbled across one that didn't sound so nice, one she felt sure the girls hadn't written.

"Oh, look here, Sydney." She pointed at the screen. "This lady—I guess she's a lady—her screen name is PhiladelphiaLadyBug—is really mad at Tony Smith. She said some ugly things. I don't think she likes him very much!"

Sydney drew near and they both read the comment.

Go ahead and write your mushy articles about Tony Smith. I won't be reading them. He is a traitor to the team. I've lived in Philadelphia all of my life and we've never had a team member I've been ashamed of until now. He needs to go back to wherever he came from—and the sooner, the better!

"Wow." Kate felt a little mad as she read the note. "That's totally mean. I understand people getting upset—after all, they've been reading all of those other blog sites and listening to that radio interview—but that was really a rude thing to say."

Thankfully, the next few comments Kate read were nice. Then she stumbled across a really, really bad one! "Oh my. This one is *awful*." She read it from start to finish, goose bumps working their way down her arms.

I don't know who started this site or why, but you will be stopped. Tony Smith is not the hero you've painted him to be. In fact, he is just the opposite. Read the web. Listen to the radio. Hear what the fans and other players have to say. Then you'll stop writing articles like this. And if you DON'T...

"If we don't?" Kate shivered a bit. "Then what?"

"Ooh, this is awful!" Sydney said. "Who does he think he is? And what is he going to do to us if we keep this blog site going? Sounds like a threat."

"It does sound like a threat. But we don't even know it's a he," Kate said. "The screen name just says PhilliesFan29."

She shook her head, a scary feeling gripping her. "Hey, didn't we see that name on one of those other blog sites we visited the other day? Seems like we did."

"Hmm." Sydney looked at it closely. "PhilliesFan29. That *does* sound familiar."

Kate quickly did a search and found several sites with the name PhilliesFan29 on them. In every case, the comments were about Tony and were very mean! She read through every one and then kept searching, searching, searching for that original site—the one they'd seen that first day. The one Andrew had told them about. Finally she found it!

"Look, Sydney! This site belongs to that man, PhilliesFan29. His whole website is mostly just mean stuff he wrote about Tony. And now it looks like he's been traveling around the web, finding every site that says anything good about Tony, and leaving ugly comments."

"The puzzle pieces are starting to come together," Sydney agreed. "PhillesFan29 is our bad guy, isn't he? He's the one who started all of the rumors about Tony, and now he's really mad because we've been saying nice things about him. I guess that got this guy all worked up." She gripped her hands together. "But what do you think he'll do? I don't like to be threatened."

"Aw, don't worry. The worst he can do is hack our site," Kate explained.

"Hack our site?" Sydney looked confused.

"Rewrite it, replacing our words with his. Or remove it from the web altogether." She flashed a confident smile. "But don't worry. I'll take care of that. I'll set up the site so, as the administrator, I have to approve whatever anyone wants to post before it's put online. That should stop him." She shook her head. "I just wish I knew who this guy was and why he would care so much about Tony Smith, of all people."

"Yeah, it's obvious he's not really after us. He's after Tony," Sydney agreed. "But why? That's the part we still have to figure out!"

"Maybe we need to dig a little deeper," Kate said. "Keep searching the web for more signs of PhilliesFan29. If we do, we might learn more."

Sydney stood and began to do her stretches.

"What are you doing?" Kate asked.

"I always exercise when I'm nervous," she explained.

"That's funny." Kate laughed. "I always eat—Twinkies, mostly. And Ding Dongs."

Sydney started doing jumping jacks, and after a couple of minutes Kate's mother stuck her head in the door. "Everything okay?" She looked at Sydney and smiled. "Ah, that explains it! I felt the floor shaking and wondered what it was."

"Oh, sorry!" Sydney stopped, looking a little embarrassed.

"No, go right ahead. I'm just happy to know everything's okay." She disappeared from view and Sydney dropped to the floor and started her sit-up routine.

Kate continued to browse the web. After a little more searching, she stumbled across a personal blog site that belonged to PhilliesFan29. She read a few words, then gasped.

"Look, Sydney! His real name is J. Kenner. Wish I knew what the *J* stands for. Oh, and look. There's even a picture of him. He's not very old, maybe late twenties. I guess the 29 in his name means he's twenty-nine years old. She stared at the photograph of the man, and a cold chill wriggled its way over her. "Ooh! Sydney!"

"What?"

"It's that man."

"*That* man? *What* man?" Sydney leaned in to have a closer look. "Who are you talking about?"

"Oh my goodness!" Kate got up and grabbed her digital camera, opening it to the picture of the man at the stadium. "This is the same man, right? The one with the MP3 player. He's wearing a different shirt and his hair is a little darker now, but I'm really, really sure it's the same guy. No doubt about it!"

"Hmm, I'm not completely sure." Sydney turned the camera to get a closer look. "It *could* be him."

"No *could be* about it. This *is* him! The guy at the stadium is J. Kenner!" Her excitement grew as she spoke. "Watch and see! Tony's going to talk to his friend at the box office and they're going to confirm it. I'd bet my hat on it!"

"Do you own a hat?" Sydney asked and then laughed. "But seriously. . .why would this guy go to all of this trouble to hurt a Phillies shortstop? It still doesn't make any sense."

"Yeah. Why pick on Tony Smith?" Kate added. "What did he ever do to J. Kenner, after all?" She racked her brain, trying to come up with something, but nothing made sense. "Maybe they were college roommates or something. Maybe. . ." She paused as an idea struck. "Maybe J. Kenner was jilted in love. Maybe Tony's wife used to be J. Kenner's girlfriend or something like that."

"You've watched too much TV." Sydney laughed and then began to pace the room. "I've seen a lot of strange stuff in my life, you know. Stranger than TV. I live in DC, after all," she said. "And being so near the White House, I hear about lots of crazy things. People just do random, nutty stuff sometimes. Maybe this J. Kenner guy was a jilted T-ball player as a kid. You never know what makes some people snap. One thing's for sure—he has to be stopped."

"Should we go to the police?" Kate asked.

"I'm not sure we have enough evidence," Sydney said. "We need proof that he's the one who recorded Tony's voice and changed it. That means. . ."

Kate gasped. "Are you saying we need to get his MP3 player? I wouldn't feel right taking it, even if he is a criminal. That would be stealing, wouldn't it?"

"Well, I was thinking of *borrowing* it," Sydney explained with a twinkle in her eye. "Not keeping it for long, anyway. Do you think Biscuit might be able to help us get the MP3 player just long enough to pull the audio files from it? He's so good at helping with things like that."

As soon as Biscuit heard his name, he joined them at the computer, whimpering. Kate reached down with her free hand and scratched him behind the ears. "Do you miss us, boy?" She gave him a tender look. "You're used to helping, aren't you? But we can't take you into the stadium, now can we?" She looked at Sydney. "So how could we do it?"

His tail wagged merrily as if he were saying, *"I'd do it if I could."*

"I guess you're right," Sydney said finally. "There's really no way to sneak a dog into Citizens Bank Park, right? They only allow service dogs."

"Service dogs? You mean, like, dogs that belong to people in the army and marines?" Kate asked.

Sydney laughed. "No, silly. I mean service dogs. The ones who travel with handicapped people. But if you don't like the idea of actually getting our hands on the MP3 player, maybe we can find a copy of the audio recording online, if that's possible. That might work just as well."

"Oh, great idea! And my dad's voice-editing software might help us tell where the words were changed. I hope so, anyway."

She quickly typed the words *Tony Smith audio clip* into her search engine. It took some browsing, but eventually they found the radio interview online.

"I feel like we've hit the jackpot," Kate whispered. "This is a gold mine!"

"Well, we prayed. . .and God answered," Sydney said. "Why are we surprised?"

"I guess I shouldn't be, but I am." Kate looked at her friend in awe. "Oh Sydney, sometimes I just need bigger faith. I need to know that God is going to do what He says He's going to do!"

"Well, this whole thing has been a real faith-builder, hasn't it?" Sydney smiled. "And you know what? Before we do one more thing, before we even listen to that audio clip, I think we need to stop and thank God. We wouldn't know any of this without Him!"

"You're so right!" Kate agreed.

The two girls bowed their heads, and with a voice as clear as crystal, Kate began to pray—thanking God for all He'd done to help them track down the man who had hurt Tony Smith. On and on she went, telling the Lord just how grateful they were!

Then, with a heart filled to overflowing with joy, she turned back to her friend. "Tomorrow's my birthday!" she said, flashing her brightest smile. "And I suddenly feel like celebrating!"

Born on the Fourth of July!

On the morning of Kate's twelfth birthday, she awoke with a smile on her face. "I can't believe it! I'm twelve! Twelve! Almost a teenager!"

She thought about all that had happened over the past week and a half. In that short amount of time, her father had received a patent for SWAT-bot. Sydney had come for a visit. And they'd almost solved a major mystery.

Of course, they still had to track down J. Kenner, but that part she would leave to the police. She'd done a lot already, after all! She had started a blog site, investigated a suspect at the stadium, and figured out the whole PhilliesFan29 angle. Almost, anyway. There was still that one little matter of learning his first name, but that would come. . .in time!

And of course, she still needed to tell her father everything she and Sydney had discovered so that he could contact the proper authorities. They would need all of the correct information to track down the bad guy, and she was happy to share what she'd learned!

However, she would have to do all of that later. Right now, there were important things to do—like celebrating her birthday!

Kate sprang out of bed and pulled the covers off of Sydney. "Wake up! Wake up! This is my big day!"

"Your big day?" Sydney groaned. "What do you mean?"

"Well, for one thing, it's my birthday," Kate said.

"I know, I know. You've told me a thousand times. Happy birthday, Kate!"

"Thank you!" She giggled. "But there's something else. Something I've been dying to tell you. It's a project my dad and I have been working on in the basement for months! A huge secret! I wasn't going to tell anyone until we worked out all of the kinks, but it's my birthday, so I feel like telling you now."

"What is it?" Sydney's nose wrinkled. "What sort of secrets have you been keeping, Kate Oliver? Better tell me. . .quick!"

Kate giggled. "I *have* been keeping secrets, but they're good ones! Instead of telling you, it might be easier to show you." She tugged on Sydney's arm until her friend sat up in the bed.

"Okay, okay!" Sydney laughed. "I guess you're in a hurry, so I'll do my exercises later."

"Don't worry about that," Kate said. "I have just the thing to help get you moving. Trust me!"

Kate practically pulled Sydney from the bed. Seconds later, the two sprinted down the stairs, and then down the next set of stairs to the basement. Biscuit followed, almost slipping on the bottom step. "Careful, boy!" Kate called out. She turned on the light and Sydney gasped.

"Kate! I've never seen so much stuff! What is all of this?"

"My dad's inventions, remember? I told you! Kind of like *Honey, I Shrunk the Kids.*"

"Oh yeah." Sydney looked around with a dazed expression on her face.

"It's an electronic wonderland down here," Kate explained. "Better than an amusement park, and all original stuff!"

"No kidding." Sydney squinted, looking beyond the bright light. "So what am I supposed to be looking at? What's the big surprise?"

"It's right here." She pointed with great joy at the robotic brace she and her father had been working on for children with muscular dystrophy. Picking it up, she explained, "See, it's a brace. Kids who have muscular problems have a hard time performing everyday tasks with their hands."

"Why?" Sydney asked, reaching to hold the brace. She looked it over carefully.

"Well, their upper arms don't work very well," Kate said. "That's why Dad and I created Robo-Brace."

"Robo-Brace?" Sydney echoed.

"Yes, well, it's a brace to help kids with their movement. When they strap this on"—she demonstrated, putting it on her arm—"they have more arm strength and flexibility. It helps them lift things too." She demonstrated, and Biscuit began to bark and then jump up and down.

"Seriously?" Sydney stared at her, amazed. "Kate, this is one of the coolest things I've ever seen. When are you going to start manufacturing them for the kids with muscular dystrophy?"

"We need to do a lot more work before we'll be ready for that. But I've been working on this idea ever since I heard Andrew's dad was a spokesman for the Muscular Dystrophy Foundation. I wanted to surprise him." She frowned. "And then when I heard they didn't want him for their spokesperson anymore, it broke my heart! We've been working so hard on this secret project!"

"Let me try it!"

"Sure!" Kate helped Sydney strap on the brace, and before long Sydney was moving her arms up, down, and all around.

"Wow, this is giving me quite a workout," Sydney said. "I can feel it in my upper arms and my shoulders."

"Which is exactly where people with muscular dystrophy are weak," Kate explained. "So now you get it!"

"I do!" Sydney giggled. "You're a genius. But what about Tony Smith? He doesn't even know about all of this? He hasn't seen Robo-Brace?"

"No, never." Kate shrugged. "We were waiting. There's just been too much going on. I didn't want to bother him during that whole rumors fiasco."

"Well, I hope you're able to show him soon!"

"I plan on it," Kate said. She glanced at her watch and then sprang into action. "But first I have to go to a super-fantabulous birthday party!"

●━━●━━●

Later that afternoon, Kate's parents took the girls, Dexter, and Andrew to Ice De-Lights, a local '50s-style soda shop that specialized in birthday parties. They ordered burgers and fries for everyone, along with a beautiful ice cream cake that read HAPPY BIRTHDAY, INSPECTOR GADGET! Kate laughed when she read it.

They hadn't been there very long when a familiar '50s song started playing. All of the waiters and waitresses gathered in a long line across the front of the restaurant and did a funny little dance. Kate couldn't stop laughing as she watched them. Then—horror of horrors!—one of the waiters asked her to join them because it was her birthday. How embarrassing! She wanted to crawl under one of the tables or run out the door. Instead, she gave it her best effort. Not that she could dance very well, but she tried!

After that, Kate just relaxed and had a great time, completely forgetting about J. Kenner or anything having to do with Tony Smith. That was, until her dad's phone rang. She could tell it was serious by the expression on his face as he talked.

"What's that?" he asked. "Are you sure?" His eyes grew very, very wide as he listened to the response from the other end of the line.

"What is it, Dad?" Kate asked, looking at her father. "What's happened?"

Kate's father ended the call and looked at all of them. "Well, that was fascinating. Andrew's dad was calling with some very interesting news."

"Interesting news?" Kate bounced up and down, more curious than ever. "Tell us, please!" she chanted. "Oh Dad, tell us what he said!"

"Yes, please, Mr. Oliver!" Andrew added, his eyes now bugging. "Tell us!"

Kate felt sure she would burst with excitement! What, oh what, had happened?

CHAPTER 14

The Plot Thickens!

Kate could hardly contain her excitement. "What did Mr. Smith say, Dad? What did he say?"

Her father clasped his hands together and smiled. "He found out the name of the man at the stadium—the one you told us about, Kate, in that seat number you wrote down. His name is James Kenner!"

"James Kenner!" Sydney and Kate stared at each other in disbelief. "Wow, I *knew* it," Kate said. "We were right about the Kenner part. And *J* is for James."

"That's just amazing," Sydney added.

"Wait. . . ." Kate's father looked confused. "You mean you girls already knew the man's name?"

"We weren't sure, but I found a blogger online with the last name Kenner," Kate explained. "He was saying lots of bad stuff about Mr. Smith. So I just put two and two together. . . ." She shrugged. "I wanted to talk to you about it this morning, but I got so busy in the basement I almost forgot!"

"Well, speaking of busy, Tony and his wife want us to meet them at their house so we can tell the police everything we know." He winked at Kate. "Do you mind interrupting your birthday party to wrap up this case? After eating the ice cream cake, I mean."

"Mind? Of course not!"

"Well, let's get this show on the road, then," Andrew said. He stood and began to sing "Happy Birthday" to Kate. She felt her cheeks grow warm with embarrassment. First the silly dance and now this? Nothing like being put on the spot in front of a whole restaurant full of people! Kate knew her friend Bailey, one of the Camp Club Girls, would love that kind of attention, but Kate usually didn't like to be noticed so much.

After the singing, Kate blew out the twelve candles on the cake, and her mother sliced it into thick pieces. She could see the yummy strawberry ice cream and chocolate cake layers as her mother laid the pieces on plates.

"Open your presents while I'm serving the cake, honey," her mother said.

First she opened the gift from her parents. Ripping the paper was always such fun! When she got the package open, Kate stared at the red Phillies T-shirt. "Oh, how funny!"

"Well, we figured it was time to start supporting our team," her father said with a wink. "But we have something else for you too."

Kate opened the second package, stunned to see a necklace with the words INSPECTOR GADGET on it in little red ruby chips, the July birthstone. She stared at her mom and dad, feeling the sting of tears in her eyes. "Oh Mom! Dad! This is the greatest! Thank you so much!"

Sydney helped her put it on, and then she opened up a small package from Andrew. He watched her carefully. "I really hope you like this," he said. "I bought it just for you."

"Thanks!" She ripped the paper off of the gift and gasped when she saw the tiny electronic baseball game inside. "Andrew, how funny!" She laughed until her sides hurt. "This is great! I can't believe you did this."

"Well, I know how much you like electronics," he said with a nod. "And I know how much you want to learn about baseball, so I figured it was the perfect gift."

"It is!"

Next she opened the present from Sydney. "Sorry, but I didn't have much time to get you anything because I left DC so quickly." Sydney shrugged. "I hope you like it."

Kate stared at the framed photograph of the Camp Club Girls and a lump rose in her throat. "Oh, it's perfect! But I don't remember taking this picture."

"It was right after we found Biscuit." Sydney pointed. "See how scraggly he looks?"

"Oh yes. He does!" Kate looked a little closer. "And he has put on a few pounds since coming to live with us. I didn't realize until now!"

Her life had changed so much since then. Still, as she stared into the faces of her friends—McKenzie, Alex, Bailey, Elizabeth, and Sydney, she had to smile. What fun they'd had solving that very first case.

Thinking about that first case got her to thinking about the second. And the third. And before long, she was bouncing up and down in her seat, ready to go. But how could she leave without eating cake? No way!

Her mother set a piece of birthday cake in front of her and she licked her lips. "This looks so good!" Kate jabbed her fork into the yummy cold cake. She took a big bite. Then another. Then another. After a few seconds, she grabbed her head. "Ow! Ow!"

"What's wrong?" Her mother looked her way.

"Brain freeze," she said.

"Ah. I get that all the time when I eat ice cream too fast," Andrew said. "Just slow down, Kate."

Slow down? Slow down? Who has time to slow down? She wanted to eat a second piece before going over to the Smiths' house, and she had to do that in a hurry.

As soon as they finished the ice cream cake, Kate grabbed her presents and headed to the van. Her father drove them to the Smiths' house in a hurry. When they arrived, the home was surrounded by police.

"Oh no!" As Kate climbed out of the van, her heart began to beat double-time as she imagined what had happened. She followed Andrew as he ran toward his parents.

"What's going on?" he hollered as they drew near.

"Yes, what's happened?" Kate echoed.

"Oh, it was terrible," Mrs. Smith said, holding her hands to her heart. "We came home from the stadium to get a bite to eat and saw that the front door had been shoved in. The alarm was going off, so I knew the police were on their way, but I was scared to go inside. Your father was brave. He went in."

"Was it James Kenner?" Kate asked, feeling jittery.

"We don't know," Mr. Smith said, shaking his head. "I went inside and checked out the place. Whoever it was tore up my office and stole some of my awards."

"Oh no!" Kate gasped. Sydney looked as if she were going to throw up.

"There's worse news." Mr. Smith looked in Kate's father's direction. "They stole SWAT-bot too."

"Stole SWAT-bot?" Sydney groaned. "Oh no!"

"Don't worry! Whoever took him won't get away for long!" Kate's dad reached for his cell phone and punched in a telephone number. Within seconds, the GPS tracking system inside of SWAT-bot gave him the robot's exact location. "They're at the corner of Cottonwood and Denning Streets," he hollered. "We have to tell the police."

Kate could hardly contain her excitement! "Oh Dad! I'm so glad you invented SWAT-bot and gave him so many cool features! You're brilliant!"

Seconds later, a policeman exited the house and listened to their excited tale. He ran for his patrol car and headed off with his sirens blaring.

Kate knew he was on his way to the corner of Cottonwood and Denning. She jumped up and down. Oh, how she wanted to get into the patrol car and help the officer!

"Why, oh why, am I only twelve?" she asked, pacing up and down the front sidewalk. "I wanted to be the one to track him down!"

"Well, you did!" Sydney said. "It was your idea to bring SWAT-bot here, wasn't it? And it was also your idea to observe the man at the stadium in the first place. You knew in your gut he was the right guy."

"And I'd be willing to bet the man who stole SWAT-bot is named James Kenner," Kate said with a sigh.

"Otherwise known as PhilliesFan29," Sydney added.

"Some fan! He's nothing but trouble!"

Several minutes later, Tony received a call from the police, telling him they had the man in custody.

"Wow, that was fast!" Kate grew more excited by the minute. "So what's his name? Were we right? Did we figure it out?"

Tony gave her a wink. "What do you think?"

"James Kenner!" Kate, Sydney, and Andrew hollered together.

Tony nodded. "You've got it. Same guy! And that Kenner fellow has a lot of explaining to do."

"Like why he caused so much trouble for you," Mrs. Smith said, giving her husband a warm embrace.

"And why he broke into our house," Mr. Smith added. "I wonder what he was looking for."

"Maybe he wanted to sell your awards to make it look like you didn't care about them," Sydney suggested. "Probably on eBay or something like that."

"That's a good idea," Tony said. "You're a good guesser, Sydney."

Her cheeks turned pink and she looked a little embarrassed, but she said a quiet "Thank you."

"Kenner will never get the chance to sell or destroy any of your things now!" Kate's father explained. "The police caught him right away."

"Thanks to SWAT-bot!" everyone said in unison.

"And thanks to the Camp Club Girls!" Tony added with a twinkle in his eye.

"Maybe things will go back to normal now," Mrs. Smith said with a nod. "That's my prayer."

"Yes, I hope so too." Tony's face beamed with joy. "I love playing for the Phillies. In fact, I don't know when I've loved the game of baseball more. And now that this episode is behind me, things are going to get even better."

"Yes, as soon as the evening news breaks the story about James Kenner, your fans will realize that you never really wanted to leave in the first place," Kate agreed. "Then life will be back to normal. Now that's worth celebrating!"

At just that moment, a string of fireworks went *Crack! Crack! Crack!* in the distance.

"Oh, that's right!" Sydney exclaimed. "It's the Fourth of July! Yankee Doodle Dandy!"

Kate looked in the distance as she heard more cracks. "I love fireworks. *Love* them! They always make me so happy!"

"I still say they're lighting fireworks just for you," her mother said, reaching to hug her. "It's a nationwide celebration for my girl!"

"Just like every year on your birthday," her dad added.

"I wish I'd been born on the Fourth of July," Sydney said with a sigh. "Must be nice to have such a huge deal made over your birthday."

They all laughed.

"Well, if you're in the mood for celebrating, it's a good thing we don't have a game tonight," Mr. Smith said. "Would you all like to be my guests for a Fourth of July pool party here? And then front-row seats as I emcee for one of the largest fireworks displays in the nation?"

"You mean a Kate Oliver *birthday* party," Kate said with a giggle.

"That too," Mrs. Smith said and winked.

"In that case, we'd love to!" Kate looked at her mother and father. "Is it okay? I only have a few more days before Sydney has to go back home, and I want to make the best of them. Please, please, please!"

"No begging necessary!" her father said. "I'd love to. I've been wanting to get to know our new friends better, anyway."

The Olivers got their swimsuits from home and then the families spent the rest of the evening together, cooking hamburgers and hot dogs on the outside grill and talking about how God had turned their situation around. Kate had a great time laughing and talking. . .and best of all, there were no bad guys to think about!

At the end of the evening, after all of the fireworks had lit up the skies, the Olivers climbed into the van to go home. As they drove, Kate asked her father a question. "What's going to happen to SWAT-bot now, Dad? The police aren't going to keep him, are they?"

"Only long enough to retrieve the information from his hard drive," her father explained. "The photos and the audio/video recording should help them prove their case against James Kenner. Well, that, and his fingerprints all over SWAT-bot."

"I'm so proud of you, Dad," Kate said, reaching to give him a hug. "If you hadn't created that little robot, the police never would have caught the bad guy."

"Aw, thanks, honey. But I was just thinking about how proud I am of *you*. You did a great job following all of the clues!"

"She's certainly a chip off the old block," Kate's mother said.

Chip off the old block? Kate wanted to ask what that meant, but Sydney interrupted her.

"When we get back to your house, don't you think we should email the other Camp Club Girls and tell them what happened?"

"What time is it?" Kate asked.

"Ten fifteen," her mother said. "And it's okay to use the computer—but not for long, okay? I know how eager you girls are to share your news."

"Thanks, Mom! I can't wait to thank my friends for their help!" Kate said. "If they hadn't worked so hard to get people to our blog site, we never would have figured out the whole PhilliesFan29 thing."

When they arrived home, the girls signed onto the internet and went straight to the Camp Club Girls chat room. They found Bailey and McKenzie already in the chat room. Kate quickly filled them in with information about James Kenner's arrest.

Bailey: *I'll text the other CCG and tell them it's solved, if that's okay with you, Birthday Girl.*
Kate: *Of course! And I'll email them with details tomorrow.*

When Kate dressed for bed, Sydney was already curled up under the covers, fast asleep. Kate slipped into the spot beside her and prayed, *Thank You, Lord, for watching over us as we solved this case. I'm so grateful that You led me to James Kenner. Lord, I pray that You will help turn things around for Tony Smith and his family. Oh, and Lord. . .*

Just then, her cell phone rang. Kate looked at the caller ID and whispered, "I'll be right back, Lord. Better get that!"

She answered right away. "What's up, Andrew?"

"I just thought you would want to know. . .James Kenner confessed to the police. He's definitely the one who's been framing my dad."

"Did he say why?" Kate asked.

"Yes. Turns out, his younger brother is a shortstop who played college ball. He was supposed to get drafted to the pros this year. And he had his heart set on the Phillies."

"But there aren't any openings for that spot, right?" Kate asked. "Is that it?"

"Yes. I guess this James Kenner guy thought he was doing his brother a favor. If he could get my dad to leave the team—drive him away with these ugly rumors—then the Phillies would need a new shortstop."

"Oh, I see," Kate said. "He thought they would pick his brother to play in your dad's place."

"I guess." Andrew sighed. "It really makes me mad, Kate. I'm having a lot of trouble not being angry at James Kenner right now. I know I'm going to have to forgive him, but it might not be easy."

"Oh, I understand. Trust me," Kate said. "But just remember. . .the Bible says not to let the sun go down on your anger. It's never good to carry a grudge. But don't worry—Kenner will pay for this crime for a long time."

"I know." Andrew paused and then added, "Kate, thank you for all of your help. It's because of you that—"

"No, not me!" Kate interrupted him. "God is the One who solved all of this. And He's a far better supersleuth than I am. He's the best, in fact!"

"You're right!" Andrew agreed.

Kate looked over at Sydney, who slept soundly on the other side of the bed. "I guess I'd better go now, Andrew. I don't want to wake up Sydney."

"I'm awake," Sydney said with a groan.

Kate giggled as she whispered into the phone, "I'll talk to you later. Right now I'd better get some rest. I only have two more days with my friend, and I want to enjoy every minute!"

CHAPTER 15

Words Have Power

On the morning after her birthday, Kate awoke before anyone else in the house. She spent several minutes lying in bed, praying silently. She didn't want to wake Sydney, after all.

Slipping quietly out of bed, she tiptoed down the stairs. Biscuit followed her, whimpering.

"I know!" she whispered. "You need to go outside!"

After letting Biscuit out, she got on the computer, excited about a brand-new idea. She signed onto the internet and immediately started composing an email to send to the Camp Club Girls, filling them all in.

Kate lost all track of time, but when she heard footsteps coming down the stairs, she glanced at the clock. Had she really been working more than an hour? Wow! The time had flown by!

Sydney sat down next to her, rubbing her eyes. "So what are you working on?" She yawned.

"Letting the CCG know what happened," Kate explained.

Sydney nodded. "It mainly happened because of you, Inspector Gadget! You're loaded with great ideas!"

Kate grabbed her necklace and held it between her fingertips with a smile. It felt good to have her friend's love and support, but it felt even better to know she'd helped track down the man who was hurting Tony Smith with his words!

Minutes later, everyone in the house awoke and came downstairs for breakfast. As Kate took a bite of her cereal, the phone rang. Her mother answered it. After a few minutes of talking, she hung up and came over to the girls with a surprised look on her face.

"It's Tony Smith," she said. "He wants to come over to talk to you two. Better hurry up and get dressed for the day! I'll tidy up the kitchen before he gets here."

Kate and Sydney scrambled from their seats and raced up the stairs.

"What do you think he wants to tell us?" Sydney asked. "I'm so curious!"

"I don't know." Kate shook her head. "But remember. . .he said he was going to surprise us with something special if we solved the case. Maybe we're about to find out what he meant by that! I can hardly wait!"

"Oh, that's right. I wonder what he's decided to do!" Sydney clasped her hands together. "It's going to be great, whatever it is!"

Kate slipped into a pair of jean shorts and grabbed her new Phillies shirt.

"There's another game tomorrow night," Kate said. "I wonder if we'll get to go."

"Oh, maybe *that's* the surprise!" Sydney said. "Maybe Tony Smith will give us tickets for one last game!"

The doorbell rang and they raced to answer the door. Mr. Smith stood there with Andrew. Kate invited them into the house. Tony greeted her parents and then turned to the girls with a broad smile.

"Remember I told you I had a special surprise for you if you solved the case?" he said.

"Of course!" Kate practically squealed.

Sydney looked at him with anticipation in her eyes. "Please tell us!"

"Yes, please tell us!" Kate echoed.

"Well. . ." He smiled, obviously trying to tease them a little. "One of you will get to toss the first pitch at tomorrow night's Phillies game."

"W–what?" Kate asked. Did he really say what she thought he had said?

"N–no way!" Sydney stammered.

Tony nodded. "You get to choose! So who's it gonna be?"

"Oh!" Kate could hardly breathe. The very idea of going onto that field in front of millions and zillions of people gave her the shivers. Why would anyone want to do such a scary thing? She'd rather solve a hundred thousand crimes before doing that!

Out of the corner of her eye, she saw Sydney. Her friend's eyes were wide and she looked like she might cry.

"I. . .I. . .I. . ." Sydney stared at Tony, her mouth wide open.

Kate laughed, realizing what she needed to say. "Sydney, it *has* to be you. I wouldn't begin to know how to throw a baseball. I'd be embarrassed to even try."

"A–are you s–sure?" Sydney stammered. "Really? Me?"

"Really!" Kate, Andrew, and Mr. Smith said in unison.

"I get to toss the first ball?" Sydney began to squeal at the top of her lungs—so loud that Kate and everyone else put their fingers in their ears. "Oh, I don't believe it!" she shouted. "I don't! I'm going to put this on my résumé. My sports résumé, I mean. Can you believe it? Me! Sydney Lincoln—tossing the opening pitch at a Phillies game. Oh Mr. Smith, how can I ever thank you? What can I ever do? Write more articles? Tell people what a great player you are? Start a fan club?"

He laughed. "No, Sydney. You've already done so much for me. Andrew told me about the Camp Club Girls. Between your work and your prayers, you guys saved my career. So you owe me nothing for this. I'm just happy that you're happy."

"Happy!" Sydney's eyes filled with tears. "Next to being in the Junior Olympics, this is the greatest thing that's ever happened to me."

She kept talking about what a wonderful experience this was going to be, but Kate hardly heard a word. She was far too excited just watching Sydney's face, and she could hardly wait to tell the other Camp Club Girls!

"Oh, speaking of great things. . ." Kate snapped her fingers as another of her brilliant beyond brilliant ideas occurred. "Mr. Smith. . ."

"Tony," he said with a grin.

"Tony, can you stay a few more minutes? My dad and I have something in the basement we need to show you."

She looked at her father for support, and he nodded as he said, "I think the timing is finally right."

"Sounds like a mystery," Tony said. "But I'm happy to take a look. I'm curious." He followed as they all clambered down the stairs and into the basement. Kate turned on the light and Tony looked around in wonder. "You have a lot of really cool things down here," he said.

"Thanks," Kate and her dad said in unison.

"But there's one thing we really have to show you," Kate explained. She reached for the Robo-Brace. "It's something my dad and I have been working on. . .together."

Tony looked at it curiously. "What's this, Kate?"

"Well, it's for children with muscular dystrophy. To help them move their arms and hands. We call it Robo-Brace."

His eyes grew wide with excitement. "Really? Show me how it works."

She did just that and Biscuit began to jump up and down, trying to get in on the fun. He went *Yap, yap, yap!* as she moved her arms this way and that way.

Tony watched with an expression of awe. "That's the most amazing thing I've ever seen. And now that the Muscular Dystrophy Foundation has asked me to continue working as a spokesperson, I'm in a great position to help you get the news out on this."

"I'm hoping to get it patented soon," Kate's dad explained.

"I'm sure you will!" Tony nodded. "It's going to help so many people!"

"I'm so glad everyone has figured out what a great guy my dad is," Andrew said. "It was really hard to hear the mean things people were saying, especially when I knew none of them were true! That James Kenner needs to go to jail for a long, long time!"

"God will handle all of that," Tony said. "I've already prayed and forgiven James Kenner. What he did was wrong, but I have to forgive him anyway."

Kate sighed. What a good man Tony Smith was! And now everyone would know it!

They all spent a little more time looking at Robo-Brace and some of her father's other inventions, and then the adults went back upstairs to have some coffee. That left Kate, Sydney, and Andrew in the basement alone.

"I really wonder why James Kenner decided to use such a mean way to pick on your dad," Sydney said. "Those rumors he started could've ruined his career."

"I know," Andrew said. "But the police explained it to us. James Kenner said that rumors were what ruined his brother's chances to get in the pros, and he wanted the same thing to happen to the man who took his place."

"Wow! See what happens when rumors get started?" Kate said. She paused a moment then thought of something. "Oh! Our rumor box! It's still upstairs with those two rumors in it. What do we do with it?"

"Hmm." Andrew shook his head. "I don't know."

"Well, all of that stuff about Tony not liking to play for the Phillies was definitely a rumor," Sydney said. "So it can stay in the box. But I think I'd better take out the one about Kate Oliver being the smartest girl in the world—especially now! That's no rumor. It's the truth!"

Kate laughed. "Trust me, that one's not true either. I'm sure there are millions of smarter people than me. But as long as we're starting good rumors, how about I start one about you?"

"Me?" Sydney shrugged. "What sort of rumor?"

"Well. . ." Kate thought about it for a minute. "I think you know more about sports than any other girl. And even though you always try to win whatever game you're playing, you're always nice to others. You play fair. And you work hard to be the best you can be!"

"That's not a rumor either." Andrew laughed. "That's just the plain, simple truth."

Kate thought about that for a moment. "I guess you're right. Maybe we don't need a rumor box at all. Maybe God just wants to remind us to be really careful every time we hear someone say something about someone else—careful to make sure it's the truth before we spread it around to others."

"Exactly!" Sydney said.

"And we also have to remember that our words have power," Kate said thoughtfully. "Whether it's a rumor. . .or mean words or even nice words. Our words make a difference to others."

"The Bible says the power of life and death is in the tongue," Sydney said. "I read that just last week. Our words will either build others up or tear them down."

"Well, I'm going to be a builder-upper, then!" Kate said with a smile. "I'm gonna watch every word that comes out of my mouth so that others won't be hurt."

Sydney nodded. "I'm going to do the same. And we can send an email to Bailey and McKenzie and the others to let them know we're going to be a rumor-free group!"

"Ooh! Maybe we should print up some T-shirts!" Kate said. "They could say 'You and Me, Rumor Free'!"

Sydney laughed. "Great idea!"

As they made their way up the stairs to join the adults, all three chanted in unison, "Rumor Free! You and Me!"

CHAPTER 16

Supersleuths Forever!

On the morning after Sydney tossed the opening pitch at the Phillies game, Kate's mother drove the girls to the train station. All along the way they laughed and talked, reliving all of the fun they'd had over the past two weeks. Kate could hardly believe so much had happened. . .and in such a short time. It felt like months had flown by, not weeks!

"Remember when you thought bases were place mats?" Sydney asked.

"Yes." Kate gave her a sheepish grin.

"And you thought the field was a court?" Sydney continued.

"I remember, I remember." Kate groaned, feeling more embarrassed than ever. "I'll be the first to admit, I didn't know anything about baseball back then."

"But you sure do now! And you were a lot of fun at last night's game. You even cheered in the right places!" Sydney said. After a pause, she gave Kate a funny look and asked, "So. . .do you like it?"

"*Like* it? Like what?" Kate asked.

"Like *baseball*!" Sydney laughed. "Are you starting to like the game?"

"Are you kidding?" Kate giggled. "I'm already thinking of an article I can add to our Phillies site. I'm going to keep it going, you know. And the Camp Club Girls will help." Her heart swelled with excitement. "I can't believe I actually like a sport." She laughed. "How funny is that?"

"Pretty funny!" her mother said from the front seat. "But it might interest you to know that I played tennis in college."

"What?" Kate sat straight up in her seat. "Why didn't you ever tell me about that?"

"Oh, I don't know," her mother said with a shrug. "Just never came up, I guess. I was also on the swim team in high school. I've always enjoyed sports."

"Well, go figure!" Kate said. "The apple *doesn't* fall far from the tree."

She got tickled by that statement and started laughing. Before long, she and Sydney were all giggles. . .until they arrived at the train station. Then their laughter quickly turned to sadness.

"I can't believe you have to go back home," Kate said, giving her friend a hug. "I don't want you to leave! I'm going to miss you so much!"

"I know," Sydney agreed. "Me too! But I need to get home to my mom. It's not easy on her, now that my dad's not there."

"I know." Kate gave her friend another hug. "Oh, but promise me we'll see each other again really soon. Promise?"

"Promise!" Sydney said, flashing a broad smile. "We're the Camp Club Girls, remember!"

"Supersleuths forever!" Kate shouted with glee.

"Supersleuths forever!" Sydney echoed.

She then looked at Kate with a twinkle in her eyes, and together they added one last line, just for fun! "Rumor Free! You and Me!"

Camp Club Girls:
Kate's Vermont Venture

Three Blind Mice

"Ahhh!" Kate Oliver screamed as she ran from the Mad River Creamery. Her heart raced a hundred miles an hour. "Wait, Sydney!"

Her friend half-turned with a frantic look on her face. She kept running, nearly slipping on the icy pavement. "We can't stop! N–not yet!"

"B–but. . .you're too fast! I can't keep up!" Kate paused to catch a few breaths. Then she ran again. The sooner she could get away from what she'd just seen. . .the better!

From behind, she heard others crying out as they ran from the building. She'd never seen so many people move so fast! Kate had a feeling none of them would ever visit the Mad River Creamery again!

Whoosh! Kate's feet hit the slippery patch of ice. She began to slip and slide all over the place.

"Nooooooo!" she hollered as her tennis shoes sailed out from underneath her. She slid a few more feet, finally plopping onto her bottom on the icy pavement. Her tiny video camera flew up in the air. Thankfully Kate caught it before it hit the ground. When she screamed, Sydney finally stopped running and turned around.

"What are you doing?" her friend asked, sprinting her way. "We've got to get out of here! I can't stand. . ." Sydney's voice began to shake. "I can't stand. . .*rats!*"

Kate shuddered and the memories flooded back. Not just one but *three* jumbo-sized rats had raced across the floor of the creamery during their tour. One had scampered across her toes! Kate shivered—partly from the cold Vermont air, and partly from remembering the sight of those horrible, ugly creatures! *Oh, how sick!* And—just in case no one believed them—she'd caught the whole thing on video!

Sydney's hand trembled as she helped Kate up. "Let's go, Kate. I'm never coming back here. Never!" Sydney's dark braids bobbed back and forth as she shook her head. Kate saw the fear in her friend's eyes.

"But I *have* to come back," Kate argued as she brushed ice off her backside. "My school report! We'll only be in Mad River Valley a week. I have to get it written! I'll never get an A in science if I don't finish it."

"Just choose a different topic. Your teacher won't care—especially if you tell her what happened!" Sydney said as they started walking. "Vermont has lots of great things you could write about. Why don't you write your essay on your aunt's inn? Or about the ski lifts? They're the coolest I've ever seen!"

Kate shrugged, still feeling sore from falling. "I don't know anything about skiing, remember? You know I'm not into sports. And nothing is scientific about my aunt's inn. This is supposed to be a *science* paper not a *What I did on my Christmas vacation* essay!"

"Well then, what about the Winter Festival?" Sydney suggested. "I read about it in the paper at the inn, and I even saw a poster advertising it. They're having all sorts of races and prizes. Maybe you can write about competition from a scientific angle."

Kate groaned. "I guess, but none of that is as exciting as the creamery. I had so many ideas for my paper, and now. . ." She sighed. "Now I probably won't even get to go back in there."

"The Mad River Creamery is exciting, all right!" Sydney agreed. "Just wait till your teacher finds out about rats in their cheese! She'll tell her students and they'll tell their parents! Before long, supermarkets won't even carry Mad River Valley products anymore."

"I guess you're right," Kate said with a shrug.

Sydney laughed. "If you *do* go back, you should get extra credit for this paper, that's all I've got to say!" Her eyes lit up. "I know! Show your teacher that video! That will get you some bonus points!"

Kate sighed. "It does creep me out to think about going back in the creamery, but I wanted to write about all the electronic gizmos they use to turn milk into cheese. It's so. . .fascinating!"

"Yes," Sydney agreed, "but *rats* are not fascinating." She squeezed her eyes shut. Opening them again, she said, "They're awful, disgusting creatures! I hope I never see another one as long as I live."

Kate laughed as she trudged along on the snow-packed sidewalk. "I've never seen you scared of anything, Sydney. You're the bravest person I know."

"Just because I'm athletic doesn't mean I like rats and snakes and stuff." Sydney shook her head. "No thank you! I'll scale the highest heights. Ski down the biggest mountain. . .but don't ask me to look at a rat! Ugh!" Her hands began to tremble.

Kate looked at her friend curiously. "Why do rats scare you so much, anyway?"

Sydney's eyes widened. "I can't believe I never told you! A couple of years ago at summer sports camp, one of the boys put a mouse in my lunch sack."

"No way!"

"Yes. I opened the bag, and the rodent stared at me with his beady eyes." Sydney's voice shook. "I threw the bag halfway across the room."

"Aw." Kate giggled. "Was the mouse okay?"

"Was the *mouse* okay?" Sydney looked at her with a stunned expression. "What about me? Why aren't you asking if *I* was okay? It scared me to death! Seriously!"

"Still, it's kinda funny," Kate said, trying not to smile.

"Well, not to me. I've never liked mice. . .or *rats*. . .since. And especially not in a creamery." Sydney shook her head. "Not that the creamery will be open for long. I'll bet the health inspector's going to come and shut the place down permanently. That's what I'd do, anyway."

"That's just so sad!" Kate sighed. "For the owners, I mean. I'd hate to be in their shoes right now!"

"Me too!" Sydney said. " 'Cause their shoes. . .and their feet. . .are still inside that awful creamery!"

Kate finally started to relax as they walked together the three blocks to her aunt and uncle's inn—the Valley View Bed and Breakfast. When they drew close to the building, Kate saw her brother Dexter outside building a snowman. "Just wait till Dex hears about the rats!"

"Hey, Dex!" Sydney hollered. "Do we have a story for you!"

The nine-year-old rose and brushed snow off his wet knees. Then he jogged toward them, his cheeks bright red from playing in the cold. "What's up?"

"We saw *rats* at the creamery!" Sydney began to tell the story with great animation. Before long, Dexter's eyes grew so wide they looked like they might pop out.

"No joke? Rats! Ooo, that's so cool!" He rubbed his hands together. "Let's go back. I want to see them. Do you think they'll let me keep one? It's been ages since I've had a pet rat!" He rattled on about how much fun it would be to share his room with a rat.

Kate shuddered. "This isn't the day to ask. They've closed the creamery for the afternoon. I bet they won't even be open tomorrow."

"And besides. . .those weren't pet rats." Sydney squeezed her eyes shut and shivered. "They're probably disease-carrying rats."

Dex scrunched up his nose and said, "Sick! Never mind, then!"

A voice rang out from the front of the inn, and Kate saw Aunt Molly at the front door, waving. Then Uncle Ollie joined her.

"Come inside, kids. Lunchtime!" Uncle Ollie hollered.

"I've made homemade vegetable soup!" Aunt Molly added. "Perfect for a cold day like this. And we have apple pie for dessert!"

"Everyone in Mad River Valley knows your Aunt Molly bakes the best apple pies around!" Uncle Ollie said with a wink.

Kate smiled at her uncle. He looked so much like her father they could almost pass for twins. Uncle Ollie was older. And mostly bald. But she still saw the family resemblance. How funny that Uncle Ollie had just married a woman named Molly! Kate still giggled when she thought about it. Ollie and Molly Oliver. Their names just tripped across her tongue.

"Apple pie!" Dexter began to run toward the house. "My favorite!"

"Mmm!" Kate smacked her lips. Aunt Molly's great cooking would surely take her mind off of what had just happened. . .unless she served cheese on top of the pie!

Inside, Kate and Sydney pulled off their mittens and scarves, snow falling on the front rug. Kate's dog, Biscuit, jumped up and down, excited to see them. Then he licked up the little puddles of water from the melting snow.

"Sorry about the mess, Aunt Molly." Kate sighed.

"Never apologize for falling snow, honey," Aunt Molly said. "I always say snowflakes are kisses from heaven. So I don't mind a little mess. You girls have just left kisses on my floor!"

"You're so sweet." Kate hugged her aunt, noticing the familiar smell of her aunt's tea rose perfume.

"So. . ." Aunt Molly flashed a warm smile as she helped Sydney with her jacket. "What do you think of Mad River Valley? Did you kids find anything exciting in our little town?"

"Oh, more than you know!" Kate shrugged off her heavy winter coat. She explained what had happened, then added, "I don't know if I can ever look at Mad River Cheddar Cheese the same way again."

"I bet supermarkets all over the country stop selling it!" Sydney added.

Her aunt's brow wrinkled. "Oh dear! I know the Hamptons, who own the creamery. They're such nice people. This is terrible. . .terrible!"

"Very strange," Uncle Ollie added, shaking his head. "Highly unusual goings-on over there lately."

Aunt Molly led the girls into the kitchen, and Kate's parents soon joined them. After they sat down at a fully laden table and asked God to bless the food, Kate told her parents about their adventurous trip, but Sydney interrupted and told the part about the rats. "It was d–d–dis–*gus*–ting!" she added.

"Not a rat fan?" Uncle Ollie asked.

Sydney shook her head. "No, sir!"

"When Dexter was younger, he had a pet rat named Cheez-It," Kate's father explained. "I'll never forget that little guy. He was pretty cute, actually."

"Only, he bit me and I started calling him Cheez-*Nips*," her mother added, then grinned. "I never could stand rats. Still can't."

Sydney shivered, but Kate laughed. "They're okay in a cage," she said, "but not running around in a creamery."

Suddenly the food didn't look very appetizing, even to Kate, who usually loved to eat. And she couldn't help but notice the cubes of cheese in the center of the table. She closed her eyes and pretended they weren't there.

Aunt Molly clucked her tongue as she scooped up big bowls of steaming vegetable soup. "That poor, poor Hampton family. Haven't they had enough trouble already? Now their creamery will be shut down. It's a shame, I tell you."

She set a bowl of soup in front of Kate, and suddenly her appetite returned. She took a yummy bite and listened to the adults talk.

"Has this happened before?" Kate's mother asked.

"Sadly, yes," Uncle Ollie said.

"This isn't the first time the health inspectors have come," Aunt Molly explained. "They've been out twice before. Can't imagine what's causing this."

"Sounds like they'll have to shut the place down permanently, then," Kate's dad said.

Aunt Molly shook her head. "Just seems so sad. I've known the Hamptons since I was young. They're good people. And the creamery has had such a great record of cleanliness. Until a week ago. First I heard about an ant infestation. Then spiders. And now. . .rats! This is all so. . .shocking. Folks around here just find this all so unbelievable!"

"Hmm." Kate pondered her aunt's words. "Why *would* they have a rat problem now, after all these years? Out of the blue? Seems. . ."

"Suspicious?" Sydney whispered.

"Yes."

"Highly unusual goings-on," her uncle added, shaking his head. "Quite odd."

Kate looked at Sydney, her excitement growing. "Are you saying what I *think* you're saying?"

"Maybe they don't *really* have a rat problem at the creamery," Sydney whispered. "Maybe someone is just trying to make it *look* like they do, to sabotage them!"

"But, why?" Kate asked. "And what can we do about it?"

"I'm not sure, but I'm gonna pray about it." Sydney nodded.

"Me too. And maybe, just maybe. . ." Kate smiled, thinking about the possibilities. This wouldn't be the first case she and Sydney had solved together. No, with the help of their friends—the Camp Club Girls—they'd almost become supersleuths! They even had a page on the internet and a chat room!

"I'm glad you're going to help figure this out," Dex said with a frantic look in his eyes. "If the Mad River Creamery shuts down, I won't be able to eat my favorite cookies 'n' cream ice cream anymore!"

"Oh, that's right." Kate clamped her hand over her mouth. "It's not just the cheese customers will be losing. . .it's ice cream too."

"And milk," her mother added. "Their milk is the best in the country."

"But I'll miss their ice cream most," Dexter said with a pout.

Kate forced a serious expression as she said, "Especially their newest flavor."

"Newest flavor?" Sydney and Dexter looked at her with curious looks on their faces.

"Rat-a-tat-tat!" She almost fell off of the chair, laughing. "Get it? *Rat-a-tat-tat!*" She doubled over with laughter.

"That's horrible, Kate Oliver!" Sydney said, standing. "I'm never going to be able to enjoy ice cream again."

"You don't eat sugar anyway," Kate said with a shrug. "You're the healthiest person I know. But me. . ." She sighed. It really would be tough for her to give up Mad River's famous ice cream.

But how could she eat it now, knowing they had a. . .what would you call it? A vermin problem. That's what they had: vermin. Vermin in Vermont.

"Ugh!" A shiver ran down her spine. Vermin in Vermont. Would she ever think of the state again without thinking of. . .rats?

Only if they solved the case!

CHAPTER 2

I Smell a Rat

After lunch, the girls took Biscuit for a walk and talked about the case.

"I wonder if this is a case of sabotage," Kate said, kicking up a pile of snow with her boot. "I think so. Don't you think?"

"Probably if they've had so many problems they've never had before. But, why?" Sydney asked, looking worried.

Kate sighed as she pulled her coat tighter to fight off the bitter cold. "We need to call the other Camp Club Girls. Surely one of them would know what to do."

Sydney giggled. "Knowing Bailey, she would also want to fly out here and join us."

Kate laughed. "Yes, and Alexis would be telling us just how much this case is like some book she read, or some movie she watched."

"Elizabeth would remind us to pray, of course," Sydney added. "And to guard what we say so that we don't falsely accuse anyone."

"Yes, and she'd probably quote that King James scripture she loves so much. . . 'Vengeance is mine; . . .saith the Lord.'" Kate smiled, just thinking about her friend. Elizabeth loved the Lord so much, and it showed in everything she said and did.

"What about McKenzie?" Sydney asked.

"She would keep searching for clues till she found the culprit!" Kate explained. "You know McKenzie! She would examine the motives of every suspect until she solved the case."

"Can we call a meeting of the Camp Club Girls in our chat room tonight?" Sydney asked. "Does the inn have internet access?"

"Uncle Ollie has a wireless router," Kate said. "I know, because I've already checked my email on my smartwatch."

"Your watch?" Sydney looked at her curiously.

"Yes, remember?" Kate stopped walking long enough to hold up her watch. "I have a smartwatch. One of my dad's students at Penn State invented it. He's a robotics professor, you know."

"I know, I know." Sydney laughed. "And you're going to be one when you grow up too!"

"Yep," Kate agreed. She looked at her watch once more. "I have to be close to a wireless signal to get online on my watch," she explained. "We're too far from the house now or I'd show you how it works."

Sydney grinned. "Okay, Inspector Gadget! I always forget you've got such cool stuff."

Kate laughed when Sydney called her by the familiar funny nickname. "Well, that's what happens when your dad is into electronics like mine is! He gives me all of his old stuff—cell phones, digital recorders, mini-cams, and all that kind of stuff—when one of his students invents something better. And this watch. . ." She glanced down at it with a smile. "It's the coolest gadget of all. I can check my email and even send instant messages with it."

"And check the time too!" Sydney chuckled. "Which is about all I can do on my watch. . .period!"

"Speaking of the time, I think it's nearly time to meet Uncle Ollie and Dad in the big red barn out back." Kate squinted to catch a glimpse of the building through the haze of the drifting snow. "They're in the workshop."

"Why are we meeting them, again?" Sydney asked.

"I think Uncle Ollie wants to introduce us to someone. There's a neighborhood boy who's been helping him with some of his projects. I think his name is Michael. We're supposed to be nice to him." She shrugged, unsure of what to say next.

"Is he cute?" Sydney asked with a twinkle in her eye.

Kate shrugged. "I don't know. Could be. I just know that Uncle Ollie said he's kind of a loner." She shivered against a suddenly cold wind that tossed some loose snow in her face.

"A loner?" Sydney wrinkled her nose. "Meaning, he doesn't have any friends? That's kind of weird."

"Maybe." Kate sighed. "Molly told me he's just sad because his grandfather died last month. So Uncle Ollie's been playing a grandfatherly role in his life. I think that's pretty nice, actually."

"Oh, I see." Sydney looped her arm through Kate's. "Well, why didn't you just say so? I'll be extra-nice to him. Poor guy."

With Biscuit on their heels, the girls trudged through the now-thick snow to get to the barn. Kate pulled back the door, amazed at what she found inside.

"Doesn't look like any barn I've ever seen!" Sydney said with a look of wonder on her face.

"I know." They stood for a moment, just taking in the sights. "Look at all of Uncle Ollie's electronics! This place is even better than my dad's workshop in our basement."

"I can sure tell your dad and his brother are related!" Sydney said.

"No kidding. Except, of course, Uncle Ollie is a lot older. And he is so smart!" Why, next to Dad, he was the smartest man Kate had ever met.

Off in the distance they heard voices. Kate followed them until they reached a small, crowded work space filled with all sorts of electronics and robotic goodies. "There you are!" she said as she caught a glimpse of her father and uncle.

A boy, about fourteen, stood in the distance. *That must be Michael.* He was tall and thin with messy hair that needed to be combed.

Michael turned to look at them with a nervous look on his face. At once, Biscuit began to growl.

How odd, Kate thought. *Biscuit gets along with everyone!*

"Stop it, Biscuit!" She tugged his leash and he stopped, but she could tell Biscuit was still uneasy. Very, very unusual. Something about this boy made Kate suspicious right away. She immediately scolded herself. *Stop it, Kate. He's never done anything to you. Be careful not to pass judgment on someone you don't even know!*

Sydney didn't seem to notice the tension in the air. She went right up to Michael and introduced herself with a welcoming smile. After taking a seat on a nearby chair, she asked, "Have you lived in the area long?"

He shrugged, but never looked her way. "I grew up in Mad River Valley. Why?"

"Oh, I just wondered." She looked around the workshop then glanced back his way. "Do you ski?"

"Of course. Who doesn't?" He looked at her as if she were crazy.

"I don't," Kate said. "Never have."

He shrugged and went back to working on some electronic contraption. "That's weird."

"So, if you ski, are you going to enter the Winter Competition?" Sydney asked.

"Maybe." He kept his eyes on his work. "I usually do, but I don't know if I feel like it this year."

"Oh, you should! It would do you good." Uncle Ollie patted Michael on the back then turned to the girls. "You should see him ski! He's the best in his age group. Wins every year."

"Humph." Sydney crossed her arms at her chest and looked him in the eye. "We'll just see about that."

"Oh yeah?" Michael turned her way. "What do you mean by that?"

"I mean, this year *I'm* entering too." Sydney nodded, as if that settled the whole thing.

"You are?" Kate turned to her friend, stunned. "Really?"

"Did you see the grand prize?" Sydney said, her voice growing more animated by the moment. "Three hundred dollars! That's exactly the amount I need to go on my mission trip to Mexico this summer."

"Oh, I see." Kate pondered that for a moment. Sydney would have a wonderful time on a mission trip. And Mexico. . .of all places! Sounded exciting.

Sydney sighed. "My mom doesn't make a lot of money." She shook her head. "And things are really tight right now. But she told me I could go if I could raise the money on my own. So, that's why I have to win that competition! I've read the article in the paper a dozen times at least. And I've stared at the poster in the front room of the inn a hundred times!"

"You have?" Kate looked at her, stunned. "Why didn't you say something sooner?"

"I don't know." Sydney looked down at the ground. "I still have to come up with the entrance fee. Twenty-five dollars. But I think my mom will send it if I ask."

"Wow." Kate stared at her friend. "So you really want to do this."

"I do."

Michael crossed his arms at his chest and stared at her. "Well, maybe I *will* enter after all. We'll just see who's the best."

"Fine." Sydney shrugged. She stuck out her hand and added, "And may the best skier win!"

Michael shook her hand then went back to his work. Kate could see now that he was putting together an electronic resistor board. *What are they building out here, anyway?* she wondered. She drew near to Sydney and whispered, "What can I do to help you win the competition?"

"Hmm." Sydney pursed her lips and squinted her eyes. "I guess you could help me find the perfect skis. I'll have to rent them, probably." A sad look came over her. "I guess that will cost even more money, so maybe not. I don't know."

"Maybe Aunt Molly can help with that," Kate suggested.

"Maybe. And then I have to find out where the competition will be held. I want to hit the slopes in advance. Get in plenty of practice." Sydney's eyes lit up. "Oh, you need to come with me!"

"Me? Put on skis? I don't know. . ." Kate hesitated. "I never. . ."

"I know you've never skied before, but there's a first time for everything. Besides, I need someone to clock my time. So you won't really be doing a lot of skiing. I think it will be good for you, Kate! You'll learn something new, and I know you love learning things."

"Maybe." Kate shrugged. "Just usually not sports! But first let's go talk to Aunt Molly and see if she knows where we can get some skis."

"Hope she has two pairs!" Sydney said, looping her arm through Kate's. "Then it'll be you and me. . .off to ski!"

Another shiver ran down Kate's spine. This one had nothing to do with the cold. How could she possibly make Sydney understand. . .she didn't like sports! Not one little bit! And the very idea of soaring down a hill with boards strapped to her feet scared her half to death!

Sighing, she headed back toward the house to ask Aunt Molly about the skis. Hopefully she would only have one pair!

The Mousetrap

Kate and Sydney tromped through the snow, finally reaching the back door of the inn, which led straight into Aunt Molly's spacious kitchen with its big, roaring fireplace. As they stomped their snow-covered boots on the mat, Biscuit jumped up and down excitedly. Must be the smell of gingerbread that had him so excited!

"Oh, yum!" Kate looked down at a large tray where several cookies were cooling. "I love these!" She pulled off her coat and hung it on the coatrack, then turned to her aunt with a "Can I have one?" grin.

"I'm glad to hear that you like gingerbread." Aunt Molly handed each of the girls a warm cookie. "Taste and see if they're any good."

"Oh, they're the best I've ever had!" Kate spoke between bites. She snapped off a little piece and handed it to Biscuit, who gobbled it up and begged for more.

"I saw that, Kate!" Aunt Molly said. "You shouldn't be giving sweets to a dog!"

"I know, I know." She sighed and pulled off her mittens. "I know I spoil him. . .way too much! But he's such a good dog, and he's been great at solving crimes, so every now and again I like to treat him."

"Treat him too much and he'll be as big around as a turkey at Thanksgiving!" Aunt Molly laughed.

"I know, I know." Kate hung her head in shame, then looked up with a grin.

"I've got some good news!" Aunt Molly said as they nibbled. "The creamery is open again. The health inspector came this morning and couldn't find any rats. In fact, they couldn't even find a hint that there had ever *been* rats. Strange, isn't it?"

"Wow! That's amazing," Kate said. "I need to go back for the tour and get some more information for my essay. Do you think Mr. Hampton would give me an interview? Maybe on video? I'd love to share it with my class. My teacher might even give me extra credit!"

"I'll call him and ask," Molly said. "Surely he will do it for me. I'm an old friend." She winked as she said the word "old" and Kate grinned.

"Do we have to go back there?" Sydney asked, looking worried. "I don't care what the health inspector said. We just saw rats in that place yesterday. Besides, I need to go skiing. I need the practice, remember?"

"Yeah." Kate leaned her elbows on the counter and sighed.

"What's wrong, Kate?" Her aunt gave her a curious look.

"Sydney wants to enter the ski competition at the Winter Festival to raise money for a mission trip to Mexico," she explained.

"Well, that's a lovely idea!" Aunt Molly stopped working long enough to grin at Sydney. "I think that's wonderful." She set two steaming mugs of hot apple cider down in front of the girls.

"Only one problem. Well, two, actually." Sydney shrugged. "I don't have any skis, and I don't have money to enter the competition. At least, not yet. I'm going to ask my mom."

"I can help with the skis. I have a wonderful pair," Aunt Molly said with a wink. "They're in the barn. Want to go see them?"

"Well, um. . ." Sydney looked a little embarrassed.

"What, honey?"

"Well, Michael is out there, and he's going to be competing against me," she explained. "So I don't really want him to see what I'm up to."

"Oh, I see!" Aunt Molly giggled. "So this is a covert operation, then?"

"Covert operation?" Kate looked at her, confused.

"Top secret mission," Aunt Molly explained. "Is that what this is?"

"Oh yes!" Kate and Sydney spoke together.

"We don't want anyone to know anything!" Sydney explained.

"Excellent idea." Aunt Molly nodded. "And I've got just the pair of skis for you. I used to ski a little, myself. These were mine from years ago. And I've even got an extra pair for you, Kate. They're not the new, expensive kind, but they will do for a beginner."

"Oh no!" Kate argued. "I don't ski, Aunt Mol. Seriously. Not ever. And I don't want to start!"

"Hmm. Well, we'll see about that." Aunt Molly snapped the leg off a gingerbread man and popped it into her mouth. "We will just see about *that*." Biscuit stood at her side whimpering until she finally gave him a tiny piece of the cookie. "Go away, goofy dog! You're going to eat me out of house and home!"

Kate looked at Sydney, hoping to convince her. "I don't mind if you go, of course. You need the practice. I don't. And maybe I can go with you tomorrow. Today I need to stay here and research cheese making for my essay paper."

Sydney rolled her eyes. "C'mon. Are you serious? You want me to believe you'd rather work on a school paper than hang out on the slopes?"

"You don't understand." A lump rose up in Kate's throat. "I *have* to get the best grade in the class because. . ." She didn't finish the sentence. No telling what Sydney and Aunt Molly would say if they knew the truth.

"Tell me, Kate." Sydney took another bite of a gingerbread man. "Why do you have to have the best one in your class? Why is it so important?"

"Because. . ." She shook her head. "Never mind. It's no big deal."

"Must be," Aunt Molly said, her eyes narrowing a bit. "Or you wouldn't have brought it up. Go ahead and tell us, Kate. Confession is good for the soul."

"Oh, okay." She bit her lip, trying to decide where to start. Surely Aunt Molly would understand. "There's this boy in my science class," Kate said, finally. "His name is Phillip. He's the smartest person I know."

"Smarter than you?" Sydney's eyes widened. "Impossible!"

Kate shrugged. "I don't know. Maybe. But we're always competing to see who gets the best grades. Kind of like you and Michael are going to do on the ski slopes. Lately, Phillip has been, well. . ." Her voice trailed off and she sighed.

"He's been getting better grades than you?" Aunt Molly asked.

"Yes, but that's not all." A lump rose in Kate's throat as she remembered the things Phillip had said. "He made fun of my last science project. I did a great job on it, and the teacher really liked it, but. . ."

"Oh honey. I'm sorry he hurt your feelings." Aunt Molly shook her head.

"I don't like to be made fun of."

"No one does," Aunt Molly explained with a sympathetic look on her face.

"He doesn't sound like a very nice guy," Sydney said.

"He's not. He even told me. . ." Kate felt the anger return as she thought about him laughing at her. "He even told me that I would never be a professor like my dad. . .because I'm a girl."

"Ah." Aunt Molly nodded and handed her another cookie. "So, you're going to try to prove him wrong by being better than him at something."

"M—maybe." She shrugged and bit off the gingerbread man's head. The yummy, warm cookie slowly dissolved in her mouth.

"Kate." Aunt Molly reached over and placed her hand gently on Kate's. "It's not wrong to want to be the best you can be. But in this case, I question your motives. You've got to examine your heart, honey."

"Examine my heart?" Kate swallowed a nibble of the cookie and took a drink of the hot apple cider. "What do you mean?"

"I mean, you need to start by forgiving Phillip for what he said."

"Oh." Kate sighed and took another sip of the cider. "I never thought about that."

"Holding a grudge isn't a good thing. Besides, the Bible says the Lord will only forgive us to the extent that we forgive others."

"W—wait. What do you mean?" Kate stared at her aunt, stunned. "You mean God won't forgive me if I don't forgive Phillip?"

"Well, Ephesians 4:32 says we should be compassionate and understanding toward others, forgiving one another quickly as God forgives us."

"Whoa." Sydney and Kate both spoke at the same time.

"Forgive quickly? But that's hard to do." Kate drew in a deep breath as she thought about it. "Sometimes it takes awhile to forgive, doesn't it?"

"Sometimes. But here's the problem with holding a grudge," Aunt Molly said. "It might start out small—like competing over whose essay is best. Then before you know it, a grudge can turn into revenge. Anger. And that's never good. So, it's better to put out that spark before it becomes a raging fire."

"Wow." Kate thought about her aunt's words as she continued to nibble on the cookie. It was all starting to make sense.

"Think of it like this." Aunt Molly appeared to be deep in thought for a moment. "Let's use what's going on at the creamery to illustrate. Imagine you're a little mouse and you see what looks like a beautiful piece of cheese. You run over to it and grab it, then. . .*snap!* You're caught in a mousetrap."

Kate nodded, "I see what you mean."

"Unforgiveness is a trap," Aunt Molly explained. "And as soon as you're caught in it, you're in trouble. So, let go. Forgive. It's always the best choice."

Kate stared at the fireplace, listening to the crackling and popping sounds the fire made. "I never thought about that before, Aunt Molly. I guess I have been holding a grudge but didn't realize it. Will God forgive me for that?"

"Of course He will! But you have to pray about it. And then—while you're at it—pray for Phillip too," her aunt said. "And you never know. . . you two might end up being friends when all is said and done."

"I can't imagine that." How could she ever be a friend to such a mean person?

"I know it seems impossible now, but trust me when I say it is possible." After a wink, Aunt Molly added, "Ask me how I know."

"How do you know?" Kate asked, nibbling on her cookie.

"Because your Uncle Ollie and I met when we were competing against each other in a square-dancing competition. We were both mighty good, though maybe I shouldn't say that."

"Oh, wow!" Kate giggled. "So, who won? You or Uncle Ollie?"

"In the long run, we *both* won," Aunt Molly explained with a sly grin. "Though it certainly didn't seem like it at the time. In the second round of the competition, my partner hurt his leg. And Ollie's partner got sick. So, we ended up competing together. . .as a team." She giggled. "And the rest is history!"

Sydney's eyes sparkled. "You fell in love on the dance floor? He danced his way into your heart?"

"Well, not that first day, but it didn't take long." Aunt Molly winked. "Ollie Oliver is a godly man and a great dancer. What a charmer!" Her cheeks turned pink, and she giggled.

Sydney sighed. "That's so sweet!" She grinned at Kate. "So maybe you and Phillip will fall in love and get married someday!"

Kate shook her head. "No way! But maybe we will end up as friends like Aunt Molly said. I just never thought about it before."

Sydney nodded. "And who knows? Maybe I'll even learn to like Michael." She shrugged. "It's possible."

"I hope so," Aunt Molly said. "That would be nice. He's such a great boy."

"Hmm." Kate wrinkled her nose. "I guess we need to give him the benefit of the doubt, even though he didn't make a very good first impression."

"I still plan to beat him in the skiing competition," Sydney said. "And I do need to practice. But I'll make you a deal, Kate. Today I'll go back to the creamery with you *one* last time. But tomorrow, you have to come skiing with me. Promise?"

Kate paused. She didn't know if she should promise such a thing or not. After all, she'd never skied before. "I—I guess so," she said, finally. "But for now, let's get back to cheese making!"

Sydney made another face then shuddered. "I sure hope there aren't any rats this time."

"Surely not," Aunt Molly said. "But if you *do* happen to see one, just remember that story I told you about the mousetrap. It's better to forgive than hold a grudge."

"It's better to forgive than hold a grudge," Kate agreed. Then, with a happy heart, she looped her arm through Sydney's and they headed back to the creamery.

The Big Cheese

Kate and Sydney walked the three blocks to the creamery with snow falling all around them.

"Don't you just love Vermont?" Sydney asked. "It's so pretty here." She began to describe the beautiful trees and the crystal-like snowflakes. On and on she went, sounding like a commercial.

"Mm-hmm. I like it here, but it's so cold!" Kate shivered.

"It's cold in Philly, where you live," Sydney said. "And in DC, where I live, it gets really cold in the wintertime. So this doesn't feel any different to me. No, I love the cold weather. And I can't wait to put on skis and glide down the mountainside. Oh, it's going to be wonderful! You're going to *love* it, Kate. I promise!"

"If you say so."

As the creamery came into view, Sydney groaned. "I can't believe I offered to come back here. This place is so scary. Do we really have to go back in there?"

"We do. But maybe we'll have a better time if we think happy thoughts," Kate suggested. "We'll focus on the good things. For example, I've been saving my allowance so I can buy different cheeses to take back to my class. You can help me decide what flavors to buy. Should I get Swiss or cheddar? And if I get cheddar, which kind? There are so many, you know." She went off on a tangent, describing her favorite kinds of cheese.

"I can't believe you're actually going to *eat* something made there." Sydney scrunched her nose. "I'd be scared to! Aren't you worried?"

"Nah," Kate said, shaking her head. "And besides, I have the *strangest* feeling about all of that, Sydney. I'm convinced someone is sabotaging the Hamptons. But, why?"

"Hmm." Sydney walked in silence a moment. "Maybe we should put McKenzie or one of the other Camp Club Girls to work, figuring out who their main competitor is. Maybe someone from another creamery is jealous and wants to put the Hamptons out of business."

Just before they entered the building, Kate caught a glimpse of someone familiar off in the distance. "Hey, look, Sydney! It's that boy. . . Michael! Are you going to tell him that you're entering the competition?"

"No way!" Sydney grabbed her arm and whispered. "It's top secret, remember? I don't want him to know."

They walked inside the store at the front of the creamery, and Kate took a deep breath. "Oh, it smells so deliciously cheesy in here!" She closed her eyes and breathed in and out a few times. "I totally believe this is what heaven it going to smell like."

Sydney grunted. "Heaven. . .smells like *cheese*? I sure hope not! Doesn't smell so good to me." After looking around the empty store, she added, "Look, Kate. Have you noticed? We're the only ones here. That should tell you something! People are scared to come back."

"Or maybe we're just early." Kate looked at her smartwatch. "Ooo! I have an email." She quickly signed online and smiled as she read a note from Bailey that said, *Have fun in Vermont!* Kate quickly typed back, *Having a blast!* then pressed the tiny SEND button.

"I don't blame people for being scared to come here," Sydney said.

Kate looked up from her watch and shrugged. "Well, let's not think about all that. Since we're here, let's sample the cheeses."

"I guess so." Sydney shrugged. "But you can do the sampling. I'll just watch."

They walked around the large glass case, looking inside. "Oh, I *love* Colby Jack!" Kate reached for her camera and took a picture of the tray filled with chunks of orange-and-white swirled cheese. Then she lifted the clear dome top from the cheese tray and took a piece. With her mouth full, she pointed at the tray next to it. "They have every kind of cheddar imaginable! Yum!" She lifted the top on that tray and took several pieces. "Wow, this is great!" She'd never seen so many different kinds of cheeses . . .and all the samples were free! But which one should she buy for her classmates?

"My favorite is the Swiss," Sydney said, taking a tiny piece. "Mom puts it on my turkey sandwiches."

"Ooo, you're making me hungry." Kate took a couple of chunks of the Swiss cheese and ate it right away. "Let's order something to eat." She pointed at the Cheese-o-Rama Snack Shack in the corner of the room. "Look! It says they make the world's best grilled-cheese sandwiches, and you can pick the kind of cheese you want. I'm going to ask for the Colby Jack on mine. What about you?"

"Kate, we just ate breakfast a couple of hours ago," Sydney said. "And then we ate your aunt's gingerbread cookies. I don't need the extra calories. And I still think we should be careful not to eat too much cheese from this place."

"Calories, schmalories." Kate shrugged. "Who cares?"

"I do." Sydney gave her a stern look. "I have to stay in shape to win that competition next weekend."

"You're already the fastest, strongest, most athletic girl I know!" Kate said. "What else do you want?"

"I want to win."

"Well, I'm not competing, and I'm hungry. Besides, it's almost lunchtime and we'll never make it back to the inn in time for Aunt Molly's food. So, let's eat!"

Kate went to the counter and ordered a cheese sandwich with a side of cheese-flavored chips. Mr. Hampton—her aunt's friend—prepared her sandwich. He looked a little worried.

As he placed her plate in front of her, Kate whispered, "Mr. Hampton, did my Aunt Molly Oliver call you?"

"She did." He gave a hint of a smile.

"Could I speak with you. . .alone?" She looked around, hoping not to be overheard, then remembered no one else was in the shop. "I'm working on a paper for school and would love to get some information—straight from the source!"

"Sure, I'd be happy to help." His shoulders sagged as he looked around the shop. "Doesn't look like we've got many customers today, anyway." He sighed. "What a mess this is! We can't afford to lose customers right now."

"I understand." Kate gave him a sympathetic look. "And I want to help you with that. In my essay I'll tell everyone how wonderful your cheeses are. That should help your business! But I'll need your help. Thanks for answering a few questions for me!"

Just then, a cheerful female voice came over the loudspeaker. "Ladies and gentlemen, the Mad River Creamery will conduct a tour of its facility in exactly ten minutes. The tour is free of charge, and complimentary cheese samples will be given along the way. Join us for the tour of a lifetime."

"It's the tour of a lifetime, all right," Sydney whispered in Kate's ear as she drew near. "Complete with rats."

"Shh!" Kate ignored her and turned her attention back to Mr. Hampton. "Maybe after the tour you could answer some questions for me? I'll be sure to give you credit in my paper. And I'll need to purchase lots of different kinds of cheeses to take back for the kids in my class, so I'll need help picking those out too."

"Of course!" he said with a smile. "I'm always happy to help a customer."

Just then, a couple more customers came through the door—a woman in a beautiful white fur coat and a man with a sour look. He shook the snow off his leather coat and looked around the shop with a frown.

"Wow, he doesn't look happy," Sydney whispered in Kate's ear. "Do you think his wife made him come?"

"I don't know." Kate stared at the man, then turned back to her sandwich. "Maybe he heard about the rats and is afraid."

"He doesn't look like the kind of man to be scared of anything. He just looks. . .mean." A look of fear came into Sydney's eyes. "I hope they're not coming on the tour with us."

The woman walked toward them and the man followed closely behind, muttering all the way.

"Uh-oh." Kate let out a nervous giggle. "Looks like they're joining us. Just smile and be friendly. Maybe they'll turn out to be nice."

"Whatever you say," Sydney whispered.

Within seconds, Kate and Sydney were tagging along behind Mr. Hampton and the two strangers into the creamery. She couldn't get rid of the nagging feeling that the man and woman were up to no good. And Sydney made her a little nervous. She wouldn't stop talking about rats.

"I can't believe I'm doing this again!" Sydney whispered. "I still have vermin-phobia after our last tour!"

"Shh." Kate turned and gave her a *please-be-quiet* look.

The girls walked from room to room, listening as Mr. Hampton explained the process of cheese making. Kate pulled out her video camera and began to film his presentation. In one room, he pointed out something he called curds and whey.

"Just like Little Miss Muffett," Kate whispered.

"What?" Sydney gave her a funny look.

"'Little Miss Muffett sat on her tuffet, eating her curds and whey.'" Kate giggled. "Now I know what curds and whey are. I never knew before. Kind of looks like cottage cheese. Kind of chunky and. . ." *Gross* was the only word that came to mind, but she didn't say it.

"Doesn't look very appetizing!" Sydney made a terrible face. "It's enough to scare me away too!"

"Well, in the nursery rhyme, a *spider* frightened Miss Muffett away," Sydney reminded her. "Not the curds and whey. And certainly not a. . . well, a you-know-what."

Mr. Hampton turned and gave her a warning look. He put a finger over his lips, then whispered, "Don't even use the *r-a-t* word. And please don't talk about spiders either. I'm having enough trouble keeping my customers without worrying them even more!" He nodded in the direction of the man and woman, who stood on the other side of the room, looking at the big machine that held the curds and whey.

Kate apologized, then added, "I'm sure your customers won't be gone for long. You have the best cheese in the state, Mr. Hampton. My mom has bought Mad River Valley Cheddar for as long as I can remember." Kate raised her voice to make sure the man and woman heard her. Sure enough, the woman looked her way. "I love, love, love cheese!" She licked her lips. "Without Mad River cheese, grilled cheese sandwiches wouldn't be the same!"

"Cheeseburgers wouldn't be as cheesy!" Mr. Hampton threw in.

"String cheese wouldn't be as. . .stringy," Sydney added, then giggled.

The woman in the white coat moved their way and nodded as she said, "Cream cheese wouldn't be as creamy."

Kate turned to the man, who crossed his arms at his chest and remained quiet. *Hmm. So, he didn't want to play along.*

Kate decided to change the subject. "This cheese making stuff looks like fun. I wish I could make cheese at home," she said with a sigh.

"Why, you can!" Mr. Hampton said. "If you have a gallon of milk, you can make a pound of cheese. You would need the help of a parent—and it takes a couple of days—but it's worth it. I can show you how to make your own cheese press, if you like."

"Would you, really?" Kate grew more excited by the moment. "Oh, I would love that. I think I'll write my paper on that, then!"

"Let's finish the tour, and then I'll show you a homemade cheese press," Mr. Hampton said. He led the way into a large room with a huge rectangular contraption filled with what looked like thick milk.

Kate looked at it, amazed. "Wow, this is huge." She'd never seen such a thing!

Mr. Hampton explained. "Yes, this is just like we talked about earlier. Once the whey is removed, the curds are pressed together, forming the cheese into shapes."

"Wow!" Kate began to videotape the process. She didn't want to miss a thing. Something caused her to turn toward the woman in the white coat. She was whispering something to the man and pointing to the curds and whey. *Hmm, I wonder what they're talking about?*

Just then Kate saw something out of the corner of her eye. She turned her camera toward the floor, just to make sure she wasn't imagining it. At that very moment, Sydney screamed. Kate jolted and almost dropped the camera.

"It's a. . .a rat!" Sydney jumped on a chair and began to squeal.

Sure enough, the brown furry critter headed right for them! He was moving so fast Kate could hardly keep up with him. For a few seconds he disappeared from view in her video camera lens, and then she caught a glimpse of him again. *Oh, gross!*

The woman began to scream at the top of her lungs and fainted. Her husband caught her just before she landed on the floor. He fanned her with the creamery brochure and called, "Abigail! Abby, wake up!"

The rat scampered close to the woman and Kate gasped. *What's going to happen next?* She whispered a quick prayer.

Holding a tight grip on the camera, Kate continued videotaping the vermin. Thankfully, he scurried to the other side of the room, leaving the woman alone. But something about the little critter seemed. . .odd. It ran in circles. Round and round it went, in a never-ending cycle. Maybe it had had too much cheese! Something was definitely wrong with it.

Mr. Hampton came around to their side of the room and his eyes grew large. "No! Not again! We took care of this. I promise! Mad River Valley Creamery doesn't have. . ." He didn't say the word. He didn't have to.

The rat finally stopped running in circles and took off under the vat of cheese. The woman regained consciousness, and Kate turned her camera in that direction. The woman began to cry out and her husband hollered, "Turn that off! I don't want you videotaping my wife!"

"Oh, I'm sorry, sir. I didn't mean any harm." Tears sprang to Kate's eyes. The man headed her way. When he got close, he grabbed her camera and shut it off, then pressed it back into her hand.

"Get on out of here, kids. . .before I lose my temper. Or maybe I'll just call the police and tell them we were being illegally videotaped!"

Sydney turned on her heels and sprinted like an Olympic track star toward the door. Kate followed, shaking like a leaf.

What a mean man! She never meant to do anything wrong! And how awful. . .to see another rat! Kate couldn't figure out why, but something about that fuzzy little creature still puzzled her.

"I'm never. . .eating. . .cheese. . .again. . .as long. . .as I. . .live!" Sydney hollered as she ran.

Kate groaned, trying to keep up. So much for helping Mr. Hampton and the Mad River Creamery. Another rat had interrupted her plans. But who was behind all of this? And why?

With the help of the other Camp Club Girls. . .she and Sydney would figure it out!

Hickory Dickory Dock

Kate and Sydney ran all the way back to the inn. When they arrived at the front door, Biscuit greeted them with wet, slobbery kisses.

"D–down, boy!" Kate panted. "N–not right now."

Between the cold air and the excitement of what had just happened, she could hardly breathe!

"Is everything okay?" Aunt Molly met them as they raced into the big room. Kate headed toward the fireplace to warm herself. "N–no," she said through chattering teeth. "We saw another r–rat!"

"Oh dear, oh dear!" Aunt Molly's cheeks flushed pink. "That's just awful! Was it inside the creamery again?"

"Y–yes!"

"Oh, how terrible!" Aunt Molly began to fan herself, looking as if she might be sick.

Kate's mother entered the room with a worried look.

"Did I hear you say something about a rat?" When Kate nodded, she said, "Honey, I don't want you and Sydney going back to that creamery. You'll just have to write your essay paper on something else, Kate."

"But that's just it." Kate sighed and plopped down on the large leather chair in front of the fireplace. "It's not dangerous at all. Something is definitely up. I can feel it in my bones!"

Aunt Molly laughed. "Oh, you can, can you? Well, what do you feel?"

"I'll know more after I look at the videotape. Do you mind if I hook my camera into your big-screen TV, Aunt Molly? I want to see everything close up."

"Ugh!" Sydney grunted. "We have to see the rat on the big screen?"

Kate laughed. "You don't have to watch."

They gathered around the television as Kate hooked up her camera. When she hit PLAY, they all watched the action.

"Here's the curds and whey part," Kate explained, pointing at the screen. "And here's the part where—"

Her mother and Aunt Molly screamed when they saw the rat run across the floor toward the woman in the white coat.

"Oh, how awful!" Aunt Molly clasped her hand over her mouth. "That poor woman."

"That man who's with her looks really angry," Kate's mother added.

"Oh, he was." Kate shivered. "But look at this."

She paused the video for a moment, focusing on the rat.

"What?" Sydney drew near, looking at the television.

Kate pointed at the pesky vermin. "Take a good look at this rat."

"Do I have to?" Sydney squeezed her eyes shut. "What about him?"

"Something about him is. . .odd. First, he's a little too big. Not your average-sized rat. Not even close!"

"Well, on your Uncle Ollie's big-screen TV, everything looks bigger than it is," Aunt Molly explained.

"Yes! Look at my ears!" Sydney laughed. "They're huge. Someone please tell me they're not that big in real life!"

"They're not, silly!" Kate groaned. "I know things appear larger than they are, but even so, this is one giant rat. And look at his fur. Have you ever seen rat fur so. . .furry?"

Sydney came a step closer and looked for a second. "No. But I'm no expert on rats."

"I've seen a few in my day," Aunt Molly said, drawing close. "And he does look a bit odd. Must be an interesting species."

"I know what it is!" Sydney said. "The rats at the creamery are well fed! That's why they're so huge!"

"Could be," Kate's mother said. "I just know we don't grow them that big in Pennsylvania!"

"Or in DC!" Sydney added.

"Most rats have really short hair," Kate observed. "And most aren't this color. This is more like the fur you'd see on a hamster or something."

"So, you think it's not a rat after all?" Sydney asked. "Maybe it's a giant hamster?"

"That's just it." She drew in a deep breath as she thought about it. "Hamsters are smaller than rats. I'm not sure what it is, but it's not a typical rat, that's for sure. I'll have to get on the internet and research all different types of rodents."

"Doesn't sound like much fun to me!" Sydney said. "We're on Christmas vacation, Kate. Remember?"

"I know, but this is really going to bother me if I don't figure it out!" Kate backed up the video and watched it again. With a sigh, she said, "Something about this frame really bothers me. After all, rats are very agile. This one isn't."

"Agile?" Sydney groaned. "I'm gonna have to look that one up in the dictionary, Kate. Why do you always use such big words?"

Aunt Molly laughed. "I hardly use that word myself!"

"Oh, sorry." Kate giggled. "I just meant most rats move fast and can make quick turns. This one. . ." She stared at the stilled photo again. "This one makes choppy movements. Jerky. You know what I mean?"

"Maybe he's had too much cheese." Sydney laughed. "That would do it. Once I ate too much string cheese, and I could barely move at all!"

"You should see me after I've had a big slice of cheesecake," Kate's mother said with a nod. "I just want to curl up in a chair with a good book!"

"Yeah, but this is different. He didn't look like he'd eaten too much. He was. . ." Kate couldn't think of what to say next. "He's shaped weird."

"Yeah, a little." Sydney shook her head. "But can we stop looking now? I've had enough of rat talk!"

"Right, right." After a moment's pause, Kate added, "Oh, I just had an idea!"

"What?" Sydney's brow wrinkled. "What are you thinking, Kate Oliver? What are you up to?"

"Well, I was just thinking this would be a great project for McKenzie," Kate explained. "She loves to search for clues. I'll send her a picture of this . . .creature. She can research it for us."

"Okay. That's a good idea." Sydney began to pace the room as she talked. "Let's send out an email to the girls and ask them to meet us in the chat room tonight at eight o'clock our time. That will give us plenty of time to hang out with your family first. What do you think?"

"Perfect."

"In the meantime," Kate's mother said, "we're still planning to go to rent a family movie and order Chinese food. Does that sound good?"

"Great! What movie?" Kate asked.

"We thought you girls could decide," her mother said. "So be thinking about it."

"Oh, I know!" Sydney clasped her hands together. "Let's rent the Nancy Drew movie. That's one of my favorites!"

"Ooo, perfect!" Kate agreed. "That should put us in the mood for solving a mystery!"

—•—•—•—

A short time later, everyone gathered around the television to watch the movie and eat Chinese food. Kate started with a big plate of moo goo gai pan, then refilled her plate with General Tso's chicken and pepper steak. Between bites, she commented on what they were watching on Uncle Ollie's big-screen TV.

"See, Sydney! See how good Nancy is at solving crimes? See that part where she kept searching for clues, even when it seemed impossible? We've got to think like that!"

"You want to be like Nancy Drew, eh?" Her father flashed an encouraging smile. "Well, you're certainly adventurous."

"And you know a lot more about technology," Sydney added. "Back when the Nancy Drew books were written, cell phones hadn't even been invented."

"No computers either," Kate's dad threw in. "And the internet was unheard of!"

"Wow!" Kate could hardly imagine a time without computers and internet. She glanced at her smartwatch, thankful for modern-day technology.

As soon as the movie ended, she glanced at the clock. "Oh, it's ten minutes till eight! Time to meet with the Camp Club Girls in our chat room!"

Sydney tagged along on her heels until they reached their room. Using her dad's laptop, Kate signed online in a flash and went to their website chat room.

As usual, Bailey was already there. The words, *Hey, what's up?* appeared on the screen.

Kate: *We need your help.*

A couple minutes later, all of the girls arrived in the chat room. After explaining what had happened at the creamery, Bailey typed, *LOL. . .I just watched* Ratatouille! *I have rats on the brain!*

Kate: *Oh, that is ironic! Didn't the rat in that movie work in a restaurant?*
Bailey: *Yes, he was a great chef.*
Kate: *Well, maybe the rats we saw at Mad River Creamery really want to become cheese-makers!*
Bailey: *LOL.*

McKenzie: *Somehow I don't think the rats are wanting to do anything but scare people! But it sounds more like someone is putting them up to it! What can we do to help?*

Kate: *McKenzie, I'm uploading a photo of the rat. I want you to take a good look at it and compare it to other rodent photos you find online. This is a weird-looking creature. We need to know for sure what it is.*

Bailey: *Icky!*

Kate: *Alexis, would you mind doing a little research online? See if you can find out any information about Mad River Creamery. See if anyone might be holding a grudge against them.*

Alex: *I'll find out who their competitors are! And I'll check to see if anyone is blogging about the creamery.*

Bailey: *I'll help with that. And I'll see if any complaints have been filed against the company, or if the cheese has ever made anyone sick.*

Elizabeth: *What about me? What can I do?*

Kate: *Can you put a prayer request on our blog site? Please let people know how much we need their prayers. Also, ask them to pray for Sydney. She's competing in a skiing competition at the Winter Festival this Saturday. If she wins, the prize money will cover the cost of her trip to Mexico this summer.*

All of the girls started chatting about Sydney's trip. When they ended, Elizabeth suggested they all pray together. She typed her prayer for all of them to see.

Elizabeth: *Lord, please show us what to do. We don't want to falsely accuse anyone. Please give us wisdom and show us who is doing this awful thing to the Hamptons. Help Kate and Sydney and keep them safe. In Jesus' name, amen.*

As she signed off of the internet, Kate thought once again about Nancy Drew and the movie they'd just watched. If Nancy could solve a crime. . .surely the Camp Club Girls could figure out who was sabotaging the Mad River Creamery!

The Rat Pack

The following morning—bright and early—Sydney came in the kitchen door, her cheeks flushed pink. She shook the snow from her jacket and pulled off her scarf. "Oh, it's beautiful out there!"

"How far did you run today?" Kate asked. Seemed like every day Sydney exercised a little more and ran a little farther!

"Only two miles." Sydney shrugged as she pulled off her scarf and gloves. "I'm out of shape. Been eating too much of your Aunt Molly's good cooking. I'm really going to have to be careful once I get back home or I'm never going to stay in tip-top shape!"

"Oh, posh!" Aunt Molly laughed. "As much as you exercise, you could stand to eat even more. Never seen anyone eat as healthy as you. Well, no one your age, anyway."

"It's important! I want to do well in the competition on Saturday." Her eyes sparkled as she added, "And, you know, I want to compete in the Olympics someday too."

"She's already been in the Junior Olympics, Aunt Molly," Kate explained. "Sydney is a serious athlete." She stressed the word *serious*.

"Well, that's wonderful." Aunt Molly patted her own round tummy and laughed. "I could stand to be more athletic. These days I just work out in the kitchen, not the gym."

"Cooking?" Sydney asked.

"No, *eating*!" Aunt Molly let out a laugh that brought Uncle Ollie in from the next room.

"What's so funny in here?" he asked.

"Aunt Molly is just telling us how she exercises," Kate said with a giggle.

"Aunt Molly. . .exercises?" Uncle Ollie looked at them with a funny expression, as if he didn't quite believe them.

Aunt Molly giggled and lifted a fork. "Like this." Opening her mouth, she pretended to eat. "I exercise my jaw." She closed her mouth and everyone laughed.

"I hope I'm as funny as you when I'm. . ." Kate stopped before finishing.

"When you're *old*, honey?" Aunt Molly laughed. "It's okay to say it. I'm no spring chicken."

"Did someone say something about old people in here?" Kate's father entered the room, yawning. "I'm feeling old and stiff. These cold mornings are really getting to me!"

"I could use a cup of coffee, myself," Kate's mother said, entering the room behind him. "Good morning, everyone!"

"Good morning, Mom." Kate reached over and gave her mom a huge hug. "We were just talking. . ."

"About me being old," Aunt Molly threw in. "But that's okay. I don't mind admitting it. Maybe I don't work out as often as I should, and maybe I can't ski like I used to when I was young, but I can certainly pay the entrance fee for Sydney to do so."

"W—what?" Sydney gave her a surprised look.

"That's right. I paid the twenty-five dollar entrance fee for you this morning," Aunt Molly said. "I prayed about it last night and felt a little nudge from the Lord to do it. Hope you don't mind."

"Mind? Mind? Oh Aunt Molly!" Sydney threw her arms around Kate's aunt and gave her a warm hug. "Of course I don't mind! How can I ever thank you? My mom will be so grateful!"

"Just go out there and ski the best you've ever skied." Aunt Molly patted Sydney on the back. "But take care of yourself. It's cold out and you'll be in unfamiliar territory."

"Where do we go?" Sydney asked. "Where's the best skiing around here?"

"You need to ski the Rat," Uncle Ollie explained. "That's where the competition will take place, and it's great for skiers at every level."

"The. . .what?" Sydney looked stunned.

"The Rat," he repeated. "That's the name of the most famous ski run around these parts."

"Ooo!" Sydney let out a grunt. "Why did they have to name it the *Rat*? Of all things!"

Uncle Ollie laughed. "I see your point. But don't let the name stop you. It's a great ski run. And if you make it from the top to bottom without falling, they give you a T-shirt." He went into another room and returned a few minutes later with a brown T-shirt in his hand. "I got this one back in the eighties when my ski legs were still strong."

"Wow." Kate laughed as she looked at the shirt that said THE RAT PACK on the front. "That's really cool, Uncle Ollie."

He turned it around and showed them the picture of the Rat on the back.

Sydney shuddered. "I never dreamed when I said I'd compete that I'd have to ski on. . .a rat!"

"It's just a name, honey," Aunt Molly said. "And besides, you'll never overcome your fear of rats without facing it head-on. So, if you're going to teach Kate to ski, the Rat is the perfect place."

Kate shook her head. "No thank you. No skiing for me, thanks. I'll just hang out here and work on my supersleuth blog site."

"Oh, come on, Kate," Sydney implored. "If I can overcome my fear of rats, you can overcome your fear of skiing! And you can work on the blog site anytime! We're on vacation now!"

"I've been a member of the Rat Pack for years," Uncle Ollie added. "We've got to keep the tradition going in our family."

"I–if I have to." Kate trembled just thinking about it!

"Aw, don't worry," Uncle Ollie said. "I wish I could go with you girls, but I've got a project going in my workshop. Should I send along your Aunt Molly as a chaperone?"

Aunt Molly laughed. "A great one I'd be! I'd probably tumble right down the hill."

"Well, maybe I could. . ." Kate's mother started the sentence, but didn't finish it.

"Could what, Mom?"

"Well, it's been years since I skied," her mom said, "but I'm willing to give it a try. To help Sydney out, of course."

"Woo-hoo! We're going skiing!" Sydney began to squeal, but Kate's insides suddenly felt squishy!

Less than an hour later, she and Sydney arrived at the ski lift, along with Kate's mom.

"Let's put our skis on before we go up," Sydney instructed.

Kate didn't have a clue how to do that, but with help from her mom, she got the long, skinny boards strapped onto her feet.

"Now what?" she asked. She wrapped her scarf around her neck as the cold wind sent an icy shiver down her spine.

"Now we go up!" Sydney pointed up the hill.

"And we have to go up. . .in *those*?" Kate felt sick to her stomach as she looked at the little chairs.

"Oh, it's a lot of fun," her mother said. "Something you'll never forget as long as you live."

"I'm sure you're right about that!" Kate said. Somehow she knew this whole experience was something she would never forget!

"This is the coolest ski lift ever!" Sydney said. "Like something out of the past. It's so cute."

"Cute?" Kate shook her head. "Doesn't look cute to me. Looks scary."

She stared up at the contraption, trying to figure out how it worked. After a minute or two, she relaxed. "It's really just a pulley system, isn't it? I know how pulleys work, so we should be safe."

"See! You just have to look at this like you do one of your science experiments, Kate," her mom said. "I'll help you into a chair, then I'll be in the one right behind you."

"Let's do it the other way around," Kate implored. "You two go first and I'll follow behind you."

"No way!" Sydney laughed. "If we do that, we'll turn around and you'll still be standing on the ground. We need to make sure you actually make it to the top of the hill."

After a groan, Kate agreed. "Just help me, okay?"

"Of course."

A few seconds later, Kate was in one of the chairs, rising up, up, up into the air.

"Wow!" she hollered, her voice echoing against the backdrop of snow. "It's beautiful up here!" She looked around, mesmerized. Everything was so white. . .so perfect. "I can't believe I never did this before. It's so fun!"

She reached inside her pocket and pulled out her tiny digital camera. Unfortunately, she quickly learned that taking photos from the air—especially when the ground was covered in glistening white snow—was almost blinding! She put the camera away and held on for dear life.

When they reached the top of the hill, Kate carefully scooted off of the chair, doing her best not to fall as the skis slipped and slid underneath her. It was so hard to balance!

"Now what?" she asked, as Sydney's feet hit the ground.

Her friend offered a playful grin. "*Now* your mom and I teach you how to ski."

"I can't promise I'll be a very good teacher," Kate's mom said, looking down the hill. "It's been awhile since I've done this. Skiing is a little scary for me too! I'm pretty wobbly!"

"I'm sure we can teach Kate what she needs to learn to make it from the top of the hill to the bottom," Sydney said. "And before long, she'll be as fast as lightning!"

"Hmm." Kate shook her head as she looked at Sydney. "I doubt that. Have I mentioned that I'm no good at sports?"

"Only a thousand times. But don't think of this as a sport." Sydney's eyes lit with excitement. "I know! Think of yourself as one of those robots you and your dad like to build down in the basement at your house in Philly."

"Huh?" Kate gave her a curious look. "Me? A robot?"

"Sure." Sydney grew more animated by the minute. "If you had to build a robot that could ski—one that could get from the top of a hill to the bottom without falling down—how would you build him?"

"Well. . ." Kate demonstrated by putting her feet together and bending her knees. "He'd have to be really flexible. And he'd have to be able to shift to the right and the left to get the right momentum going, so his knees would have to bend. And he'd have to have a way to come to a quick stop, so I'd have to build him ankles that turned so he could stop in a hurry!"

"Exactly!" Sydney giggled. "You've got it! Just pretend *you're* that robot."

Kate laughed. "Okay. So what would you name me?"

"Hmm." Sydney paused, deep in thought. After a moment her eyes lit up. "I know! We'll call you Snow-bot!"

"Snow-bot it is!" Kate nodded. "So, show me what to do, O Sports Star, you!"

Sydney looked at her with a grin. "I can't believe I'm saying this, but let's hit the Rat!"

Kate looked down at the track winding alongside some trees. "Where does it lead?"

"Who cares?" Sydney called out. "That's half the fun. . .finding out! So, c'mon! Let's go!"

Just as they started to push off, a boy whizzed by them. He wore a red jacket and cap, but looked familiar. Kate watched as he soared down the hill, faster than anyone else.

"Oh, look, Kate!" Sydney pointed with a worried look. "It's that boy. . . Michael."

"I wonder what he's doing here." Kate frowned. Hopefully he wasn't really going to enter the competition. Sydney needed to win, after all!

"He's a great skier." Sydney watched him closely as he zipped down the hill, moving gracefully around every curve. "Doesn't look like he needs the practice." They watched him ski all the way from the top of the hill to the first curve, where they lost sight of him. At that point, Kate groaned.

"Wow." She didn't know what else to say. Michael *was* good.

"I'll bet he already has his Rat Pack T-shirt," Sydney said with a sigh. "He probably has a whole drawer full! Let's face it. . .I'll never win that competition on Saturday if he skis."

"Don't say that," Kate's mother said. "I'll bet you're just as fast!"

"Probably even faster," Kate added. "I don't know anyone who can run as fast as you. So surely you're just as fast on skis!"

"Only one way to know for sure." Sydney's expression brightened. "Let's go!"

She pushed off and led the way. Kate looked down, took a deep breath, said a little prayer, and then inched her way forward with her mother at her side.

To her surprise, she went slip-sliding down the tiny hill without falling. In fact, she went even faster than her mother, who tumbled into the snow at the first big curve.

Down, down, down Kate went. . .feeling almost like a bird taking flight. The cold wind blew against her cheeks, but she didn't mind. And though skiing was a little scary, Kate had to admit it was a lot more fun than she expected. *Maybe I really am a Snow-bot!*

On the other hand. . .she looked ahead. Sydney had almost made it to the bottom of the hill. Kate had almost caught up with her when something caught her attention. "Look out!"

Kate swerved to the right to avoid hitting a baby fawn. She tumbled head over heels, hollering the whole way. *Thump!* She ran straight into Sydney, who also took a tumble. Thankfully, Kate wasn't hurt. But when she looked up, Sydney was sitting in the snow, holding her ankle.

"Oh man!" Sydney's eyes glistened with tears.

"What is it?" Kate asked, drawing close.

Sydney groaned. "My ankle hurts. I guess I twisted it."

"How bad is it?" Kate knelt down in the snow, shivering from the cold. "Is it my fault? Did I hit you with my skis?"

"No, you didn't hit me. It's my own fault. I wasn't paying attention."

"Is it really bad?"

"I think I can walk on it." Sydney took a few steps, groaning the whole way. Each step looked more painful than the one before it.

"Do you think it's broken?" Kate asked. *Poor Sydney!*

"No. It's just twisted. I'm sure it'll be fine. When I get back to the inn, I'll put some ice on it and elevate it." After a few more steps, Sydney added, "Sure hope this doesn't keep me from being in the competition."

"We'll pray about that," Kate said. "The Lord knows you need that money for the mission trip. He's going to provide it one way or another."

Mrs. Oliver arrived. She took one look at Sydney and apologized. "I'm sorry we got separated! I made it down around the next curve before I realized you weren't with me. I took a little tumble, then came back up to look for you." She looked at the tears in Sydney's eyes and gasped. "Have you hurt yourself, honey?"

"A little," Sydney said. "My ankle hurts. I don't think it's very bad, but we should probably go back to the inn, just in case."

She hobbled beside Kate as they walked back to the car. Just as the girls reached the parking lot, Michael passed by. He gave them a funny look, but kept walking without speaking a word.

"Hey, there's Michael again." Kate watched as he disappeared into a crowd of people. *Something about that boy seems. . .weird.* Just as quickly, she was reminded not to judge him before knowing all the facts.

"He's really going to beat me now, especially if I'm injured." Sydney groaned.

"Don't talk like that!" Kate said. "You'll be fine. And you were almost to the bottom of the hill when I knocked you down. It's wasn't your fault."

"No, you don't understand. It was already hurting before that. When I rounded the first turn, I think I twisted it!"

"When we get back to the inn, we'll elevate your ankle," Kate's mom said. "I'm sure it'll be fine in no time."

They drove back to the inn, where Aunt Molly greeted them with hot chocolate and peanut butter cookies, straight from the oven. She scolded Sydney, her gray curls bobbing up and down. "Sydney, you need to be careful! You could have hurt yourself out there."

"Oh, I'm fine." She forced a smile, but Kate could tell her friend was really in pain.

"Still, I've been skiing for years and I've never gotten hurt before." Sydney groaned. "It would have to happen the day I'm trying to teach Kate."

"I'm not a very good student." Kate shrugged. "I'm the reason she fell in the first place." She buried her face in her hands, trying to stop the tears. "I told you I was no good at sports!"

"Of course you are! You were doing a great job," Sydney said. "And I think you would have passed me too!"

"You do?" Kate looked at her, stunned.

"I do." Sydney nodded. "So, don't be so hard on yourself!"

"You're a natural, Kate!" her mother added. "You need to stop saying you're no good at sports."

"Saying we're no good at sports is an Oliver family trait." Aunt Molly laughed. "Most of us in the Oliver family are more into technology." She turned to Kate. "Did you know your Uncle Ollie is working on a new mixer for the creamery? Michael's been helping him."

"Michael sure isn't helping him today," Sydney explained. "We just saw him skiing. He's really, really good."

"Ah." Aunt Molly nodded. "He's decided to enter the competition, then."

"I guess."

"Well, don't fret, Sydney. Let's just pray and see what God does. In the meantime, you girls scoot on out to the barn and take a plate of these cookies to your Uncle Ollie. They're his favorite."

"Maybe I can help him with his project," Kate said, growing excited. "I'd love to see all of the gadgets he's working on out there. Maybe I'll learn something new!"

Sydney laughed. "That sounds just like something you'd say, Kate. You're always more excited about learning than anything else."

"That's a special gift God has given her," Aunt Molly explained. "He's gifted her with. . ."

"Lots of brains?" Sydney asked.

Everyone laughed.

"Well, I *do* get a pretty big head sometimes," Kate said with a giggle, "especially when it comes to my science projects. But that doesn't mean I have more brains than anyone else."

"Still, you're the smartest girl in our club," Sydney said. "And I just know you'll figure out what's going on at the creamery. Before long this mystery will be solved."

"Yes, but who knows if the creamery will reopen." Aunt Molly sighed. "I talked to Geneva Hampton today, and she said the county health inspector is coming back for another inspection. Everyone is nervous they won't pass this time around."

"I still say there was something strange about that rat on the video," Kate said. "It looked different from other rats I've seen. I can't wait to hear back from McKenzie."

She thought about it as she trudged through the snow to get to the barn, where Uncle Ollie greeted her with a smile. Enough worrying about rats! For the rest of the day, she just wanted to do what she did best. . .work on gadgets and gizmos!

Hi-Ho, the Dairy-O

After the long day of skiing and helping Uncle Ollie in the barn, Kate finally fell asleep. Every muscle in her body ached from skiing, so she tossed and turned all night trying to get comfortable.

When she finally did fall into a deep sleep, Kate had a crazy dream. She was skiing through the Mad River Creamery, chasing rats! At the end of the dream, she fell into a humongous vat of curds and whey. For some reason, the woman in the white fur coat was swimming in there too with the mean man! And Michael was standing nearby with skis in his hand, talking about what a great competitor he was.

When she finally awoke, Kate found herself quoting the lines from "Little Miss Muffett." Totally strange!

She rubbed her eyes and looked at the clock. Seven thirty in the morning? Too early to be up, especially on a vacation.

She rolled over in the bed, wondering where Sydney was. Had she been swallowed by a giant rat, perhaps?

Kate rose from the bed, brushed her teeth, and dressed in her warmest clothes. She had a feeling she knew just where Sydney would be. Sydney's foot had felt back to normal when they went to bed the night before. Minutes later—after shivering her way through several snowdrifts—Kate arrived in the barn and made her way back beyond Uncle Ollie's workshop to the small gym in the back. Uncle Ollie had added the gym, primarily for guests, a few years earlier. Sure enough, Sydney was on the treadmill. She looked at Kate and smiled, but never stopped walking.

"Hey, you're up early." Sydney dabbed at her forehead with a cloth.

"So are you." Kate yawned. "But you actually look like you're happy about it. I still want to be in bed!"

"I get up early every day now. Got to stay in shape, you know." Sydney stopped the treadmill and turned to face her. "Morning is the best time to exercise. It wakes up your body and gives you the energy to face the rest of the day. But the roads were icy this morning, so I decided this would be safer since my ankle is still a little weak. Uncle Ollie said it would be okay."

"He's probably just happy someone is actually using his workout room." Kate looked out of the window back toward the inn. In the early morning light, it looked even more beautiful, especially with snow stacked up in lovely white piles all around. "But can we talk about working out later? Aunt Molly is making oatmeal, and I never like to think about exercising and eating at the same time! Makes me nervous. Besides, I'd rather eat any day!"

"I suppose." Sydney shrugged, stepping off the machine. "I can eat oatmeal. It's loaded with fiber and lots of vitamins. That's what I need to stay in shape for the competition. I just have to cut back on the brown sugar and butter, that's all."

Kate slapped herself in the forehead. "Good grief."

They trekked through the snow to the back door. As Kate swung it open, the wonderful aroma of cinnamon greeted them. "Yum!" Her tummy rumbled.

Minutes later they sat at the table. Kate warmed her hands against the steaming bowl of oatmeal. She breathed deeply, loving the smell of the cinnamon.

"I want to go back to the Rat today," Sydney said, taking a bite of her oatmeal.

Kate started to grumble, but then remembered how much she had enjoyed skiing. *Maybe I need to stop saying I'm no good at sports! I actually found one I like!* She took a bite of the oatmeal, smiling as she tasted the sugar, cinnamon, and butter. *Mmm. Aunt Molly knows just how I like it!*

Sydney fixed her own bowl, careful to add only the tiniest bit of brown sugar. Kate sighed as she watched her friend. Maybe if she tried—really, really tried—she could be athletic like Sydney.

Or not.

Thankfully, her little brother interrupted her thoughts. "I'm gonna build another snowman," Dexter said. "My other one fell over last night. Besides, he didn't look very good. He was kind of lumpy, and his nose fell off. I heard one of the kids in the neighborhood laughing at him. I think I'd better start over."

"You go right ahead and build a new one, honey," Aunt Molly said. "But remember to forgive those kids who made fun of you first!"

"I will." He nodded and skipped off to play outside.

Aunt Molly looked at Kate and winked. "You know what I always say. . . 'A snowman is the perfect man. He's very well rounded and comes with his own broom.'"

Kate laughed. "You're so funny, Aunt Molly."

"Why, thank you very much." Her aunt handed her a mug of hot cocoa.

"I want to go back to the creamery today," Kate said, then sipped the yummy cocoa.

"Go back?" Sydney gave her a funny look. "But it's closed down, right?"

"I don't mean go inside. I just want to look around outside. To. . ."

"Snoop?" Sydney asked. "Is that what you mean?" She paused for a moment then added, "I know what you're up to, Kate Oliver. You're determined, aren't you?"

"Well, maybe a little." Kate shrugged. "We'll only be in town till the end of the week, and I want to solve this case. If we spend all of our time practicing for the competition, we won't figure out who's sabotaging the creamery."

"Or *if* someone's sabotaging them," her aunt reminded her. "We still don't know."

"And we never will if Sydney and I don't get busy."

"True, true," Aunt Molly said.

Just then, Kate remembered something. "Before we leave, I need to check my email to see if any of the other Camp Club Girls have written." She signed online and checked her email.

The first was from McKenzie:

Been checking every species of rodent on the web. Gross! The creature in the photo you sent has the body of a rat, but is a lot larger. It also has unusual fur. I can't find any other critters with fur like that! I will keep researching, I promise! In the meantime, keep me updated!

The next email was from Alexis:

Kate and Sydney, I have been researching the Mad River Valley Creamery. It's been in the area for over seventy years— owned by the Hampton family. The current owners—Luke and Geneva Hampton—inherited it from Luke's parents in 1986. Sales last year were higher than ever before. There is another creamery called Cheese De-Lite in a town about fifty miles away. Their sales aren't as high as Mad River's, but they claim to have the best cheese in the country. Cheese De-Lite is

owned by Mark and Abigail Collingsworth. Their photos are
on their company's website.

Kate clicked the link and tried to go to the website Alexis was talking about, but just then the internet stopped working. With a sigh, she rose from her seat. "I guess we should really get over to the creamery anyway. We can go skiing tomorrow, I promise."

The girls bundled up in their heavy coats and grabbed scarves and mittens.

"It's extra-cold out today," Kate's mother said, "so don't stay out long. Promise?"

"I promise, Mom." Kate kissed her mother on the cheek. "Please pray for us, okay? I want to solve this case!"

"I will, honey. I'll pray that the Lord reveals every hidden thing! Oh, and take Biscuit with you. I'll feel safer knowing he's there. He's a great watchdog! Just make sure he's wearing his sweater."

"And a great crime solver!" Sydney added.

"Okay." Kate reached for Biscuit's leash. He jumped up and down, excited to be going with them.

Minutes later, the girls were on their way to the creamery. Kate noticed how much colder it felt today. "M–man!" she said with chattering teeth. "Maybe we picked the wrong day for this!" She clung tight to Biscuit's leash and kept an eye on him.

"It's perfect ski weather." Sydney took a couple of steps, then slid a little. "Whoa." She paused to rub her ankle. "I've got to be more careful on this weak ankle! I almost fell."

"Better watch out! We've got to get that ankle healed by Saturday, so no more falling!" Kate said.

When they arrived at the creamery, they found it closed, just as Kate suspected. There were no cars out front—not even the Hamptons' SUV.

"So sad," she said, shaking her head.

"Now what do we do?" Sydney pulled her scarf tighter and looked at Kate. "How can we snoop if the place is closed down?"

"Let's go around back. We've never seen the back of the building before."

"You're not thinking of sneaking inside, are you?" Sydney asked. "'Cause if you are. . ."

"No, no. I wouldn't do that. I'm just looking to see. . ." Kate shrugged. "I don't know. Something. Anything."

Biscuit tugged on the leash, leading them to the back of the creamery.

Once there, they looked at anything and everything—the doors, windows, even the alleyway behind the back parking lot. All the while, Biscuit kept his nose to the ground sniffing, sniffing, sniffing. Kate wondered what he might be smelling. *Probably all of that cheese!*

"This place is huge!" Sydney said. "I had no idea it went back this far."

"It *is* big. And it's different from any building I've ever seen before." Kate pointed. "Oh, look. There's the Dumpster."

"So?" Sydney gave her a funny look. "You're not going to make me climb in and look for evidence, are you?"

"No." Kate laughed. "But it would make a funny picture to send the other girls. I'm just looking to see evidence of rodents."

"Rodents. . .gross!" Sydney shuddered. "You think they've been hiding out in the Dumpster?"

"If they're looking for leftovers!" Kate giggled.

"Dis–*gus*–ting!" Sydney said, then laughed.

They looked all around the Dumpster, but saw nothing suspicious. Kate even checked the edges of the building, finally noticing some footprints in the snow. "Oh Sydney, check this out. These look like tennis shoe prints."

"So?" Sydney shrugged. "Mr. Hampton probably wears tennis shoes."

"No, he wears hiking boots. I remember looking the other day. These prints start at the edge of the parking lot and go all the way to the back door." Kate pulled on the door handle, but it didn't open. "Hmm. Locked." Biscuit began to whimper and pawed at the door. "Looks like he wants in there too."

"He's a cheese-a-holic!" Sydney said. "He wants inside so he can eat all of the cheese!"

Kate laughed and said, "Probably," then pulled Biscuit away from the building.

"Lots of people probably use that door," Sydney said, rubbing her hands together.

"I don't think so." Kate shook her head, deep in thought. This looked like the kind of door that rarely got used. "Maybe someone snuck in through this door to put rats inside."

"If so, wouldn't we see evidence of the rats? Maybe. . .droppings." Sydney looked like she might be sick as she said the word.

"Ooo, so true!" Kate dropped to her knees and looked around. After a few minutes she rose back up again and shrugged. "Don't see anything."

Pulling out her camera, she began to take pictures of the footprints. "At least we have this evidence."

"Little good it does us," Sydney said. "Just footprints in the snow. Big deal."

"But it might be a big deal," Kate reminded her. "You never know."

She snapped several photographs as she followed the trail of footprints back to the edge of the parking lot. "They disappear right here." She sighed. "Oh well."

An idea came to her. "If we measure the footprints, we should be able to determine the shoe size."

"How will that help?" Sydney asked, wrinkling her nose in confusion.

"It will help us eliminate suspects," Kate explained.

"Are you saying you have a measuring tape with you?" Sydney looked at her as if she didn't believe such a thing was possible.

"I do! It's a digital measuring tape and it records the measurements. I can't believe I haven't shown it to you before." She pulled it out of her pocket and measured the prints. "Hmm. It's 10.31 inches. I wonder what size that is."

"Well, it's not as big as your dad's shoes," Sydney observed. "But it's lots bigger than Dexter's." She stuck her foot in the footprint and shrugged. "Bigger than mine too, and I've got pretty big feet!"

"I'm guessing it's a size eight or nine in a men's shoe," Kate said, putting the digital measuring tape away. "But we can ask my dad later."

Her cell phone rang, startling her. Kate looked at the number and smiled when she saw it was her dad. "Hi, Dad! Wow, that's a crazy coincidence! I was just talking about you."

"You were?" He laughed. "Good things, I hope."

"I need your help. We've measured some footprints. They're 10.31 inches long. What size man's shoe would that be?"

"Hmm. I might have to look that one up on the internet," he said. "Or, measure my own feet! But before I do that, let me tell you why I'm calling. We've decided to go to the restaurant in town for lunch. Want me to swing by and pick you girls up?"

"Oh, we can walk," Kate said, her teeth chattering.

"No, honey. The temperature has really dropped. Your mother is worried you and Sydney will get frostbite. We're coming by that way, so meet us out front. Besides, we'll need to drop Biscuit back off at the inn before going to the restaurant. Oh, and Kate. . ."

"Yes, Dad?"

"How's the investigation going?"

She sighed. "Other than a few footprints, we haven't found anything

139

suspicious. This case might just turn out to be a dead end. Maybe the creamery isn't being sabotaged, after all."

"Well, don't sound so depressed about that!" He laughed. "We want a happily-ever-after ending to this Christmas vacation, don't we?"

"Sure. But if there's really no case to solve, then I've wasted a lot of hours on our family vacation when I should have been hanging out with my family. And I've spent way too much time outdoors when I could have been sitting next to the fireplace drinking Aunt Molly's hot cocoa."

"Aw, honey, your mother and I know how much you girls love to investigate. So you go right ahead and do what comes naturally."

"Are you calling me a natural-born snoop?" Kate asked.

"If the shoe fits. . ." He laughed again. "But I am a little concerned about how much time you kids have been spending outdoors in this weather. I don't want you catching cold. . .especially right before Christmas!"

"Yes, and poor Biscuit is shivering," Kate said. "I feel bad for him. We should buy him a thicker sweater!"

"We'll do that," her dad said. "In the meantime, we'll be by to pick you girls up in about ten minutes."

"Okay, Dad. Oh, and Dad?"

"Yes, honey?"

"I love you. Thanks so much for understanding."

"Love you too, kiddo."

As they ended the call, something caught Kate's attention. A car pulled around the back of the creamery through the alley. She and Sydney slipped behind a Dumpster and watched. Kate did her best to keep Biscuit quiet, but he kept whimpering. "Hush, boy!" she whispered.

"Wow, that's a great car. A Jaguar!" Sydney whispered, her eyes wide with excitement. "Do you suppose the Hamptons own a car that fancy?"

Kate shook her head. "They don't seem the type. Besides, I saw Mr. Hampton drive away in an SUV the other day, not a Jaguar."

"Seems kind of weird that a fancy car like that would be in an alley behind a creamery," Sydney said. She peeked out once again, then pulled her head back with a worried look on her face. "We'd better be careful. I think they're slowing down."

The tires crunched against the icy pavement, finally stopping. A woman stepped out and looked around in every direction, then signaled and a man got out. Biscuit began to growl. Kate pulled on his leash to get him to stop, but he refused.

Kate gasped. "Do you see who that is?" she whispered. "It's the woman who fainted the other day. . .and her husband."

"Oh yeah." Sydney squinted. "The woman in the expensive coat and the man with the sour look on his face." Sydney paused a moment to look at them. "Ooo! He looked this way. I hope he didn't see us."

They watched as the man and woman walked across the back of the building. He seemed to be looking for something. At one point, he stood on his toes and tried to look into a window. Biscuit yipped, but Kate tapped him on the nose and whispered, "Shush!"

"Why do you suppose that man is looking inside?" Kate whispered to Sydney. "He just went on the tour the other day, so he knows what the building looks like on the inside."

"I don't know," Sydney said. "But it's really suspicious. Oh!" She paused, then looked at Kate with a gleam in her eye. "Kate, look! He's wearing tennis shoes!"

Kate squinted to see the man's white tennis shoes.

"Wow!" she whispered. "You're right."

That didn't necessarily make him a suspect, but it did make her wonder!

They continued to watch the man. He put his hand on the doorknob of the back door and tried it, but it wouldn't turn. Once again, Biscuit started to growl. Kate tried to quiet him. "He's trying to break in!" she whispered.

"We don't know that for sure," Sydney said. "After all, we tried that knob too, and we weren't trying to break in."

"True." Kate shook her head as she watched the man. He walked to another window and looked inside, then continued across the icy parking lot to the side of the building.

"It's like he's looking over every detail of the building," Sydney whispered. "Like he's scoping it out. But, why?"

"I wish I knew! Something is odd about him, for sure," Kate said.

"Do you think they have something to do with the rats?" Sydney asked. "Maybe we should find out who these people are and see if there's any connection."

Just then Kate's cell phone rang. . .loudly! Then Biscuit started barking even more loudly!

"Oh no!" she whispered. She reached to silence the phone, but the man turned and looked in their direction. "Hush, Biscuit! Hush!" Kate pressed the IGNORE button on her phone and took a couple of deep breaths. "Look the other way. Look the other way," she whispered as she watched the man.

However, instead of looking the other way. . .he began to walk right toward them! Kate's heart felt like it might explode.

"Lord, help us!" she whispered. "Please!"

CHAPTER 8

The Plot Thickens

Kate's heart raced as the stranger's shoes crunched through the snow in their direction. *Oh no! Please turn around!*

"What is it, Mark?" the woman called out. "What are you doing over there?"

"I heard something behind the Dumpster," he hollered back. "I'm checking it out."

Kate squatted and tried to hide on the farthest side of the Dumpster, praying he wouldn't see them. Unfortunately, the closer he came, the more Biscuit growled.

Just when Kate was sure they would be discovered, a car horn beeped from the front of the creamery.

"It's Dad!" Kate mouthed to Sydney.

The woman hollered out, "Mark! C'mon, let's get out of here before we get caught!"

"I'm out of here!" The man ran back toward his car, and the woman joined him. Seconds later, they went speeding off.

The car disappeared back into the alleyway and Biscuit ran after it, barking at the top of his lungs. Kate sat shivering behind the Dumpster. "I c–can't b–believe they didn't c–catch us."

"I know! That scared me *so* bad!" Sydney said, her eyes wide with fear. "I've never been that scared!"

"Me either! What do you think they were doing here?" Kate asked. "Do you think they put the rats in the store the other day? Seems pretty obvious, if they did!"

"I don't know, but it sure is suspicious!" Sydney said. She glanced Kate's way, still looking nervous. "Oh, by the way, who called?"

Kate glanced at the caller ID on the phone. "Bailey. I'll call her back later. No time to talk right now!"

"Just wait till she hears what she interrupted!" Sydney said.

The girls heard a horn honk again.

"That's my dad," Kate said. "He's probably getting worried. Let's make a run for it!"

Sydney took off running and Kate followed. As always, she could barely keep up with her friend. "I've. . .been. . .eating. . .too. . .much. . . cheese!" she said as she slid back and forth across the slippery pavement. "It's. . .slowing. . .me. . .down!"

"Just. . .keep. . .going!" Sydney called out. "You'll make it!"

As they rounded the front of the building, the girls saw the Olivers' car. Kate was never so happy to see her parents. She opened the car door and climbed in, happy to find it warm inside. Biscuit jumped in on top of her, his wet paws making her colder than ever. "Sit, boy!"

He curled up next to her on the seat, panting.

"I th–thought I w–was going to f–freeze out there!" she said with chattering teeth. Her hands were shaking so hard, she could barely close the door.

"So, any more suspicious stuff to report?" Dexter asked, looking up from his handheld video game.

"Is there ever!" Kate told the whole story about the man and the woman.

Her mother gave her a stern look.

"Kate Oliver, this is getting dangerous. You're in over your head. I think it's time to call the police."

"I understand your concerns." Kate's father reached over to pat her hand. "But let's not get too worked up. It was just a car in a parking lot. No one set off any alarms or anything. And the girls are fine." He looked at them both. "You are fine, aren't you?"

Kate nodded and Sydney muttered a quick, "Uh-huh." However, inside, Kate still felt like a bowl full of jelly! She quivered all over! Was it from the cold. . .or fear?

"We'd better get Biscuit back to the inn," Kate's mother said. "He looks tired."

Minutes later, they dropped him off at the inn. The adults chatted all the way to the restaurant, but Kate couldn't seem to say a word. Instead, she just kept thinking about the man. Why was he scoping out the building? Were the footprints his? He was wearing tennis shoes, after all.

They arrived at the restaurant in just a few minutes. As they started to get out of the car, Kate's father turned her way.

"Before we go inside, give me your digital measuring tape and I'll measure my feet," he said.

"Why in the world would you do that?" Kate's mother asked. "And in a restaurant parking lot, of all places!"

"I'm trying to help Kate solve a big case!" He pulled off his shoes and Kate handed him the measuring tape. After a moment, he said, "My feet are 10.7 inches long and I wear a size ten. So I'm going to guess your suspect is probably a size nine in a men's shoe."

"What makes you think it's a man?" Aunt Molly asked. "Maybe that woman with the white coat has extra-large feet!"

"Good point." Kate shrugged. "We really don't know." As they walked into the restaurant, she leaned over and whispered to Sydney, "Hey, what size feet do you think that man had? The one behind the creamery, I mean."

"I wasn't looking at his feet, Kate," Sydney said, shaking her head. "Honestly! I was too busy trying not to get caught!"

"Yeah, me too." Kate sighed, then whispered a prayer of thanks. *Thank You, Lord, that we didn't get hurt back there. Thanks for sending my dad at just the right moment!*

As they entered the restaurant, Kate's wrist began to buzz. "Oh! I have an email on my smartwatch." As they waited to be seated, she checked it.

"Who was it?" Sydney asked.

"Elizabeth. She just wanted to let us know she was praying for us this morning."

"Wow!" Sydney smiled. "I'm glad she was! What a cool coincidence! We really needed it, didn't we? Her timing was perfect!"

"It sure was!" Kate agreed.

"That's how God works," Aunt Molly said with a nod. "He works out every detail in His perfect timing."

The hostess led the Oliver family to a booth, and everyone sat down. As soon as she got the menu, Kate began to look it over. Her stomach was rumbling, and she could hardly wait to eat!

Just then she heard a familiar voice. Looking up, she saw Michael in the next booth, talking to the waitress.

"Hi, Michael," Kate called out. She waved, trying to be friendly.

He looked her way and nodded, then turned back to his handheld video game, not even pretending to be nice.

"Humph." Kate crossed her arms at her chest.

"Be quick to forgive, honey," Aunt Molly reminded her. "Even when others don't respond the way they should. That's the perfect time to forgive. . .before you get upset."

"Yes, but he *never* responds the way he should," Sydney said quietly.

"And have you noticed he never looks happy?"

"And why is he sitting all alone in a restaurant?" Kate asked. "That's weird."

"Oh, I can explain that part. His mother is a waitress here." Aunt Molly pointed at a woman with dark hair pulled back in a ponytail. "That's who he was talking to. Her name is Maggie. She's worked here for as long as I can remember, so Michael spends a lot of his free time here. Keeps him from being lonely, I guess."

"I see." Kate raised her menu, trying to hide the fact that she was snooping.

"The poor kid's been through a lot," Uncle Ollie said with a sad look on his face. "His dad left when he was only three, and now, of course, Michael has lost his grandpa. So anything we can do to keep him from being too lonely is a good thing."

"Oh, I know, but there's something about him that worries me." Sydney shook her head. "I don't know what it is, exactly. Just. . .something."

"Are you worried he'll beat you in the contest?" Uncle Ollie asked with a mischievous twinkle in his eye. "'Cause I have it on good authority you're pretty fast. I wouldn't worry if I were you."

"Oh, I'm not worried. I promise."

Kate looked at her friend, wishing she could read her thoughts.

Uncle Ollie rose from his seat and invited Michael to join them at their table. He came, but he didn't look happy. When he sat next to Kate, she tried to smile. . .tried to be friendly. But he didn't make it easy! He sat there like a bump on a log, just staring at his Nintendo Switch while everyone else talked.

Kate's cell phone rang, and she looked at the number. "Oh, it's Bailey! I forgot to call her back." She looked at her mother and asked, "Can I answer it? Do you mind?"

"Go ahead, honey," her mom said. "Just don't be long. We need to order our food soon."

Kate nodded, then answered the phone with a smile. "Hey, Bailey! What's up?"

"I found some information online," Bailey said, sounding breathless and overly excited, as always. "Did you know the Mad River Creamery fired their security guard several months ago?"

"No. How did you find that out?"

"I googled the name *Mad River Creamery* and went to every site that came up. Every one. Way down on the list I found a blog site that belongs to some nameless person, complaining about someone being fired from the creamery this past summer."

"Really? But you don't know who owns that blog? That's weird."

"Really weird!" Bailey said. "It was all very suspicious. Just sort of a warning for readers to stay away from the creamery. I guess this person was the one who got fired. Or maybe a relative or a friend. . .something like that."

"Ooo, the plot thickens!" Kate looked at Sydney in anticipation and whispered, "There's more to this than meets the eye!"

Sydney looked surprised, but didn't say anything. Instead, she stared at Michael out of the corner of her eye, as if she didn't trust him.

"Did the website mention anything about rats?" Kate asked Bailey.

As she said the word *rats*, everyone at the table looked her way. Kate's mother shook her head, as if to say, *This is not appropriate dinner table conversation, Kate!* Kate mouthed the words "I'm sorry," then put her hand over her mouth, waiting for Bailey's response.

After a moment, Bailey said, "No, but there was plenty of stuff on there about getting even!"

"Very suspicious. Makes me wonder. . ." Kate started to say more, but noticed the look on her mom's face. "Bailey, can I call you back later? We're in a restaurant right now, and I need to order my meal."

"Sure. I'll text you if I find out anything else."

"Please do."

Kate ended the call and turned back to everyone at the table with a cheery voice. "So, what's everyone going to order? I'm starved!" She opened the menu and pointed to a large baked potato with all of the trimmings. "Mmm! This looks good. I'm going to get this." After a moment, her gaze shifted to a picture of roast beef with mashed potatoes and gravy. "Or this! Yummy! I haven't had roast and potatoes in ages. And can we order dessert after, Mom? I'm starved!"

She pointed to a picture of coconut cream pie. "They have my favorite!"

"I like the cherry pie," Dexter said, pointing at another picture.

"Their apple pie is great," Uncle Ollie added, "but not as great as your Aunt Molly's!"

"Pie has a lot of empty calories, Kate," Sydney whispered. "It's not really good for you."

"Empty?" Kate looked at her friend, curious.

"That just means it's not really good for you, but it's fattening," Sydney explained. "Most sweets are nothing but empty calories."

"Oh." Kate closed the menu and thought about that for a minute. Finally, she cheered up. "But I feel full after I eat pie, not empty. So it can't be all bad, right?" She flashed a smile at Sydney, who laughed.

"I love you, Kate," Sydney said. "You always see the good in everything."

"Especially in food!" Kate giggled. "And I'm starving right now!"

"Solving mysteries makes you hungry, eh?" her father asked. "That's my girl. But you'll never *really* starve, that's for sure!"

"Nope! I have the best appetite in town."

"And the best nose for snooping," her mother added. "And I'm assuming Bailey was calling with news about the creamery?"

"Well, yes, but. . ." She shrugged. "I don't want to bother you guys with this while we're eating."

"Tell us," Aunt Molly said. "We want to know."

"Well, Bailey thinks maybe she's stumbled across a clue. Something that will help us figure out who's sabotaging the creamery."

"*If* someone's sabotaging the creamery," Aunt Molly reminded her. "We still don't know for sure."

"Yes." Kate nodded. "That's true." Even as she spoke the words, however, she knew that it *was* true. Someone was trying to sabotage the creamery. And she would figure out who. . .and why!

"What's the deal with you girls?" Michael rolled his eyes. "Why is it so important to figure this out? What are you trying to prove, anyway?"

"Trying to prove?" Kate asked, confused. "Nothing, really."

"We just like to help people." Sydney shrugged. "It's what we do."

"And they're good at it!" Dexter added.

Michael rolled his eyes. "Why do you want to help those Hamptons?" He muttered something under his breath.

"Don't you like the Hamptons?" she asked.

Instead of answering, he got up and left the restaurant without even saying good-bye.

"Well, that was strange," Aunt Molly said with a stunned expression.

"Very!" Kate's mother added.

"Not like him at all," Ollie added. "In fact, I've never seen this side of him. Very odd."

"I'm telling you, something about that boy bothers me," Sydney added. "I can't put my finger on it, but he's just. . .weird." After a second, she looked ashamed. "I'm sorry. I shouldn't have said that. I'm trying not to judge people, and look what I just did." She sighed.

"We all make mistakes," Kate added, "but you're right about the fact that something about him seems suspicious."

Thankfully, the waitress showed up at the table.

"Hi, Maggie!" Aunt Molly said with a smile. "Good to see you."

"Well, it's great to see you too," she said. "You're my favorite customers, you know."

"She says that to all of her customers," Uncle Ollie whispered in Kate's ear.

"I heard that, Ollie Oliver, and you know it's not true!" Maggie grinned. "You folks are my very favorite." She looked around and asked, "Hey, what happened to that son of mine? I thought I saw him sitting here with you."

"He was." Uncle Ollie shook his head. "Not sure what happened, but he left in a hurry."

"Hmm." She shook her head. "He's been acting mighty strange since my pop. . ." Maggie's eyes filled with tears, and Kate suddenly felt very sorry for her.

"I'm sorry," Kate said, feeling a lump grow in her throat. How terrible it must be to lose your father! She looked over at her dad and tried—just for a moment—to imagine it. The idea was so painful she pushed it away immediately.

"Sorry to get all emotional on you." Maggie wiped the tears out of her eyes with the back of her hand and smiled. "What would you like to order, folks?"

Kate ordered the soup and sandwich combo, then listened as everyone else ordered. Everything sounded so good! At the end, she changed her order to a burger and fries to match her dad's.

While they waited for the food, Sydney changed the topic to the upcoming competition.

"Do you think you're ready, honey?" Aunt Molly asked.

"I don't know. I've only had one practice," Sydney said. "But Kate and I are going back to the Rat tomorrow so I can try again."

"I'm glad you're learning to ski, Kate," Aunt Molly said. "And you never know. . .we may turn you into a sports fan after all!"

"That would be the day!" Kate's father said. "My girl is far too busy helping me with all of my gadgets and gizmos to think about sports when we're home. That's one reason I'm glad we're in Mad River Valley. She can stop thinking about electronics and start thinking about just being a kid!"

Kate shrugged. "Skiing is okay, but you know me, Dad. I'd rather be working on one of the robots with you."

After a moment's pause, she added, "Oh, and by the way. . .speaking of robots. . ." She went on to tell him Sydney's idea about the snow-bot.

"Snow-bot?" He looked at her with a sparkle in his eyes. "What a marvelous idea. Maybe when we get home, we could actually build a little snow-bot and use it for ski demonstrations! Can't you see it now?" He went off on a tangent, talking about how they could sell the robot to people who wanted to learn how to ski.

"Wonderful idea!" Uncle Ollie threw in.

"Hey, it was my idea," Sydney said with a pretend pout. "If you make millions off of this robot, do I get some of the profits?"

"Of course, of course!" Kate's dad laughed. "You'll get a percentage and so will Kate. Who knows. . ." He grinned from ear to ear. "Snow-bot might just be a big hit!"

"Oh, I hope so!"

Everyone went on to talk about skiing, but Kate's thoughts were on something else. She kept thinking about what happened at the creamery. The man and woman in the car. . .what were they doing there? Something about them just didn't seem right. And what was up with those footprints? Did they belong to the man. . .or someone else? How would she ever find out?

Glancing out the window, she happened to notice Michael passing by. The minute she saw him, a chill came over her. Something about him made her very nervous. Very nervous, indeed.

With a sigh, she turned back to her family and friends, determined to stay focused on the important things. *Lord, don't ever let me forget the people who are right in front of me! They're more important than any case!*

Right now, the investigation could wait!

CHAPTER 9

Lost in the Maze

On Friday, just one day before the big competition, Kate went with Sydney to ski one more time. This time she wasn't as nervous as before. In fact, she almost looked forward to it.

"I'm getting faster every time!" Sydney said, looking more confident than she had in days. "But there are still a couple of areas that slow me down. I need to figure out how to pick up speed in those places!"

"Yes, there are some crazy twists and turns on the course," Kate agreed. After all, she'd already fallen several times and had the bruises to prove it!

"I think I can make it to the bottom without falling this time," Sydney said. "But I want to increase my speed in the tricky places. So let's do our best to get to the bottom in record time today, okay?"

"Sure. And I'll time us." Kate pointed to her super-duper watch. "I'll bet you're the fastest one out there!"

"Hardly!" Sydney laughed. "But maybe I'll do better today than last time."

The girls dressed in their warmest clothes and prepared to head off to the slopes.

"Do you think you'll be okay without me?" Kate's mom asked. "Molly and I have plans to visit Michael's mother today. She seems a little lonely, so we want to cheer her up by taking her to the tearoom for some girl time."

"That's sweet, Mom," Kate said. "But don't worry about us. Mad River Valley is a safe place. Nothing'll happen."

"They'll be fine," Aunt Molly assured her. "It's a safe course, and lots of people are around. Don't fret!"

"Well, just stay as warm as you can." Kate's mom handed her some money. "And if you get cold, go inside and buy some hot chocolate. Promise? And don't forget to call if you need anything. We're just a few minutes away."

"I promise, Mom." Kate grinned. "But don't worry! I'm twelve now, remember? And it's not like I haven't been to the slopes before. We just went the other day. This time I'm sure it will be even easier than before."

"I know, but it's hard to watch your children grow up and do things on their own!" Kate's mom shrugged and her eyes misted.

Kate gave her a hug and whispered, "I promise not to grow up *too* fast." She wondered what it would feel like to be a mom, watching your child do something alone for the first time.

A few minutes later, Uncle Ollie drove Kate and Sydney to the ski area. As he stopped the car, he gave them a warning. "We're expecting more snow this afternoon, girls, so finish skiing early. I'll be here to pick you up at two o'clock. I think that will give you plenty of time. Try to be here waiting so I don't have to come looking for you."

"We'll be here!" Kate said. She waved good-bye as she and Sydney headed across the parking lot with their skis.

When they arrived at the ski lift, this time Kate wasn't as scared to get on it. In fact, she looked forward to it. As they rode up, up, up the hill, she breathed in the fresh morning air and hollered, "I love it here!" to Sydney, who was in the seat below hers. Her voice echoed against the snow-packed mountain. *This place doesn't just look awesome; it sounds awesome!* she thought.

Finally, they reached the top of the slope. Even though Kate wanted to ski, she still felt a little nervous. She and Sydney made their way to the Rat, and Sydney looked at her with a grin. "I'm overcoming my fear of rats by skiing here!"

"Me too!" Kate giggled. "Funny, huh? Think of all the stories we'll have to tell the other girls!"

Kate rubbed her gloved hands together for warmth before reaching for her poles. Then she and Sydney took off soaring down the hill. The crisp, cold wind whipped at her face, making it tingle. In fact, it was so cold that her arms and legs began to ache.

The first big turn caught Kate off guard, and she almost fell. Thankfully, she got control of herself and made it without tumbling. A short time later, she came to a small drop-off.

"Woo!" she hollered as she soared into the air, then landed gracefully below. *I can't believe I did that!*

Now for the hard part. The next part of the course was filled with twists and turns, and there were some trees ahead. *Better steer clear of those, for sure!*

She bent her knees and leaned into the course, picking up speed as she rounded the first sharp turn. Then the second. As she came to the section of trees, she leaned to the left to avoid them.

Just as Kate sailed into a clearing, she heard a terrible cry. To her left, Sydney tumbled head over heels into the snow.

"Oh no!" Kate got so distracted watching her friend that she lost her footing and tipped over sideways. She landed on her bottom in the snow. It didn't hurt too badly, but then she rolled a couple of times and banged her elbow into a rock. "Ouch!"

Finally coming to a stop, she pulled off her skis and ran to Sydney's side. "Are you okay? What's happened?"

Sydney sat in the snow, gripping her ankle with tears streaming down her face. "Oh Kate. It's my ankle! It's worse! *Much* worse. I think I've really hurt it this time!"

"What did you do?"

"I don't know. It was already hurting this morning when I walked on the treadmill. I guess I should have told someone, but I didn't. I thought I could make it stronger by walking on it, but I guess I was wrong."

"Oh Sydney!"

"I feel like I've twisted it again. But it hurts so bad! Much worse than before."

"What should we do?" Kate asked, looking around. Oh, if only someone else would come by and offer to help! What made her think they could come to the slopes alone?

"I. . .I think we need to go back," Sydney stammered. "Do you mind?"

"Of course not!" Kate looked around again, hoping for some help. The mountainside remained empty. The only thing she heard was the sound of her voice echoing against the snow. "Will we have to walk down to the bottom?"

"I guess." Sydney looked around. "But I don't think I'll make it, to be honest. Maybe there's a trail closer to the trees. It's too dangerous to be out in the open like this. Any moment a skier could come flying down the hill and run us over!"

"Oh, I never thought of that!" Kate held tight to her limping friend's arm and led her to some trees.

When they got there, Sydney gripped her ankle and began to cry harder. "I can't believe I did this! I'm never going to get to go on my mission trip now."

"Don't worry about that right now," Kate said. "One thing at a time."

She looked around, a little confused about where they were. Just then a bit of falling snow caught her attention. "Oh no! It's snowing again. Uncle Ollie said it wasn't supposed to snow till this afternoon."

"That's not good, Kate. We can't get stuck out here in the snow, especially if my ankle is too weak to go to the bottom of the hill!"

"I know, but what can we do?" Kate started to tremble.

"We've got to get back to the parking lot somehow." Sydney dabbed at her eyes with gloved hands. "Do you think you can help me?"

"I'll try." Kate looked around. "But which way is the parking lot? I'm confused."

"I think it's east?" Sydney looked up with pain in her eyes. "Do you have a compass?"

"Yes." Kate pulled out her digital measuring tape with the built-in compass. "Okay, east is this way." She pointed to their left. "You're sure it's east, right?"

"I think so." Sydney shrugged. "But right now I'm in so much pain, I'm not sure about anything."

A cold wind blew over them, making an eerie sound against the backdrop of the mountain. Kate shivered.

"Wow. That was creepy. Sounded like the mountain was crying."

"No, I'm the only one crying," Sydney said, forcing a smile.

"Would it be better if I went after someone to help carry you back?" Kate offered. She hated to leave Sydney here, but she didn't know what else to do.

"No, I think I can hop on my good foot, as long as we go slow. Just help me, Kate. Please." Sydney rose to her feet, almost falling over. She leaned against Kate.

"Take slow, steady steps," Kate said. "And let me do most of the work."

She had never seen Sydney like this before. Usually Sydney was the one running races or playing sports. But now—with an injured ankle— would she even be able to ski in the competition? It was only a couple of days away. What would happen if she didn't win the three hundred dollars? Would she get to go on the mission trip?

After the girls had been walking a few minutes, the snow began to fall even harder.

"It—it's blinding me," Kate said, shivering. "I can't see more than a few feet."

"And I'm getting colder by the minute," Sydney added. "It's making my ankle hurt worse."

They followed what looked like a trail. It wound in and out, in and out, and seemed to lead absolutely nowhere. They faced dead ends at every turn!

"Now I know what a mouse feels like, hunting for cheese in a maze," Kate said, then groaned. "No wonder they call this slope the Rat. It just like being trapped inside a gigantic trap!"

Minutes later, Sydney shook her head. "I have to stop for a minute, Kate. It hurts too much to keep going. Stop. Please."

"Of course." Kate stopped, grateful to find a spot under some trees where the snow was packed tight. After watching Sydney rub her ankle, Kate had an idea. "Oh, I can't believe I didn't think of this sooner!"

"What?"

"I have a GPS tracker on my cell phone. I can type in the name of the lodge next to the parking lot, and the tracker will lead us back. . .no problem."

The wind began to howl louder and louder, and the girls huddled together. Off in the distance, the skies began to look heavy and gray.

Kate opened her phone and waited for a signal. "Come on." She shook the phone, frustrated. "Work! Please work!" A few seconds later, she had a faint signal. Kate quickly typed in the name of the lodge.

"Pray, Sydney," she said. "This has to work."

"Okay. I'm praying." Sydney's eyes were filled with tears, and Kate knew her ankle must really be hurting. Sydney never complained!

A couple of minutes later, just as Kate started to get her hopes up, she lost the signal on her phone. She closed it with a sigh. "What's the point of having GPS tracking if I can't get a signal?"

A burst of cold air caught her by surprise, and she began to shake. "Is it getting colder, or am I just imagining it?"

"I–it's g–getting c–colder. And the snow is really coming down now. See?" Sydney pointed to the skies, then huddled next to Kate, shaking. She closed her eyes. "I don't know why, but I'm suddenly getting tired."

"It's the altitude. And the dark skies."

Kate looked up. The sky hung heavy over them, a sure sign that a heavy snowfall was on its way.

"W–what are we going to do?" Sydney broke down in tears.

Kate had never seen this side of Sydney before. Usually her friend was the strong one. . .the brave one.

Now I have to be strong and brave!

"They're going to find us," Kate said, doing her best to sound confident. "We've got the transmitters on our snow boots, remember? That's the very best tracking device."

"Yes, but your Uncle Ollie's not coming back till two o'clock," Sydney reminded her. "It will be hours before they even realize we're missing. No one will know to look for a signal till then, and I'll be frozen stiff by two o'clock!"

"Don't say that!" Just the thought of it sent a shiver down Kate's spine.

"I'm sorry." Sydney pulled at the scarf around her neck. "I don't know why I'm so scared."

"It's normal when things go wrong. Just keep praying, Sydney."

"I need to," her friend said. "My throat is starting to feel funny. And my eyes sting from the ice."

"Would you be okay for a minute if I went to look for someone to help?" Kate asked. "I'll come right back, I promise."

Sydney leaned against the tree and nodded. "Just promise you won't stay gone long. And leave a trail so you know how to get back to me. I don't want to get stuck out here alone."

"Me either. I'll follow my footprints back." As soon as Kate spoke the word *footprints*, she remembered the footprints they'd found behind the creamery. Would they ever figure out who was sabotaging the Hamptons?

This isn't the time to worry about that!

Kate hated to leave her friend, but she wanted to check something. If she was remembering correctly, there was an old red barn just south of here. She'd seen it yesterday when the skies were clear. If they could just make it to that barn, they could warm up. And maybe she could get better reception there too. If so, she could call her father or Uncle Ollie on her cell phone. They would come in a hurry!

A few minutes later, Kate found a trail. It wound through tangles of brush and snowcapped trees. She turned to the right and then the left, trying to get her bearings. *Lord, help me. Please.* A tree branch slapped her in the face, and snow flew everywhere.

"Oh!" The pain shot through her cheek, and she ducked to wedge her way underneath the low snow-covered branches.

A few seconds later, she heard the strangest sound. . .like something falling and hitting the earth below. Taking a step, she heard a *c-ra-ack!* The ground underneath her shifted, and she started to tumble forward!

Down, down, down she went. . .praying all the way!

Along Came a Spider

Kate tumbled down through several layers of snow and ice until she landed with a *thud* on an icy patch of ground. She rubbed at her backside and cried out in pain. "Oh, help!" Right away, she began to pray. "Lord, get me out of here. Please!"

Pushing her weight backward, she landed on sturdy ground. However, the place where she stood just seconds before collapsed. Down, down, down it went, making a crashing sound below.

She peeked over the edge, realizing she'd almost stepped off the edge of a drop-off. Somehow she had stopped. . .just in time! Kate's heart thumped hard against her chest. How close she'd come to falling! Another look convinced her it was a long way to the bottom. *I could have died!* Something—or *Someone*—had saved her, just in the nick of time!

And where was the crackling sound coming from? She still heard it off in the distance. Squinting against the blinding snow, she saw something that looked like a frozen waterfall to her right. Pieces of the ice had broken off and fallen into the spot way down below. The frozen water led down to the place where she might have landed, if she'd taken one more step.

Whoa! Talk about a long drop! Thank You, Lord! You saved my life.

Kate scooted backward on her bottom, finally confident enough to try to stand. Only one problem. Her clothes were now damp and so cold. Straightening her legs was tough. And her feet suddenly ached. "Lord, just a few more minutes," she whispered. "I have to find a safe place."

Struggling against the strong wind, she kept her balance. Kate tried her cell phone once more. No signal. Determined to succeed, she turned toward the right. *I can do all things through Christ who strengthens me. I can do all things through Christ who strengthens me.*

For whatever reason, she thought about Phillip and her science project. Suddenly—with her life in jeopardy—it seemed so silly to hold a grudge against someone else. Really, the only thing that mattered right now was getting help for Sydney!

After a few treks through the deepening snow, Kate finally caught a glimpse of something red in the distance. "Oh, good!"

An old, dilapidated barn stood alone against the backdrop of white snow.

It's a long way away, but I think we can make it.

She used her own footprints to run back to Sydney. Kate found her in tears, seated on the ground next to a tree.

"I've found a safer place to wait," Kate explained. "Do you think you can take a few steps with my help, as long as they're not downhill?"

" 'I can do all things through Christ who strengthens me,' " Sydney spoke above the rising winds. "That was our Bible verse a couple of weeks ago in Sunday school."

"Wow! That's amazing! I was just quoting that verse!"

With Kate's help, Sydney rose and leaned against her. Together they took their first steps through the mounds of snow.

" 'I can do all things through Christ who strengthens me,' " Sydney said.

" 'I can do all things through Christ who strengthens me,' " Kate echoed.

They continued saying the words until they drew closer, closer, closer to the old red barn. Finally they reached the door.

"It looks really old, Kate," Sydney said. "I don't even think that door will open. The hinges are broken."

"It *has* to open. It just has to." Kate reached for the door, praying all the time. After a struggle, she managed to get it open. "There! See!"

"Oh, it's dark in here." Sydney took a few hobbling steps inside, and Kate followed her.

"I wish we had a flashlight. It's kind of creepy."

"You don't think there are any. . ." Sydney's voice trailed off.

"What?" Kate asked.

"Rats?" Sydney whispered.

Kate shuddered. "Oh, I didn't think of that. How strange would that be? To find rats here."

She squinted, her eyes finally getting adjusted to the dark. "Ooo! This place is filled with spiderwebs!"

She found herself caught in one and began to bat at it, pulling it apart. "Gross!"

"This is so creepy!" Sydney said. "I don't like spiders any more than I do rats. But this place is filled with them. Look!" She pointed as a large spider crawled up the wall. "Remember your Aunt Molly said the creamery had spiders too? I wonder if they were this big?"

"I don't know. But, look, Sydney. There are some mounds of hay over there." Kate pointed, getting more excited by the minute. "If we can get down inside the hay, I think we'll warm up. Then I'll try to use my phone again."

The girls had just settled down into the soft, cushy straw, when Kate thought she saw the door crack open. "W–who is it?" she called out. She began to shake all over!

The door slammed shut, making a clacking noise as the wind caught it and pushed it back and forth.

"Do you think that was a person?" Sydney asked. "Or maybe just the wind?"

"I'm too scared to look!" Kate pinched her eyes shut and sat in fear for a moment. Then, just as quickly, she felt courageous. "I'm tired of being a scaredy-cat! I'm going to look." She ran over to the door and inched it open. Staring out onto the open expanse of snow, she thought she caught a glimpse of someone.

"Come and help us!" she called out.

The person—who looked like a boy or maybe even a man—disappeared in the distance. He wore a dark jacket and carried a big backpack. But why would he be hanging out at an empty, abandoned barn? And what was in the backpack?

Or was he even real? Kate turned back to Sydney and sighed.

"Who was it?" her friend asked.

"I don't know." Kate rubbed at her eyes. "Maybe it was no one! Have you ever heard of a mirage?"

"A mirage?" Sydney yawned. "Like something you see only in your imagination, but it seems so real you actually think it *is* real?"

"Right." Kate shrugged. "First it looked like someone. . .then it didn't. Maybe my overactive imagination is working overtime! My mom accuses me of that sometimes."

With the door still cracked, Kate opened the phone and saw a tiny signal. The GPS tracking system opened, but the signal faded almost immediately. Kate prayed a silent prayer: *Lord, I'm scared. And I don't know what to do. But I know You do. Help us, Lord. Please! I'm starting to imagine things—and they're not good!*

"My ankle hurts even more." Sydney's voice sounded weak. "And I'm getting so tired. Feels like it's nighttime, but it's barely even noon. Right?"

"Right. But I'm getting sleepy too," Kate agreed with a yawn. "Maybe it's because it's so dark in here." She walked back over to the straw and curled up next to Sydney. She wanted to rest, but visions of spiders and spiderwebs kept her awake. What if she dozed off and one of those creepy crawlers crawled into her hair? Or down her arm! Ooo! What a terrible thought!

Minutes later, Kate's eyes grew heavier, heavier, heavier. Though she tried to fight the sleepiness, before she realized it, her eyes were closing—and she was sound asleep. She dreamed of rats and spiders, all chasing her down a big hill!

Kate couldn't be sure how much time passed, or if she was dreaming. But at some point, she heard the sound of a man's voice outside the barn and the sound of a dog barking. It sounded like a distant echo, like something from a dream.

"W—what is that?" She sat up, trying to figure out where she was. She could only make out shadows in the dark barn, but she definitely heard sounds coming from outside. The barking continued, sounding more and more familiar!

"Biscuit!" Was she dreaming? It sounded like her canine companion!

"Is anyone in there?" a man's booming voice rang out.

Kate jumped up, her eyes still heavy with sleep. "Sydney! They've found us."

Sydney awakened and rubbed her eyes. "W—what? Who's found us?"

"Sounds like Pop and Uncle Ollie!" Kate tried to stand but could hardly move, she was so cold. Every joint and muscle ached.

"We're in here!" she called out. "Help us, please!"

"We're here! We're here!" Sydney called out, sounding hoarse and tired.

The door to the barn swung wide, and Kate's father stood there. Uncle Ollie appeared next to him with Biscuit at his side. The dog ran straight for Kate, jumping into the pile of hay and spreading it everywhere.

"Kate!" her father called out, his voice cracking with emotion. "I was so scared!"

"Pop! I'm so glad you're here! How did you know where to find us? I couldn't use my phone."

"Michael came and got us," Uncle Ollie explained. "He told us you were here."

"Michael?" Kate and Sydney spoke at the same time.

"How did he know we were here?" Kate asked, more confused than ever.

Uncle Ollie shrugged. "I'm not sure. He just said he saw you girls go into the old red barn on the south side of the pass. He was worried you might be in trouble."

"We *were* in trouble, so why didn't he come inside and talk to us?" Sydney asked. "That doesn't make any sense! He left us all by ourselves."

Uncle Ollie shrugged. "I don't know. I just know that he saved your lives by telling us you were here! We owe him our thanks."

"Humph." Sydney crossed her arms and made a face.

Biscuit jumped up and down, licking Kate in the face.

"He's happy to see you!" Uncle Ollie said with a nod.

"I'm happy to see him too. I. . .I wasn't sure I ever would again." Kate burst into tears at once, realizing just how scared she'd been.

"How will we get back to the inn?" Sydney asked, looking nervous. "My ankle is injured. And I think it's really bad this time." Her tears started up again.

"Oh, we're on the snowmobiles," Kate's father explained. "But if you're injured, we'd better take you to the emergency room as soon as we get back to town."

Sydney's tears started flowing when she heard the words *emergency room*. "I'm never going to get to ski in the competition now. I can't believe this!"

"Remember, 'all things work together for good to them that love God, to them who are called according to his purpose,'" Uncle Ollie reminded her. "God will use this situation in a good way. Just watch and see."

"I don't see how He can, but I'm going to choose to believe that," Sydney said with a sigh.

Minutes later the girls climbed aboard the snowmobiles. Kate rode behind her father, and Sydney rode behind Uncle Ollie. As they made their way up one hill and down another, Kate thought about everything that had happened that day. Sydney's ankle. Almost falling down into a frozen creek. Finding refuge in a barn. Michael.

Hmm. Thinking of Michael raised so many questions. He hadn't been a mirage after all. But why didn't he stop to talk to them? Why did he run off, even if it was to get help?

Something about that boy just seems wrong.

As soon as they arrived at the inn, Kate's mother and aunt Molly ran out to greet them. The girls were showered with kisses, then Kate's mom called Sydney's mother on the phone to tell her what had happened.

She gave them permission to take Sydney to the emergency room, and the girls and Mrs. Oliver piled into the car. As soon as they got inside the car, Kate finally felt free to cry. Oh, what a day it had been! Her tears flowed—partly in relief for being safe and partly because of the things she had faced earlier in the day.

Just then, her cell phone beeped. *Now I get a signal!* She glanced down, noticing a text message had come in from Elizabeth. Strangely, it was a scripture verse, the same one she and Sydney had been quoting all day.

Kate almost cried as she read the words: I CAN DO ALL THINGS THROUGH CHRIST WHO STRENGTHENS ME.

Somehow she knew this was more than a coincidence.

Curds and Whey

Later that evening, after returning from the emergency room, Kate and Sydney enjoyed a quiet evening with the family. Thankfully, Sydney's ankle wasn't broken, though the doctor said it was a bad sprain. After putting a splint on it, he warned Sydney to stay off it for at least two weeks and to keep it elevated. She didn't care for that idea very much.

"That's my whole Christmas break!" she had argued. Still, she had no choice. Under Aunt Molly's watchful eye, Sydney kept it elevated for the rest of the day and kept ice packs on it. Every time she started to put it down, Aunt Molly would tell her she was going to call her mama. Then Sydney would put it back up again and groan.

As they ate their dinner, Kate kept thinking about the skiing competition. What a shame! Three hundred dollars lost! Sydney wouldn't get to go on her mission trip now, after all. But what could be done about it? And with Sydney's ankle in such bad shape, would they ever figure out what was going on at the creamery? Surely Kate's parents wouldn't let her go alone to snoop, not after what happened today!

After a wonderful meal, everyone relaxed around the fireplace and told stories. Kate told everything that had happened to them on the ski course, right down to the point where she almost fell into the frozen creek. Her mother's eyes filled with tears.

"Oh, I should have gone with you! I can't believe I let you go without an adult. Can you ever forgive me for letting you go alone?"

Kate rushed to her mom's side and leaned against her. "There's nothing to forgive, Mom! We wanted to go by ourselves, remember? But I forgive you, anyway. . .if it makes you feel better! I've learned to forgive quickly and not to hold a grudge!" She gave her mom a squeeze. "Not that I could ever hold a grudge against you—even if you did do something wrong, which you didn't!"

"Thank you, sweetie," her mother said, giving her a kiss on the forehead. "That makes me feel better."

"Forgiving quickly is always a good plan," her father said. "Remember that time I had to forgive the man who claimed he invented one of my robots?"

"Oh, that's right," Kate said. "I'd forgotten about that."

"And remember the time that woman backed out of her parking space and hit my car?" Kate's mom said. "She wasn't very nice about it, and neither was the insurance company—but I had to forgive."

"I remember it was tough—especially because she wasn't nice about it." Kate shook her head, wondering how some people could be so mean. *Why can't everyone just be nice. . .like my mom and dad?*

"Once, someone found my checking account number and stole some money from my bank account," Uncle Ollie said. "He took hundreds of dollars and I was really mad. At first. But I got over it. I read that verse about forgiving as Jesus forgives and decided it wasn't worth holding a grudge."

"It never is," Aunt Molly said. She turned to Kate with a wink. "And I'm sure you've already forgiven the boy in your class who made fun of you, haven't you, honey?"

"Yes." Kate nodded. "I've forgiven him."

Sydney groaned and everyone looked her way.

"What's wrong?" Kate's mom asked with a worried look on her face. "Are you in pain?"

"No." Sydney looked sad. "I guess I just have to learn to forgive myself. I got so excited, thinking I could win that contest, that I put all my hopes in myself instead of in God. And I let myself down by getting hurt."

"You can hardly be mad at yourself for getting hurt!" Aunt Molly said. "That just doesn't make sense!"

"Oh, I know. But I'm disappointed in myself because I was *so* sure I was going to win the prize." Sydney shrugged. "Just goes to show you I was putting my trust in the wrong person. Me." She looked at the floor, her eyes filling with tears. "I guess I do that a lot, actually. I'm pretty good at sports, so sometimes I think I can do things on my own without God's help. I forget that He's the one in charge."

"I think we all do that sometimes," Uncle Ollie admitted. "But God always forgives us, if we ask."

"I will. I promise." Sydney smiled. "And if He wants me to go on that mission trip, I'll go—one way or the other."

"That's right! He always makes a way where there seems to be no way,"

Kate's dad said. "That's a promise from the Bible. And you know God's promises are true. He is faithful to do what He says He's going to do."

Sydney nodded and smiled for the first time all evening. "I feel so much better. Thank you for reminding me. I needed to hear that!"

Kate didn't say anything, but she was glad for the reminder too.

After dinner, they all gathered in the big central room, where they ate large slices of warm apple pie and drank apple cider flavored with cinnamon sticks. As Kate leaned back against the super-sized pillows on the sofa, she looked around the room and thanked God for the special people in her life. She also thanked Him for protecting her and getting her back to her family safely.

For a moment—a brief moment—she felt a little sad. After all, they only had three more days in Mad River Valley. She and Sydney hadn't solved the mystery, and now Sydney wasn't going to get to ski. Looked like things weren't working out the way they'd hoped. Still, she had to believe God would work everything together for His good, just like Uncle Ollie said.

"A penny for your thoughts, Kate," Aunt Molly said with a hint of a smile.

Kate turned to her with a grin. "Oh, I'm just thinking of how God always has bigger and better plans than we do!"

"He sure does!" Aunt Molly agreed. "And I have a sneaking suspicion He's got more plans ahead than you know!"

Kate thought about that. Maybe Aunt Molly was right. Maybe there were plenty of adventures ahead!

A couple of hours later everyone headed off to bed.

"It's been a long day," Aunt Molly said with a yawn. "I'm going to sleep like a bug in a rug tonight."

"Ooo! Did you have to say that?" Kate said. "Thinking of bugs reminds me of all those spiders we saw today in that old barn!"

"Sorry, kiddo," said Aunt Molly. "I'm going to sleep well tonight."

"I'm not sleepy at all," Kate admitted. "My mind is still going, going, going! I can't seem to stop thinking about everything."

"Well, try to get some rest anyway, honey," her mother said. "You need to enjoy our last few days in Vermont, and that won't happen if you don't get enough sleep."

Kate and Sydney dressed for bed and then climbed under the covers. Kate tossed and turned for at least an hour. She finally gave up and kicked off the blanket.

"What's up?" Sydney asked, opening one eye.

"It doesn't matter how hard I try, I just can't go to sleep," Kate said with a loud sigh.

"How come?" Sydney asked with a yawn.

"I have too much on my mind. Things are all jumbled up."

"Really? What do you mean?"

"My thoughts must look kind of like the curds and whey in that big container at the creamery. Everything is all mixed up. Lumpy."

Sydney chuckled. "Sounds funny, but I'm not really sure what you're talking about."

"Well, I have a lot on my mind. The competition. The creamery. The picture of that rat. The woman in the white coat. . .and her husband. Michael and the barn filled with spiders." She shook her head. "It's just a lot to think about. I'm having trouble falling asleep with my mind whirling like this."

"Well, try counting sheep," Sydney suggested.

Kate pulled the blanket back up and closed her eyes, but for some reason, all she saw were rats and spiders. "Ugh!" She tried to fall asleep with her eyes open, but that didn't work either. Suddenly, Kate sat up in the bed and gasped. "Sydney! I just remembered something!"

Sydney rolled over in the bed and groaned. "We're never going to get any sleep!"

"I know, but this is important!"

"What is it?"

"The man behind the creamery. . .the one with the woman in the white coat. . ."

"What about him?" Sydney asked with a yawn.

"His name was *Mark*." Kate pushed the covers back once more, suddenly very nervous. "Remember? The woman called him by that name!"

"So?"

"So, Alexis said *Mark* was the name of the man who owns Cheese De-Lite, Mad River's main competitor. Right?"

"Ah." Sydney sat up in the bed. "That's right. And didn't she say his picture was on the website?"

"Yes, I think so. There's only one way to know for sure!"

The girls sprang from the bed and tiptoed out into the great room of the inn, where Uncle Ollie kept two computers for guests to use. Kate quickly signed online and typed in "*Cheese De-Lite.*" When the web page came up, she gasped.

"Oh Sydney, look!" She pointed at the screen. Right there—in living color—was a professional photo of the man and the woman they'd seen on the tour that day, and again behind the creamery. "Mark and Abigail Collingsworth, owners of Cheese De-Lite in central Vermont." Kate shook her head as she read the words aloud. "Do you think they. . ."

"I don't know." Sydney began to pace back and forth. "I suppose it's possible. Maybe they want to make Mad River Creamery look bad so they can steal their customers."

"Seems weird." Kate thought about it. "Why would they go to such trouble? Why not just hire an advertising firm to come up with better commercials or something?" She began to list several different possibilities, but none of them made sense.

"I don't know." Sydney shrugged.

Kate shook her head and continued to stare at the photo. "I just have the strangest feeling about these two. I can't put my finger on it."

"What are you thinking?" Sydney asked. "Tell me. . .please!"

Just then a light snapped on in the room. "What in the world are you girls doing up after midnight?"

Kate turned when she heard her dad's voice. "Oh Dad, I'm sorry! We didn't mean to wake you up, but we just found another piece to the puzzle!"

All of the noise woke up Biscuit, who began to yap and run in circles. Before long, Uncle Ollie came into the room. Then Kate's mom. Then Aunt Molly. Then Dexter, who rubbed his eyes and looked at them all like he thought it was morning.

"What's happening, girls?" Aunt Molly said, rubbing the sleep from her eyes.

Kate turned her attention to the website, showing it to the others.

"Do these people look familiar to you?" she asked.

"Not at all." Aunt Molly squinted. "Wish I had my glasses on. . .I'd be able to see better. But they don't look familiar to me. What about you, Ollie? Do you know these folks?"

"I don't recognize them." He snapped his fingers. "But, come to think of it, I did hear Michael say some couple was snooping around town, asking a lot of questions about the creamery."

"Michael said that?" Kate released a breath, then leaned back in her chair.

"Yes."

Even stranger. "This is Mark Collingsworth," Kate explained, pointing at the picture of the man. "And his wife, Abby."

"What about them?" Aunt Molly asked.

"They own a creamery about fifty miles away. A competitor. This is the man Sydney and I saw the other day behind the building. And this woman was with him."

"Wow. Very suspicious." Uncle Ollie nodded. "We'll have to call the Hamptons in the morning and tell them." He scratched his bald head and pursed his lips. "Do you think he and his wife are the ones sabotaging the creamery?"

Kate sighed. "Maybe. I'm not sure. We don't really have any proof, and I hate to accuse someone unless I know for sure."

"We just know they were doing something behind the building that day," Sydney added.

"Well, let's talk about this in the morning," Kate's dad said with a yawn. "There's no point trying to solve a mystery in the middle of the night. We all need our rest, especially if we're going to go to the Winter Festival."

Kate's heart twisted at his words. If Sydney couldn't compete, what was the point in going?

Just as the girls crawled back into bed once more, Sydney sat up with a silly grin on her face. "I have a brilliant beyond brilliant idea!"

"What is it?" Kate asked, yawning.

"Just because *I* can't enter the competition doesn't mean *you* can't."

"W–what?" Kate sat straight up and stared at her friend in disbelief. "Did you just say what I thought you said? You want me to take your place in the competition?"

"Sure! Why not? You did a great job skiing down the Rat. And I'd be willing to bet the people in charge of the festival will transfer my entry fee to you once they hear that I'm injured."

"But, why?"

"Because. . ." Sydney took her hand and gently squeezed it. "I think it would be good for you. For ages now I've heard you say you're no good at sports. I really think you would do a great job and it would prove—once and for all—that you can overcome your fear of sports."

"But. . .a competition?" Kate shivered just thinking about it. "That's not the best place to prove something to myself."

"Don't you see, Kate?" Sydney said. "The only person you'd be competing against is yourself. This wouldn't have to be about anyone else. Just you. Face your fears head-on like I did. Ski down that mountain and you'll be a winner, no matter how fast you go. See what I'm saying?"

"I guess so." Kate pulled the covers up and leaned back against her pillows. "But I'll have to pray about it. I just don't know yet. I'll let you know in the morning, okay?"

"Okay." Sydney chuckled. "But get ready, Kate! I have a feeling you're going to be skiing tomorrow afternoon."

As Kate closed her eyes, she tried to picture herself sailing down a mountain. For some reason, every time she thought about it, she pictured Michael. . .whizzing by her, going a hundred miles an hour.

Thinking of Michael made her wonder—once again—why he'd been at the old spider-filled barn. Just a coincidence, or were there darker forces at work? And why had he left them there without saying a word? Very strange, even for him!

Kate's eyes grew heavy and she finally drifted off to sleep, dreaming dreams of red barns, snow-covered mountains. . .and rats. Big, hairy rats.

CHAPTER 12

Racing the Rat

Kate stood at the top of the hill, staring down. Somewhere between her middle of the night conversation with Sydney and now, she had decided to do it. She'd entered the skiing competition. And now, looking at the steep hill below, she was finally ready to face her biggest fear. "I can do this! I can do all things through Christ Jesus who strengthens me!"

Off in the distance, she heard Sydney's voice calling out. "Go, Inspector Gadget! Ski the Rat!"

"You can do it, honey." Her mother's voice echoed across the packed snow.

"Join the Rat Pack!" Uncle Ollie threw in his two cents' worth.

Hearing the words *Rat Pack* reminded Kate that they hadn't yet solved the mystery about the creamery. Thinking about the creamery made her think of the woman in the white coat and the man with the sour expression on his face. Thinking of the man and woman reminded her of the day she and Sydney had hidden behind the Dumpster. And for some reason, thinking of the Dumpster reminded her of Bailey and how her phone rang at just the right—er, *wrong*—time.

"Why am I thinking about that right now?" Kate scolded herself. "I'm supposed to be getting ready to ski, not solve a crime!"

She took her place and tried to prepare herself the best she could.

"I can't believe I'm doing this. I can't believe I'm doing this!" Kate bent her knees and looked down at the long, slender skis. "Lord," she prayed, her eyes now closed, "help me get to the bottom without falling. Oh, and Lord, if You could help me win, I promise to use the money to bless someone else!"

She opened her eyes and looked at the hill below. "It's just a hill. And I'm just like a little robot, about to glide from the top of the hill to the bottom. No big deal! What am I so worried about?"

Of course, there was that part where hundreds of people were watching her, but once she got started, she wouldn't have time to even think about them. No, all she had to think about was getting to the bottom without falling!

At the *pop* of the starter's pistol, Kate dug her poles into the snow and pushed off. As she began to sail down the hill, the cold wind whipped at her face. In fact, the wind was so strong it nearly knocked her down a time or two. Thankfully she managed to stay on her feet!

She came to the first curve and bent her knees, leaning into it. "C'mon, Snow-bot!" she whispered. "You can do this!"

Kate managed to straighten out her position after making the curve. . . without falling! "Woo-hoo!" she called out to no one but the wind. "I did it!" Up ahead she saw a sharp curve to the left. "Uh-oh." She whispered another prayer, then bent her knees to make it around the turn.

Picking up speed, she almost lost control. After a bit of wobbling, she sailed on down, down, down. The trees off in the distance seemed to fly by, their snow-covered branches nothing but a blur.

For a moment, she remembered what had happened yesterday. . .how Sydney had injured her ankle in that very spot. How Kate had searched for a trail through those trees to find help. How they'd ended up in an old red barn with spiders. How Michael was there with his backpack on.

Michael. Hmm.

"Don't think about that right now!" Kate whispered to herself. "Just stay focused! Stay focused!"

After a couple more twists and turns, the bottom of the hill was in sight. Kate crouched a bit, trying to get more speed.

"C'mon, c'mon!" With faster speed than ever, she soared over the finish line, then—like a good robot would do—turned her feet to come to an abrupt stop. Kate's heart raced a hundred miles an hour.

"I did it! I did it!" She pulled off her goggles and began to cheer at the top of her lungs. She could hear the roar of the crowd and felt a little embarrassed. Kate put her hands over her mouth and giggled. Making it to the bottom without falling felt so good! And Sydney was right! She *had* proven something to herself.

I'm not bad at sports! I need to stop saying that!

One by one, she watched the other skiers in her age group. A couple of them fell. One of them made it all the way to the bottom, but didn't seem to be moving as fast. One girl was really, really good. Kate watched her as she came sailing down the hill. Her bright blue snowsuit stood out against the bright white snow.

"Wow, she looks like a pro." At the very last minute, the girl lost control of her skis and went sprawling in the snow.

"Oh man! I hope she's okay," Kate whispered.

Thankfully, the girl rose to her feet and raised her hand to show everyone she wasn't injured. Everyone cheered and she skied down to the bottom of the hill and took a bow.

Finally it was Michael's turn. Kate had almost forgotten he was competing until she saw him. She could hear Uncle Ollie's cheers off in the distance.

Michael is really blessed to have Uncle Ollie in his life. He needs someone like that to support him.

Michael started off well and even made the first curve with no problem. But then, at the second big turn, he almost lost his footing. Thankfully, he didn't fall, but it did slow him down a little. He still skied very well, and Kate knew he'd made up for the lost time. At least, it seemed like it! She was surprised when she saw his time come up on the board. *Oh wow. It took him almost a full second longer to reach the bottom than me. Weird.*

Only one skier was left. Kate watched as the boy sailed down the hill like a professional skier.

"Wow, he's so good!" She watched in awe as he gracefully moved back and forth on his skis. Then, just before he reached the final turn, his skis somehow bumped up against each other and he toppled over! A loud gasp went up from the crowd.

"Oh, that's terrible!" Kate covered her eyes, not wanting to look. Hopefully he wasn't badly hurt.

It took a couple of minutes for him to stand, but he finally managed. The crowd applauded his efforts, and he responded with a dramatic bow. Kate laughed. *He's a great sport!*

After that, everything seemed to move in slow motion. Kate heard her name announced over the loudspeaker. "The winner of this year's Winter Festival junior level competition is twelve-year-old Kate Oliver from Philadelphia, Pennsylvania!"

It almost felt like they were calling someone else's name.

"Me?" she whispered. "I won?" Kate could hardly believe it! The whole thing seemed impossible. . .like a dream. Only this *wasn't* a dream! It was true. Every bit of it!

An older man gestured for her to come to the stage, which she did with shaking knees. She climbed a few stairs and stood before the people.

"Kate Oliver, congratulations on skiing the Rat! You're now an official member of the Rat Pack!" He handed her a T-shirt and opened it to show the icky-looking rat on the back.

Kate giggled and took the shirt. "Thank you so much!" She searched for Uncle Ollie in the crowd. When she found him, she held up the shirt and grinned.

"The Winter Festival of Mad River Valley is proud to give you this trophy for your performance today." The man standing next to Kate gave her a big silver trophy with two skis on top. "And of course. . ." the man continued, handing her a check, "the grand prize of three hundred dollars!"

Kate gripped the check in her hand and whispered a prayer. "Oh, thank You, Lord! I know just what to do with this!"

The crowd started applauding, and Kate felt her cheeks warm up. They always did that when she was embarrassed. No doubt they were as red as tomatoes!

She looked through all of the people till she found her family and Sydney standing off to the left of the stage. Getting down the stairs was the easy part. Making her way through the crowd—with so many people patting her on the back and saying congratulations—was a lot harder than she imagined!

Finally she saw her mother. "Oh Kate! You were wonderful! Congratulations! We're so proud of you!"

"I knew you could do it!" her dad hollered.

The others in her family gathered around, looking at the trophy. Kate held it up for all to see.

"She's a beauty!" Uncle Ollie said.

"That's the coolest trophy I've ever seen!" Dexter added.

"Wonderful, wonderful!" Aunt Molly added. "I'm tickled pink, honey. And even more tickled that you were wearing my old skis! What an honor!"

Biscuit jumped up and down in excitement. Kate reached down to scratch him behind the ears. "I know, boy! You're so excited!"

Sydney came hobbling toward her on her sore ankle. "Oh Kate! I'm so proud of you! You're the fastest skier here."

Kate shook her head. "I still don't know how it's possible. And I know for a fact that your time would have been better than mine, if only. . ." She looked down at her friend's ankle and sighed.

"No *if onlys* today," Sydney said with a happy nod. "Today we're *all* winners."

Off in the distance, Michael walked by, his shoulders slumped forward in defeat. Kate noticed the sour look on his face. He looked her way and glared at her.

Wow. Not everyone is acting like a winner, Kate thought.

He reached underneath the stage and pulled out his backpack, but as he started to put it on, something fell out of it. Something small. And furry.

"Is that what I think it is, or is my imagination acting up again?" Kate whispered.

At once, Biscuit went crazy! He ran toward the small fuzzy critter, barking like a maniac. Only when Kate took a second look, did she realize for sure just what she was looking at! Right away, she began to scream!

"It's. . .it's. . .a. . .*rat*!"

The Mouse Takes the Cheese

As soon as Kate shouted, Michael dropped his backpack into the snow and began to run away from the crowd. Kate had never seen anyone move that fast! He shot through the throng of people, heading toward the lodge.

"Oh, I wish I could run!" Sydney said, wringing her hands together. "This bum ankle of mine won't let me!"

Kate raced after Biscuit, who now stood at the edge of the snow barking like a maniac. She couldn't blame him! *Did I really see what I thought I saw? Did a rat. . .a real, live rat. . .just fall out of Michael's backpack?*

As she got closer to the stage, she glanced down to see what Biscuit held in his mouth. He yanked it around to the right, then the left, then the right, then the left.

"Oh, gross! If it was a rat, it's a goner now!" Kate didn't want to touch it. *Oh, how disgusting!*

A crowd gathered around. "Look, everyone!" Dexter shouted. "Biscuit caught a rat. Good boy!"

"A rat?" one man said with a smirk on his face. "How ironic!"

It took Kate a minute to realize what he meant. They were standing at the bottom of the Rat ski course, after all.

People began to laugh, but Kate didn't feel like joining them. Not yet, anyway. She had a sinking feeling.

"Look!" another man called out. "This dog is going crazy!"

Biscuit continued his chewing and chomping frenzy, and Kate actually felt sorry for the poor little rat. What a terrible way to die!

She grabbed the dog by his collar and scolded him. "Biscuit, let go! Stop! Enough already!"

After a couple of seconds, he finally dropped the furry little thing. Kate gasped when she looked down and saw. . .metal pieces? *Metal pieces inside a rat? What?*

"What is that?" Sydney hobbled up beside her.

"Oh, wow, Kate!" Sydney looked shocked. "It's not a real rat at all. It's a little. . ."

"Robot," Kate whispered. "It's a robotic rat! No wonder it ran in crazy circles that day at the creamery. And no wonder McKenzie couldn't find a photo of another rat that looked like this one. It's not real. It never was." Relief swept over her. "That means they never really had a rat infestation at the creamery. Not real rats, anyway. Just robotic ones. But why? Why would Michael do this?"

Uncle Ollie reached down into the snow to pick up the robotic rat, which Biscuit had almost destroyed. He rolled it from one hand to another, looking it over. "I don't believe this. I really don't believe this. I'm the one who taught him how to build robots, but I never dreamed he would take the things I'd taught him and use them to hurt someone!"

"There were three rats that first day at the creamery," Sydney said, reaching for Michael's backpack. "So there must be at least two more inside!" She looked up at Uncle Ollie. "Is it okay to open it and look inside to see?"

"I give you permission." Michael's mother, Maggie, drew near. "We need to know for sure before. . ." Her eyes filled with tears, and Kate suddenly felt very sorry for her.

Poor woman! She's still sad about her dad dying, and now this!

Mr. and Mrs. Hampton walked up. They both looked completely shocked.

Sydney reached inside the backpack and came out with not just one but two furry critters! As soon as she saw them, she began to scream. "Ooo! More rats!"

One of them flew up into the air, then hit the ground. Kate reached down and grabbed it. "But they're not real. See?" She rolled it around in her hand. "I can feel the metal parts inside. And look, here's where the batteries go." She showed everyone the belly of the rat.

By now, several people had gathered.

"Step back, everyone!" Mr. Hampton said, drawing near. "Step back!"

He approached Kate and took the rats from her, examining them carefully. "Whose bag is this?" he asked, pointing to the backpack.

"It belongs to my son, Michael," Maggie said with tears in her eyes.

"Where did he go?" Mr. Hampton looked around. "Is he still here?"

"I saw him running toward the lodge," an older woman said. "He was going mighty fast!"

Mr. Hampton and Uncle Ollie led the way to the lodge. Kate and her family trudged along behind him in the snow. Kate prayed all the way.

Lord, please let Michael still be there. And help us understand why he would do something like this to the Hamptons!

As they entered the main room of the lodge, Kate saw Michael sitting in front of the fireplace. As soon as he heard everyone come in the door, he turned and looked their way. Kate couldn't help but notice he had tears in his eyes.

What's up with that? What secrets are you hiding, Michael?

Mr. Hampton walked straight over to him and dropped the backpack down on the floor. "Is this yours, son?"

"Yes, sir." Michael looked down at the ground.

"And these, um, rats. They're yours?" Mr. Hampton continued.

Michael hung his head in shame. "Yes, sir. I made them. In my basement."

Maggie walked to his side and slipped an arm over his shoulder. "Michael, we just need the truth. Are you the one who. . ." Her voice cracked. "Are you the one who put the rats in the creamery?"

Kate's heart twisted as he gave a slow nod and then began to cry.

Why would he do such a thing? That's horrible!

Michael turned to Uncle Ollie, talking a mile a minute. "You don't understand what they did to my grandpa!"

With an angry look on his face, he pointed to Mr. and Mrs. Hampton, who stood in silence listening to him. "My Grandpa Joe worked for them for years as a security guard. He was a good man. . ." Michael's voice cracked. "But they fired him! Fired him. For no good reason. He needed that job. We had bills to pay!"

Mr. Hampton looked stunned. "We had good reasons for firing him, Michael, whether you know it or not."

Michael shook his head, growing angrier by the moment. "After he lost his job, Grandpa started getting sick. I know it was because he was so depressed. He was never the same after that. And my mom had to work harder than ever to pay for his medical bills."

Michael began to shake uncontrollably. Kate watched as he clenched his fists.

"So you wanted to get even with them?" Uncle Ollie asked. "You sabotaged the creamery to get even?"

Michael nodded. "I. . .wanted to bring them down! They hurt my grandpa, and I wanted to hurt them!"

Ooo! Kate thought about the scripture she had learned from Aunt Molly. *So that's what happens when you hold a grudge! People really do end up getting hurt!*

"What did you do, son?" Uncle Ollie asked. "Tell me everything."

"I. . .I went to the old barn on the south slope and got lots of spiders. I set them loose in the creamery. But I could tell that wasn't going to be enough to convince people, so I. . ." He shook his head, then stared at Uncle Ollie. "I used what you taught me about robots. Made three of them. Figured if I could. . ." He paused and shook his head. "I just wanted sales to go down at the creamery. I wanted to hurt the Hamptons like they hurt us!"

Michael's mother drew near and wrapped Michael in her arms. "Oh honey," she spoke with tears in her eyes. "First of all, it's wrong to get even with people, even if they really do hurt you. But in this case, you're completely mistaken! The Hamptons are good people."

"No, they're not!" He looked at his mother like she was crazy.

"Oh Michael, there's so much you don't know about your grandpa. He was a good man, but in those last few months before he lost his job, he was already very sick. The Hamptons didn't know it, of course. He didn't want them to know."

"What do you mean, Mom?"

"He told me he'd been falling asleep on the job. A lot. It was probably the medication he was on. I always suspected that, of course. And he never told the Hamptons he was on medicine for his weak heart, so they never knew. He didn't want anyone to know."

Geneva Hampton began to cry. "I always thought there was something more going on with Joe. He kept falling asleep on the job. But I didn't realize he was on medication!"

"He was," Maggie said. "And mighty strong medicine, at that." She turned back to Michael to finish the story. "One night your grandpa fell asleep on the job. It had happened before, but this time a fire broke out in the area where the cows were kept."

"I remember that night," Uncle Ollie said, scratching his head. "It was a close call! The Hamptons could have lost all of their cows that night."

"And it was your grandpa's fault," Maggie said softly to Michael.

Michael shook his head. "Why didn't you ever tell me this? Why did you let me think. . ." He looked up at Mr. and Mrs. Hampton and shook his head. "I just thought they were being mean to him. Now I don't know what to think."

"I think we're all confused and hurt," Uncle Ollie said. "And when we're hurt, we often do things we don't mean to do. I once heard a pastor say, 'Hurt people hurt people.' And it's so true."

Mr. Hampton shook his head, looking more than a little upset. "Oh,

I feel terrible! I wish I had known about Joe's heart condition! We could have worked something out. Maybe cut back on his hours or something."

"No, he was really too frail to be working, anyway," Maggie said. "That's why I tried to pick up so many extra hours at the diner. I figured the more money I made, the less he would have to worry about finances. We were doing okay, until. . ."

"Until he had the heart attack?" Uncle Ollie asked.

Maggie nodded. "Yes. Then I knew. . ." She began to cry and Kate reached over to wrap her arms around her. "That's when I knew he would never work again. At that point, I just wanted to see him get better, to come back home."

"We just wanted everything to be. . .normal," Michael said, his eyes glistening with tears. "But then. . ."

"Well, we all know what happened next." Maggie sniffled then wiped her nose with a tissue. "He went to be with Jesus. And, of course, he's in heaven celebrating right now, but we still miss him so much."

"Enough to do some really dumb things." Michael kicked at a pile of snow with the toe of his tennis shoe. "I. . .I'm so sorry. I really thought you guys fired Gramps because. . .well, because you didn't like him."

"Oh no, honey!" Geneva Hampton wrapped her arms around his shoulders. "We loved your grandpa. And we were concerned about him. That's really why we let him go. Though he never told us about his illness, we knew something was wrong and we decided the job was putting too much stress on him."

"You did the right thing," Maggie said. "It wounded his pride a little, but he needed the rest."

Michael looked at Mr. Hampton with tears in his eyes. "Can you ever forgive me? I'm so sorry."

"Of course we forgive you, Michael," Mr. Hampton said. "It would be wrong to hold a grudge."

"I'll do everything I can to make this better," Michael said with a hopeful look in his eye. "I know! I'll come to work for you. You won't have to pay me or anything. I'll work in the factory every afternoon to make up for what I've done. And I'll tell everyone I know to buy Mad River Valley cheese!"

Mr. Hampton laughed. "Well, we can always use the help, but you're a little young to be working, aren't you?"

Michael shook his head. "I'm turning fifteen in a week! I can have a job if my mom says so, right? I just want to make up for what I've done. I . . .I can't believe I let my anger get control of me like that. Next time I'm going to wait till I have all of the facts before acting!"

"Great plan!" Mr. Hampton gave him a pat on the back. "Now, I have an idea! Geneva made a huge pot of cheddar cheese soup for the festival. It's out in the car. Are you folks hungry?"

"Cheddar cheese soup?" Kate's stomach rumbled, just thinking about it. Man, did that ever sound good!

She turned to Sydney with a smile on her face and whispered, "I can't believe it! We were right! The creamery was being sabotaged!"

Just as quickly, she thought about the woman in the white coat and her husband. If Michael was the one who'd sabotaged the creamery, who were they. . .and what were they doing in Mad River Valley?

Christmas in Vermont

On the day after the big Winter Festival, Kate went to church with her family. She knew their time in Vermont was drawing to a close, and she wanted to enjoy every moment. She couldn't have been more surprised to hear the preacher's topic of the day: forgiveness. What a fun coincidence. Of course, Aunt Molly called it a *God*-incidence. Kate couldn't help but agree!

A couple of times during the service, Kate looked at Maggie and Michael who sat in the row beside them. He really seemed to pay attention to the sermon. And she felt pretty sure he'd learned his lesson about forgiveness.

But, had *she*?

As soon as they arrived back at the inn, they all ate lunch together, then Aunt Molly and Kate's mother washed the dishes. Sydney settled into a chair across from Uncle Ollie to talk about sports, and Kate. . .well, Kate had something specific on her mind. There was something she needed to do. Something she should have done days before.

Heading over to Uncle Ollie's computer, she signed into her email account. Then, thinking carefully about each word, she began to type.

Dear Phillip,

I'm in Mad River Valley, Vermont, on Christmas vacation with my family. I've been working on my science project. It's all about cheese! (Boy, have I learned a LOT!) I'm sure you're hard at work on your project back in Philly or wherever you're spending your vacation. Hope you're having fun!

I just want you to know that I'm sorry if I ever did anything to make you feel like you're not as smart as me. I think you're so smart and should have told you so instead of always trying to make it look like I'm the best!

When you made fun of my project a few weeks ago, it hurt my feelings, but I have forgiven you. Will you forgive me for the mean things I was thinking about you since then? Please? When I get back to school, I'm going to ask Mrs. Mueller if we can work together on our next project. The Bible says that one can put a thousand to flight but two can put ten *thousand to flight. That's kind of a fancy way of saying we can do more if we work together!*

I learned a lot about that this week in Vermont. I worked with my friend Sydney and together we accomplished great things. I can't wait to tell you all about it! The rest of the school year is going to be better if we're friends!

See you soon! Kate Oliver

She read over the email once or twice, then pressed the SEND button.

Just then, Kate heard her mother's voice behind her. "What are you doing, honey? The others are waiting to open Christmas presents!"

"Oh, just taking care of something I should have done days ago." Kate turned around and smiled at her mom, feeling contentment in her heart. "Forgiving someone. Or rather, *letting* that someone know I've forgiven him!"

"Wow. Well, I can think of no greater Christmas gift than that. You know, honey, God is in the forgiving business. That's why He sent His Son, Jesus, as a baby in a manger. He knew that we—His children—all needed a Savior."

Kate nodded. "I know. But I'm glad you reminded me. I'll never look at the baby in the manger the same again, Mom!"

In the next room, Kate heard voices raised in song. Aunt Molly warbled, "Deck the halls with boughs of holly" at the top of her lungs, and the others soon joined in.

"Come and join us, honey," her mother said, extending her hand. "We've got some celebrating to do. And lots of presents to open!"

"Yes, we do!" Kate thought about all of the victories of the past week as she made her way into the great room, where flames lit the fireplace and her family members sang in several keys at once! In one week's time she had solved a mystery, won a competition, and forgiven Phillip. *That's a lot, Lord!*

Only one thing left to do. . .and oh, what fun it was going to be! Talk about a merry Christmas!

One by one the family members opened presents. Kate was tickled to get so many fun gifts—a hand-knitted scarf from Aunt Molly, a great journal from Sydney, and lots of cool things from her mom and dad. Even Dexter gave her a great present—a cool new digital recorder.

Finally the moment arrived. . .the one Kate had been waiting for. She watched as Sydney opened the gift she had so carefully wrapped. Everyone's eyes nearly popped when they saw the three hundred dollars in cash inside.

"W—what?" Sydney looked at her, stunned. "What have you done, Kate?"

"It's my Christmas gift to you!" she exclaimed. "The *only* reason I agreed to take your place in the competition was to help you go on your mission trip. Of course, I never dreamed I would actually win. . .but I did! It was a huge blessing for both of us! Don't you see? Now you can go to Mexico."

"B—but. . .I didn't earn this money." Sydney tried to hand it back to her. "*You* did."

"No, the way I look at it, it's really a miracle I made it from the top of the Rat to the bottom without falling on my face and embarrassing myself in front of hundreds of people! So, we'll call that our miracle money. And I can think of no better way to spend my miracle money than on a mission trip!"

"A—are you sure?" Sydney stammered.

"Sure I'm sure! Take it. Go to Mexico. Have the time of your life." Kate leaned over and whispered, "Just don't have any big adventures without me, okay?"

"Okay! I'll try!" Sydney giggled and hugged the gift tightly. "Oh, I don't believe it! Can I call my mom? Would that be okay?"

"Of course, honey." Aunt Molly pointed to the phone. "You go right ahead. But the rest of us still have presents to open."

Sydney headed over to the phone to make the call. Kate could hear her squeals as she shared the story with her mother. Oh, how wonderful it felt. . .to be able to do something so fun for a friend!

Several minutes later, after everyone had opened all of the Christmas gifts, Kate heard singing at the door. At least, she *thought* it was singing. Sounded a little off-key to her!

"Sounds like carolers!" Uncle Ollie said.

He opened the door and Kate smiled as she saw Mr. and Mrs. Hampton outside, along with Michael and his mother. Together, the four of them sang "The First Noel" really, really loud. Oh, what a wonderful sound, to hear their voices raised in harmony! A little off-key, but harmony, just the same!

Thank You, God! Kate giggled. *This is what happens when people forgive one another! You fix their broken relationships!*

After they finished singing, Aunt Molly invited them inside. "You're just in time!" she said. "We baked snickerdoodles and I've made wassail! Let's celebrate together!"

"We have a lot to celebrate, don't we?" Mr. Hampton said, smiling at Michael. "God has done such wondrous things this Christmas season. He's brought us all closer together and given us plenty of reasons to look ahead to a bright new year!"

"Yes, He has," Mrs. Hampton agreed with a twinkle in her eye.

They had all settled into chairs around the dining room table to eat cookies and drink wassail when Mr. Hampton cleared his throat to get the attention of everyone in the room. "I have some news," he said, clasping his hands together.

Everyone looked his way. Kate could hardly wait to hear what he had to say. She hoped it was good news!

"Geneva and I are selling the creamery!" Mr. Hampton grinned from ear to ear.

"W–what?" Everyone spoke in unison.

"Are you kidding?" Uncle Ollie asked.

"Please say this is a joke!" Aunt Molly added. "We don't want you to move away!"

"We're not moving away," he said. "I promise!"

"Oh Mr. Hampton. . .please don't give up just because your sales are down right now," Michael begged. "I'll do anything. . .everything to help you get them up again."

Mr. Hampton laughed. "No, you don't understand. Geneva and I are ready to retire. And we have no children to pass the business to. God never blessed us with a son or a daughter. A wonderful couple from central Vermont has been talking with us about buying the place. In fact, I think you met them, girls. They were on the tour that day. . ."

"Abigail and Mark Collingsworth?" Kate stammered.

"Why, yes." Geneva Hampton looked stunned. "How did you know their names? That's amazing."

"Oh, trust me," Sydney said. "We know a lot more than that about them. They already own a creamery called Cheese De-Lite about fifty miles from here. They're Mad River's main competitors."

"Not anymore!" Geneva Hampton laughed. "They're moving their operation to Mad River Valley. From now on, there will be no Cheese De-Lite. But they will bring their signature cheese flavor with them. . .the low-fat version of cheddar."

"Low-fat cheese?" Kate wrinkled her nose. "No wonder that man has such a sour look on his face. That doesn't sound very yummy."

"No, he had a sour look on his face because he *really* thought we had rats at the creamery," Mrs. Hampton said with a laugh. "We had a hard time convincing him it wasn't true! But now that he knows the real story, he's made us an offer. And it's a good one. So the next time you see him, he will be smiling, I'm sure!"

"Still, low-fat cheese?" Kate said. "Icky!"

"Hey, we have to cut back on our calories every way we can!" Sydney said. After a sheepish look, she added, "Well, at least *I* do, if I'm going to be a sports star!"

Kate sighed. "I guess I'd better cut back on calories too. Skiing was a lot of fun. You never know, I may end up liking sports too! Wouldn't that be something!"

"I can hardly wait to tell the other Camp Club Girls!" Sydney laughed. "Can you imagine the look on Bailey's face when she hears you won a skiing competition!"

"And what about McKenzie! She's going to flip!" Kate chuckled just thinking about it. "I'm excited to tell Elizabeth. I know she's been praying. I always feel better, knowing she's praying."

"Me too," Sydney observed. "And I always feel better when I'm spending time with you. That's why. . ." Her eyes filled with tears. "That's why I'm so sad this week is almost over! We have to go home soon!"

"Let's spend every minute together. . .having fun!" Kate said.

●—●—●

A few minutes later, Michael asked if he could speak to Kate in private. She sat next to him on the couch wondering why he had such an embarrassed look on his face.

"You know, I bragged a lot about how fast I am on the slopes," he said.

"Yes, you did," Kate agreed. "But you *are* fast. I saw you with my own eyes."

"Yes, but I saw *you* too! And you're amazing, Kate! Really amazing."

"You think so?" She felt her cheeks turn warm as an embarrassed feeling came over her.

"I know so." He grinned. "Are you coming back to Mad River Valley next winter? If so, I'd better start practicing now if I'm ever going to beat you."

Kate laughed long and loud at that one. "How funny! A boy actually thinks I'm good at sports! That's hysterical!" She giggled. "I don't know if

I'll compete next year. I liked it more when I was skiing for fun. But I'm sure we'll come back for a visit if Aunt Molly and Uncle Ollie invite us!"

"Oh, you're *always* welcome!" Aunt Molly said, sweeping Kate into her arms. "Please come and see me as often as you like."

"Yes, I feel sure there are lots of mysteries to solve in Mad River Valley," Uncle Ollie said.

"Like who ate all the snickerdoodles when I wasn't looking," Maggie said, looking at Uncle Ollie.

"Or who put too much cheese in the fondue," Michael threw in.

"Or who used my treadmill when I wasn't looking!" Uncle Ollie added, looking at Sydney.

"Wasn't me!" Aunt Molly proclaimed.

They all laughed at that one.

"It doesn't matter where Kate goes, adventure always seems to follow," her dad said. "She's my little supersleuth!"

"I just *love* adventure!" Kate said. "Love, love, love it!"

She and Sydney spent the next few minutes telling everyone about some of the cases they had solved with the Camp Club Girls. On and on their stories went, filling the ears of everyone in the room.

When she finished, her dad looked at her, beaming with pride. "I'm so proud of you, Kate."

"Here's to Inspector Gadget!" Sydney raised her glass of wassail.

Seconds later, everyone joined her, offering up a toast to Kate. She felt all warm and tingly inside. Solving mysteries made her feel good from the top of her head to the bottom of her toes.

But what made her feel even better—much, much better, in fact—was forgiving Phillip. Perhaps that had been the greatest lesson of all this week. Never again would she hold a grudge. No, from now on she would forgive. . .quickly!

"Be kind to one another, tenderhearted, forgiving one another, even as God in Christ forgave you." Kate smiled as she whispered the words. Yes, from now on, she would always be quick to forgive!

Aunt Molly stood and began to sing "Joy to the World." Uncle Ollie joined her, then Mr. and Mrs. Hampton. Before long, most everyone was singing, even Michael.

Sydney leaned over and whispered in Kate's ear. "We solved another case, Kate! Can you believe it?"

"Yep!" Turning to her friend, Kate whispered the words they loved so much: "Supersleuths forever!"

Sydney winked and added, "Forever and ever!"

Kate nodded, then happened to look over at the little manger scene on the fireplace mantel. She focused on the babe inside, remembering what her mother had said. *He came to forgive,* she reminded herself.

With a *very* merry heart, Kate lifted her voice and began to sing!

Camp Club Girls:
Kate and the
Wyoming Fossil Fiasco

Water, Water Everywhere!

"Kate, watch out!"

Kate Oliver jerked her arm back as she heard her teacher's voice.

Kaboosh! A large glass of water tumbled over, landing directly on the fossil plate she had just unpacked from a large wooden box.

"Oh no!" Kate squeezed her eyes shut. Surely she did *not* just spill water on a priceless artifact, thousands of years old!

"Quick. Let me dry it." Mrs. Smith, Kate's teacher, grabbed a paper towel and ran toward Kate.

Kate backed away, shaking so hard her knees knocked. "I–I'm so sorry! I didn't mean to spill it."

Of all things! She had come to the museum to help her teacher. And now she'd destroyed something of great value! Why oh why did things like this always seem to happen to her?

"It's not your fault, Kate," Mrs. Smith said. "I left my glass of water sitting there. I only have myself to blame."

"Still. . ." Kate's glasses slipped down her nose, and she pushed them back into place. Tears filled her eyes as she watched her teacher. How would the museum ever replace something so valuable? And would Mrs. Smith lose her new job as museum curator? A shiver ran down the twelve-year-old's spine.

"Please, Lord, don't let that happen!" she whispered.

"Wait a minute. . ." Mrs. Smith shook her head as she dabbed the fossil plate with the paper towel. "Something is very wrong here."

Kate leaned forward to look. "W–what is it?"

"A glass of water couldn't possibly harm *real* fossils," Mrs. Smith explained. "But look at this." She pulled the towel away and Kate gasped. The fossil imprint appeared to be dissolving, slowly melting away before her eyes.

"I don't understand." Kate took her finger and twisted a strand of her blond hair, something she often did when she was nervous.

"Neither do I," Mrs. Smith said as she pulled off her latex gloves. "But I'm going to get to the bottom of this." When her hands were free of the gloves, she pulled out a magnifying glass and examined the fossil plate. After a moment, she whispered, "Oh my. This doesn't look good."

Kate grew more curious by the moment.

"Kate, see what you think." Mrs. Smith handed her the magnifying glass. Kate peered through it, taking a close look.

"Very interesting," she said. "They look like grains of sand, only maybe a little bigger."

Kate reached into her backpack and pulled out a miniature digital camera, just one of her many electronic gadgets. She zoomed in and began taking photos, documenting the changes in the fossil as they occurred. She had a feeling these photos would come in handy later.

"Up close it doesn't even look real. Funny that I never noticed it before." Mrs. Smith touched a spot where the water had landed, then stuck her finger in her mouth. Her eyes grew wide as she looked at Kate. "You've got to be kidding me!"

"What?" Kate asked. "What is it?"

Her teacher gasped. "Brown sugar!"

"No way!" Kate took one final picture of Mrs. Smith with her finger in her mouth. "The fossil plates are. . .fake?"

"Looks that way." Her teacher put down the magnifying glass and shook her head. "I don't believe it. I simply don't believe it. These plates are on loan to the museum from a quarry in Wyoming. We're expecting hundreds of guests to visit the museum to see them. And now we find out they're not even real? This is terrible news!" She reached for a piece of paper and began to fan herself. "Is it getting hot in here?"

Kate shook her head. "Not really." She put her camera away and then looked at her teacher, trying to figure out how she could help.

"I must be nervous." Mrs. Smith paced the room. "What am I going to do?"

She paused and looked at Kate. "This exhibition was supposed to be the biggest thing to happen to our museum in years. People were coming from all over the country to see these fossils. Oh, why does something like this have to happen my first week as curator? Why?"

"I don't know, but I would sure like to get to the bottom of this," Kate said. "So if you don't mind. . ." She pressed her hand inside the backpack fishing around for something. Finally she came up with the tiny finger print kit.

Mrs. Smith looked at her, stunned. "You just *happen* to have a fingerprint kit in your backpack?"

"Yes." Kate giggled. "I always carry it with me. I never know when there's going to be a mystery to solve or a criminal to catch."

"You solve mysteries?" Mrs. Smith looked confused. "And you catch criminals?"

Kate nodded and smiled, "Along with a bunch of others called the Camp Club Girls."

She would have plenty of time to explain later. Right now she had work to do. She pulled out several other gadgets, starting with a tiny digital recorder. "I'd like to record our conversation, Mrs. Smith. You might say something important to the case."

"Case?"

"Sure. I have a feeling this is going to be a very exciting one, but I need to keep track of the information, and recording it is the best way."

"I suppose that would be fine." Mrs. Smith shrugged.

Kate turned on the recorder and set it on a nearby table, asking her teacher questions about the fossil plates. Then she pulled something that looked like an ink pen from her backpack.

Mrs. Smith looked at her curiously. "Do you need to write something?"

"No, this isn't really a pen." Kate wiggled her eyebrows and smiled. "It's a text reader. Look." She took the pen-like device and ran it along the edge of the wooden box the fossil plates had been packed in. It recorded the words STONE'S THROW QUARRY, WYOMING'S FOSSIL FANTASY LAND.

"Very clever," Mrs. Smith said with a nod.

After recording a few more words from the side of the box, Kate turned her attention back to her backpack. She pulled out the smartwatch her father had given her.

Her teacher looked at Kate's gadgets, her brow wrinkling in confusion. "Why do you have all of these things, Kate? Do you really solve mysteries, or is this some sort of game?"

Kate shook her head. "It's no game. And it looks like we have a doozy of a mystery here. But to solve it, I need to contact the other Camp Club Girls."

"Camp Club Girls? I'm not sure I understand. Who are the Camp Club Girls?"

"We're a group of girls who all met at Discovery Lake Camp awhile back," Kate explained. "We solve mysteries together. If anyone can get to the bottom of this, the Camp Club Girls can."

Mrs. Smith's eyes grew wide. "Really? Do you think you could help figure out who did this? That's a lot to ask of a group of girls your age."

"You would be surprised what the Camp Club Girls can do with the Lord's help!" Kate went to work, lifting fingerprints from the edges of the fossil plate. Before long, she had a couple of great ones. "Perfect. Now, if it's okay with you, I need to send an email to the girls in the club to see if they can help."

"Well, sure," Mrs. Smith said. "I guess that would be okay. Do you need to use one of the museum's computers to get online? I'm sure I could arrange that."

"No thanks." Kate pulled off her latex gloves and opened her wristwatch. "I can send emails on my smartwatch."

"You. . .you can?" Mrs. Smith did not look convinced.

Kate typed out a quick note to the girls:

Emergency! Need help cracking a fake fossil case! Meet me in our chat room at 7:00 p.m. eastern time.

She closed the watch and smiled at her teacher. "Don't worry, Mrs. Smith," she said, trying to sound brave. "The Camp Club Girls are on the case! We'll figure out this fossil fiasco in no time!"

With the tip of her finger, she reached to touch the ruined fossil plate then stuck her finger in her mouth, tasting the sweetness of the brown sugar. These plates might not be the real deal, but they sure were tasty. And Kate was convinced they contained clues to help unravel the mystery.

Suddenly, she could hardly wait to get started!

CHAPTER 2

A Sweet Adventure

The fossil fiasco gave Kate and the Camp Club Girls an exciting new puzzle to solve. She could hardly wait! Surely, with the Lord's help, they would crack this case wide open! She thought about this all the way home from the museum.

As Kate ate dinner with her parents that evening, she filled them in on what had happened. "I felt terrible when I spilled the water," she said. "But Mrs. Smith said it wasn't my fault."

"I'm sure she felt awful for leaving her glass so close to the fossil plates," Kate's mother said. "I guess it just goes to show you how careful you have to be around things of value."

"But look on the bright side, Kate," her father added. "If you hadn't spilled water on them, she might have never discovered they were fake. The whole thing could have been a huge embarrassment to your teacher if the exhibition had moved forward and someone discovered the forgery after the fact. People who paid money to see the fossils would have been angry to find out they'd been lied to. So you probably saved the day, whether you realize it or not."

"I never thought of that!" Kate suddenly felt better. "I guess it's a good thing we found out now instead of later." She took a couple of bites of mashed potatoes, then leaned back in her chair, thinking about her father's words. Maybe spilling that water *had* saved the day, after all.

Her little brother Dexter took a bite of meatloaf, then talked with his mouth full. "Kate, can I help you and the Camp Club Girls with this case?"

She shrugged. "Probably, Dex. But I need to talk to the other girls." Kate glanced at the wall clock, startled to find it was fifteen minutes till seven.

Her dad changed the topic of conversation, talking about the family's upcoming vacation to Colorado, but Kate had a hard time paying attention.

She only had one thing on her mind right now. . .getting online to meet the other Camp Club Girls in their internet chat room.

A few minutes later, after eating a second helping of meatloaf and mashed potatoes, Kate headed upstairs. She glanced at her reflection in the large round mirror that hung on the wall. Her shoulder-length blond hair was a little messy, but she didn't really mind. After all, she couldn't be a supersleuth and have perfect hair at the same time, could she? Still, she needed to do something about her glasses, which had slipped down her nose again. Kate pushed them back up with her finger and shrugged.

"C'mon, Biscuit!" She looked down at her dog. His tail waved merrily as he followed her up the stairs. Biscuit could always tell when they were about to set off on an adventure. He was a great mystery-solving dog and had even helped the girls before. Maybe he could help this time too.

When she reached the top of the stairs, Kate turned to walk down the long hall toward her bedroom and almost tripped over Robby, the robovac. As always, Biscuit barked at the little robotic vacuum cleaner and Kate scolded him. "I would think by now you would be used to Robby, Biscuit! Stop barking."

The pooch tucked his tail between his legs and followed her to her bedroom. Once there, Kate grabbed her new laptop—the one her father had given her. It was super-duper fast and Kate was so thankful that it had wireless internet connection so she could use it anywhere in the house. Kate signed online, realizing the other Camp Club Girls were waiting for her in the chat room—Bailey, the youngest, twelve-year-old Sydney, and Elizabeth, the oldest of the girls. Somehow, knowing they were on the case made everything better.

Kate: *K8 here. Everyone else here?*
Sydney: *I'm here.*
Bailey: *So am I! Ready for adventure!*
Elizabeth: *I really want to help. Just tell me what I can do.*
Alexis: *Yes, this sounds really curious. But we need to know more before we can help you.*
McKenzie: *Kate, can you tell us more about the fake fossils? Your email didn't have much information.*

Kate quickly explained what had happened at the museum, typing as fast as her fingers could go. She told them every detail—about the accident with the water, the fake fossils, and her teacher's fears that she might lose her new job.

Kate: *I think we can start by figuring out where Stone's Throw Quarry is. I saw the name on the packing crates. That's where the fossils are from.*

McKenzie: *Ooh, hang on a minute. I think I'm on to something. There's a Stone's Throw Quarry south of Yellowstone National Park, just a few hours from where I live. I'm looking at their website now.*

Seconds later, she pasted in the link and before long Kate clicked it, watching as the colorful site appeared.

Kate: *Wow. Looks like a great place. This is cool. Stone's Throw hosts a three-day fossil camp for kids, week after next. I wonder. . . Our family is supposed to leave in a couple of days to go on a trip to Rocky Mountain National Park in Colorado. Maybe I could talk my mom and dad into driving up to Yellowstone National Park afterwards so I could go to that fossil camp. They could set up their tent at the park and McKenzie and I could go to the camp hosted by the quarry. I'll bet if we spent a few days there, I could take some fingerprints and compare them to the ones I got today. Maybe we could figure out who forged the fossils!*

Bailey: *Forged the fossils. That's funny.*

Kate: *If we don't figure this out, Mrs. Smith could lose her new job at the museum. And the museum will lose a lot of visitors. We've got to find the real fossils and get them to the museum in time for the exhibition.*

McKenzie: *I would love to help. I'll have to ask my parents, of course. Maybe they would like to go to Yellowstone too. It's one of my dad's favorite places and he's been talking about going on a vacation soon.*

Kate: *Great! Just pray that my mom and dad like the idea.*

She tucked a loose blond hair behind her ear.

"That your mom and dad like *what* idea?" Her mother's voice rang out from behind her.

Kate turned and faced her mom with an embarrassed smile. "Oh, hi, Mom."

"Hi to you too. What have you and the other girls come up with, and how does the plan involve your father and me?"

"Oh, it's the best idea ever," Kate said, giving her mom a hopeful smile. "I need to go to a fossil hunting camp in Wyoming week after next."

"Wyoming?" Her mother stared at her, looking a little stunned. "But we're not going to Wyoming. We're going to Colorado."

Kate flashed another smile, hoping to convince her mom. "Think about it. Wyoming would be a great place to visit. You and Dad can camp out at Yellowstone National Park with Dex while I'm at fossil camp. I know how much you've always wanted to do that."

"Honey, we're going to *Rocky Mountain* National Park in Colorado," her mother explained. "Not Yellowstone."

"Can't we do both?" Kate asked. "Please? Oh please?"

"Kate, you don't seriously think. . ." Her mother shook her head. "Oh never mind. I can see that you *do* think we might consider this." After a pause, she said, "Well I promise to talk to your father about it. But don't get your hopes up. I'm not sure your father will like the idea. It's a long drive from Rocky Mountain National Park to Yellowstone."

"But it will be so worth it if I can help my teacher figure out who did this," Kate said. "Besides, it would be a great adventure. And I know Dex would love it." She smiled as she mentioned her little brother's name. Just as quickly, her smile disappeared as she realized he would probably want to go to the quarry camp too. How could the girls ever solve a mystery with her little brother tagging along?

Kate's mother left the room, and Kate realized the girls had gone on chatting without her. She skimmed their posts, getting caught up.

McKenzie: *This is what we'll do. K8 and I will go to the camp and figure out who would want to forge a fossil and why.*

Sydney: *And the rest of us will help too! We'll figure this out!*

Bailey: *I wish I could go to fossil camp with you! But I know my mom won't let me.*

Alexis: *This whole thing reminds me of a documentary I saw last year with my dad. I'm going to watch it again. Maybe it will give us some clues.*

Sydney: *I'm going to research the quarry online before you get there. So call me, okay?*

Kate: *Okay.*

Elizabeth: *This reminds me a little of the story of Jacob and Esau from the Old Testament. Do you remember that one? Jacob pretended to be his brother Esau so that he could steal his birthright. He put on animal skins to try to fool his dad into thinking he was really his brother.*

Kate: *Oh that's right. And his dad, Isaac, fell for it,didn't he?*

Elizabeth: *Yes. Sometimes pretenders get away with things. A lot of people are really good at faking it.*

McKenzie: *Some aren't so good. That's why we have to figure this out!*

Elizabeth: *I'm going to read that story again tonight. And I will pray. Maybe the Lord will drop some clues in our lap and we can solve this case.*

Kate: *I'll be in touch. We'll figure this out!*

Bailey: *Yes, send us text messages. Or call.*

Kate: *Maybe we'll have wireless internet access too. But we'll stay in touch, I promise. Now pray that my parents say yes.*

The girls said their goodbyes and Kate signed off-line. Then she curled up on the bed with Biscuit at her side. She hugged him. "What do you think, Wonder Dog? Are you ready for a fossil-tastic adventure?"

He reached up to lick her face and she giggled. Looked like Biscuit was ready to go! Now if only her parents would join the fun!

Kate Goes to Yellowstone

Just a week and a half after the fossil fiasco, Kate's father drove the family's van to the entrance of Yellowstone National Park. He had agreed that after a week in Colorado, the Oliver clan would go to Wyoming so Kate could go to fossil camp. Talk about an answer to prayer!

As they entered the park, her father shook his head. "I still can't believe you talked me into this."

"But we'll have so much fun!" Kate gave him an encouraging smile.

"You're probably right." He steered their van toward the campsite. They arrived moments later and worked together to unload and set up the family's large tent.

"I want to go to fossil camp too," Dexter grumbled. "It's not fair that Mom and Dad won't let me."

"Who knows? You may have an adventure of your own, here at Yellowstone," Kate said. Leaning closer, she whispered, "You know there are bears here, right?"

"Bears?" He reached for the video camera and held it up. "If I see one, I'll tape it! Maybe I'll make a movie to show my friends. I'll call it. . . *Un-bear-able!*"

Kate laughed until her sides hurt. Suddenly she didn't feel so bad about leaving Dexter here while she went to fossil camp.

An hour later, McKenzie's family arrived. Kate smiled as her friend climbed out of their large RV. She could hardly believe how much older McKenzie looked. At thirteen, McKenzie was the second oldest of the Camp Club Girls. She was much taller than last time.

McKenzie wore her red hair pulled back in a ponytail and freckles dotted her cheeks. The freckles were the only thing Kate and McKenzie had in common. Well, the only thing except their faith and their love of crime solving!

"It's so great to see you again!" McKenzie hugged Kate. Then she scratched Biscuit behind the ears. "And it's supergreat to see Biscuit too. I've missed you, boy!"

He rolled over on his back, begging for his tummy to be rubbed.

"Okay, you silly thing." McKenzie laughed as she knelt to tickle his tummy. "I never could keep from spoiling you."

The happy pooch rolled in the dirt, glad to get so much attention.

"I'm so happy your parents agreed to come!" Kate said. "Can you believe we're really here?"

"No, but I'm so glad!" McKenzie looked up from tickling Biscuit's tummy and grinned. "Oh Kate, we'll have the best time in the world. Fossil camp. Can you believe we actually get to go?"

McKenzie's mother walked up. "I can't believe we let you girls talk us into this," she said.

After the Phillipses got settled in, the two families gathered around the campfire, where they roasted hot dogs and nibbled on potato chips. Kate ate her first hot dog then reached for another.

After eating hot dogs, they roasted marshmallows. Kate ate three in a row then smacked her lips. "Man! Those were good!"

"Tell us the whole story about why we've come to Wyoming, Kate," Mrs. Phillips said. "What happened with your teacher at the museum, and what are you and McKenzie hoping to find on your adventure at the quarry?"

Kate put down her stick. "Well, my science teacher, Mrs. Smith, just got a new job at the Museum of Natural Science in Philadelphia. She's a curator."

"What's a curator?" Dexter asked, looking up from his sticky marshmallow.

"A curator is the one in charge of the projects," Kate explained. "She organizes the collections. Mrs. Smith was organizing the new fossil collection and it turned out to be fake."

"Oh I see." Dexter swallowed the rest of his marshmallow, licked his fingers, and went back to playing with his Gameboy.

"Tell us again how you found out they were fake," Mrs. Phillips said.

"We were unpacking the fossils from their boxes when I accidentally spilled a glass of water on one of them," Kate explained.

Mr. Phillips shrugged. "A little water shouldn't hurt anything."

"That's just it," Kate said. "The imprint began to melt and Mrs. Smith realized the fossils weren't fossils at all. We looked closer and found out someone had forged them!"

"Out of sand?" Mr. Phillips asked. "I suppose that would be the obvious choice."

"No." Kate shook her head. "You'll never believe it. Brown sugar!"

"Oh my." Mrs. Phillips looked stunned. "Must be someone who really knows his or her fossils to disguise brown sugar that well."

"Yes, a real pro," Kate's father agreed. "I think you girls need to keep your eyes open for people who have worked at the quarry a long time. Maybe you will find your suspect that way."

"Maybe," Kate said. "Or maybe the bad guy—or girl—doesn't work at the quarry at all. Maybe it's someone on the outside."

"What makes you think that?" her mother asked.

"Sydney did some research and sent me a list of other quarries in Wyoming that compete with Stone's Throw."

"I see," her mother said. "Could be a competitor, trying to make Stone's Throw look bad."

"Exactly." Kate nodded. "Sydney also sent me a bunch of information about the type of fossils found at Stone's Throw and where they're sold, so we have a lot of information to go on."

"That's why we have to go to the quarry," McKenzie said. "To figure all of this out."

"I just hope we can crack this case," Kate said. "I don't want Mrs. Smith to lose her job. I got an email from her just yesterday. She said that the board members at the museum are holding a special meeting next week. Some of them are holding her responsible for this, but it's not her fault. She had no idea those fossils were fake until I spilled the water."

"Well of course she didn't. How could she?" McKenzie asked. "It's not like anyone goes around licking fossils or pouring water on them!"

"Still, we have to figure this out before that meeting," Kate explained. "If so, we can save the day."

"Remember, honey, only God can truly save the day." Kate's mother reached to give her a hug. "He uses us to touch others' lives, but ultimately only He can work the miracles, not us."

Kate nodded. "Thanks, Mom. Just keep praying, okay?"

"I will, honey."

"And we will do what we can to help too," Mr. Phillips said. "Tomorrow, when we drop you off at the quarry for fossil camp, we'll go on the tour. Maybe we can unearth some helpful information." He laughed and then slapped his knee. "Get it? *Unearth* some helpful information?"

Kate giggled.

"I'm sure McKenzie will be a big help to you, Kate," Mrs. Phillips said.

"She always has a way of digging deep to find answers."

"Digging deep! That's a good one!" Mr. Phillips slapped his knee again. "Man! We're on a roll, aren't we?"

Everyone had a good laugh. It made Kate feel terrific to know their parents were excited about this. Now, if only she and McKenzie and the other Camp Club Girls could actually solve this case in time for Mrs. Smith to keep her job. . .then all would be well!

CHAPTER 4

Fossil-tastic Fun!

The next morning, Kate's dad drove the girls to Stone's Throw Quarry, about an hour away from Yellowstone. Mr. Phillips went along for the ride. So did Dexter. Kate could hardly contain her excitement, not just about the camp, which started at ten o'clock, but about spending time with McKenzie too. All along the way, she kept in touch with the other Camp Club Girls by sending text messages to keep them updated.

"Elizabeth says she's praying for us," Kate whispered to McKenzie.

"And Bailey says to have fun!" McKenzie added, looking up from her phone.

The girls giggled.

Just then, Kate received an email on her smartwatch. She looked up at McKenzie, wide-eyed. "Sydney says to drink lots of water because we're at a higher elevation."

"Oooh, good idea." McKenzie nodded. "If anyone would know about that kind of stuff, Sydney would."

Kate typed a response to Sydney's email then sent it. "There. I told her we would use sunscreen and drink lots of water."

"Don't you just love technology?" Kate's father said. "Here we are, in the middle of Wyoming, and the girls can stay in touch with their friends all over the country by text messages or emails."

"Oh, that's nothing," Kate said. "Just wait till tonight! We're doing another internet chat with our friends. It'll be great. They're all on the case."

"I love it." McKenzie's father smiled. "Back when we were their age, we didn't even have cell phones."

"You didn't?" Dexter looked at them, clearly stunned. "How did you talk to people?"

"Well for one thing, we spent a lot more time talking to the people we were actually with," Mr. Phillips said. "If we had an emergency while driving down the road, we would stop and use a pay phone."

"Pay phone?" Dexter shrugged. "What's that?"

Kate's father laughed. "Never mind, son. Just trust us when we say that times have changed."

Dexter crossed his arms and leaned against the seat with a sour look.

Kate glanced his way, concerned. "Everything okay, Dex?"

"I just wish I could go with you to camp. You and McKenzie are going to have a lot of fun solving mysteries."

"Maybe next time," Kate said. She didn't worry too much about her little brother. He would have a lot of fun at Yellowstone. "Think of all the bears you're going to see," she whispered.

His eyes grew large.

When they arrived at the quarry, Kate looked around, surprised by what she saw. Or rather, what she *didn't* see. To their right she noticed a boring-looking building and to the left, a parking lot. "Doesn't look very exciting," she said. "Pretty dull looking, actually."

"Yeah." McKenzie bit her lip and shrugged. "Hope we didn't make a mistake in coming."

"Looks can be deceiving," Mr. Phillips said. "You might be surprised what you find hiding under rocks or bushes." His wiggled his eyebrows and the girls laughed.

They got out of the car and Kate looked at her watch. "Looks like we're right on time."

"And it looks like we have just enough time to get you girls settled in before going on the tour," Mr. Phillips said. He looked at Kate's dad. "Are you game?"

"I'd love to go on the tour before we drive back," Kate's father said with a nod. "I've been working on a project with my robotics students back in Pennsylvania, and a trip to the quarry would help me think more creatively."

The girls made their way to the building with their dads behind them. They followed the signs that read CAMPERS SIGN IN HERE. As they joined a long line of other campers, the boy in front of Kate turned to look at her.

"You here for camp?" he asked, nudging up his glasses with his finger.

"Yes." She nodded. "I'm Kate and this is McKenzie."

"I'm Joel." He gave them a nod, then raked his fingers through his dark, curly hair. "I come every summer. This is my favorite camp."

"You go to other camps too?" she asked.

"Sure." He shrugged. "Math camp. Science camp. Band camp. But this is the best."

"Well this is our first time," McKenzie explained. "And we have a lot to learn."

"I see." His brow wrinkled. "Newcomers. Well, welcome. If you have any questions about fossils, ask me. I'm your guy."

"He's your guy all right," McKenzie whispered in Kate's ear. "Sounds like you two have a lot in common."

"W—what?" Kate could hardly believe McKenzie would say such a thing!

McKenzie winked then looked from one to the other. Kate's stomach fluttered. How embarrassing! She hoped Joel hadn't heard. Or Dexter! He would tease her nonstop if he thought she was interested in a boy!

"You're both very scientific," McKenzie whispered. "And I'll bet he would love your electronic gadgets."

Thankfully the line moved forward. Before long a young man with a nametag that read CONNER greeted them.

"Welcome, ladies! And you are. . . ?"

"I'm Kate Oliver and this is McKenzie Phillips," Kate said. "We're first-time campers."

"Welcome to the best fossil-tastic adventure ever!" Conner said. "You girls are in for a real treat. Want me to help you get checked in?"

"Please," McKenzie said.

He gave them each a clipboard. "Just fill out these forms for me. You can turn them back in here at the desk when you're done."

Kate nodded and took the paperwork, which she filled out lickety-split. McKenzie took a little longer. When they finished, they returned to the desk and Kate's father paid her tuition. McKenzie's father paid for hers as well.

"What about the tour, Dad?" Dexter asked. "You promised we could go!"

"There's a tour starting in ten minutes," Conner said. "I'll be leading it."

"How long does it last?" McKenzie asked. "Do we have time to go with our dads before camp starts?"

"Yes, it's just a thirty minute tour of the quarry, which is behind this building," Conner said. "When you're done, meet Megan at the bunkhouse, and she will get you settled in." He pointed to a pretty young woman in her twenties with blond hair and a bright smile.

She drew near. "Did someone call my name?"

"I was just telling our new campers to meet you at the bunkhouse after the tour," Conner said. "This is their first time at Stone's Throw."

"Welcome." Megan extended her hand and Kate shook it. "I'm Megan Jenkins."

"Megan's father, Mr. Jenkins, owns the quarry," Conner explained.

"That's right." Megan nodded. "I grew up just a couple of miles from here. Spent my childhood digging for fossils with my dad."

Kate smiled at the pretty blond. "I'm Kate Oliver and this is my friend McKenzie."

"We're glad you could join us at fossil camp," Megan said. "Enjoy the tour, and when you're done, I'll be at the bunkhouse to help you get settled in. We'll be great friends!"

"Thanks." Kate had a feeling she was right. They were going to be great friends.

The girls and their fathers walked to a sign with the words TOUR GROUPS on it. Then they went on the tour, which Conner led. They started by touring the museum. Kate noticed a room near the front that was open to the public, but another behind it said EMPLOYEES ONLY. Curiosity got the better of her. She tiptoed to the door, slipping away from the others on the tour. Unfortunately, it was locked. She wouldn't find out what was behind it. At least not today.

Next Conner led the way to the quarry's closest excavation site. He talked to the group about some great fossils that paleontologists had found there, and told them about a few that he had found as a teenager.

"I used to love to come here as a kid," he said. "There's just something about this place that really gets under your skin."

"Under your skin?" Dexter whispered, looking at his arms. "What does that mean?"

"He means once you come here you have to keep coming back. . .it's that much fun," McKenzie explained.

Dexter pouted.

Kate did her best to pay attention to Conner. He seemed like a great guy, and he certainly knew a lot about fossils! Maybe she could learn a few things from him.

When the tour ended, she hugged her father. "Dad, thanks so much for letting me come here. I'm going to have a blast."

"You're welcome, honey." He smiled down at her. "It looks like you'll be in good hands."

Both girls said their goodbyes, and then headed to the bunkhouse to join Megan. She greeted them with a broad smile and a bubbly "Hello!" Once inside, she led them to their room, where three other campers were unloading their backpacks. Kate sized them up. The tall one with brown hair was probably twelve or thirteen. The short one with red hair and freckles was probably ten. And the one with the blond ponytail? She looked like the oldest of them all. . .maybe fifteen.

Megan quickly made the introductions. She pointed first to the girl with the blond ponytail. "Kate and McKenzie, I'd like you to meet Lauren." She gestured next to the brunette. "This is Ginny." Finally she pointed to the cute little redhead. "And this is Patti."

Patti nodded. "Nice to meet you."

"Nice to meet you too," Kate added. She couldn't help but smile. Meeting these girls reminded her of that day at Discovery Lake Camp when she first met McKenzie, Bailey, Elizabeth, and the others. Camp was always such a great place to make new friends.

After a few pleasant words, Kate and McKenzie started unloading their things.

"Did you bring everything on the list?" McKenzie asked, opening her backpack.

Kate went through the items, one by one. "I've got my sunscreen and sun hat. Comfy clothes. Sleeping bag and pillow. Backpack. Gloves. Hiking shoes. Toothbrush. Toothpaste. Shampoo." She looked at McKenzie. "Did I forget anything?"

"Yes!" Her friend looked shocked. "What about your gadgets?"

"Oh, I have all of those in this bag." Kate lifted her backpack where she'd put all of the good stuff—her laptop, the digital recorder, the text-reader pen, and much, much more. "I've got a GPS system on my phone in case we get lost," she said. "And I brought my laptop. I hope they let me use it." She looked at Megan, who flashed a smile.

"Sure. Those things are fine. We've got no problem with technology at fossil camp. In fact, the people who run the place encourage the campers to use all the technology they can to learn more while they're here. So internet access is a plus."

Kate nodded. "Speaking of the internet, we hoped to have a video chat with some friends tonight on my laptop." She gazed at Megan, more curious than ever. "Is that allowed?"

"As long as you do so before lights-out, it shouldn't be a problem," Megan said. "But trust me, if you girls get too rowdy after lights-out, that's a different story." She grinned. "I'm a pretty easygoing counselor, but I like my beauty sleep."

Kate laughed. Megan didn't look like she needed any beauty sleep. In fact, Kate couldn't help but hope she'd look like Megan when she got older.

"I brought lots of snacks too!" Kate said, opening another, smaller bag. She dumped out dozens of candy bars, cookies, and chips.

Kate quickly ate a candy bar and tossed the wrapper in the trash.

Then she put all the rest of her snacks away for later. In the meantime, she listened as McKenzie and Megan kept talking.

"Are you bunking in here with us?" McKenzie asked.

"Yes," Megan said. "And Conner bunks with the guys. If you need anything or have any questions, just ask."

"So what happens first?" McKenzie asked, glancing at her watch. "It's five after ten. Aren't we supposed to be doing something?"

"Conner is going to meet us at the excavation site at eleven o'clock," Megan said. "We'll give the campers some instructions before we break for lunch. There's a lot to learn before we begin."

"I'm sure!" Kate laughed. "I feel like I don't know anything about excavations!"

Lauren headed off with Ginny and Patti behind her. As they left their room, Kate glanced over and saw a Bible on Megan's bunk. She looked at her counselor with a smile. "Megan, you're a Christian?" she asked.

"I am." Megan flashed a broad smile. "You are too?"

"Both of us," McKenzie said. "We met at a Christian camp awhile back."

"I'm so glad to hear this." Megan reached over and rested her hand on Kate's shoulder. "I always pray that the Lord will send just the right people to fossil camp. Looks like you're both here for a reason."

"Oh, we came to solve a mystery," Kate said. She quickly explained what had happened with the fake fossils, and Megan's eyes grew wide.

"You're saying the fossil plates that came from Stone's Throw were fake?" She paused then added, "I wonder if my dad already knows. He's been acting kind of down lately. This might explain it."

Kate nodded. "Our friends, the Camp Club Girls, are trying to figure out who would forge the fossils. . .and why. And I need to do it before my teacher loses her job!"

"Wow." Megan drew in a deep breath. "You really have a mystery on your hands, don't you." She paused once again. "But maybe the Lord has brought you here for more than that."

"What do you mean?" Kate asked.

"I mean a lot of kids come here to dig for fossils, but they end up digging for something else instead. Maybe there are some life lessons the Lord wants to teach you while you're here."

"Could be." McKenzie nodded.

"And who knows. . .maybe He wants you to do a little digging in His Word while you're here too," Megan said with a twinkle in her eye. "Did you bring your Bibles with you?"

McKenzie nodded. "I did."

"I use an online Bible," Kate said. "I can read it on my phone or my laptop."

"Well, do this then," Megan said. "Every morning when you wake up, spend a little time digging in the Word before you pull out your chisel and dig in the rock. I have no doubt the Lord will reveal more than fossils to you while you're here."

"Good advice," McKenzie said.

"We'll do it!" Kate added.

Somehow the idea that the Lord had more in mind only made this adventure even more exciting.

CHAPTER 5

Digging In

When the campers reached the excavation site, McKenzie glanced at Kate and grinned. "Look, there's that guy we met earlier." She nodded to Joel.

Kate looked at his jacket, hiking boots, and hard hat. "Man, he looks like he's ready to go. I can sure tell he's done this before."

"Looks like fun," McKenzie said. "And check out his backpack. It's huge. Must be loaded with equipment."

"Maybe he knows something we don't!" Kate mumbled. She looked at the rest of the campers, trying to size them up. Most were about her age. A couple were older, though, including Joel.

He looked her way, smiled, and then stepped in her direction. "This is always my favorite part. . .listening to Conner and Megan explain about the tools and safety gear."

"You really *do* come here a lot," McKenzie said, looking puzzled. "You know everyone by name?"

He grinned. "Yeah. I want to be a paleontologist someday, so I've been coming to fossil camp every summer since I was ten."

Kate thought about his words for a moment. If he had been coming to the camp for several years, maybe he could help solve the mystery of the fake fossil plates. She asked, "How old are you now?"

"Fourteen." He paused. "Well, almost fourteen. My birthday isn't until September. But even after I'm too old for this camp, I'm going to keep coming because there's so much to learn. No matter how much I study, I always find out more when I come to camp. Fossils are so exciting."

Kate sighed. "I don't know anything about fossils."

"Me either," McKenzie said.

"Just hang out with me," Joel said as he grabbed his backpack.

"Yes, Joel is the person to learn from," Megan said, drawing near. "He's discovered some of the best fossils at the quarry over the past three years.

If you want to see them, visit our display area."

"Really?" Kate stared at him with new appreciation. "So you're famous!"

His cheeks turned red. "Famous? No. But maybe someday I will be." He smiled in Conner's direction. "Like Conner. I want to be like him."

"You want to be like him?" Kate's eyes narrowed as she thought about this.

"Yes, he's the best here," Joel said with an admiring look on his face.

"Hey, what about me?" Megan pouted.

Joel grinned. "Sorry. You're great too, Megan. It's just that Conner is so talented, and he's discovered some of the most valuable fossils on the property."

"It's true." Megan nodded. "Conner really knows his stuff, so if you girls have any questions I can't answer, I'll send you to him." She smiled. "But remember what I said about Joel. He knows almost as much as the counselors, so you might start by asking him your questions. And in case you didn't notice his stuff in the museum the day you arrived, you might look again."

Joel's cheeks turned even redder. "I'd love to help. Just let me know if you need anything."

"Thanks." Kate thought about that for a minute. Before long, suspicions set in. Perhaps Joel wasn't just a camper. Maybe he was a spy. She gazed at him, her eyes narrowing. Yes, maybe he had been sent from some other quarry to scope out the place. She would have to keep an eye on him over the next few days to see if he acted strange.

Conner joined the conversation. "Several paleontologists have taken an interest in Joel's work," he said. "Just ask Megan's father, who owns the quarry."

Megan nodded. "Some of the fossils Joel has found are really valuable. You can see them in the museum with his name next to them."

McKenzie's brow wrinkled. "But I thought we got to keep any fossils we found," she said. "Isn't that part of the purpose of this? To go home with real fossils?"

"Some you can keep and some you can't," Megan said. "It just depends on what you find."

"The fee we paid for the camp only allows us to collect common specimens," Joel explained. "If we discover something rare, it belongs to the state of Wyoming and has to stay here in the museum."

"Wow," Kate said. "I didn't know that."

He nodded. "That's right. And they take it very seriously. No one steals any fossils from Stone's Throw."

Kate wanted to say, "Oh yes they do!" but held her tongue. Surely someone here at Stone's Throw Quarry was stealing the real fossils and replacing them with fakes. But who? And why?

She didn't have much time to think about it. Conner called the group to the side of the hill and got everyone quieted down as he spoke.

"Welcome, everyone. In case you haven't already heard, my name is Conner Alexander and I'm a counselor here at Stone's Throw, as well as a paleontologist. I used to be a camper just like you." He grinned. "So, you never know, one day you might end up working here too."

"I hope so," Joel whispered. "That's my goal."

"Hmm." Kate grew more suspicious than ever. Maybe Joel was just pretending to like Conner. Maybe he wanted to work here so he could steal the real fossils and replace them with fakes. She grew more nervous as she thought about it. Just as quickly, she scolded herself. *You don't even know Joel! Why would you suspect him of anything?*

"Everyone pay attention." Conner clapped his hands. "We have a lot to discuss. I want to go over all of our rules and talk to you about what you will wear on the excavation site. We want everyone to be safe." He opened a large crate and pulled out a yellow hard hat and a bright colored jacket. "You campers will wear these at all times."

"Ooo, a hard hat!" Kate took the bright yellow hat as Megan handed it to her and plopped it on her head. "Ouch. Man, that really is hard."

"Safety equipment is so important here at Stone's Throw because you never know when we'll come across falling rocks," Conner explained. "And staying with the group is critical too. We don't want to run the risk of anyone getting lost."

"We're also giving you these backpacks to carry your tools in," Megan said. "Any you might have brought from home probably aren't strong enough to hold your accessories and any rocks you might pick up. Remember, many of the rocks will be dirty or muddy."

"Ugh." McKenzie sighed. "So much for staying clean."

"Take a look at your tools now," Conner said.

Kate looked inside her backpack, pulling out a hammer and chisel. "Wow. Cool." She suddenly felt like a real paleontologist.

"Make sure the hammer you've received is the right weight for you," Conner said. "It can't be too heavy or too light. You'll use it to pound on rocks."

Kate decided hers was just right. Not too big. Not too small. She felt like Goldilocks.

"Next, carefully pull the chisel out of the bag," Conner instructed.

Kate gingerly lifted the chisel from the backpack, her eyes growing wide as she examined it. "Wow."

"Most of your work will be done with this chisel," Conner explained. "You will use it to remove fossils from the surrounding environment. A large chisel, like the one you're holding now, will be used for most of your work. But there's a smaller chisel in the bag to help you handle the more precise work. It will come in handy too."

"Why?" A younger camper asked.

"A lot of fossils are still buried in stone under many layers of rock. In order to get to them we have to very carefully remove the stone. It's a long and tedious process. I'm warning you now that if you are impatient, these next few days will be very difficult for you."

"I'm pretty patient," Kate whispered. "So I should be okay."

McKenzie shrugged. "I hope I am. I guess we'll find out!"

As Kate looked at her tools, she thought about Mrs. Smith and wondered what she was doing today. How Mrs. Smith would have enjoyed this adventure! Kate could just picture her now, chiseling the stone in search of fossils to put in the museum. How fun!

As she held the chisel in her hand, Kate was reminded of Megan's words. Not only would she dig for fossils this week, she would also dig deep in her Bible to see what she might discover there too! Of course, she wouldn't need a chisel for that!

Conner continued his teaching, and Kate did her best to pay attention. "There are a couple of other tools in the bag that will come in handy," he said. "You won't always need a hammer or chisel to remove the fossil from its surroundings. You might just need an instrument called a steel point. And of course a brush will come in handy. You'll use it to clean dust and other debris from the fossil."

Kate held up her brush and examined it closely. "Hmm." Things were getting more interesting by the minute.

"There are a handful of other items in your bag," Megan said. "A magnifying lens, of course. And a tiny container of superglue to secure broken fossils. Only use the superglue in case of an emergency. We've also given you foam sheets to wrap your samples in, and elastic bands to secure the foam sheets so that nothing gets broken. You will also find a couple of small boxes to carry tiny samples, as well as plastic bags. Any questions?"

A couple of the kids raised their hands, but Kate was too excited looking at her chisel to ask any questions. She pulled out her tiny digital camera and took a picture.

"I see that Kate has her camera," Megan said.

Kate looked up, embarrassed.

"That's okay, Kate. We encourage you to bring a digital camera so that you can take pictures of the specimens as you find them."

"Whew." Kate smiled. "I thought I was in trouble." She reached into her pocket and pulled out the tiny digital recorder. "Is it okay to use this to record my thoughts when I find something?"

"Of course!" Megan nodded. "Really, the only way you can get in trouble around here is by going off away from the group."

"Or going into the private rooms in the museum," Conner added, suddenly looking a little nervous. "There are a few areas where only quarry staff can go. Just keep an eye out for the NO CAMPERS ALLOWED signs and you'll do just fine."

"Can we make phone calls?" Kate asked.

"Yeah, what if we need to call our parents or something?" McKenzie asked.

"Just make sure you let us know first," Megan said.

Conner nodded. "Yes, and if there's something important enough for your parents to know, we need to know first, especially if you're not feeling well. And speaking of which, I guess it's about time we went over our safety requirements so that you can stay healthy and safe while you're with us."

"I want to check to make sure you're all wearing proper footwear," Megan said. "Boots are best."

She examined everyone's feet. Kate giggled as she looked down at her hiking boots. They didn't come in very handy back home in Philadelphia, but here, they were perfect!

"Your boots are excellent for this environment, Kate," Megan said, giving them a closer look. "Walking boots protect campers from ankle sprains and keep you from slipping on wet surfaces."

"Wet surfaces?" McKenzie looked up at the sky. "It's not even raining."

"No, but where we're going, some of the terrain will still be covered in morning dew or will be damp from yesterday's light rainfall. We can never be too careful."

"Now, let's talk about eye and hand protection." Megan held up a pair of safety goggles. "Safety glasses must be worn any time you're hammering rocks. Splinters can be very dangerous." She held up a pair of gloves. "These will keep your hands from getting blisters while you're hammering. There's nothing worse than blisters when you've still got work to do. Trust me."

Kate thought about what Sydney had said about wearing sunscreen and drinking lots of water. Thank goodness she had come prepared.

Looked like she and McKenzie were going to have to be extra careful this week. Fossil camp just might turn out to be a little dangerous!

She listened closely as Conner and Megan gave them the rest of their instructions. As she did, Kate couldn't help but think about the Camp Club Girls. She wondered what they were doing right now. Was Elizabeth reading that Bible story about Jacob and Esau, trying to get some answers? Had Alex learned anything from her documentary? Would Sydney have any advice about the quarry? Was Bailey pouting because she didn't get to come to fossil camp?

If only she could talk to them right now!

"Kate, would you like to be the first to try out your tools?"

She startled to attention as she heard Conner's voice.

"I. . .I'm sorry. What?"

He gave her a funny look. "Were you daydreaming? I was asking if you would like to be the first one to use your tools to excavate."

"Um, sure." She reached for her chisel and moved to a spot next to him. Then, as he instructed, she began to chip away at the ground. Kate whispered up a prayer, asking the Lord to help her during this very exciting week. What would He unearth? Only time would tell!

CHAPTER 6

Unearthing New Clues

After just a few minutes of digging, Conner and Megan dismissed the campers to the main building for lunch. Kate's tummy grumbled in anticipation. She could hardly wait to eat.

McKenzie looked her way. "What did it feel like, Kate?" she asked. "Using the chisel, I mean."

Kate shrugged. "I didn't really get to dig long enough to find anything, but it was fun."

"It was just a practice run," Megan said, stepping alongside her. "We always choose one camper to demonstrate. You did great! I have a feeling you'll do fine at excavating."

"If I can just pay attention," Kate said, then laughed.

"What do you mean?" Megan looked at her curiously.

"I just mean that my mind wanders," Kate explained. "I'm usually thinking of other things and other people." *Like my teacher. And the Camp Club Girls. And Dexter.* For some reason, she couldn't help feeling a little guilty about the fact that she was having so much fun and he was back at Yellowstone without her.

"Well, I don't know about you, but I was thinking about lunch!" Megan laughed. She hollered out to the group. "Follow me to the lunchroom, everyone!"

They walked around the back of the building, past a door that read PRIVATE, and kept going until they came to a door leading to the lunchroom. As they entered, Joel walked beside Kate and McKenzie.

"Did you have fun?" he asked.

"Yes." Kate nodded. "Can I ask you a question, Joel?"

"Sure." He shrugged.

"Can you tell me about the fossils you've found? The valuable ones, I mean. And don't leave out a thing. I have a lot to learn and I have a feeling you could teach me what I need to know."

He nodded. "Sure, but it might be easier to show you. After lunch I'll take you into the museum as we can talk about the fossils I found and actually see them at the same time. Like I said, the most valuable ones are still here. I couldn't take them with me."

McKenzie's eyes widened. "I still can't get over the fact that you're just a camper like us, but you actually have fossils on display here. That's so cool."

He shrugged. "It's really not that big of a deal."

"Not that big of a deal?" Kate stared at him. How could he say that? "Those fossils were buried deep in the earth thousands of years ago! Of course it's a big deal."

When he shrugged again, she thought about how strange he was acting. Maybe her feelings about him earlier were right. Something about this guy was suspicious. Maybe Joel really wanted Conner's job. Maybe he was really the one who had forged the fossils. But why would he do such a thing? To make someone else look bad, perhaps? None of this made sense. And if he did do it, how would she ever prove it? There was only one way. She had to win his confidence. And then she had to somehow get his fingerprints.

Kate and McKenzie got their trays and walked to the lunch counter to get their food.

"I'm starving!" Kate said. "I can't wait to eat my lunch. Then I'm going back to the cabin and eat some of the cookies my mom packed for me." She gazed at the plate, confused. "What *is* this stuff?" she asked.

"Oh, they always give us fun stuff at mealtime," Joel explained. He pointed to the fish sticks. "They call these *Knightia* Nuggets. Get it?" She shook her head. "You know. *Knightia*," Joel repeated.

When she shook her head a second time, he explained. "*Knightia* is an extinct species of fish, found in Wyoming. They're trying to be funny and clever. Today it's fish. Tomorrow they'll probably serve us chicken legs and call them dinosaur bones. It's supposed to get us in the mood to excavate."

"Oooh, I see." Kate smiled.

"Very funny." McKenzie led the way to the table and sat down.

As they ate, the girls from Kate and McKenzie's dorm all gathered around with their food. One of them—what was her name, again? Lauren? Yes, Lauren. She acted as if she had a little crush on Joel. Not that he noticed. He just kept talking about fossils, fossils, and more fossils. Half of the things he talked about Kate could figure out. The rest? Well, some of it just didn't make sense. This guy really knew his stuff!

"Do you feel like you have a lot to learn?" McKenzie whispered in Kate's ear.

She nodded. "Yes, and I don't think a three-day camp is long enough! I never realized how little I knew about all of this. But I'm willing to learn."

"Me too." McKenzie nodded. "And I can't wait to share what we learn with the other Camp Club Girls."

They enjoyed their lunch and getting to know the others. Kate especially liked Patti, who kept them entertained with stories about her friends at school.

"She reminds me of Bailey," McKenzie whispered.

"I know!" Kate grinned. "I was just thinking the same thing."

Before long, McKenzie told the others about Kate's gadgets. "You should see all of her stuff!" she said. "She has a pen that records text, a miniature camera, a digital recorder, and a watch that sends emails."

"No way." Joel looked at her as if he didn't quite believe it.

"It's true." Kate lifted her wrist and showed off the watch. "I'll send an email right now."

"You're kidding, right?" Lauren asked, looking stunned.

"Nope." She typed a quick email to Elizabeth.

Thanks for your prayers. We made it to the quarry safely.

Then she pushed the tiny SEND button. Joel looked on, still not looking convinced.

A couple of minutes later, the little watch let out a beep and she pushed a button, showing off Elizabeth's email response.

Glad you made it. Talk to you tonight online!

"See!" She held her watch up for Joel to read the note. He shook his head. "Man. That's really something. What else have you got?"

"Oh, bunches of stuff. My dad is a robotics professor. You should see the cool electronics we have at home. Robots galore!"

"No way." Joel stared at her. "Are you serious?"

"Yep. We even have a robotic security system. And a robovac to clean our carpets. His name is Robby."

"Her dad always gives her the neatest things," McKenzie explained.

"Well, sometimes his students invent things and we end up with the beta versions."

"What's your favorite thing?" he asked.

"Hmm." She thought about it for a minute before answering. "Probably the smartwatch. But I love my mirrored sunglasses too. They've come in really handy."

"Did you bring them with you?"

"Sure." She shrugged. "I'll wear them to the dig this afternoon if you like."

"That would be cool." He gave her an admiring look and she felt embarrassed. She finished up her meal then quickly changed the subject.

"Do we have time to look in the museum before we head back out to the excavation site?"

"Plenty of time," he said. "They always give us an hour break after lunch, anyway. Would you like to go look at my fossils now?"

"Sure. Why not."

Kate and McKenzie trudged along on his heels as he led the way to the small museum. As they walked inside, Kate noticed an older man with thinning hair carrying some large boxes. He was dressed in dark pants and a Stone's Throw work shirt. Both were wrinkled and dirty. And his hair—what little of it there was—was sticking up on top of his head. In fact, it looked like it hadn't been combed all day.

The sour-faced man grunted as the kids walked by. "You kids watch where you're going and stay out of my way," he mumbled. He began to mutter something under his breath about how kids were always getting under his feet, and Kate took a giant step away from him. She wondered why he was in such a terrible mood.

"Who is that guy?" she whispered as they turned toward the first display.

"Oh, that's Gus," Joel said with a shrug. "He's only been here a couple of years. Gus is the one who packs and ships the fossils. If I were you, I wouldn't bother him. He's a little cranky."

The older man almost dropped one of the boxes.

"See what you did?" he said with a grunt. "You kids made me lose my train of thought. I almost dropped this."

He carried the boxes to the door marked PRIVATE, then put them down on the ground to open it. Seconds later, he disappeared inside.

"What's he cranky about?" McKenzie asked. "We didn't do anything to him."

"I know." Joel shook his head. "I've never been able to figure him out. Trust me. No one has."

"Still, he needs to be nicer to people," Kate said. "There's no excuse for being so mean."

"Sounds like he's got a great job," McKenzie added. "I think it would be fun to prepare the fossils and ship them all over the country. I think it would be a blast. A person with a job like that should be in a good mood!"

"I know." Joel shook his head. "I've never understood why, but he's always moody. I've just learned to stay away from him. And trust me, I've been coming here for years, so I know what I'm talking about. Everyone around here calls him Grumpy Gus."

Kate frowned. "Maybe he's in a bad mood because people stay away from him. I'll be extra nice to him for the next few days and see if I can get him to smile."

"Good luck with that!" Joel laughed. "You won't be the first person to try, and you certainly won't be the last. But I'll bet you can't get him to smile, Kate."

"Oh really!" She took those words as a challenge. Before fossil camp was over, she would get Grumpy Gus to smile, no doubt about it.

As they entered the museum, she looked at the door the older man had walked through. "What's back there?" she asked.

"That's where Gus works," Joel explained. "I've only been back there a couple of times. If you want to know more, ask Conner. He hangs out in there a lot. It's where the fossils are cleaned and prepared for packing."

Kate nodded, but didn't say anything. She couldn't help but try to figure out what lay behind that door with the word PRIVATE on it.

McKenzie cleared her throat and Kate looked her way. "What?" she mouthed.

"I'll tell you later," McKenzie whispered. "Something about that man seemed suspicious. Maybe we can talk about it later this evening when we're alone."

Kate felt a shiver run up her spine and she nodded. Something about Grumpy Gus made her very nervous too.

They wandered through the museum, looking at all of the displays. "I wish I had more time to explain all of this," Joel said. "But it'll have to be a fast tour."

"That's okay." Kate gave him a warm smile. "We're just happy to be here."

"Thanks." He looked embarrassed. "Remember I talked about the *Knightia* at lunch? This is a sample."

"Wow." Kate stared at it, mesmerized. "It's so. . .perfect."

"Yep." He nodded. "And over here we have several other species of fish. "The *Mioplosus*. The *Diplomystus*."

"Goodness." Kate shook her head. However did he remember those complex words?

After looking at several specimens, they reached the far wall. Joel looked around, his brow wrinkling in confusion. "That's weird," he said.

"What?" McKenzie asked.

"Well, the stingray fossil that I discovered is usually mounted in a box right here, but it's missing. Conner never mentioned anything about taking it down. It's the most valuable fossil of all the ones I've found, so I'm especially proud of it."

"Seems odd that the most valuable one is missing," Kate said, growing more suspicious by the minute. Had Grumpy Gus stolen it? Her imagination almost ran away with her as she thought about the possibilities. Kate pulled out her camera.

"What are you taking a picture of?" McKenzie asked. "There's nothing there to photograph."

"Sure there is." She pointed to the plaque that read HELIOBATIS STINGRAY.

"Why take a picture of that?" Joel asked.

"For research."

He shrugged. "I don't see the point." Shaking his head, he added, "I just wish I knew what happened to my stingray specimen. I dug for hours to get that one. . .and now it's gone."

"Are you worried that someone stole your fossil, Joel?" McKenzie asked.

He shrugged. "I don't know. Could be they've loaned it out to another museum. They do that a lot."

"I know," Kate added. "My teacher is a curator at the science museum in Philadelphia, where I live."

"You're kidding." He gave her an admiring look. "That's impressive."

"I help her sometimes." Kate shrugged. "For fun."

She didn't tell him about the fake fossils they'd discovered. No point in sharing too much information, just in case.

Joel sat on a nearby bench, looking sad. Kate sat down beside him.

"What are you really worried about?" she asked. "You have something on your mind. I can tell."

He sighed. "This is the deal. Every year the quarry offers a six-week internship to one camper who shows potential. A couple of famous paleontologists are coming to spend the rest of the summer, and I wanted to spend it with them. Can you imagine what an honor that would be?"

"Um, sure." Kate shrugged. Might sound like fun to Joel, but she couldn't imagine spending the whole summer outside digging with chisels in the rock and the dirt.

Joel rose and started to pace back and forth, his brow wrinkled. "That fossil is my best sample. How will they ever know what I'm capable of if it's gone?" He continued to pace.

"Are you worried some other camper will get the internship?" Kate asked.

"Maybe. It's pretty complicated," he explained. "This internship is open to kids all over the world. More than three hundred teenagers have competed for this honor. I really thought I stood a chance. . .until now. Now I'm ready to give up."

"Give up?" McKenzie gave him a curious look. "Over a missing fossil?"

"That stingray fossil is my biggest achievement and now it's gone. There's no proof that I discovered it. It's like someone just walked away with the proof that I'm valuable. That I'm worth anything."

Kate gasped. "Well, of course you're valuable!" She looked at him, stunned, not quite believing he had said that. "You're one of God's kids. We're all valuable in His sight."

Joel shrugged. "You don't get it, Kate. Where I come from, you have to prove yourself. In my house, you have to get straight As on your report card or make the honor roll at school to get noticed."

"But that doesn't prove you're valuable," McKenzie argued. "Even if you got Bs or struggled in school, you would still be valuable to God."

"Try telling that to my teachers and parents. You girls just don't understand." Joel plopped back down on the bench and sighed.

"I do." Kate sat next to him. "My dad is really, really smart. He's a professor, remember? But he would be the first to tell you that our real value comes from God."

She pointed at the wall. "All of these things are worth a lot of money. I know that. But I also know that you're more valuable to God than all of them put together. And you don't have to prove anything to Him. He loves you, even if you're not always the one who gets the internship or gets straight As."

Joel bit his lip and Kate could tell he was really thinking about what she had said. After a while, he shrugged. "I guess. If you say so." He gave her a funny look then glanced at the clock on the wall. "Oh no! It's five minutes till two. We've got to get back out to the site. This is the best part. The excavation begins right away!"

"Do I have time to get my mirrored sunglasses?" Kate asked.

"Only if you hurry!"

The kids took off running toward the quarry as fast as their legs could go!

CHAPTER 7

The Big Dig

Kate ran behind Joel and McKenzie, stopping to get her sunglasses out of the bunkhouse. She arrived at the excavation site huffing and puffing, but right on time.

"Take a look around you," Conner said to the group as he gestured to a large open field. "It's hard to believe, but this area used to be a lake."

Kate paused for a few breaths, then paid close attention.

"Wow. We're standing in the middle of a dried up lake," McKenzie whispered. "Good thing I brought my swimsuit!" She laughed and Kate giggled.

"This region of Wyoming is loaded with fossil specimens," Conner explained. "Thousands of years ago rains would fall and the water would flow down the mountain, forming lakes."

Megan stepped up beside him. "Another theory is that the whole earth was covered in water during the Genesis flood, creating the perfect environment for fish."

"The Genesis flood?" Patti, the little girl with the red hair and freckles, looked confused.

"You know," Kate threw in. "The story of Noah and the ark. It rained for forty days and nights."

"I remember hearing that story in kids' church," Lauren said, tossing her hair. "Can you imagine being on that ark with all of those stinky animals?" She made a face and pinched her nose. "Gross!"

This got all of the girls tickled and before long, everyone was laughing. Well, everyone but Kate. She was still thinking about what Megan had said.

"Regardless," Conner said. "The waters dried. When that happened, millions of fish died in just a short period of time."

"How sad," Kate whispered.

"Because of that, this area is rich in fish fossils," Conner said. "That's good news for us, since that's what we're searching for today." He gestured to his right. "Layers of mud covered up the dead fish of course, but then volcanic activity occurred."

"Volcanoes?" McKenzie looked very, very nervous. Her eyes grew big.

"That happened a long time ago," Conner explained. "Not anymore."

"Whew." McKenzie looked relieved.

"Anyway, the volcanic activity exposed the fish fossils. And thousands upon thousands of them are still here, waiting to be discovered. . .by you!"

"Wow." Kate could hardly believe it. Would she really find a fossil? If so, would she get to keep it, or would they put it in a box and hang it on a wall in the museum? Suddenly she could hardly wait to get started.

"I know you kids are anxious," Conner said. "But there are a few things we need to cover before we actually start digging." He held up something small. Kate took a couple of steps toward him to see what it was.

"This is a *Mioplosus* specimen. They are very common in this region. I'm going to explain how it became a fossil, so pay close attention."

Kate drew near, more excited than ever.

"There are five phases to fossilization," Conner explained. "You might need your notepads for this one. You'll want to remember all of this for later on."

Kate leaned over to Megan and whispered, "Can I use my digital recorder?"

"Of course," Megan nodded. "He'll cover a lot of material, so taking notes would be tough anyway."

Kate reached inside her backpack and came out with the tiny black digital recorder and turned it on.

Conner held up the fossil and explained. "The first phase of fossilization is death," he said. "Let's say, for example, that a fish dies, then drifts to the bottom of the lake. After scavengers get a hold of it, the skeleton is the only thing that remains."

"Gross," McKenzie whispered. "Doesn't sound very appetizing."

"Oh, but that's the most important part," Joel said softly. "Sometimes bad things have to happen in order for good things to come out of them."

"Hmm." Kate thought about his words. Sometimes life was like that. Bad things happened. . .then good things came out of the bad.

"After death comes the deposition stage," Conner explained. "During this phase, the sand and silt cover up the shell over a period of time, building several layers."

"Those layers protect the shell from damage," Kate whispered. "I read all about it online."

"Yeah, I saw a video in my science class about this," McKenzie whispered back. "After hundreds of years, the shell is way below the surface. No one even knows it's there."

"Right." Kate nodded. "Sometimes for thousands of years. Can you imagine?"

McKenzie shook her head.

Kate was lost in her thoughts when Conner started talking once again.

"After the deposition comes the third phase," he explained. "We call this permineralization."

"Per-mineralization?" Little Patti shook her head. "I hope I don't have to spell that word later. I'll never get it right."

Megan offered a smile. "Break the word down into parts. Per-mineral-iz-a-tion. It just means the shell goes through a bunch of changes over time. Before long, the original shell becomes hard, like a rock."

"Why didn't he just say that?" Patti mumbled.

Conner went on to talk about that process, but Kate was distracted, watching Joel, who was scribbling notes in his notebook. He really was taking this seriously. She felt bad for him, knowing his fossils were missing. On the other hand, maybe they really had just been loaned to another museum. She hoped so, anyway.

Conner continued explaining how fossils were made, and Kate tried to pay attention, even though some of what he said didn't make much sense.

"The fourth phase is erosion," Conner said. "Wind, ice, sun, and rain begin to take their toll on the fossil, changing it."

"Everything changes over time," Joel whispered, still scribbling in his notebook.

Kate looked over at McKenzie, who had changed so much over the past year, and nodded. "Yep. It's true," she whispered.

Conner continued to talk. "Finally, the last phase. Exposure. Exposure comes when a paleontologist locates the fossil. It is removed from the ground and is cleaned up."

"That's what I do," Joel said, squaring his shoulders. "Finding them is the best part!"

Kate tried to pay attention, but every time she thought about someone cleaning the fossils, she remembered Grumpy Gus. What did he do behind closed doors besides cleaning and packing fossils? Did he have a mold and several bags of brown sugar, perhaps? Did he take the real fossil plates and sell them illegally and pocket the money? Was he the one who had stolen Joel's fossils? Was he the one responsible for what happened to poor Mrs. Smith?

Kate's imagination began to work overtime as she thought about it.

"After a fossil is exposed, we look at it under a magnifying lens," Megan said. "Examine every square inch of it."

"That's the fun part," Joel whispered. "Seeing everything close up. Have you ever looked at a fossil through a magnifying lens? It's really cool."

"Yes, actually, I. . ." she started to tell him about that day at the museum with her teacher, but stopped. No, she couldn't give away too much information just yet. After all, she still wasn't sure who she could trust. Joel might look like a good guy, but he could be faking it. She needed to be on the lookout for fakes. . .no doubt about that.

"How big are fossils, anyway?" McKenzie asked.

"Oh, they come in all shapes and sizes," Conner explained. "Some are so tiny you can only see them with a magnifying lens, and some are huge. Some of the bigger ones include bones belonging to dinosaurs."

"Wow." The girl's eyes grew wide at this news. "Really?"

Conner nodded.

Kate raised her hand. "Excuse me, but can I ask a question?"

"Sure," Conner said.

"What happens to the fossils when they leave the quarry? Do you sell them?"

Conner appeared to be thinking about his answer. "As we've discussed, many of the fossils are quite valuable. Those stay here at the museum but are often loaned to other museums around the country. People all over the country enjoy looking at Stone's Throw fossils. They're quite popular."

When they're real, Kate thought.

"You'd be very surprised at just how valuable some of these fossils are," he added. "And how rare."

"So valuable and rare that someone wants to steal them and keep the money for themselves!" McKenzie whispered.

Kate nodded, then looked at Joel. She couldn't stop thinking about the missing stingray. Was Joel the victim? Or was he somehow involved in all of this? Only time would tell.

"Okay, kids!" Megan clapped her hands to get their attention. "It's time to get suited up! We're going to start our first dig. So grab those hard hats! Put on those safety goggles! Let's get digging!"

Kate scrambled into her bright orange jacket, put on her yellow hard hat, and grabbed her goggles. After securing them, she reached for her backpack and pulled out the larger chisel.

"I'm ready!" she said with a giggle.

The next hour was spent digging. At first, it seemed easy. But after a while, Kate's arms got really tired. "I don't think I could be a paleontologist," she whispered to McKenzie. "My arms aren't strong enough!"

"What would Elizabeth say to that?" McKenzie whispered back.

"I know, I know." Kate laughed. "She would say, 'I can do all things through Christ who strengthens me.'"

"And she's right," McKenzie said. "Besides. . ." She flexed the muscles in her upper arm. "We're getting stronger every day."

"Getting stronger every day. I like that." Kate nodded, and then slowly began to dig again.

Before long, one of the girls hollered, and Kate turned around, curious.

"I found one!" Lauren said with a joyous look. "I really, really found one! Look everyone!"

They all drew near and examined the fossil.

"It's broken, but it's still really cool." She held it out for Conner to examine.

"Yes, that's a *Knightia*," he said. "They are very common here in Wyoming. Nicely done, Lauren. You're the first to unearth a fossil, so you'll get the privilege of leading one of the teams in the treasure hunt tomorrow morning."

"Aw man." Kate shrugged. "Wish I'd been the first."

"What would Elizabeth say?" McKenzie asked her again.

Kate grinned. "She would quote the scripture 'But many who are first will be last, and the last first.'"

"Exactly." McKenzie nodded. "So let's remember that. And just because we're not the first to discover a fossil doesn't mean we won't figure out who forged the ones at your teacher's museum. We're here for a reason, Kate, and I truly believe the Lord will do something very exciting!"

Kate was starting to nod when something—or rather, someone—in the distance caught her eye. "Look, McKenzie!" She pointed as an older man disappeared behind the trees to their left. "Was that Grumpy Gus?"

"No idea. I didn't get a good look."

Kate reached into her bag and came up with her teensy-tiny binoculars. She pulled off her safety glasses and peered into the binoculars, trying to see into the forest. Yes, sure enough, a man was running, hiding from tree to tree. She couldn't tell for sure, but it looked like Gus. He was wearing the same color shirt, anyway.

"Something is very suspicious here, McKenzie," she whispered. "Very suspicious, indeed!"

CHAPTER 8

Camp Club Girls to the Rescue!

Later that evening, the campers headed into the dining hall. Something smelled really good!

"What's for dinner?" Kate asked as they sat down at the table.

"Just as I predicted." Joel held up a chicken leg. "Dinosaur bones. *Tyrannosaurus rex!*"

McKenzie shook her head as she picked up the piece of chicken. "Doesn't look like any *Tyrannosaurus rex* I've ever seen!"

"Exactly." Joel slapped himself in the head and Kate laughed.

"Well, the cook has a great sense of humor, anyway!" she said.

She got into the line to get her food but something caught her eye. "McKenzie!" She elbowed her friend.

"Ouch!" McKenzie rubbed her side. "What is it, Kate?"

"Look." She pointed at Gus, who carried a large bag of brown sugar.

"Ooo." McKenzie nodded. "And look, Kate. . .he's headed away from the kitchen, not toward it. Isn't that strange?"

"Very."

"What are you girls talking about?" Lauren stepped into line behind them and started chatting about the fossil she had found. Before long, as they talked, Kate almost forgot about Gus. Almost.

When she got back to the table with her food, Kate joined a fun conversation with Joel and the other campers, laughing and talking about their adventures at the camp. Someone in the room started clapping, so she looked up, curious.

"We have a wonderful treat for you kids tonight," Megan said, getting everyone's attention. "I want to introduce someone very special to me."

An older man entered the room. He had soft white hair and wore blue jeans and a button-up cowboy shirt. His long white mustache and beard reminded Kate of someone from an old movie. And his leathery, tanned skin surely proved that he spent a lot of time in the sun.

"This is my father, Gerald Jenkins," Megan said proudly. "He is the owner of Stone's Throw Quarry."

"Wow." So this was Megan's dad.

Mr. Jenkins joined the campers, answering many of their questions. Kate finally worked up the courage to ask her question, but waited until the others were distracted, so they wouldn't hear her.

"Mr. Jenkins?" She spoke softly and he looked her way. "My name is Kate Oliver. I live in Philadelphia and my teacher works for the Museum of Natural Science as a curator."

"Ah." He nodded. "I can guess what you're about to ask."

Kate bit her lip, trying to decide how much to share. Finally she could take it no longer and blurted out her question. "Do you know about the fake fossils that my teacher and I found? If so, do you have any idea who forged them?"

"Yes, I know all about it," he said, keeping his voice low. "Your teacher called last week. I contacted the police and they've been out to take a report. But I can't figure out who is doing this to us. We've been sabotaged, for sure."

"You haven't seen anyone with brown sugar? Or anyone acting strangely?" *Like Grumpy Gus, for instance?*

"Not on the property. And I've looked, trust me." He shook his head. "I'm here all day every day and haven't seen anything suspicious."

She thought about telling Mr. Jenkins that she and McKenzie had just seen Gus carrying a large bag of brown sugar, but didn't. Not yet, anyway. She had to be sure she could trust him first.

He shook his head and his eyes grew misty. "I feel terrible about what happened," Mr. Jenkins said. "But I feel even worse when I think about the fact that someone stole the original fossil plates from us. They're worth a lot of money."

"What would a person do with stolen fossils, anyway?" Kate asked.

"Oh, all sorts of things. They're valued all over the world, so maybe they sold them to an underground ring of fossil thieves."

"Ooo, sounds scary."

"Another theory is that they are holding them for ransom. Maybe to try to bribe me in some way."

"Why would someone do that?" Kate asked.

He shrugged. "I don't know. I can only tell you that I've been praying about this all week, ever since I got the call from your teacher." He smiled at Kate. "We'll figure out who did this. . .with the Lord's help. Those fossils will return home to Stone's Throw, and I'll send them to your teacher for the exhibit. You just wait and see."

"I hope you're right." She paused a moment, then looked into his kind eyes. "Can I ask you one more question?"

"Sure."

"Joel is a great camper and he knows so much."

"Oh yes, he's one of the best," Mr. Jenkins agreed.

Kate bit her lip as she tried to decide how much to say next. "He's worried he won't get the internship because his stingray fossil is gone."

"What?" Mr. Jenkins looked stunned. "The stingray is missing too?"

Kate nodded. "We don't know that it's officially missing. I was hoping you loaned it to another museum."

"No." He shook his head. "We often loan out fossils, as you know, but everything is written on a schedule. I don't remember anything about the stingray being loaned out. Very strange."

"Well if you go into the museum, you'll see that it's missing," Kate said.

"I'll do that right now," he said. He nodded. "Thank you for the information, Kate."

"You're welcome, sir. Thanks for letting us come to your great quarry!"

After she finished eating, Kate headed back to the cabin with McKenzie at her side.

"So what did Mr. Jenkins say?" McKenzie asked.

"He knows all about the fake fossils," she said. "And he says he's praying about it." She paused a moment. "He didn't seem to know anything about the missing stingray though."

"Odd, isn't it?" McKenzie observed. "People who work right here don't seem to notice much, do they?"

"Wow." Kate paused to think about that. "You might be on to something there, McKenzie. We saw Grumpy Gus walking across the dining hall with a bag of brown sugar, and yet Mr. Jenkins says he's been watching, but hasn't seen anything suspicious. What's up with that?"

"Right." McKenzie paused. "What if Mr. Jenkins is only pretending to be concerned? What if he's really the one who did all of this?"

"Why would he sabotage his own quarry?" Kate asked. "Doesn't make any sense."

"Sure it does." McKenzie nodded. "It's a great scam. He makes money by selling the real fossils to the bad guys and makes money by selling the fakes to legitimate businesses. That's a lot of money!"

"I don't know, McKenzie." Kate shook her head as they entered the cabin, then paused to give her a serious look. "It would break Megan's heart to find out that her dad was doing something illegal."

"True." McKenzie sighed.

Kate walked over to her bunk and sat down, whispering so the other girls wouldn't hear. "I'm not really accusing Mr. Jenkins. I'm just thinking out loud. Trying to figure who did this."

"I know. And the suspects are piling up." McKenzie reached for a rubber band and pulled her hair up into a ponytail. "But that's why we're meeting with the other Camp Club Girls tonight in the chat room, right?" She paused. "I can't wait to tell them what we found out today."

"Before we talk to them, can I ask you a question?" Kate asked.

"Sure."

"Remember you said there was something suspicious about Gus? What did you mean?"

"Oh. . ." McKenzie's brow wrinkled. "I just noticed his clothes were really wrinkled, like maybe he slept in them or something."

"I noticed that too!" Kate said. "It was a little strange, wasn't it?"

"Yes. What kind of a person is so busy that he can't even change into pajamas to sleep?" McKenzie said. "It makes me think he's up to something in the middle of the night."

"Ooo, I see." Kate nodded.

"Maybe." McKenzie nodded. "The wrinkles in his clothes make me wonder."

"Well, we can ask the other girls their opinion."

"What other girls?" Patti asked, plopping on Kate's bed. "What are you girls whispering about, anyway?"

"Yes, what's up with you two?" Lauren asked, joining them. "You've been acting mighty suspicious!"

"Oh, I, um. . ." Kate paused and looked at McKenzie. She didn't know how much she should share with these girls. After all, she barely knew them!

"Kate and I are on a secret adventure," McKenzie said. "We'll tell you all about it tomorrow or the next day."

"But we leave day after tomorrow," Patti argued. "I don't want to wait till then to find out your secret! Tell me now."

Kate shook her head. "What's the point in calling it a secret if I tell it? But I will give you a clue. We're trying to solve a mystery. Trying to figure something out."

"Hmm. A mystery." Patti sighed. "How can I help you if I don't know what it is?"

Kate shrugged. Thankfully, her phone rang at that very moment, interrupting their conversation. She was surprised to hear Alexis's voice on the other end of the line.

"Kate, I know we're meeting with the others online in a few minutes, but I wanted to talk to you first. This is important."

"Sure." Kate rose from the bunk and went outside the cabin so that she could speak to Alexis privately. "What's up?"

"I've been doing some research on the staff at Stone's Throw," Alexis said. "I got the idea after watching that Paleo-World documentary again."

"What did you find out?"

"All of their pictures are on the website, along with their names. There's a fellow name Gerald Jenkins who owns the place."

"That's Megan's father," Kate said. "Megan is our counselor."

"Right. Megan Jenkins. She was practically raised at the quarry. And there's a guy named Conner who has all sorts of degrees. He's a paleontologist."

"He's really young," Kate said. "Probably just twenty-five or so."

"From what I can gather, he's really smart. He started as an intern at the quarry a long time ago, and now he's back, working as a counselor."

"Right," Kate said. "Anything else?"

"Yes." Alexis's voice grew more serious. "There's a guy named Gus who seemed a little suspicious to me."

Kate's heart began to thump. "He seems odd to us too!" she said. "What did you find out about him?"

"Well, I don't want to scare you, but he used to work for another quarry and he got fired. I read about it online. There was a big write-up in the paper a couple of years back. I had to dig deep to find it."

"Dig deep?" Kate couldn't help but smile as Alexis used the words she'd been hearing so much. "Do you know why he was fired?"

"Something to do with some fossils that were accidentally destroyed. Just promise me you'll be careful around him, okay? I would feel terrible if something happened to you girls."

"I'm sure we'll be fine," Kate said. "But we'll be extra careful, just in case. And Alex. . .thank you for calling and telling me that."

"You're welcome. I'll keep researching online to see if I can find out anything else about him."

"Thanks. See you online in a few minutes," Kate said. As she clicked the END button on her phone, Megan walked by.

"Well hello, Kate. Everything okay?"

"Y–yes." She forced a smile. She didn't want Megan to know she suspected anyone just yet. "I was talking to my friend Alex."

"Friends are an important part of our lives, aren't they?" Megan smiled. "God has blessed me with such great friends over the years."

She began to talk about her best friend—someone named Julia—and Kate sighed in relief. At least Megan hadn't asked about the case!

A few minutes later, Kate and McKenzie sat on Kate's bed with the laptop open.

"I sure hope the Wi-Fi is strong," Kate mumbled. "The other girls are probably already in the chat room waiting on us."

Thankfully, she signed on with no problem at all. Less than a minute later, she was in the chat room and could see that all of the others were already there, just as she predicted. Kate typed while McKenzie looked on.

Bailey: *Hi, K8!*
Elizabeth: *Having a fossil-tastic adventure?*
Kate: *Yes. We've learned a lot already!*
Sydney: *About the case, I hope. I've been working hard on this end!*
Kate: *Good. Before we get started, I wanted to ask a favor. I'm going to upload a picture that I took today. I need someone to spend a little time looking up this fossil online to see if you can locate it. It's missing from the quarry's museum.*

She quickly uploaded the picture of the tiny stingray sign.

Bailey: *What is that, Kate?*
Elizabeth: *Yes, I've never seen anything like that.*
Kate: *It's a very valuable fossil that one of the campers—a guy named Joel—unearthed last summer. For the past year it's been on display in the museum. But today, when he went to show it to me, he noticed it was missing. We don't know if someone took it down for a reason or if it's been stolen.*
Alexis: *Why not just ask someone?*
Kate: *I don't want to raise any red flags. But it makes me curious, especially in light of the forged fossils. Maybe this is a bigger case than we thought! I'm hoping one of you can figure out what happened to it. Maybe if we can track down that fossil, we'll find our answer.*
Sydney: *Leave it to me. I'll find that missing stingray if I have to swim upstream to do it!*

McKenzie laughed at that one.

Elizabeth: *I've been reading the story of Jacob and Esau a lot over the past week or so. And I've prayed and prayed, asking the Lord to show me how it fits with this case.*
Kate: *What has He shown you?*
Elizabeth: *Only that we have to be careful not to be fooled by people who are pretending to be something they're not. Sometimes people put on a big smile and act nice, but on the inside they're really not.*

A shiver ran down Kate's spine. She thought at once of Grumpy Gus. Maybe Elizabeth was right. Maybe he was on the run from the law. Maybe he was just pretending to be a quarry worker.

On the other hand, what about Mr. Jenkins? Sometimes the most honest-looking person turned out to be the real bad guy.

And then there was Joel! Hadn't she already suspected him?

Kate: *I'm so confused. The list of suspects is growing by the minute. I sure hope we can figure this out. Only two more days of camp left! I brought my fingerprinting kit, so I hope to lift some prints soon.*
Alexis: *My uncle works in a fingerprinting lab. Maybe he would help.*
Kate: *Great idea!*
Sydney: *We'll figure this out! We're the Camp Club Girls, after all!*
Elizabeth: *And we have the Lord on our side. There's power when people agree in prayer!*

"She's right," McKenzie told Kate. "Six of us are all agreeing and praying!"

"True." Kate smiled, suddenly feeling better. She glanced at the screen, noticing Bailey's next comment:

Bailey: *I wish I could be there with you. How is Biscuit?*
Kate: *He's with my parents. He's not here.*
Bailey: *Not there? How do you expect to solve a mystery without him?*

"She's right, you know," McKenzie said, reading over her shoulder.

"Things would be easier with Biscuit here."

Kate sighed. "Megan was really nice to say I could use my gadgets. I don't think she would be as nice if I asked to bring my dog to fossil camp!"

"You never know." McKenzie shrugged. "Maybe you could ask your dad to bring him when he picks us up. Might be fun. Ask Megan first, though."

"I'll do that." Kate turned her attention back to the screen, smiling as she read Elizabeth's last line.

> Elizabeth: *I have to sign off now, but I will be praying. Remember that Jacob and Esau story. Don't let anyone fool you into thinking they're something—or someone—they're not. Okay?*

All of the girls said their goodbyes and before long the chat room was empty. Kate turned to McKenzie and sighed. "Looks like we've got to be extra careful, now that the suspects are piling up."

"Suspects?" Patti's voice rang out. "What do you mean?" She sat on the edge of Kate's bed.

"Yes," Lauren said, joining them. "Sounds like this secret thing you're working on is getting exciting. Are you sure you can't tell us something about it?"

Kate shook her head. "I promise we'll tell you later. Right now I need to pray about all of this."

"Did I hear someone say something about praying?" Megan's voice rang out as she entered the room, her hair still wet from the shower.

"Yes." Kate nodded. "I've got a lot on my mind."

"Well prayer is the answer." Megan winked. Drawing near to Kate, she whispered, "Remember what I told you earlier today. Spend some time digging in your Bible while you're here. Do a little excavation in the scriptures. I think God will shine some light on your situation. . . whatever it is."

Kate nodded. "Okay. I'll do it." She smiled at her counselor, and then thought about all of the questions rolling around in her mind. Who forged the fossils? Why was Gus so grumpy? Was Joel somehow involved in all of this? And what about Mr. Jenkins? Was he just pretending not to know who replaced the real fossils with fakes?

Kate padded off to the showers, her mind reeling in several directions at once. Tonight she had more questions than answers. Hopefully, tomorrow she would have more answers than questions.

CHAPTER 9

Sugar, Sugar

Early the next morning—long before the sun came up—a loud clanging woke Kate.

"What is that?" she grumbled, sitting up in the bed.

"It's the quarry bell," Megan said, stretching. "It goes off every morning at five thirty."

"F–five thirty?" McKenzie bounded up from her slumber. "A–are you kidding me?"

"Nope." Megan laughed. "I'm used to it."

"Well I'm not." Kate yawned.

"Why are we up at five thirty?" Lauren asked from a bed on the other side of the room.

Megan yawned. "It's better to work early in the morning before it gets too hot. Besides, we have a busy day planned for you kids. The sooner we get going, the more we'll accomplish."

"Ugh." Kate rolled over in the bed and pulled the covers up over her head, wishing she could catch a few more Zs. Unfortunately, the bell started clanging again. She pushed the covers back and got out of bed, heading into the bathroom to change into her clothes.

"What time is breakfast?" she heard McKenzie asking Megan.

"Six o'clock. And the excavation begins at seven," Megan explained. "But I think that still leaves you girls plenty of time to read your Bibles and pray, if you'd like to do that before breakfast."

Kate yawned as she thought about the busy day ahead. She was tempted to skip her Bible reading and just go straight to breakfast, but decided against it. Maybe God had something He wanted to show her in the Bible. She reached for her laptop and signed on to the internet, going at once to her favorite online Bible site.

"Where is the story of Jacob and Esau again?" she whispered to McKenzie.

"I think it's in Genesis. . .right?" McKenzie didn't look convinced.

"Maybe." Kate began to type in the words Jacob and Esau until the scripture came up. "It's Genesis, chapter 25," she said. Skimming over it was the easy part. Trying to figure out what a story about two brothers had to do with this case was quite another! She read the story more carefully the second time, really thinking about it as she did.

"So Jacob wanted something that rightfully belonged to his brother Esau. He wanted his birthright. . .right?"

"I think that's it," McKenzie said.

"To get it, Jacob dressed up in a hairy costume and pretended to be Esau so his father would give him the blessing that really belonged to his brother." She stopped reading and thought. "Sometimes people really *do* pretend to be one thing when they're really another," she whispered. "People aren't always who we think they are."

"Are you thinking of someone in particular?" McKenzie whispered.

"Maybe." She shook her head. Who did she suspect the most, after all? Gus? Mr. Jenkins? Joel? It would be hard to say at this point.

She wrapped up her Bible study and walked to the dining hall with the others. Once inside, Kate noticed Gus standing near the kitchen door. She nudged McKenzie.

"Look. There he is again."

"He still looks grumpy," McKenzie said. "I think we need to stay away from him."

"I'm not so sure." Kate paused. "Hey, I have an idea." She looked down at her lunch tray and saw the two doughnuts. "I'm going to try an experiment. Watch and see. I'll make him smile."

McKenzie shook her head. "I don't think so, Kate."

"It never hurts to try." Kate walked over to him, and he looked up from his work.

"What do you need, kid?" he asked.

"Oh, nothing. I just wanted to give you something." She reached out showed him the doughnut. He looked at her with a stunned expression.

"What's that for?"

Kate shrugged. "Just because. I thought you might like it."

"Well I don't. I'm diabetic. Can't eat sugar. What are you trying to do? Kill me? Did some of those kids tell you to do that?"

She put the doughnut back on her tray, suddenly nervous. "No. No one said a word about it. And I'm sorry. I didn't know you were diabetic. I was just trying to be nice."

"Well be nice to someone else. I have work to do."

"But. . ." She watched as he disappeared through the door with the No CAMPERS ALLOWED sign above it. As he disappeared from sight, a creepy feeling came over her. She still wondered what he did back in that room. Sure, he probably shipped fossils. But what else?

"That didn't go very well, did it?" McKenzie asked, drawing near.

"No." Kate shook her head. "He's diabetic. Who knew?"

"Oh, wow. And you offered him sugar, of all things."

"Yes, he thought I did it on purpose. Can you believe that?"

"Well maybe other people have been mean to him," McKenzie said. "You never know."

"Maybe." Kate sighed. "But McKenzie. If he's diabetic, why was he carrying around a jumbo-sized bag of brown sugar yesterday? Answer that."

McKenzie shrugged. "I have no idea, but you're right. It doesn't make sense! I will say this, though, if he's claiming to be a diabetic, that's the perfect cover."

"What do you mean?" Kate asked.

"I mean, no one would ever suspect a diabetic of using sugar to forge anything. See?"

"Ooo yeah. Good point." Kate nodded. "Gus will be a tough nut to crack. But I feel like we need to know more about him."

"It's getting more and more obvious that he is behind this, don't you think?" McKenzie asked.

Kate shrugged. "Maybe. Only time will tell. One thing is for sure. He has access. He's in that room all alone."

"True."

A familiar voice interrupted their conversation. Conner walked by carrying a large bag. "Hey, kids." He flashed a warm smile. "What did you think of the breakfast?"

"Good." Kate nodded. "I really liked the doughnuts."

"Doughnuts?" He held one up. "Girls, these aren't doughnuts. They're life preservers!" Conner doubled over in laughter and before long they all joined him.

"He's really funny," Kate whispered.

"Yeah," McKenzie nodded. "And he's a great counselor too. I heard some of the guys talking about him yesterday. They really like him a lot."

"Just like we like Megan."

Conner shifted his bag to his other arm. "We're going to have a great morning, but I need to drop off these samples first. See you soon." He walked through the door into the private area.

"Maybe Conner will catch Grumpy Gus in the act," Kate whispered.

"Maybe." McKenzie shrugged.

Kate yawned as Megan passed by.

"Sleepy, Kate?" her counselor asked.

"Sort of."

"Didn't you sleep well?"

"Not really." She shook her head.

"Miss your family?" Megan asked.

"Sort of, but I have something else on my mind. It's hard to sleep when your thoughts are tumbling around in your head."

"Anything I can do to help?" Megan asked.

Kate shook her head, knowing better than to say too much.

Megan said, "The second day at fossil camp is always the best. We're going to have a treasure hunt."

"Treasure hunt?" McKenzie looked confused.

"Yes, we'll divide the campers into two teams—boys and girls. I'll lead the girls' team and Conner will lead the boys'. We'll give you kids a list of fossils—three different kinds—and the first team to find all three wins."

She began to talk about the treasure hunt so much that Kate found it hard to focus. She kept yawning. Hopefully she would wake up before heading out to excavate. She needed to pay close attention today. Surely an adventure lay ahead!

The Treasure Hunt

As the campers gathered at the excavation site, Conner turned to them with a smile.

"I have some news for you," he said. "Most of you know Joel." He gestured to Joel, whose cheeks turned red.

"Because of Joel's skill in locating valuable fossils, he's our resident 'rock' star." Conner slapped his knee and laughed. "Get it? Rock star?"

Kate laughed. So did McKenzie. But not Megan. She rolled her eyes and whispered, "Don't let Conner distract you. He's just trying to get you girls worked up to think the boys are better than you are. He pulls something like this at every camp."

Kate giggled. "I won't let him get to me, I promise."

Conner rubbed his hands together in excitement. "What we're about to do is my favorite thing at fossil camp. We're going to have a treasure hunt."

"Let's divide into teams," Megan instructed. "Girls, come and get in line behind me, and boys, you line up behind Conner."

Everyone quickly got into place.

"I can tell you're excited," Conner said. "But try to stay calm, cool, and collected. That's the best way to win this challenge." He reached for his clipboard and pulled off two pieces of paper. "Each team has a list of three items. Three different kinds of fossils—*Mioplosus*, *Phareodus*, and *Knightia*. You will see the pictures here." He turned the paper to face them. "The first team to return here to this spot with all three fossils will win."

"What do we win?" McKenzie asked.

Conner's face lit with excitement. "The winning team gets to go into the prep room to watch me clean and prepare the fossils. Then we'll show you the process of packaging and shipping them all over the world."

He began to talk about all of the work that went on in the quarry's prep lab, how the lab tech worked carefully to remove rock from ancient fossils, then prepared them for handling. The whole thing sounded really complicated. . .and exciting!

Kate's heart began to race. How wonderful it would be to get in that room! She would take her fingerprint tape and look for prints. Maybe they would match the ones on the fossils back home. Then perhaps Alexis's uncle could help the girls figure out whose prints they were!

"Conner does most of his work in that room," Megan said. "He's one of the best in the nation. He gets the fossils stabilized, cleaned, and prepared. Then Gus—I believe some of you met him—gets the fossils packaged to send out."

"We've got to get in that room!" McKenzie whispered. "So let's win the treasure hunt."

Kate nodded.

"It's really an amazing honor," Joel explained. "I've only been in there a couple of times over the years. The prep lab is usually off-limits to campers and quarry guests. But it's by far the coolest place here." He began to explain the process of cleaning the fossils, but Kate couldn't keep up with him, he was talking so fast.

"All we have to do is win the treasure hunt," Kate said. "And then I'll get to see it for myself."

"Not possible!" He laughed. "Sorry, girls, but this is my specialty. I'll find all three specimens before you find even one!"

"Campers, let's get suited up," Megan announced as she handed out hard hats, vests, and jackets. Then she gave the campers their backpacks, which were loaded down with tools.

"I feel like I gain ten pounds when I put this on," Patti complained as she struggled to get the backpack in place.

"Just think of how strong your muscles are getting," Megan said with a wink.

Kate couldn't help but think of Dexter. He would have loved this part. Maybe she could do more than win the treasure hunt today. Maybe she would locate a fossil that she could give him. . .something really special. That would make him feel better about not being there. And maybe—she grew more excited as she thought about it—maybe she and McKenzie would find enough fossils for each of the Camp Club Girls too! Wouldn't Bailey and the others love that!

"Everybody ready?" Conner hollered.

When the campers cheered, Conner lifted his hand and hollered, "On your mark, get set. . ." As he shouted "go!" he dropped his hand. The girls took off running toward the dry lake bed and the boys headed off to the field to their right.

When they arrived, Kate and the others paused to catch their breath. She didn't want to start out feeling so winded, especially when she hadn't had much sleep.

"I'm going to dig for a *Mioplosus*," Lauren said. "My brother found one of those last year when he came to camp."

"I would suggest starting with the *Knightia*," Megan said. "The quarry is filled with them."

Kate watched out of the corner of her eye as Joel went to work with his large chisel. "Man, he's fast," she whispered to McKenzie. "He really knows what he's doing."

"You won't find any fossils if you spend all of your time worrying about how much better he is than us," McKenzie whispered back.

"I know you're in a hurry to get started," Megan said, "but I always like to say a few words before the hunt begins. If you listen to my advice, you'll be more likely to find fossils quickly."

Kate paid close attention.

"Okay, girls, this is what you do." Megan's voice grew serious. "Notice that this whole area is filled with flat slabs of rock. It was formed a long time ago on the bed of the lake."

"Bed of the lake," Kate whispered. Sounded funny.

"You heard Conner explain yesterday how fossils are made. Can you remind me how the fossils got here, in the dry lake bed?"

Kate raised her hand. "Yes. When a fish died, it would sink to the bottom of the lake, then get covered with mud, just like Conner talked about yesterday."

"That's right," Megan said. "And over a long period of time, the lake dried up and the mud turned to stone. So buried deep within those slabs of stone are priceless treasures. In order to find them, you have to pick up the rock and split it. You might be surprised at what you find inside."

Kate paused to think about how life was sometimes like that. Sometimes you really thought you knew someone. . .knew them really well. Then, after a little digging, you learned something else entirely new about them. For example, after a little digging, she had learned that McKenzie snored. Only a little, but still it was a snore. And hadn't she learned a lot about each of the Camp Club Girls since they started solving mysteries together?

"This is one of the things I love most about leading excavations," Megan said. "Sometimes I look around at all of the reminders of life that came before us, thousands of years ago. It's pretty amazing, really, when you think about it. We can hold the past in our hands." She looked at the group, her eyes getting a little misty. "Then I look at all of you campers and I realize that I'm looking at our future. So the past and future come together every year when we lead these excavations. That means so much to me."

"Oh wow." Kate swallowed hard. How interesting, to think that she was part of a project that represented the future. Carrying on a project with fossils formed thousands of years ago.

"When I look at all of you, I also realize that each of you is a treasure, far more valuable than anything we could ever find in the stones here. You are created in God's image. His imprint is in your heart."

Kate smiled as she thought of that. Her mom often told her how much she was loved. Still, it felt good to have someone she barely knew tell her just how precious she was. Megan's words made her day!

"Now go dig up some fossils," Megan said. "But while you do, remember how valuable you are. How priceless."

Kate headed off with her chisel in hand. She found a spot and began to dig. All around her the other girls were laughing and talking, but she didn't join in. Who had time to chat with so much at stake? She had to find those fossils to win the prize! Then she and McKenzie could figure out who was forging the fossils and help Mrs. Smith keep her job.

The morning passed with the girls working extra hard. Kate let out a holler as she located a *Knightia* and the girls all cheered. However, off in the distance they heard the boys cheering too.

"Sounds like we're tied!" Megan said. "So keep at it, girls. You can do this."

About a half hour later Lauren located a *Mioplosus*. She beamed with joy as she held it up for all to see. "I knew it!" she said. "I knew I would find one!"

"You did a great job!" Megan said, examining the fossil. "I'm so proud of you. Now if we can just find the *Phareodus*. Then you girls will win the treasure hunt and you can tour the prep lab!"

From the other side of the dry lake bed, Kate heard Joel's voice ring out. "I found it!" he shouted. "I found the *Phareodus*!"

"We have all three!" another one of the boys hollered. "The boys win!"

They began to cheer. Kate let go of her chisel, watching it drop to the ground. "They. . .they beat us?"

McKenzie sighed. "Looks like it."

"But how will we ever get into that back room now?" Kate whispered.

"This whole trip to Wyoming will be a waste."

McKenzie looked at her, clearly confused. "What do you mean?"

"We asked our families to come to Wyoming because we thought we could solve this case. But we can't, unless we get into that room."

"You don't know that."

Kate plopped down on the edge of a large rock. "I just don't like to disappoint anyone, especially the Camp Club Girls. They're working hard to figure this out. But we need to do our part too. And digging in the ground isn't enough. We need to get into the secret, hidden places in the quarry to know what really goes on here."

"Kate, don't get discouraged," McKenzie said. "We'll figure out who did this with the Lord's guidance. But we have to have faith. It won't help anything to give up."

"I just knew the girls were going to win," Kate said sadly. "And since we didn't, well, it just makes me a little mad. I guess I have a bad attitude."

Megan walked up and gave Kate a curious look. "Bad attitude? Who has a bad attitude?"

"Me." Kate sighed as she shrugged out of her backpack. "I must be a sore loser."

Megan laughed. "I've seen a few of those over the years so you're certainly not the first, and I'm sure you won't be the last." She paused. "I think about it this way, Kate. You know how fossils are really imprints?"

"Sure." Kate shrugged, not sure what this had to do with anything.

"We leave an imprint on others with our attitude," Megan said. "Good or bad. A little bit of us rubs off on them. So when you react with an attitude to something—good or bad—it's like you're creating a. . ." She paused and appeared to be thinking about what to say. "Like a fossil on the heart, if that makes any sense."

At once, a feeling of shame washed over Kate.

"I'm so sorry, Megan. I have had a bad attitude today." She turned to McKenzie. "My faith has been a little low. I guess I just don't see how God is going to solve this."

"Honey, if anyone knows how to dig deep, it's the Lord." Megan patted her shoulder then headed off to join the others.

In the distance, lightning flashed and the girls heard a roar of thunder.

"Oh man. Looks like a storm," Kate said. She grabbed her backpack. "Better get back inside. I don't want my stuff to get wet." She pulled off her smartwatch and tucked it into the backpack to keep it safe, just in case rain fell.

"Race you back to the dorm!" Joel hollered out as he ran by.

Kate took off running behind him. If she couldn't beat him at excavating, maybe she could beat him at racing!

Sure enough, she started gaining on him. By the time they reached the building, she was a few feet ahead of him. She finally stopped, huffing and puffing. Joel grinned as he stopped next to her.

"My backpack is heavier," he explained with a sly wink. "Must be all of those fossils I found today."

Kate and McKenzie groaned.

"I'm just kidding." Joel flashed a smile. "Just a little friendly competition, girls. But seriously, I'm really proud of you. . .especially you, Kate. I understand you found the first *Knightia*. Excavating must come naturally to you."

"I'm not sure it does," she said. "But I did have a lot of fun." She thought about that as they headed into the cabin to get cleaned up. So what if they didn't win? She had learned a lot—about fossils and about her heart.

CHAPTER 11

Curiosity Kicks In

A flash of lightning lit the skies as the girls entered their cabin.

Kate shivered. "Looks like we ended our treasure hunt just in time."

Patti shook her head. "I don't like storms. I hope it doesn't. . ." Just then a loud peal of thunder shook the building. Her lips quivered as she said, "Th–thunder!"

"The storms up here can get pretty intense," Megan said. "So stay indoors."

"Do we have time to shower before lunch?" Kate asked. "I'm sticky and sweaty."

"Me too," Lauren said. "I've got to get into clean clothes."

"You have plenty of time," Megan said. "Go ahead and shower, then let's sit and talk awhile before lunch. We have plenty of time, and I want to get to know you girls better."

As Kate grabbed clean clothes, she noticed a text message on her phone.

"Who's it from?" McKenzie asked, drawing near.

"Looks like it's from Sydney." She pressed a couple of buttons and read the message. "Oooh, look, McKenzie."

"Located the missing stingray fossil at a museum in Vancouver." Kate read the words then looked at McKenzie, stunned. "Joel's missing fossil is in Vancouver, Canada? What's it doing there?"

McKenzie shrugged. "I don't know. Maybe the people at Stone's Throw are loaning it to them. Probably isn't any big deal."

Kate shook her head. "Then why doesn't Mr. Jenkins know about it? He owns this place." She lowered her voice. "Unless—he's behind all of this."

She glanced at Megan and thought about how sad the counselor would be to find out her father was a bad guy!

"I don't know, Kate," McKenzie whispered. "I still suspect Grumpy

Gus. That makes more sense to me, especially since we saw him with the brown sugar."

"Maybe. But I'm going to ask Sydney to check on one more thing. I need to know how long that stingray fossil has been there, and I need to make sure it's the real deal. Maybe that fossil in Vancouver is a fake, just like the one in Philadelphia."

"So if the one in Vancouver is fake, then where's the real one?"

"Hmm." Kate bit her lip. "I think there's an underground ring of thieves. Maybe Grumpy Gus is just one of many. And maybe. . ." She snapped her fingers as an idea came to her. "Maybe he hasn't had time to sell that one yet. He could be hiding it here somewhere. Maybe that's what he was doing in the woods yesterday, finding the perfect place to hide it."

McKenzie shrugged. "I guess that's possible."

Kate began to pace the room. "If only we'd won the treasure hunt! Then we could have gone into the shipping room instead of the boys. I would have looked for brown sugar. . .or something else to incriminate Grumpy Gus."

McKenzie sighed. "This really stinks. We're getting close to solving the case and can't even get into the room where the forgeries are taking place."

"Maybe we can." Kate chewed on her fingernail, deep in thought.

"What do you mean?"

Kate lowered her voice. "Tonight, after everyone goes to bed, we can go to the shipping room and look around. I'll take my fingerprinting kit and see if there are any prints I can lift."

McKenzie's eyes grew wide. "What if we get caught?"

"We won't. I have an idea. I'll take my little video camera in there too. I'll find a place to leave it so that we can record Gus. Then we'll have the proof." She looked at McKenzie as a peal of thunder cracked overhead. "You know," she whispered, "there's really only one way we're ever going to solve this."

"Ooh?"

"Yes." She leaned in close and whispered, "If we do make it into that room, we'll do some serious digging. We need to know if the fossils they're sending out are the real thing or if they're made out of sugar."

"But how do we get in there?" McKenzie whispered.

"I noticed there's a back door leading to that room too. And when we came across the parking lot after the treasure hunt, that door was propped open with a large stone. Maybe it still is."

McKenzie shook her head. "I don't know, Kate. I want to pray about this while I take my shower."

Kate thought about the case as she showered, and she prayed too. The last thing she wanted to do was to falsely accuse someone. But with the clock ticking away, the girls had very little time to solve this case. Desperate times called for desperate measures. That's what Kate's mom always said anyway.

But how desperate? Should they really sneak out of the cabin and try to enter the prep room? Something about that felt wrong and even a little scary. However, the idea of not solving the case felt even more wrong.

By the time she ended her shower, Kate had talked herself into it. Tonight, while everyone else was asleep, she would take her fingerprint kit, her video camera, and several other gadgets, and she would go into the prep room. . .to see what she could see. Hopefully it would help solve the case.

After showering, the girls dressed for lunch. Megan gestured for them to sit on her bed.

"I just wanted to say something, campers," she said with a smile. "I see a lot of campers come through here and you girls are great! I hate to play favorites, but I'm so happy to be your counselor this week."

Kate reached to hug her. "We're happy to be here. And thank you so much for being a great counselor, Megan."

"It's easy when your campers are as good as mine are." Megan winked and they all smiled.

Soon the campers were sitting in Conner's class on the various types of fossils. Then, as the evening wore into the night, Kate couldn't stop wondering what Grumpy Gus was up to in that back room. With her curiosity getting the better of her, she knew there was only one way to find out. She had to get inside that room, no matter what!

Night Crawlers

"Shh!" Kate used the tiny flashlight on the end of her ink pen to guide the way across the dark quarry parking lot toward the main building. Every step made her a little more nervous than the one before. What were they thinking. . .coming outside in the middle of the night? What would Megan say if she caught them?

Still, they didn't have any other choice, did they? Fossil camp ended tomorrow. If they didn't locate a few more clues tonight, there might not be enough time tomorrow to really figure things out. And Kate couldn't bear the thought of leaving without knowing who forged the fossils. So in spite of her fears, they headed toward the main building. Hopefully, they would make it inside without getting caught. Thank goodness the storm had passed!

"I'm trying to be quiet," McKenzie whispered, "but I just tripped over a rock and it scared me. Everything about being out here scares me. Aren't you frightened?"

"'I can do all things through Christ who strengthens me!'" Kate said. "That's the scripture Elizabeth gave me and I'm just going to keep saying it!"

"'I can do all things through Christ who strengthens me,'" McKenzie repeated several times in a row.

"Not so loud!" Kate whispered. "Someone might hear us."

A coyote's howl stopped them in their tracks.

"D—did you h—hear that?" McKenzie asked.

Kate nodded but kept walking. "Yes. But we can't stop now. C'mon. We're almost at the building."

When they reached the back of the main building, she stopped at the door, praying it was still propped open.

"Oooh, great news!" she whispered, pointing to it. "Let's go inside."

McKenzie took hold of her arm. "Kate, are you sure? If the door's open that probably means someone is inside."

Kate nodded, hoping to convince herself. As she opened the door, it creaked. The girls tiptoed inside, and their eyes adjusted to the dim lighting. The girls realized they were in a tiny enclosed hallway. At the end of the hallway, they saw another door with a see-through glass window in it.

On the other side of the glass, they glimpsed someone moving. A man. The room was dimly lit, so they couldn't tell who it was. Kate ducked and grabbed McKenzie's arm, pulling her down too. Kate reached into her bag and grabbed her digital camera.

"If you take pictures through the glass, he'll see you," McKenzie whispered.

"I won't stand up to take the pictures. . .and I'll turn off the flash so he won't see anything. Watch and see." Still kneeling, Kate lifted the camera to the bottom of the glass window. "Say a little prayer, McKenzie."

"Trust me, I've been praying ever since we left our cabin."

Kate snapped several photographs, holding the camera at different angles.

"Now what?" McKenzie asked.

"Now we look at the pictures." She quickly scrolled through the pictures she'd just taken. Several weren't very good. But a couple of them showed a large fossil plate.

"Yep, that's him all right," Kate whispered. "I wish I could zoom in the photo to see if that fossil plate is real or not."

"Can we do that on your computer?" McKenzie asked.

"Yes, but I don't want to go back to the cabin just yet." She patted her backpack. "I brought my fingerprint kit. I need to get inside to lift some prints and see if they match the ones on the fossil plate in Philadelphia."

"How can we get in there with someone working?" McKenzie whispered. "It's impossible."

"Maybe he—or she—will leave. You could distract him and I'll go inside."

"Distract him?" McKenzie asked. "H—how?"

"Go to the window on the other side of the room and tap on it. He'll go to the window and I'll slip in and do my work."

"Kate, that's scary." McKenzie paused, and then said, "Okay, okay. I'll do it. But I'm not happy about it."

She slipped out of the back door into the darkness. Kate peeked through the glass pane into the room where the man worked in the shadows. After a few moments, she heard McKenzie tapping on the window and saw the man look up from his work. Unfortunately, he didn't head toward the window. . .he came toward the door!

Kate ran into the parking lot. She called out to McKenzie and soon the two of them were standing in silence at the back of the building in complete darkness. Her heart pounded so loudly she could hear it in her ears. Still, they hadn't gotten caught. That was good.

"Why is it suddenly so dark out here?" McKenzie whispered.

"Someone turned out the light," Kate responded. "Maybe he's trying to spook us."

"Well, it's working!"

The girls stood frozen in their tracks. After a while, they heard a sound at the back door and realized the man—whoever he was—had gone back inside.

"I guess we're safe," McKenzie said with a sigh. "But I'm all turned around now that it's so dark out here. What about you?"

"Yeah, me too." Kate took a couple of steps to her left. "I think our dorm is this way," she whispered. "Isn't that right?"

"I'm not sure."

They took a couple of steps together and crashed into a trash can. Kate held her breath, hoping no one would notice.

"I don't think we're going the right way," McKenzie whispered. "How will we ever find our way back to the dorm now, Kate?"

"Hmm." Kate paused. "Oh, I know! I have a GPS tracking system on my phone. It's really detailed, so I think it will guide us." She turned it on and within minutes they were headed the right way. Though they bumped into a few things on the way to the cabin, the girls finally made it back safely.

"I don't ever want to be scared like that again!" Kate whispered as they entered the cabin.

The girls tiptoed to their bunks, careful not to wake the others. Kate bumped her toe on the edge of the bed and almost yelped, but stopped herself. If only she could stop her hands from shaking and her knees from knocking!

After fetching her laptop and a bag of chips, she gestured for McKenzie to meet her in the bathroom. There, she plugged her camera into her laptop and downloaded the photos. She opened a photo of a fossil plate.

"That's what I wanted to see," she whispered. "That plate."

She zoomed in. . .close. . .closer. . .closer. . .until she finally got a good look at the fossil plate.

"Hmm." McKenzie shook her head. "When you zoom in on it, it doesn't look like the others in the museum."

"No kidding." Kate opened her bag of chips. "But it looks just like the one I spilled water on that day I was with my teacher. Look here." She searched her computer until she found the copies of the photos she'd taken with her camera that day at the museum. She placed the photos side by side. Sure enough, they looked alike!

"The fossils Grumpy Gus is shipping *are* fakes, just as we suspected," Kate said, taking a bite of a salty chip. "No doubt about that. And I'd guess they're made out of brown sugar, just like these." She pointed to the photo of the ruined fossil plate.

"So it's true." McKenzie bit her lip. "He's shipping fakes. But how do we know he made them, or even knows they're fake?"

"Ooo, look at this one!" She pointed to a picture that showed a man's legs. A man wearing blue jeans. "Does Gus wear jeans? I can't remember."

McKenzie shrugged. "I don't know. I never paid attention."

"I wish we could've gotten in the room so I could've gotten those fingerprints." Kate sighed, and pressed a couple more chips in her mouth.

"Maybe we can do that tomorrow." McKenzie yawned. "But can we talk about this in the morning, Kate? It's really late and I'm so tired."

"What in the world are you girls doing up in the middle of the night?" Kate looked sheepishly at Megan. "Oh, we, um. . ."

Megan knelt beside her and looked at the computer screen. "And what were you talking about? You found out something about the fake fossils?"

"Sort of." Kate's heart began to thump. She wanted to tell Megan everything. . .but could she trust her? It was getting harder to know who to trust.

"We have some pictures of someone packing fake fossils to be shipped out," she explained. "We're not sure who it is, but we're sure the fossils are forged. They look just like the brown sugar ones my teacher and I discovered back home in Philly."

"And where did you get these photos?"

"Well, we. . .um. . ." McKenzie's gaze shifted to the ground.

"From the cleaning and shipping room," Kate explained. "I took the pictures."

Megan's brow wrinkled. "Surely you weren't really outside in the middle of the night."

"Well, we, um. . ." Kate sighed.

"Look, I'm all for crime solving," Megan said. "But remember the one rule I told you not to break? You're *not* to go off by yourself. It's too dangerous. And to go off by yourself at night makes it even more dangerous. We have coyotes here."

"I know." A shiver ran down Kate's spine. "We heard them."

"Well you're very fortunate to be back in one piece," Megan said. "But you broke a quarry rule, and I'm really disappointed in you."

Kate's eyes filled with tears right away. "I'm sorry, Megan. And I'm sorry about going outside too. It was a little scary, being out there all alone. We should have asked you to come with us, but I didn't really want anyone to know what we were doing until we had the proof."

"And this is your proof?" Megan asked, pointing to the computer screen. "Pictures of someone packing fossils?" She examined the photo again. "I'm not even sure who that is, to be honest."

"Don't you see?" Kate said. "We know the fossils are forged. And we know Gus is the one who usually packs them. Doesn't that make him guilty?"

Megan shook her head and rubbed her eyes. "I don't like to accuse anyone without proof. And if I'm going to accuse anyone of anything tonight, it's going to be you two. You broke the rules. I have no choice but to tell Conner and my dad and let them decide if you should be reprimanded or not."

"R—reprimanded?" Kate's eyes filled with tears. "Really?"

"Well, yes. There are always consequences for our actions, Kate. You broke the rules."

"I—I suppose so." She began to cry. "I've never done anything like this before, Megan. I'm so sorry. But we have to figure this out by tomorrow because my teacher is going to lose her job."

"You can't fix everything for everyone, Kate," Megan said. "Some cases aren't yours to solve."

Some cases aren't yours to solve.

Kate dropped into bed, Megan's words tumbling in her head. Maybe her counselor was right. Maybe she *wasn't* supposed to solve this.

But if she wasn't, why did she feel as if she was?

She squeezed her eyes shut, but kept hearing the sound of the coyotes howling, which caused her to tremble all over again!

With images of a man in blue jeans still floating through her brain, Kate finally fell into a troubled sleep.

Digging Deeper

Early the next morning Kate got a phone call from Sydney. Still half-asleep, she answered. "H–hello?"

"Kate, you won't believe it!"

"What is it, Sydney?"

"I called that museum in Vancouver," Sydney explained. "Well actually, my mom called for me. She told them our suspicions about the stingray fossil and guess what?"

"The one they have on display is a fake?" Kate asked.

"That's right. It's a fake!" Sydney squealed. "So the real one is still out there. . .somewhere. Oh, and guess what?"

"What?"

"When we asked them who authorized the fossil to come to them, they didn't have a name. They just said it was a man from Stone's Throw Quarry who set the whole thing up."

Kate sighed. "Well, that could be anyone."

"I know. But we're getting close, Kate. I can feel it!"

"All I feel"—Kate let out a long yawn—"is tired! But thanks for calling, Sydney. This is our last day, so we have to figure this out right away!"

They ended the call and Kate took a shower. Then she and McKenzie searched for Joel. They found him in the dining hall, eating breakfast alone. Most of the others weren't awake yet.

Plopping down at the table, Kate said, "I need to talk to you." She eyed one of his doughnuts, which he gave to her. She popped it into her mouth, enjoying the gooey sweetness. "Yum."

"What do you need to talk about?" Joel looked curious and pressed another doughnut into his mouth.

"We have some news for you." McKenzie sat on the other side of him.

Kate told him all about Sydney's call—every last detail. The more she talked, the more upset Joel got.

"Wait." He stood and began to pace the room. "You're saying that not only is my stingray missing, someone has forged it and sent the forgery to a museum in Canada?"

"That's right." Kate nodded, feeling a lump rise up in her throat. "But stay calm, Joel."

"How can I stay calm? I'm never going to get the internship now. Maybe Mr. Jenkins will think I faked the fossil myself. Maybe he'll think I'm behind this."

"No one will suspect you," McKenzie said.

Kate paused. "Well that's not completely true. I actually suspected him."

"W—what?" Joel said.

She told him about Mrs. Smith's forged fossil and he stared at her, his eyes narrowing.

"You thought I had something to do with that, Kate? You think I would forge fossils and sell them?"

"Well, I. . ." She shook her head. "Oh, I don't know, Joel. I was confused. You have access to the room where this is taking place. And you have motive."

"I—I do?" He looked confused.

"Well sure," Kate said. "You're trying to get that internship. I thought maybe you would do *anything* to get it."

He raked his fingers through his hair and then stared at them once again. "I'd do almost anything to win the internship, but not that. I wouldn't stoop to illegal activity. Besides, I love the Jenkins family. I would never put the quarry at risk. Never." His voice shook with emotion, and Kate suddenly felt awful for accusing him in the first place.

"Let's just forget I said anything about it, okay?" Kate said. "Will you forgive me for suspecting you?"

"Well sure," he said. "But if *you* suspect me, maybe others do too."

Megan walked into the room just then. "What are you kids talking about? You look pretty intense."

"Megan, we're getting more clues about the fake fossils," Kate explained. "And I'm more curious than ever about who is doing this. We found out that Joel's stingray fossil, which turned up at a museum in Vancouver, was also forged, just like the ones at the museum in Philly."

"Oh no." Megan sat down. "I wonder if my dad knows." She shook her head. "If we don't get this straightened out, our quarry will have a bad reputation. We can't risk that. People all over the country love us, and we want them to know they can trust us."

"There's really only one way," Joel said. "We have to figure this out. . . and fast!"

"Yes, camp ends this afternoon," Kate reminded them. "So we have to work super fast."

"I'll tell you what. . ." Megan shook her head. "I probably shouldn't do this, but I'll help you kids figure this out. I'll do it to help my dad. . . and you."

"That's awesome, Megan," Kate said. "But how?"

"Easy. We'll walk straight into the clean and prep room and see for ourselves. I'll take you there, but we'll have to wait until late this afternoon while the others are at the excavation site."

"We. . .all four of us?" McKenzie asked.

"Well sure. All you had to do was ask," Megan said. "I would have taken you there all along."

Kate slapped herself in the head. "I don't believe it. You're so great, Megan. I thought you would be mad at us after last night."

"What did you do last night?" Joel asked.

Kate filled him in and his eyes grew wide. "You went outside in the dark? With all the coyotes hanging around?"

"Y–yeah," McKenzie agreed. "We didn't know about the coyotes or we wouldn't have gone."

"We think we'll figure this out once we get in the room," Kate said. "Is it okay to bring my camera and some of my other gadgets?"

"Sure." Megan shrugged. "I don't see why not." She paused a moment, then looked at the girls. "Can I ask you a question?"

"Yes." McKenzie and Kate both spoke at the same time.

"Do you think Gus is the one doing this?"

Kate shrugged. "Maybe."

The wrinkle in Megan's brow grew deeper. "Well, before you judge him too harshly, I think you kids need to know something about him."

"O–okay." Kate gave her a curious look.

"Here's the deal," Megan said. "About two years ago when my dad first met Gus, we fell in love with him. . .and his wife, Jeannie. She was bubbly and fun and always made us laugh."

"I didn't know Gus was married," Joel said. "I've never met his wife."

Megan paused. "Gus and Jeannie were on a road trip to Colorado, carrying some expensive fossils from the quarry where he used to work. Gus was driving the car at the time, and they had a terrible accident late at night."

Kate gasped. "Really? What happened?"

"A driver fell asleep at the wheel and hit Gus's car. Jeannie was badly hurt."

"Oh Megan, that's awful!" Kate said.

"Yes. She spent a long time in the hospital—several months. She's been in a rehab facility ever since. Gus goes to see her every day. I understand the hospital is very expensive."

Kate looked at McKenzie and mouthed the word, *"Wow!"* Maybe Gus forged the fossils and sold them to make the money he needed for his wife's care.

"On top of all this, the quarry he used to work for fired him because the fossils he was delivering were ruined in the accident."

"That doesn't seem fair," McKenzie said. "Why would they fire him when the accident wasn't his fault?"

"I don't know." Megan shook her head. "But my father felt sorry for Gus and gave him the job here. And even though he's kind of grumpy, we love him very much. He's like a grandfather to me."

Megan started to go on but got distracted by the other campers entering the dining room. Megan headed off in search of Conner.

After she left, Kate turned to McKenzie and Joel. "What did you think of that?"

"Megan obviously thinks Gus is innocent," McKenzie said. "She feels sorry for him because of what happened. I don't blame her. It's a sad story."

"Yes, but. . ."

Joel's eyes narrowed. "I think there's more to the story than meets the eye."

"He has motive," Kate said. "And he obviously needs money."

"Exactly." McKenzie nodded.

"And he does work in that room all alone." Kate's tummy rumbled. "I guess we can talk more about this over some food. I'm so busy solving mysteries that I don't have time to eat. That's inexcusable!"

They all laughed.

After breakfast, the campers headed across the parking lot. Kate saw Gus entering the back door of the building. Something about seeing him troubled her, but she couldn't put her finger on it. It was probably the story Megan had told about what had happened to his wife.

Watch out, Kate, she scolded herself. *Don't start feeling sorry for him!*

Still, something about seeing him today put things in a new light. She pondered that for a minute, trying to make sense of her feelings.

Suddenly Kate snapped her fingers as she realized what had been bothering her so much. "McKenzie!"

"What?"

"Did you see Gus just now?"

"Sure." McKenzie shrugged. "What about him?"

"Did you notice what he was wearing?"

McKenzie's eyes grew wide. "Now that you mention it, yes. He was wearing the quarry uniform—brown pants and a tan shirt."

"*Not* blue jeans," Kate said. "The person in the picture I took last night was definitely wearing jeans."

"Yes, but that picture was taken in the middle of the night," McKenzie said. "So he probably doesn't wear his uniform when he goes to the quarry in the middle of the night to pack the forged fossils. In fact, it's more likely he would wear regular clothes if he's doing something sneaky."

"I suppose." Just one more thing for Kate to think about. But with so little time left, her thoughts were now tumbling around in her head faster than she could keep up with them. If she and McKenzie ever needed prayer. . .now was the time!

CHAPTER 14

The Plot Thickens

Just after breakfast, when the others went to watch a video on the quarry's history, Megan led the way to the prep room. "It's quiet in here during this time of day. Gus does most of his work during the afternoon."

"And in the middle of the night," Kate added.

"The middle of the night?" Megan looked at her curiously. "Are you saying that because you think it was Gus in the pictures you took last night?"

Kate nodded. "Yes."

"Well we don't know that for sure," Megan said. "And remember the story I told you about Gus. We need to assume he is innocent until proven guilty."

"Okay." Kate sighed. Still, she would prove once and for all that Gus did this. Maybe. "Megan, do you mind if I use my fingerprint kit?" Kate asked when they were inside the room.

Megan shrugged. "I don't mind. But remember, Kate, lots of people come in and out of this room, not just Gus. So any prints you lift might belong to other people."

Kate nodded. "I know. I just need to compare the prints to the ones on the fossil plate back in Philadelphia."

She reached in her backpack, pulled out the fingerprint kit and went to work. "Oooh, this is the perfect spot!" She pressed the fingerprint tape down on the table and lifted a perfect print. Kate could hardly wait to compare it to the ones from the ruined fossil back in Philly.

"Here's another one, Kate." McKenzie pointed to a shipping label on a wooden crate. "Might as well get it too!"

They spent the next five minutes lifting all sorts of fingerprints. Megan watched at the door, in case anyone decided to come in the room.

Just as Kate finished with the last print, she heard a familiar voice.

"What are you girls doing in here?"

Conner. Hopefully he wouldn't be too upset that Megan had let them in the room.

Megan flashed a smile. "Oh, hey, Conner. What are you doing here? Aren't you supposed to be with the kids?"

"I had something to take care of first." He looked at her curiously. "Aren't these girls supposed to be watching the video too?"

"I'll send them in there when we're done," Megan said with a nod. "Something came up and I needed to. . ."

"Needed to what?" He drew near, a concerned look on his face.

"Well I offered to help the girls with something."

Kate tucked the fingerprint kit into her backpack. No point in saying too much.

Just then, the door to the room opened and Grumpy Gus stepped inside. Kate's breath caught in her throat. *Oh no! Caught!*

"What's going on in here, a party?" he asked. "You people filling my work space for some reason?"

"Well actually, we were. . ." Megan stopped before finishing her sentence.

"She's giving us a tour," Kate said.

"You know how I feel about kids in my work space." Gus looked grumpier than ever. "I don't like them in here."

"Yes, get these campers out of here, Megan," Conner said. He gave her a warning look but Kate still had a couple of questions that needed to be answered, so she jumped right in.

"Can I ask you a question?" She drew near Conner. "What happened to Joel's stingray fossil? It's disappeared from the museum."

"It has not," he said with the wave of a hand. "I had a request from a museum in Vancouver, so I asked Gus to send it."

"I packed it up a week ago and shipped it," Gus said. "Why are you asking?"

"Oh, no reason." Kate shrugged and tried to look calm, though her insides were trembling. She didn't mention that the fossil in Vancouver was a fake.

"You kids get on out of here," Gus said. "I have work to do and I can't do it with you underfoot."

As he shooed them out of the room, Kate had a brilliant idea. She deliberately left her backpack sitting on the floor next to the lab table. Following Megan out of the back door, she tried to still her shaking hands. She whispered the verse that Elizabeth had given her—the one about being able to do all things through Christ who strengthened her—and took a deep breath.

They stepped out into the bright sunlight and Kate planned her next words. She started with two simple ones: "Oh dear."

"What is it, Kate?" Megan looked her way.

"I, um, I left something in the room."

"What?" Megan asked.

"My backpack," she said. "I left it. It'll only take a minute."

Megan held open the door and Kate ran back inside.

"What are you doing in here, kid?" Gus said, looking her way. "I told you that I have work to do."

"Oh, I know." She flashed a smile. "I just came back to get my backpack. Sorry."

Gus grunted and walked to the other side of the room to lift a packing crate. Kate took advantage of the fact that his back was turned and reached inside her backpack, quickly pulling out the tiny digital recorder. She set it in the corner behind a stack of trays and positioned it to face Gus's worktable.

Oh, I hope this works!

She glanced across the room at Gus, who was now heading her way. "Get on out of here, kid. I don't need you leaving stuff in here for me to trip over."

"Yes, sir." She lifted her backpack to show him that she was ready to leave and he grunted again. She was pretty sure she heard him mutter something about kids always getting in his way, but she didn't take the time to listen. No, she had something else to take care of now. Something very important.

She raced back outside, and approached McKenzie and Megan, now out of breath. "I—I need to go back to the cabin and look at these prints," she said. "Is that okay?"

"Yes. I'll walk you there. Then McKenzie and I will join the others in the video room. What are you thinking, Kate?"

"I need to figure out if the fingerprints match. And then, um. . ." She fiddled with her backpack, growing nervous.

"What?" Megan asked.

"Then I need to figure out a way to get back in the shipping room to fetch my video camera, which I just hid behind some trays."

"Brilliant, Kate!" McKenzie clapped her hands together.

Megan laughed. "Wow. You really have done this case-solving thing before, haven't you?"

Kate nodded. "I have. But this time is a little more nerve-racking!"

They walked back to the cabin together, and then Megan and McKenzie headed to the video room. Kate pulled out her fingerprint kit and examined the prints she had taken that day at the museum. Then she compared them to the ones she had taken today.

The ones from the lab table were a perfect match. Bingo! So were the ones from the shipping crate. Obviously the same person who packed the crate was the one who had forged the fossils, right?

Hmm. She paused to think about that. Like Megan said, more than one person worked in the shipping room. How would she ever know for sure whose fingerprints these were? She would have to print each person who worked in the room. In fact, she would have to print every person who ever went in that room.

Kate pulled out her cell phone and took several pictures of the fingerprints and sent them by picture message to Alexis. "Maybe her uncle can run these prints and tell us who committed the crime," Kate said to herself.

She put all of the items back in her backpack. Then she leaned back against the pillows and began to pray.

"Lord, if You want me to solve this case, I'm really, really going to need Your help. I know the prints match, but I don't know whose prints they are. Lord, can You show us who did this? Was it Gus? Or was it someone else?"

As she continued to pray, Kate's eyes grew heavy. She drifted off into a hazy sleep. She woke almost an hour later! "Oh no! What have I done?" Just as she scrambled to her feet, her phone rang. She looked at the number, recognizing it right away. Elizabeth.

Kate answered with a quick, "Hello?"

"Kate, I was praying for you this morning," Elizabeth said. "And I felt like I was supposed to call and tell you to be extra careful today. I have the strongest feeling someone is pretending to be something they're not."

"Like that Jacob and Esau story," Kate said. "You know what? I think you're right. I've been wondering about something all morning long." She quickly told Elizabeth her suspicions and her friend agreed to pray. In fact, she decided they should stop to pray, right then and there. Over the phone.

"Lord, You know who did this," Elizabeth prayed. "And You know the truth from a lie. We ask that You give Kate and McKenzie wisdom to know the difference today. Help them solve this case, Lord. Amen!"

"Amen!" Kate echoed.

By the time she hung up the phone, she felt energized to finish what she had started. She would figure out who was Jacob and who was Esau. And when she got it figured out, she'd know exactly who had forged those fossils . . .and why!

Putting the Pieces Together

Kate spent the rest of the morning at the excavation site with Megan and the other campers. Conner didn't come because he had other work to do, so it was a quiet day with the boys and girls working together. No competition this time.

Kate really enjoyed her last day digging for fossils, but her mind was on other things. She couldn't stop thinking about the video camera she'd left in the workroom. And she couldn't stop thinking about Gus's brown pants. Something about all of this left her feeling very confused. Mixed up. In fact, the more she thought about it, the more she wondered if they'd had the wrong person all along.

A thousand thoughts rolled through her brain, but only one really made sense. In fact, the more she thought about it, the more sense it made. But how could she prove it? Only one way. Alexis's uncle would have to prove that the fingerprints belonged to the right person.

"Hey, what's up with you today?" Joel asked, drawing near. "You're really quiet. That's not like you."

"I, um, have a lot on my mind." She happened to notice he was wearing blue jeans. Then again, so were all of the other boys. And Conner. She remembered seeing him in blue jeans earlier today. Then again, he never seemed to wear the quarry uniform, did he?

When the kids took a break for lunch, Kate saw Mr. Jenkins cross the dining hall. Like most of the others, he wore blue jeans. However, she no longer suspected him. After much thought and prayer, she felt he could be trusted. She rose from her place at the table and met him on the opposite side of the room, away from the other campers.

"Mr. Jenkins, I think I'm getting close to figuring this out, but I need your help one more time."

"Oh?"

"Yes, I'm pretty sure I know who's been forging the fossils, and I think the proof is in the workroom."

"What kind of proof?"

"Hopefully a video of someone doing something suspicious. But we won't know for sure until I look at the video. I was wondering if you'd go retrieve my camera for me. I would like to go back to the cabin to watch it after lunch."

"Of course." He nodded. "Now, where is this camera you've hidden?"

"I hid it behind several trays."

"Very crafty!" He grinned. "Okay. I'll go in there and get the camera, but give me a few minutes. I have to talk to Megan first." He disappeared into the kitchen and was gone several minutes. Then Kate watched him walk across the dining hall toward the workroom. She prayed he would be able to get the camera without anyone noticing.

Sure enough, he came out a few minutes later with a paper lunch sack in his hand.

"I think this is yours," he said, placing the lunch bag on the table.

Kate grinned and whispered, "Thanks."

"What is that?" McKenzie asked, taking the seat next to her. "Did you pack your lunch?"

"Not exactly." She giggled then whispered, "It's my video camera." She looked up as Conner entered the dining hall and sat with the boys. "Come with me to the cabin, McKenzie. We still have a case to solve."

They ran across the parking lot together, straight to their cabin. Once inside, Kate plopped on her bunk. She could hardly wait to watch the video. She tried to click on the camera, but it wouldn't come on.

"Don't tell me!" she groaned. "The battery is dead. I should've thought of that. I left it running for too long."

"Did you bring the charger?" McKenzie asked.

"Yes, but it will take awhile to charge." She scrambled off the bunk and looked through her duffel bag until she found the charger. Plugging it in, she sighed. "Everything seems to be taking so long."

"Remember, patience is a virtue!" McKenzie said. "Good things come to those who wait."

"I'm just not very good at waiting." A few minutes later she checked the camera and it came on. "Awesome!" With her fingers trembling, she rewound the camera to the beginning.

"Ooo, what is that?" McKenzie asked, pointing at the screen.

"Well you can see the edge of the trays," Kate said. "I hid the camera behind them. So we're not going to be able to see much, but maybe we'll hear something suspicious."

She listened closely as a man's voice rang out.

"That's Gus," she said.

"Who's he talking to?"

"Hmm." Kate listened a bit closer. "Sounds familiar." Another moment later, she recognized the other voice. "Oh, that's Conner."

"Gus is saying something to him, but I can't make it out."

Kate backed up the video and listened closely. Off in the distance, faint as a whisper, she heard Gus say, "Conner, I'm surprised you're still going strong today. Didn't you work through the night?"

McKenzie's eyes grew as wide as saucers. "No way! Conner was the one in the room last night?"

"Sounds like it." Kate's stomach began to get butterflies. This confirmed what she had been thinking all morning. She kept watching and listening to the video, hoping to learn more.

"What is Conner saying?" McKenzie asked. "I can't make it out."

"Sounds like Conner is telling Gus to take a break. Telling him that he will take over for a while."

"Ooo, I think I heard the door close," McKenzie added. "Do you think Gus left the room?"

"Maybe, but look." Kate pointed at the screen. "You can see a man's legs, but I'm not sure whose they are! The picture is fuzzy."

McKenzie squinted and took a closer look. "That has to be Conner. Gus is wearing his uniform today, remember?"

"Oh right!" Kate watched as the man in the blue jeans walked by. For a while the room grew silent. Then she heard Conner speaking again. This time his words were a lot clearer, thank goodness.

"Who is he talking to?" McKenzie asked. "There's no one in the room with him."

"Maybe there is!" Kate whispered. "Maybe someone else came in." She listened closely as Conner said something about fossils.

"Ooo, I know!" McKenzie snapped her fingers. "He's talking to someone on the phone. Has to be, because we can only hear what Conner is saying, not what the other person is saying."

"I think you're right," Kate agreed. "But it's hard to tell what he's talking about."

They listened a little bit longer, and Kate gasped when she heard Conner start to laugh. He said something that sounded like, "We got away with it."

"Did he really just say 'we got away with it'?" McKenzie asked. "Or am I imagining things?"

"That's what I thought he said too!" Kate nodded. She pushed the REWIND button on the video camera and played that part over again. Sure enough, it really sounded like those were his words. She rewound it and played it once more, this time slowing down the speed. "Weeee. . . goooooooot. . .a. . .way. . .with. . .it." Plain as day!

After that, Conner's words were a little muffled, but the girls could understand part of it, especially when he said, "Meet me in the parking lot at three, but watch out. Some kids are snooping around, so we have to be careful this time."

McKenzie gasped. "Oh Kate!"

After that, the screen went black.

"Must be when the battery died." Kate let out an exaggerated sigh. "But at least we know Conner is up to something here."

"I just don't believe it!" McKenzie looked stunned. "Why Conner? He's got a great job here at the quarry. Paleontologists make a good living. Why would he need to forge the fossils and sell them illegally?"

"I don't know. But I've had a funny feeling all morning that he's our bad guy. He's been pretending to be something—or someone—he's not." Kate filled McKenzie in on Elizabeth's phone call earlier this morning and McKenzie looked stunned.

"Wow."

"Yeah," Kate nodded. "So I've been praying all morning that God would reveal the truth, and now I'm pretty sure He has. Just one last thing we have to do. We have to pray that Alex's uncle is able to run the fingerprints through the computer before we leave the camp today. Otherwise we won't be able to prove anything."

"Maybe we can," McKenzie said. "Come with me." She grabbed Kate's hand and ran in the direction of the dining hall. Once inside, she passed the other kids and went into the kitchen. The cook looked over at the girls with a surprised look on his face.

"What's up, kids?"

"I just have a quick question," McKenzie said. "Might sound kind of silly, but has anyone who works at the quarry ever come into the kitchen to borrow any brown sugar?"

"Brown sugar?" The cook shrugged. "Yeah. Why?"

"Do you remember who?"

"Well sure," he said. "Conner. It's the funniest thing. I've never heard of anyone who uses brown sugar in his coffee, but Conner does. He seems to love just nibbling on the stuff too. So he's always in here looking for sugar."

"Bingo!" Kate yelled. She grabbed McKenzie by the hand and they ran out of the kitchen, hollering "Thank you!" to the cook as they ran.

"What do we do now?" McKenzie asked.

Kate glanced at the clock. "Hmm. It's two o'clock. Dad should be here at three to pick us up."

"That's the same time Conner is going to pass the real fossils off to whoever he was talking to on the phone," McKenzie whispered. "What do we do now?"

"Now we tell Mr. Jenkins," Kate said. "And then he calls the police. Looks like the Camp Club Girls have found their man!"

Biscuit to the Rescue!

Kate and McKenzie found Mr. Jenkins in the dining hall chatting with several campers.

"Could I talk to you again, sir?" Kate asked anxiously.

"Well sure, Kate."

"In your offie?" she said. "And please bring Megan."

"Well sure." He leaned over with a twinkle in his eye. "I have a feeling you're going to share some big news."

"The biggest news ever!" she whispered in response.

Minutes later Mr. Jenkins took a seat at his desk, and Megan sat in a chair nearby. Kate and McKenzie paced the room.

"What is it, Kate?" Megan asked. "You're making me nervous!"

Kate glanced at the clock on the wall—2:10. "We don't have much time. We have to call the police."

"Police?" Megan asked. "Why?"

Kate pointed to Mr. Jenkins's television. "Do you mind if I plug in my video camera so I can show you something?"

"Be my guest."

Seconds later, they were all watching the video together. Dismay filled Megan's voice. "Oh, I don't believe it! Not Conner! He's my friend! I trusted him!"

"Looks like he fooled us." Mr. Jenkins reached for the phone and dialed 911. Kate could hear him talking to the police. She hated to interrupt, but felt it was important.

"Mr. Jenkins, tell them to come a couple of minutes after three. You need to catch him in the act if you want the charges to stick."

"Good idea." He nodded and conveyed his wishes to the police, who agreed to come at five minutes after three.

"What do we do now?" McKenzie asked.

"Conner is teaching the final session in the dining hall," Megan said. "Let's all go back in there and act like nothing is unusual. Just be ourselves."

"This will be the best acting job of my life!" Kate said. She looked at Mr. Jenkins and Megan and said, "But I am sorry that the bad guy turned out to be one of your employees. I'm sure this is really hard to hear."

"It is," Mr. Jenkins said. A puzzled look crossed his face. "I'm so disappointed. I've been mentoring Conner for years. He's like a son to me. It breaks my heart that he would steal from me."

"I just can't believe he was pretending to be something he wasn't all of this time." Megan shook her head and brushed away some tears. "I will never understand that."

Kate thought of the story of Jacob and Esau once again. How interesting that Conner was a fake, just like the brother in the story!

The girls walked into the dining hall and took their seats at the table. Conner looked at them with a troubled glance as he saw Mr. Jenkins and Megan enter the room behind Kate and McKenzie.

"He's nervous," Kate whispered. "I think he knows something's up."

She listened as he gave his final speech—something about the work paleontologists were doing with fossils around the world—but was distracted when a text message came through on her phone. She tried not to look obvious as she opened the phone, but it was hard! Kate almost swallowed her bubble gum when she read the text from Alexis: KATE, THE PRINTS DON'T BELONG TO GUS. THEY BELONG TO CONNER. HE'S BEEN IN TROUBLE FOR SOME PETTY THEFT BEFORE, SO THE FINGERPRINTS WERE IN THE DATABASE.

Kate passed the phone to Mr. Jenkins, who sat behind her. He read the words and pursed his lips, then passed the phone back to her.

When the session came to an end at 2:45, the campers were dismissed to load their gear and prepare for their parents' arrivals. Kate grew more excited by the moment. Any time now, the police would be here. And her father. She prayed for God's protection over everyone involved.

At exactly 2:55 she and McKenzie walked to the front parking lot with Mr. Jenkins and Megan nearby. She smiled as a familiar RV pulled into the parking lot.

"Hey, my dad brought the RV!" McKenzie said. "Cool."

"Perfect to hide behind!" Kate added.

They greeted their family members. Dex looked excited to see them. So did Biscuit, who jumped up and down.

"Be still, boy," Kate said. "We don't have time for you to go crazy right now!"

"Did you have a good time girls?" Kate's father asked.

"Did you figure out who forged the fossils?" Dex added.

"Yes," Kate whispered. "But we can't really talk about it yet." She looked up at her father. "Dad, we need to stay a few more minutes. I promise it won't take too long."

He shrugged. "If it will help you girls out, sure."

Kate looked across the parking lot as an unfamiliar car pulled up. She watched Conner emerge from the trees on the far side of the parking lot with something large in his hand. A briefcase, maybe?

"McKenzie, look!" She reached for her camera and snapped pictures.

"Kate, what in the world is happening?" her mother asked.

"I promise I'll tell you everything!" She kept taking pictures. "But right now we have to wait on the police!"

"The police?" Mrs. Phillips fanned herself.

The man in the car pulled close to Conner and popped open his trunk. At that moment, Mr. Jenkins headed their way. Kate prayed for his protection. When he arrived next to Conner, the men began to argue. Kate watched in horror as Conner ran toward the trees. She glanced at Biscuit and hollered, "Biscuit! Go get him, boy!"

Biscuit the Wonder Dog took off running across the parking lot. He caught up with Conner just as a patrol car pulled into the parking lot, sirens wailing. Biscuit grabbed hold of Conner's jeans with his teeth and held on for dear life.

"Let go of me, you dumb dog!" Conner yelled. He shook his leg and Biscuit bounced a little, but held on tight, yanking this way and that.

Seconds later the police caught up with Conner. One of them patted Biscuit on the head. "Good boy, puppy," he said, scratching him behind the ears.

"His name is Biscuit the Wonder Dog!" Kate called out. "He's a crime-solving dog!" She took a few steps toward the officers, but they gestured for the kids to keep their distance.

"Stay over there," the officer called out. "We'll get statements from you after."

Kate nodded. She knew better than to interrupt a crime scene! Biscuit ran to her and she hugged him.

"Good puppy, Wonder Dog!"

She and McKenzie peeked around the edge of the RV, watching the police arrest Conner. As they did, several of the other campers drew near.

"What in the world is going on?" Lauren asked.

"Yeah, why are the police talking to Conner?" Patti asked.

Joel simply shook his head, a sad look in his eyes. Finally he whispered, "I don't believe it. I really don't believe it. I thought Conner was a great guy."

Kate shrugged. "Even really great people make mistakes."

"And this was a big one!" McKenzie added.

The police now put Conner in the back of the patrol car with the other man and pulled out of the parking lot. Mr. Jenkins walked toward the campers with a sad look on his face.

"You'll never believe what the police just found in Conner's trunk," he said.

"Brown sugar?" McKenzie and Kate spoke in unison.

"Actually, they did find traces of brown sugar, but that's not what I'm talking about," Mr. Jenkins said. "They found the actual stingray fossil and a little black book with phone numbers of the people Conner has been selling the real fossils to. It's an underground ring of fossil thieves."

"I knew it!" Kate turned to McKenzie with a smile. "The Camp Club Girls were right! He was selling the real fossils to make money."

"Have you ever heard of an artist named Jean Van Horn?"

"I have," Megan said, her eyes growing wide. "He's Conner's best friend."

"Well apparently he's been using the real fossils for artwork. It's a common practice, but not one that many people know much about. They take the fossils and turn them into art masterpieces, then sell them for hundreds of thousands of dollars. The stolen fossils are so beautifully disguised when the artist is done with them that they're not even recognizable."

"Wow." Kate shook her head. "That's amazing."

"Thankfully Conner confessed to the officer," Mr. Jenkins said, looking at Kate. "And when I asked him about the fossils that were supposed to be sent to your teacher's museum in Philadelphia, he promised to tell the police where they are."

"Yea!" Kate hollered. "Mrs. Smith's job is saved!"

"Thanks to you girls." He smiled at Kate and McKenzie. "You're the real heroes here."

"Nah." Kate felt her cheeks turn warm with embarrassment.

Mr. Jenkins nodded. "Yes you are! And I should offer a reward for those fossils."

"Oh no, sir!" Kate said. "We didn't do this for a reward. We did it to help you and so my teacher could keep her job at the museum."

"Then at least let me offer you kids some ice cream before you go," he said with a twinkle in his eye. "It's the least I can do!"

All of the campers went back inside the dining hall for ice cream sundaes. As they ate, Megan drew near, still looking a little sad.

"I still can't believe it was Conner. He was my friend." She sighed.

"I'm sure you're really disappointed," McKenzie said.

"I am." She paused. "You know, all of this talk about fake fossils has reminded me of something."

"What's that?" Kate looked her way.

"Well the Bible says we're supposed to let our yes be yes and our no be no. In other words, we're supposed to be who we say we are. No faking it."

"Ah." Kate nodded.

"Just seems like so many people say they're Christians, but don't really act like it. Or maybe sometimes they fake it when they're around their church friends, but when they're at school or hanging out with another crowd, they act differently."

"I know what you mean," McKenzie said. "One of my friends from church is like that. I've tried to talk to her about it, but she still keeps on pretending when she's around the kids at church. I see what she's like at school, and she's really different."

"Maybe there's a lesson to be learned from this fossil fiasco," Megan said with a sigh. "Maybe God is trying to show us that it's so important to be the real deal. Genuine."

Kate nodded. "No fakes!"

"That's right." Megan nodded. "No fakes. You know why? Because it dishonors Him when we pretend to be something we're not. And if we think others won't notice, we're wrong! People are pretty good at spotting fakers."

"That's true," McKenzie said.

Kate noticed Joel standing to the side, very quiet, staring at the ground.

"You okay, Joel?" she asked, drawing near.

He shrugged. "I don't know."

"What do you mean? You know everything!" She gave him a warm smile.

"No I don't." He shook his head. "I mean, I know some things. Scientific things. Things about fossils. But I don't really know what you're talking about."

"What do you mean?"

He shrugged. "I go to church on Sundays with my mom and dad. And I even go to Sunday school. But mostly it's to make my parents happy, or to hang out with friends. I'm not really going for any reason other than that."

"Wow." Kate paused before responding. At least he was being honest about it! "You know what, Joel?" she said at last. "I'm really proud of you. You didn't have to tell me that. You could have just gone on pretending. But you were honest."

"Yeah, I guess so." He took a seat, looking more defeated. "But watching you and McKenzie the past few days has shown me something. You two are the real deal. You really love God. It's obvious."

Kate got a happy tingly feeling all over. "Thank you, Joel."

He paused, then gave her a hopeful look. "I guess what I'm trying to say is, you two aren't fakers, but I am."

"Ah." Kate didn't say anything more. She wanted to give him a chance to finish.

"I don't want to fake it anymore," Joel said.

"Have you ever asked Jesus to live in your heart?" McKenzie asked, drawing near. "If you give your heart to Him, He will show you how to live a real Christian life, one where you don't have to pretend."

Joel shook his head. "No, I never did that. I just go to church, like I said."

"Well going to church isn't what makes you a Christian," Kate explained. "The only thing that really gives you a real relationship with God is making Jesus Lord of your life. When you do that, everything becomes *very* real, trust me!"

McKenzie nodded. "She's right, Joel. You won't have to fake it anymore."

He gave her a curious look. "So, um, how do I do that?"

"You can pray and ask Jesus to come into your heart," Kate explained.

He shrugged. "I, um. . .well, I don't know how to do that."

Kate smiled, and thought about Elizabeth at once. Elizabeth would say, "Kate, don't ever be afraid to stop what you're doing and pray for someone, even if it's in a public place."

With a happy heart, Kate did just that.

CHAPTER 17

A Fossil on the Heart

After praying with Joel to accept Jesus, Kate felt like singing! She felt like dancing and jumping for joy. Was this how God felt too? Probably! The angels in heaven were probably throwing a party right now!

Kate's mother drew near. "Honey, I hate to rush you, but we have to get back to Yellowstone soon. Tonight is our last evening with the Phillips family, and we want to have a big campfire and let you and McKenzie tell us the whole story of how you caught the forger."

Kate nodded. "Okay, Mom. I'll be right there. I just need to talk to one last person. Can you give us about five minutes?"

"Sure." Her mother gave her a warm hug. "And in case I haven't said it yet, I'm so proud of you!"

"The Camp Club Girls did it together!" Kate said with a nod.

Her mother headed to the RV, and Kate walked with McKenzie and Joel into the museum, looking for Gus. Kate spotted him at last.

"Gus, could we talk to you for a minute?" she asked.

He shook his head. "I'm busy, kid."

"It will only take a minute. Please?" She looked into his tired eyes and he shrugged.

"I guess. But make it quick."

"I. . .we. . .just wanted to tell you something," Kate explained. "We wanted to tell you how happy we are that you work here. You do a great job for the quarry and we appreciate you."

He stared at her suspiciously. "Who told you to say this?"

"No one," McKenzie said. "We just wanted you to know, that's all."

Gus ran his fingers through his thinning hair and looked at them as if he didn't quite believe them. "You mean, you're just saying this to be nice?"

"Well sure," Kate said. "When someone does a great job, it's always a good idea to let them know."

"If you think I'm so great, then why were you kids snooping around this place at night, hoping to catch me doing something wrong?" he asked. "I know all about it."

"Sorry about that." Kate sighed. "We were just trying to figure out who was making the fake fossils."

"I know, I know." Gus put his hands up. "You thought it was me. But now I have something to tell you."

"Oh?" Kate gave him a curious look. "What is it?"

"I suspected Conner of foul play all along," Gus said. "I've been keeping an eye on him for weeks, documenting suspicious activity."

"No way!" Kate crossed her arms at her chest and stared at him. "Were you in the woods one day when we were excavating? I thought I saw you."

"Yes, I followed him out there that day because I'd found a large bag of brown sugar hidden in the closet in my workroom earlier in the day. I took it to the kitchen, thinking maybe one of our cooks had misplaced it, but they thought I was crazy, so I took it back to the workroom."

"Wow. So that explains why we saw you walk through the dining hall with a bag of brown sugar," Kate said.

"Yes." He sighed. "Something told me Conner was up to no good, but I couldn't prove it. I hated to go to Mr. Jenkins without any proof."

"I see." She paused then looked at him. "Are you saying you knew all along that the fossils you were sending out were fake, but you sent them anyway?"

"No." He laughed. "I only began to suspect it when you kids started following me. I overheard something you said to Mr. Jenkins. Just enough to get me curious. And to be honest, I was worried about Joel's missing stingray, but I hadn't said anything about it."

"Wow. So we were all worried about the same thing," Kate said. "To think we could have been working together!"

"Yep." Gus grinned—the first smile she'd seen from him. "Would you kids like a proper tour of my workroom? A lot of interesting things go on back there."

Kate looked up at him, stunned at his kind gesture. "Really?"

"Really." He nodded and grinned.

"That would be great. We can't take long, though, because my parents are waiting."

"They can come too," Gus said. "Run and fetch them."

Kate did just that, and before long, both families were crammed into the tiny work space.

As Gus showed them around, he was all smiles. "Wow. He's really great," Kate whispered to McKenzie.

Kate thought about everything that had happened. How she had misjudged people!

The tour ended after just a few minutes, and it was time to leave the quarry. Kate had a hard time saying goodbye to everyone, especially Megan and Joel.

"Promise you'll write?" Joel asked.

"I will. And you let me know if you get that internship."

"Oh, I forgot to tell you! Mr. Jenkins told me this morning that I did!" Joel's faced beamed. "Isn't that terrific news?"

"Awesome!" Kate turned to Megan, feeling tears well up in her eyes. She reached to hug her counselor goodbye and whispered, "I'm going to miss you so much."

"I'm going to miss you too," Megan said. "And I can never thank you enough for helping solve this case, girls," she said, reaching for McKenzie with her other arm. "I hope you'll come back."

Kate nodded. "Maybe we'll get to come back someday and bring our friends. You'll love Elizabeth. And Sydney and Alex and Bailey. . ." On and on she went, singing the praises of the Camp Club Girls.

Finally Kate's mother interrupted her. "I'm so sorry, honey, but we really have to go."

"Okay." Kate sighed and gave the quarry one last look before they climbed into the RV. As they pulled out of the parking lot, she felt the sting of tears in her eyes but quickly brushed them aside. No tears today. This was a happy day.

"Mom, would it be okay if I called Mrs. Smith?" Kate asked. "I want to tell her what happened."

"Yes, it's fine," her mother said. "I know she'll be very relieved."

Kate spent the next ten minutes on the phone with her teacher, who was thrilled to get the news, especially when she heard that the real fossils had been located and would be sent to the Philadelphia museum in a few days.

"Kate, you did it! You solved the case *and* saved the day."

"I hate to disagree with you, Mrs. Smith," Kate said, "but only God can save the day. I am glad He chose to use the Camp Club Girls to help, though!"

"Me too." Her teacher laughed then thanked her once again for helping out.

Kate ended the call, then looked at McKenzie. "Now we need to call the other girls and let them know what happened!"

"Yes, they'll be so excited!" McKenzie added.

"Awesome! Let's do a conference call."

Minutes later, Kate had all of the Camp Club Girls on the line. Everyone was so excited that they talked on top of each other.

Kate held the phone in her hand and McKenzie leaned in close to hear everything.

"We have so much to tell you!" Kate said. "We figured out who forged the fossils!"

"No way!" Bailey let out a loud squeal. Kate pulled the phone away from her ear and rubbed it, then laughed.

"Yes. And you're never going to believe who it was. The very last person on planet earth that we would have ever suspected—Conner! Alex already knows because her uncle helped us run the fingerprints, but I wanted to tell the rest of you."

Kate quickly relayed the rest of the story, giving the girls all of the details then thanking each of the girls for her help.

"Oh wow, that's unbelievable!" Sydney said. "Conner seemed so trustworthy."

"I know," Kate said. "He's a respected paleontologist and a counselor to the boys. That's why I never considered him. But in the end, that's who it turned out to be."

"So Gus wasn't the one after all?" Bailey asked.

"No, it looks like we judged a book by its cover. . .and we were wrong," Kate answered.

"What do you mean?" Sydney asked.

"I saw a grumpy older man in wrinkled clothes and thought he was a bad guy. Turns out he's just a man who is hurting. His poor wife is in a rehab hospital because of a terrible car accident. Instead of judging Grumpy Gus, I should have shared God's love with him." Even as she spoke the words, Kate felt guilty.

"Don't let her fool you," McKenzie said. "Kate *did* show him God's love. Every time she passed by, she smiled and talked to him. That's a lot more than most of the other campers did."

It warmed Kate's heart to hear McKenzie's words, but she still felt bad.

"Remember what happened in the story of Jacob and Esau," Elizabeth said. "Even though Jacob made some mistakes, God still made something good out of the situation. That's how the Lord works. You watch and see."

"O—okay. I will."

"I see one good thing that came out of it already," Sydney said. "You suspected the wrong person, but your suspicions led to the right person.

Don't you find that interesting?"

"Yes." Kate couldn't help but smile. "I learned a big lesson."

"What's that?" Alexis asked.

"Megan told me on the day of the treasure hunt that we each leave an imprint on others with our attitude. She called it a fossil on the heart."

"Ooo, I like that," Elizabeth said. "A fossil on the heart."

"When my attitude is good, I leave a good imprint and when my attitude is bad, well. . ." Kate paused and sighed. "Let's just say that sometimes I leave a negative imprint."

Sydney laughed. "Kate, don't be so hard on yourself. You're one of the sweetest girls I know. You've left a great imprint on my heart. And on Bailey's. And Elizabeth's." She began to talk nonstop about how each of the Camp Club Girls had left a different imprint. Before long, Kate was laughing. The Camp Club Girls all started laughing and talking and soon got really loud. Kate's mom gave her a warning look.

Kate ended the call just as they arrived at their campsite at Yellowstone. The sun was starting to set in the west, painting the sky the most brilliant colors Kate had ever seen.

She and the others climbed out of the RV and stretched their legs.

"I'm so hungry!" she said. "What's for dinner?"

"We're grilling hamburgers and hot dogs," her mother said. "You girls can help."

Kate and McKenzie helped their mothers get the meal ready. As they worked, Dexter drew near, his eyes wide with excitement.

"Kate, you'll never believe what happened when you were gone."

"What?" She looked at her little brother.

"Yesterday morning we had a bear. He came right to the edge of our tent."

"No way!"

"It's true," her mother said. "I think someone. . ." she looked at Dexter, "someone left the bag of marshmallows out. And a little bear cub found it at the campsite, just a few feet from our tent."

"I wish you could've seen it, Kate," Dexter said with a grin. "I came out of the tent and caught him in the act."

"What did you do?"

"Well, I read online not to ever spook a bear, so I stayed quiet. For a minute or two he didn't know I was there."

"We watched the whole thing from our tent," her father said. "The cub was so busy eating marshmallows that he wasn't paying attention to anything. But as soon as he saw Dex, he took a couple of steps in his direction."

"Then what?" Kate could hardly believe it.

Dexter shook his head. "I stood frozen like a statue."

"We all prayed silently," her mother said. "The Lord answered our prayers. The bear ate that last marshmallow and then took off into the trees."

"When he left we ran and got inside the van," Dexter said. "Just in case he came back."

Kate's father said, "He didn't come back. He went off, probably looking for more food."

"I'm so glad I didn't go to fossil camp with you," Dexter said. "I would have missed the whole thing."

"See!" Kate laughed. "I told you God had an adventure in store for you."

When everyone gathered around the campfire with food, between mouthfuls of their yummy burgers, Kate and McKenzie told them the whole story. Afterward, one thing stood out above all the others. Kate still heard Megan's words echoing in her ears. . ."*We leave an imprint on others with our attitude. A little bit of us rubs off on them. So, when you react with an attitude to something—good or bad—it's like you're creating a fossil on the heart.*"

"A fossil on the heart," Kate whispered once again.

This was *one* lesson she knew she would never forget.

Camp Club Girls:
Kate and the Pennsylvania
Pretzel Pickle

CHAPTER 1

And the Winner Is. . .

Kate stood on the huge stage with an overhead spotlight nearly blinding her. She waved at thousands of adoring, cheering fans. Her heart soared with excitement as the thunderous applause rang out. She tiptoed to reach the microphone behind the podium. She spoke, her voice quivering.

"T–thank you so much for giving me this award." She held up the huge trophy with the words Best Young Inventor engraved on it, and the audience cheered once again.

"I. . .I'm so grateful," she continued. "I accept it on behalf of all of the young inventors around the globe!" She turned to Mr. Peterson, the man who had just handed her the trophy and smiled. "And thanks to the committee for choosing me. I pray the Turbo Heat-Freeze is the first of many more inventions to come!"

Mr. Peterson stepped to the microphone and faced the crowd. "One more round of applause for Kate Oliver, Pennsylvania's Young Inventor of the Year!"

The crowd members rose to their feet as their applause grew louder. Kate felt her cheeks turn warm with embarrassment. Never in her wildest dreams had she ever imagined standing here in front of so many people! And what an honor!

"Three cheers for Kate! Three cheers for Kate!" rang out from the front row. She smiled at her parents, who sat with her little brother, Dexter, at their side. She waved, nearly tripping as she turned to walk to the edge of the stage. As she did, cameras flashed with dozens of people taking her picture. She walked down the steps, nearly dropping her large trophy.

"Careful, Kate," she whispered to herself. "You don't want to fall in front of thousands of people!"

"Kate, Kate, Kate!" Dexter's voice rang out above the crowd.

She smiled at her brother and waved, suddenly feeling a little strange.

"Kate!" he called out again. "Kate Oliver!"

Or was it Dexter? Suddenly, she wasn't so sure anymore.

"Kate! Kate Oliver!"

"Hmm?" The room grew fuzzy.

"Kate, wake up!"

"W–what?" She stirred in her seat, coming awake. She blinked her eyes several times and her classmates came into view. She looked around and realized she was at school. . .in her science class. Oh no! Had she really fallen asleep in class? What a crazy dream she'd had! One of the best ever!

"Kate Oliver. Have you been staying up late?" her teacher Mrs. Abercrombie asked with a stern look on her face.

"Oh, y–yes," she stammered as she rubbed her eyes. "I'm sorry. I've been perfecting my invention, the Turbo Heat-Freeze. The one I entered in our school's science fair last week."

"Yes," Her teacher nodded. "That's exactly why I wanted you to be wide awake when I made my announcement."

"Announcement?" Kate's heart pounded in excitement.

Mrs. Abercrombie walked to the front of the room. "Okay, now that Kate has joined us, we are ready to begin. Class, all of the science teachers at our school have judged the science fair entries, and I am happy to announce the winners. Would the following students come to the front of the room?"

Kate sat straight up in her chair, growing more and more excited. "Please, please, please!" she whispered.

Mrs. Abercrombie called the first name: "James Maddoux."

Kate sighed but never lost her focus on the front of the room.

"Jenny Padilla," Mrs. Abercrombie said next.

Kate watched her friend Jenny walk to the front of the classroom. Jenny was one of the best science students ever!

Mrs. Abercrombie next called another boy's name: "Phillip Johnson."

Kate watched as Phillip, the class's brainiest boy, walked to the front. Her heart twisted a little as she watched him. It seemed as if she and Phillip always ended up competing for the top spot.

"Kate Oliver."

Finally! Kate joined the others, her heart beating a mile a minute.

Mrs. Abercrombie faced them all. "Taking fourth place with her invention, the Shop-Vac Hover Craft," is Jenny Padilla. She handed Jenny a certificate as the other students clapped.

"In third place is James Maddoux for his invention: the battery-powered dust-mop."

Kate could hardly breathe. This meant it was down to two—she and Phillip were competing again for the top spot.

"Our runner-up turned in a great invention," Mrs. Abercrombie said, looking at them both. "The judges were very impressed."

Kate felt her heart sink a little as her teacher looked her way. Had she come in second place. . .again?

"The Weather-Cast Watch won rave reviews with the judges," Mrs. Abercrombie said. "Phillip, you are our second place winner this year."

Instead of smiling, Phillip looked a little upset as he reached to take his certificate. He looked at Kate, but only for a second. She didn't have time to think about it, though. Not now! She was about to be declared the winner of the science fair!

Sure enough, Mrs. Abercrombie held out a framed certificate in one hand and a small trophy in the other as she said, "Kate Oliver has won this year's science fair with her invention, the Turbo Heat-Freeze. And as the winner, she has been chosen to represent our school at the Young Inventors' Festival in Hershey, Pennsylvania, over spring break."

Everyone in the classroom began to clap, and Kate grinned. She reached to take the certificate and the trophy as Mrs. Abercrombie whispered, "Now you see why I needed you to be wide awake."

"Yes, thank you so much!" Kate laughed. "I'm so excited!"

"Now, I have some more good news." Mrs. Abercrombie looked at Phillip. "The school has decided to send both our first place winner and our second place winner this year. So, Phillip, you will be going too!"

His sour expression lifted at once. He smiled and whispered, "Thank you."

The bell rang, and the class ended. Kate slipped on her backpack, then headed out into the hallway with the trophy and framed certificate in hand. Every few seconds another student stopped her, offering congratulations. She couldn't stop smiling.

The next couple of classes seemed to drag by, but Kate's mind wasn't on her studies for once. She could hardly wait to get home to tell her parents. And, of course, she would have to send an email out to all of the Camp Club girls—Alex, McKenzie, Bailey, Sydney, and Elizabeth. These were the special friends from around the United States that she'd met at Discovery Lake Camp. There they'd solved the first of many mysteries together. They would certainly celebrate this victory with her.

Finally the school day came to an end. Kate rode the bus home, holding tightly to the trophy. She noticed Phillip sitting across from her with a scowl on his face, but what could she do? She wasn't bragging, after all.

Just holding the trophy she'd rightfully won. Besides, he would be going to the competition too.

She sighed as she thought about that word: *competition*. Kate had never really considered herself as a person trying to win over anyone else. But these days she found herself competing. . .a lot.

When she arrived home, Kate entered the house and found her mother at the stove, stirring a pot of soup. The delicious smell of chicken filled the room.

She put the trophy behind her back and grinned as she spoke. "Mom!"

Her mother turned and smiled. "Kate, you startled me."

"Sorry."

Her mother gave her a suspicious look. "What are you hiding behind your back? What's up?"

Kate pulled the trophy from behind her back and her mother grinned. "Oh honey. I'm so proud of you. You've won the science fair!"

"It's more than that, Mom," Kate said. "I'm going to represent the school at the Young Inventors' Festival in Hershey in two weeks. Please say we can go!"

"I'll have to check with your father," her mother said. "But I don't see why it would be a problem. And you know how much I love chocolate, so going to Hershey is always fun."

Hershey, Pennsylvania was the place where all the famous chocolate was created. Chocolate bars, chocolate kisses. . . Kate's mouth began to water at the thought.

Mrs. Oliver snapped her fingers. "Oh, I know! Since it's over spring break, why not invite one of the Camp Club Girls to join you?"

"Oooh, what a fun idea!" Kate thought about it for a moment. "You know who I think I'll ask? Alex. She's so much fun and she's so encouraging. She always looks on the bright side. She'd be the perfect one to have along."

"Great idea!" her mother said. "And while you're at it, why not invite her parents too? Hershey is a great place, and it's not just about chocolate—though that's my favorite part, of course. They've got a wonderful amusement park too. It's call Hersheypark."

"Sounds too good to be true! I'll look it up online after I talk to Alex and the other Camp Club Girls." Kate reached for her handy-dandy cell phone as she marched up the stairs toward her room and punched in Alex's number. Her friend answered on the third ring.

"Hello?"

"Alex! This is Kate! You're never going to believe what happened." The words spilled out of Kate's mouth so fast she could hardly keep up with them. She told Alex the whole story—about winning the science fair, about being invited to the Young Inventors' Festival. Everything.

In the middle of it all, her friend laughed. "Whoa, whoa, whoa! I can't keep up with you, Kate!"

"Sorry." Kate giggled as she plopped onto the bed. Biscuit started to whimper, so she reached down and picked him up, putting him on the bed beside her.

"Let's start over again. You want me to go where with you?" Alex asked. "Hershey, Pennsylvania? The place where they make all of the chocolate?"

"Yes!" Kate practically squealed, causing Biscuit to dive under the covers. "You'll never believe it. Of all the people in my school, I was chosen to represent the students at the young inventor's contest. And Hershey is close to Amish country, so if you come with us, we'll get to go to Paradise."

"Paradise?" Alex laughed. "We're going to heaven?"

"No." Kate laughed. "Paradise, Pennsylvania. It's a little town in Lancaster County, just a couple of hours from my house in Philly. I've been there dozens of times. The last time, I visited several pretzel factories."

"I always knew you loved pretzels," Alex said. "But I didn't realize you loved them that much."

"Oh yes." Kate looked up at the poster on her wall, smiling as she read the words: BAKE A BETTER PRETZEL AND THE WORLD WILL BEAT A PATHWAY TO YOUR KITCHEN. "I'm crazy about pretzels. Hard crunchy ones. Soft chewy ones. You name it. . .I eat them!" She paused for a moment, realizing pretzels weren't her only weakness. These days, she'd been snacking on anything and everything—chocolate, sour candies, chips, and more. In fact, her jeans were starting to get a little tight, now that she thought about it.

Alex kept on talking. "Wow. You've already been to Amish country? That's really neat. I've only read about the Amish in books. Their lifestyle is very different." She began to talk at length about what it would be like to live without electricity and cars, but Kate's thoughts had already drifted. She couldn't help but think about her invention.

"Amish country is where I came up with the idea for my Turbo Heat-Freeze," Kate explained. "It happened at a pretzel factory run by two sisters. I can't wait to go back and show them in person."

"I see." Alex paused. "So, you want me to be there with you in Hershey when you win the whole thing, and then we'll celebrate by eating pretzels in Amish country afterwards?"

Kate giggled. "Do you think I'll win?"

"You're the smartest person I know," Alex said. "But I can't say for sure that you'll win, because I haven't seen your invention yet. What is a Turbo Heat-Freeze, anyway?"

Kate started to tell her, but then decided not to. Not yet, anyway. "Ooh, I don't want to give it away. It's a big surprise. Just ask your mom if you can come, okay? I think you would love the town of Hershey. It's the best!"

"Well, you know I try to eat healthy foods," Alex said. "But I love chocolate too. It sounds great. Besides, this would be the perfect opportunity for me to tape some episodes of my cable column documentary, 'From a Kid's Eye View.' "

She began to talk about all of the things she could tape while there— the various competitors involved in the festival, the rides at the Hershey amusement park, and even the people who lived and worked in the town of Hershey.

"Can you imagine living in a town filled with chocolate?" Kate asked. "It would be like a taste of heaven on earth!"

Alex giggled. "Must be wonderful. I can hardly wait to get there. I wonder if we'll get tired of chocolate after a while."

"Never!" Kate laughed. "Impossible!" After a little more chatter, she ended the call, and then got on the internet to research Hershey and Amish country. As the Hershey site opened, Kate smiled. "This will be a blast!"

She looked at the page describing Hersheypark, the town's theme park.

Just then, an Instant Message came through. Kate smiled when she saw it was Bailey, the youngest of the Camp Club Girls.

Bailey: *Whatcha doing?*
Kate: *Researching Hershey, Pennsylvania.*

Kate explained her reason and Bailey congratulated her. Before long, the two of them were both reading about Hersheypark and other fun things to do in the town.

Bailey: *Oh Kate, you'll have the best time ever! I wish I could go too! I'm so excited for you and Alex. Be sure to ride the sooperdooperLooper roller coaster!*
Kate: *I will. I'm sure that will be my favorite!*
Bailey: *I'll call the other Camp Club Girls and ask them to pray for you. Maybe if we all pray, you will win the big prize!*

Kate started to tell her about the dream she'd had, but was distracted by Biscuit, who rolled over, begging for his tummy to be rubbed.

Kate: *Bailey, I have to go. A spoiled little dog wants attention.*
Bailey: *Gotcha. Well, have fun!*

With those words, Bailey disappeared.

Kate closed the laptop and leaned back against the pillows on her bed with a sigh. Biscuit licked her nose and she laughed. "What do you think, boy? Ready for another adventure?" Kate and the girls had found Biscuit while on their first mystery at camp. Kate had gotten to keep the dog, and he'd even helped the girls solve some mysteries.

He snuggled closer to her, wriggling like crazy, and Kate couldn't stop laughing.

"Okay, okay!" she said at last. "Hang on for the ride, boy! I have a feeling this trip to Hershey is going to be filled with surprises!"

She also suspected they'd encounter several tasty opportunities along the way. . .and not just the chocolate kind. Surely this trip would be one she wouldn't soon forget!

CHAPTER 2

A Sweet Reunion

Two weeks later, Kate and her family arrived in Hershey.

"Did you see what that sign said?" her brother hollered as they entered the town. "Hershey, Pennsylvania, the Sweetest Place on Earth!"

"I saw it!" Kate laughed. "And I'll bet it's true."

"I can't wait to go to Hersheypark," Dexter said. "It'll be a blast."

"Hershey has a lot of wonderful things to offer," Kate's mom said. "There are strolling bands, concerts, even a chocolate spa. I might have to check that one out!"

Kate's father laughed. "I'm eager to see how the rides at the amusement park are constructed. I brought my camera to take pictures."

Kate grinned as she thought about how different her family members were. Her dad loved figuring out how things were made.

As they settled into their room, Kate peered out the window. Unfortunately it was cloudy. She could barely make out the top of the roller coaster. Not that anyone was on it in the rain. All the rides were shut down due to the weather. Bummer.

"Come and look out of the window, Dex!" she said. "You can see the sooperdooperLooper from here. You have to look hard to see it through the fog, but it's there."

Dexter whistled as he glimpsed it. "Man! It's huge. I'll bet it's really fast. And scary."

"Doesn't seem scary to me," Kate said. "It looks like fun!"

Biscuit whimpered in his crate. "Ready to come, boy?" Kate looked around the hotel room. "You have to promise to behave while we're here. Don't break anything. . .and don't have any puppy accidents!"

A beep sounded, and Kate scrambled to get her cell phone. "Ooh! It's a text message from Alex. She and her parents just arrived. They're in room 389."

"Great," Kate's mother said. "See if they want to join us for lunch in the dining room and then we can all go to the exhibition hall together. You can show everyone your little oven freezer thing."

Kate looked at her mother. "It's a Turbo Heat-Freeze, Mom," she reminded her.

"Right." Her mother nodded. "Turbo Heat-Freeze."

She gestured for Kate to sit beside her on the bed. "And in case I've forgotten to say it recently, I'm so proud of you, Kate. I should have known you would turn out to be an inventor like your father is. You've always been such a smart, creative girl."

Kate giggled. She loved being compared to her father. He was the smartest person she knew. Maybe that's why she had become so competitive with Phillip lately. She wanted to show her dad that she was smart. . .and inventive. That way he would be really proud of her.

Just then Mr. Oliver came into the room carrying a bucket of ice.

"Somebody talking about me behind me back?" her father asked with a twinkle in his eye.

"In a good way, Dad," Kate said, running to give him a hug. "Mom was just telling me that I take after you because I like to invent things."

"And because of all of those gadgets of yours." Her mother pointed to Kate's backpack. "Did you bring them with you?"

"Of course!" Kate opened the bag and stuck her hand inside. She took out the tiny black digital recorder. Next she found her teensy-tiny digital camera. Kate then reached for her text reader, which looked like an ink pen. She ran it along the words in the hotel's Bible and it recorded the scripture from Romans 12:3: *Because of the privilege and authority God has given me, I give each of you this warning: Don't think you are better than you really are. Be honest in your evaluation of yourselves, measuring yourselves by the faith God has given us."*

Kate nodded. Perhaps God was trying to share a message with her! Winning the competition would be fun, but what would it prove, really? All of the people in the contest were talented and had great ideas.

Kate reached for her cell phone. It might come in handy while here. So might the next gadget she pulled out.

Kate stared at the smartwatch her father had given her the year before. She could hardly believe it was possible to check her email or browse the web on a wristwatch, but it always came in handy.

Finally, Kate pulled out a pair of mirrored sunglasses, smiling as she put them on. "Yep. You really can see what's going on behind you when you're wearing these. Cool."

"I'm not sure why you brought it all here with you," her mother said. "Are you expecting to solve some sort of mystery while here?"

Kate shrugged as she pulled off the sunglasses and tucked them back into the bag. "You never know. It's good to always be prepared." She had the strangest feeling she needed to be ready for anything this week, though she wasn't sure why.

A few minutes later Kate tagged along on her parents' heels as they walked to the hotel's beautiful dining room. Alex and her parents arrived moments later.

Kate greeted her friend with squeals and laughter.

"Look at you!" she said. "You look so great!"

"So do you," Alex responded. "I like your new glasses. They're really cute."

"Thanks." Kate shrugged. She didn't really mind wearing glasses. They made her feel smart, in fact.

"This was such a great idea, Kate," Alex said. "This part of the country is beautiful. My mom loves it already."

"It's true," Mrs. Howell said, smiling at Kate. "We've been needing to get away for a while, and spring break was the perfect opportunity. And what woman doesn't like chocolate?" She laughed aloud and everyone joined her.

"I only have one complaint," Mr. Howell said. "It's been hot and muggy for spring."

"Yes, does it always rain like this?" Mrs. Howell asked. "I do hope the weather clears up."

Kate's mother shook her head. "We've had a lot of rain lately and you're right. . .it's exceptionally warm for spring. I wish we could have offered you better weather."

"Well, we can't blame anyone for the rain," Alex's mother said, then laughed. "At least it's not snow. And besides, we'll be indoors at the exhibition hall much of the time. I can't wait to see what Kate and the other young inventors have come up with. I'm sure it will be wonderful."

When the waitress came to take their order, Kate chose a hamburger with extra bacon, along with an order of fries and a soda.

As they ate and everyone chatted, Kate was so excited she could hardly sit still long enough to eat. She wanted to get to the exhibition hall right away to show the others her invention. And she could hardly wait to show Alex the pretzel factory!

Lunchtime seemed to fly by, and before she could count to ten, Kate found herself in the exhibition hall, checking in. Above them hung a large sign: THE YOUNG INVENTORS' FESTIVAL, SPONSORED BY THE MILTON HERSHEY SCHOOL.

"Oh, I read all about that school online," she said. "They do great things for kids in need."

"Wonderful!" Alex said. "That makes it even better!"

Kate picked up a packet with her name on it, smiling as she pulled out the badge.

"You're official!" her mother said, helping her clip the badge into place. "You're a true young inventor."

Kate beamed and felt a sense of joy wash over her. "I know it's true what the Bible says, Mom. God really does give us the desires of our heart. I've always wanted to invent things. . .like dad does."

"Speaking of inventions. . ." Alex's face lit up. "When are you going to show me this invention of yours, the one that's going to win the whole thing? I brought my video camera so I could get some footage for my column." She held up the tiny video camera and grinned.

"We don't know that it's going to win anything," Kate whispered. "But I did have a dream that I won the grand prize!" She told Alex about her dream and how she woke up in class afterwards.

"I think it would be totally awesome if you won," Alex said.

Kate shrugged, thinking about the verse she'd just read on her text reader. She didn't really consider herself better than others, so what did it matter if she won the big prize or not?

"Where's your invention?" Alex asked.

"Oh, it's already on display," Kate said. "Come with me." They walked down the long aisle of other inventions.

"Ooh, what's that?" Alex asked, pointing at a lamp made out of old car parts.

"I think it's a living room lamp," Kate said with a giggle. "Pretty clever, right?"

"No kidding. Everything here is clever. And to think kids invented all of these things. Pretty impressive."

Kate smiled. "I'm sure a few of them had a little help from their parents."

"Did you?"

Kate shrugged. "Well, you know my dad is a robotics professor, so I've learned a lot from him over the years. But I can honestly say that this invention is completely mine. He didn't help with it." She led the way to the booth where the Turbo Heat-Freeze was on display and pointed at it. "This is it."

"Wow." Alex gave her a funny look. "It kind of looks like an Easy Bake Oven."

Kate laughed. "There's a reason for that. It started out as one. But not anymore!" She drew near. "I call this my Turbo Heat-Freeze."

"Heat-Freeze?" Alex looked confused. "I don't get it."

"It's an oven and a freezer in one," Kate explained. "The left side heats and the right side cools."

Alex leaned down and looked closer. "No way. Show me how it works, Kate."

"Okay." She placed several bite-size pieces of a soft pretzel in the tiny easy-bake pan then laid a piece of chocolate bark on top. "Watch this." She put the pan in the little oven and began to count. "One, two, three, four, five. . ."

Alex joined her. "Six, seven, eight, nine, ten."

Kate reached in to grab the pan from the other side and Alex gasped. "Kate, use a pot-holder. You're going to burn your hand!"

"No I'm not." She shook her head. Kate held up the little pan, showing her friend the little pretzel bites, which were each coated in just the right amount of chocolate. "It's not hot at all, and the chocolate is perfectly hardened." She passed the cold pan to Alex.

"Wow!"

"Have a taste," Kate said.

Alex shook her head. "I really shouldn't. You know I try to eat healthy."

"Just one little bite," Kate suggested.

"Okay." Alex reached down and took a bite of one of the pretzels, then looked up, her eyes wide. "Oh Kate! This is fantabulous. Seriously, it's the perfect blend of salty and sweet. And I love the fact that you've used soft pretzel bites. This is so much yummier than those chocolate-covered pretzels you can buy at the grocery store."

"I know." Kate laughed. "My dad said the same thing. But my mom says the peppermint version is best."

"Peppermint?" Alex looked at her with a wrinkled brow.

"Yep. Watch this." Kate reached for another pan, adding several pretzel bites. Then she lifted up something that looked like a white chocolate bar with bits of red running through it. "This is peppermint bark."

"Mmm. Sounds yummy."

"It is. It's white chocolate with crushed peppermint candies." Kate laid it on top of the pretzel bites, then put it in the oven and counted to ten. She pulled it out, completely cooled, and handed one of the delights to her friend.

Alex's eyes widened as she bit into the tasty concoction. "Oh Kate! This tastes like Christmas!"

"I know." Kate giggled. "My mom served them to our guests last December. And this is just the tip of the iceberg. I've also used dark chocolate, caramel, and all sorts of other things to coat the pretzels. But my absolute favorite is melted jellybeans because they come in so many flavors. The possibilities are endless."

"Your invention works the same with the jelly beans?" Alex asked. "No way!"

"Yes, it's always the same," Kate explained. "The machine rapidly melts the candy, then hardens it just as quickly. And the really cool part is, you can use specialized pans to solidify the candy-covered pretzels in whatever shape you want. Look at this." She held up a tiny pan her father had designed with several star shapes.

"Are you serious?" Alex did not look convinced. "The candies are going to come out shaped like stars?"

"Sure." Kate put one pretzel bite in each star-shaped hole then reached for the bag of jellybeans. "What's your favorite flavor?" she asked.

"Mmm. I like watermelon best," Alex said. "But I can't imagine a watermelon jellybean with a soft pretzel bite inside."

"You never know until you try it." Kate added three watermelon-flavored jellybeans on top of one of the pretzel bites. "I like strawberry, myself." She added a couple of strawberry flavored jellybeans on top of another pretzel bite.

"Let's go crazy with the rest," Alex said. "Try all sorts of different flavors."

Kate nodded as she added jellybeans to the rest of the star-shaped holes. "Okay, are you ready to watch the magic?"

Alex nodded.

Kate put the tray in the oven and counted to ten. Then, just as the little bell went off, she pulled it out of the other side. True to her word, the jellybeans had melted, and then re-hardened around the pretzel bites, creating colorful star shapes.

"This is a non-stick pan, so they pop right out," Kate said. She turned it upside down and sure enough, a dozen brightly colored candies easily fell out. She nibbled the strawberry one, savoring the sticky goodness and the chewy, salty pretzel inside. "Mmm."

"Mmm is right!" Alex said, chomping down on the watermelon one. "I'm going to have the cinnamon," she said, grabbing a red one.

"Hey, I thought you said you were eating healthy?" Kate said.

"Oh, yeah." Alex shrugged and then laughed. "I'll have a salad for lunch to make up for it."

A few minutes later, the girls were a giggly mess, their fingers covered in drippy, sticky sweetness. Alex wiped off her hands and reached for her video camera.

"I can't believe I almost forgot to tape this!" she said. She videotaped several minutes of Kate demonstrating her Turbo Heat-Freeze then finally clicked the camera off. "Okay, enough taping! Back to eating. I need to try the sour apple next."

"Apples are fruit, right?" Kate asked, and then giggled. "That means they're healthy."

Alex laughed. "I don't think apple candy is the same thing as a real apple, Kate, but good try!"

She put the camera down and reached inside the bag of jellybeans, still grinning.

"Speaking of sour apples. . ." Kate nudged her and pointed to Phillip, who entered the booth next to them with his parents.

"Who is that?" Alex asked. She raised her eyebrows. "Do you have a crush on him or something?"

"No way. That's Phillip. He doesn't like me. . .at all!"

He turned her way, his smile fading the moment he laid eyes on her invention.

As he passed by he whispered, "Just wait, Kate Oliver. You might have won the science fair, but I'm going to be the big winner at this competition. I'm going to come out on top. . .no matter what it takes."

A little shiver ran down Kate's spine as she thought about his words. Why did he have to be at war? Couldn't they just be friends? Why did he always have to prove that he was better than she was?

Thankfully, her mother's voice interrupted her thoughts.

"We've decided to take a trip to Amish country when you're done here," her mom said. "It's time to stop at that pretzel factory you love so much!"

"Yes!" Kate's heart soared with anticipation. Finally! She would get to take Alex to meet two of her favorite people in the world—the two ladies who owned the Twisted Twins pretzel factory. And while she and Alex were there, they could buy a couple of yummy pretzels. Kate's mouth watered just thinking about them.

"Go ahead and set up your table properly," her mother said, looking at the mess they'd made. "Then you girls can spend a few minutes looking at the other inventions." She leaned close and whispered, "There's more here than candy, you know."

Kate giggled. As much as she wanted to see the ladies who ran the pretzel factory, it was far more important to stay focused right now. She needed to remember why she'd come to Hershey, after all.

As if Phillip would let her forget. As she glanced his way, he mouthed the words, *"I'm going to win!"* and gave her a creepy look. Kate sighed and stared at the Turbo Heat-Freeze. It was a great invention, but would the judges think so? Only time would tell. In the meantime, she had some pretzels to eat!

CHAPTER 3

Tasty News

Kate and Alex straightened the table, then walked through the hall, checking out the other inventions. She couldn't remember ever seeing so many unusual and inventive things under one roof. A lot of super-intelligent students were part of the exhibition, and their inventions were so clever! How her little Turbo Heat-Freeze could compare, she wasn't sure. Still, she was happy to be considered for the prize. What an honor!

She saw people from every state in the United States. Maggie from Texas had something called a ball hopper, which picked up tennis balls from the court. Lilliana from Hawaii had a battery-powered lei, which lit up and played Hawaiian music. Kate was especially interested in the tri-fold movie camera a girl from California had invented. How very cool. . . and how unique!

Yes, unique was truly the word. Kate was having far too much fun just seeing how talented all of the kids were. It was great to be one of the group.

"Thank You, Lord, for letting me come here," she whispered. "This is the coolest thing ever!"

A man wearing a shirt with the Hershey's logo on it stopped by. A smile lit his face when he saw the name on her badge.

"Kate Oliver! I'm happy to meet you at last!"

Kate looked up. The man standing next to her had eyes the color of the sky and soft, wrinkly skin. She especially liked his white mustache and beard. He looked a little like Santa Claus was imagined to look, now that she thought about it. She stared at him a bit longer, realizing he looked just like the man in her dream—the one who had handed her the trophy!

"My name is Kris Carmichael," he said, extending his hand. "I am the Program Director for Hershey. I'm also the director of the Young Inventors' Festival, and we're so happy to have you here representing your school."

"Oh, thank you, sir," she said, trying to hide her embarrassment. "I'm so excited!" She shook his hand, noticing how tiny her hand felt in his. In fact, everything about her felt small next to this large man with the booming voice and bright smile.

"What have we here?" Mr. Carmichael asked, looking at Kate's invention.

She quickly explained the Turbo Heat-Freeze, and he looked very interested.

"This sounds a little like the process we use at the Hershey factory, but appears to work on a much faster scale. Very interesting. Based on first impressions, I would have to say that the Turbo Heat-Freeze will revolutionize the candy-making industry because it cuts down on the heating and cooling time. And it softens the candy without fully melting it, which is quite clever. I'm not sure I've ever seen anything with these capabilities, to be honest."

Kate felt her cheeks heat up with embarrassment. "Thank you, Mr. Carmichael."

"My pleasure. I never mind talking about young geniuses."

"Oooh, she is a genius, isn't she?" Alex said with a smile. "The Camp Club Girls are so proud of her."

"Camp Club Girls?" Mr. Carmichael gave her an odd look. "Who are they?"

"Oh, we're a group of girls who met at camp," Kate explained. "Alex, Elizabeth, Bailey, Sydney, McKenzie, and me. We solve mysteries together."

"Mysteries, eh?" He gave her a curious look. "Found anything mysterious here at Hershey?"

"Not yet, sir," she said and then leaned in to whisper, "but I'm sure we will. Mysteries seem to follow us wherever we go."

He had a good laugh at that one. "Well I wish you the best—with your invention and your mystery solving. And when you see those other Camp Club Girls next time, tell them to eat more chocolate."

"Oh, that's not possible, sir," Alex said, rubbing her stomach. "We already eat more chocolate than most kids."

"Especially me," Kate said and then laughed.

He grinned. "That's what we like to hear. As long as people go on loving chocolate, Hershey will go on making it."

"Then you can count on making it forever," Kate said, "because I'm sure I'll love it that long. Maybe longer."

"Do you think there'll be chocolate in heaven?" Alex asked, reaching for her video camera. "And before you answer, would you mind if I videotaped what you're about to say?"

"I suppose that would be all right." Mr. Carmichael cleared his throat and adjusted his shirt collar. "How do I look?"

"Fine, sir," Kate said.

Alex spoke loudly as the video camera ran. "I'm here at the famous Hershey's chocolate factory with Mr. Carmichael, who is heading up the Young Inventors' Festival. I've just asked him if he believes there will be chocolate in heaven." She drew nearer to him and said, "Please tell our viewers what you think, Mr. Carmichael."

"Well. . ." His cheeks turned red, and he looked a little embarrassed. "I hope so," he said at last. "I would imagine there's a chocolate river in heaven with a beautiful waterfall that never stops flowing. Wouldn't you?"

"Yum!" Kate licked her lips, envisioning it. Surely if God could make streets of gold, He could make a river of chocolate, right? And in heaven, they wouldn't even need the Turbo Heat-Freeze. Surely everything there would be far better than anything she could invent, anyway!

"Thank you for that exciting answer," Alex said, and then turned off the camera. She grinned at Mr. Carmichael.

"Well, speaking of chocolate," he said, turning to Kate, "I do hope you can join the other competitors at the amusement park on the last day of the competition, after the winner is announced."

"We plan to, if the weather is good," Kate responded. "It's done nothing but rain since we got here."

"Yes, and it's exceptionally hot for this time of year," he added. "Very odd."

"Speaking of the amusement park, that reminds me. I forgot to say thank you for the tickets," Kate said. "It was so nice of the festival people to provide tickets for everyone in my family."

"Our pleasure." The wrinkles around his eyes grew more pronounced as he smiled. "We know that young inventors love adventure, and Hershey's amusement park is loaded with adventure."

She nodded. "I can't wait to find out for myself!"

"Well, you're a talented young inventor, Kate Oliver." He gave her another encouraging smile. "Perhaps you'll work for us some day!"

He turned to walk away, but then looked back, giving the Turbo Heat-Freeze one last admiring glance.

"I think he's interested in it, Kate," Alex whispered. "And who knows? Maybe the people at Hershey *will* hire you one day. You could end up working here when you're grown up."

"I would love that. It would give me the opportunity to invent more things!" She gave her table one last glance then took a few steps through the crowd of people. "Can you imagine how much chocolate I could eat if I worked here?" They both laughed. "But seriously, I've already been exploring the idea of making a candy that the Hershey's people would love using those tiny square pretzels. You know the ones I'm talking about, right? They're crunchy, not soft."

"Waffle pretzels?" Alex asked, her nose slightly wrinkled. "They're sold in a bag at the store?" She continued to walk beside Kate, though it was difficult to stay together in the crowd.

"Yes. That's right." Kate said. "I got the idea after eating a candy my aunt made last Christmas. You take one of those little waffle pretzels and put a Hershey's Kiss on top then you put it on a cookie sheet and place it in the oven. You can use a Hershey's Hug, if you like white and dark chocolate mixed together. Anyway, you leave it in there for about four or five minutes until it softens. Then you pull it out of the oven before it melts and let it cool to re-harden. But first you press a Reese's Pieces candy on top."

She started walking again, suddenly feeling hungry.

"Mmm. Chocolate *and* peanut butter," Alex said, then licked her lips. "Sounds divine. Like a Reese's Peanut Butter Cup, only with a pretzel bottom."

"Right." Kate nodded as she continued to walk. "My aunt even made a few of those pretzel candies using Hershey's Kisses with caramel centers. I remember they were really yummy and gooey."

"Oh wow. I never thought of that!" Alex's eyes grew wide and she grinned. "Sounds amazing!"

"Yes, the possibilities are endless because I can make them in ten seconds in the Turbo Heat-Freeze. No need for a regular oven anymore." Kate grew more and more animated as excitement kicked in. "And it's really cool because Hugs and Kisses come in so many different flavors now."

"I wonder why the people at Hershey don't mass-produce that pretzel kiss recipe," Alex said. "Surely they have to know about it."

Kate stopped walking and turned to face her. "With my invention, they *could.*"

"Oooh, Kate!" Alex looked at her and nodded. "I see what you mean. You want to show them how quickly it could be done in your Turbo Heat-Freeze machine? Then maybe they'll be even more interested?"

"Exactly!" Kate nodded. "Maybe I'll get the chance before the competition ends. And who knows. . ." she leaned in to whisper, "maybe you're right. Maybe I will work here someday!"

Her mind reeled with possibilities as they continued walking. In fact, she found herself so distracted that she almost ran into a girl about her age. Kate tried not to stare at the girl's navy blue dress and stiff white cap.

"Look at that girl," Alex whispered, giving Kate a nudge with her elbow. "She must be Amish. Look at what she's wearing."

"Mm-hmm." Kate nodded. "I think it's interesting that several competitors are from the Amish community. They don't use electricity, but they're still inventive."

"I guess you would have to be if you didn't have electricity," Alex said, and then laughed. "Can you imagine living without it?"

"No, but I guess it would be like camping."

"Not exactly," Kate's father said, drawing near with her mother. "The Amish have created their own sort of technology. Nothing rustic about it."

He went on to talk about what life was like in Amish households and how beautiful the Amish farmlands were, but Kate wasn't really paying attention. She was too busy looking at Phillip, who passed with a bag in his hand. She smiled warmly, hoping he would return it with a smile of his own. Instead, his eyes narrowed and he turned to look the other way.

"Everything okay?" Alex asked, giving her a nudge.

"Hmm? Oh, yeah. Sure." Kate shrugged. She wasn't going to let a competitive boy ruin a perfectly good day. Not when so many exciting things lay ahead!

"Kate, are you nearly ready to go?" Her mother's voice rang out. "We need to head out to the pretzel factory now."

"Yes! Just let me take care of a couple of more things at my table." She began to work at tidying up as well as she could and making sure she had all of the supplies she would need for the next day's preliminary round of judging.

With newfound excitement, Kate headed off to a pretzel wonderland!

All Twisted

Kate and Alex shared a quick lunch with their parents then climbed into the Oliver's van for the drive to Amish country. Kate's mom and dad sat near the front, chatting with Alex's parents. Dexter sat in back with the girls. Kate and Alex spent the time laughing and talking about the adventures they'd had since meeting at camp. Dexter got bored with their conversation and started playing a video game.

A couple of times Kate glanced out the window of the van, noticing the scenery. Amish country was very beautiful.

It seemed like no time at all before they arrived at familiar building with the words TWISTED TWINS on front.

"So this is what a pretzel factory looks like," Alex said, her eyes growing large. "I pictured it to be really big for some reason."

"Well, this is a family-run place," Kate's mother explained. "So it's not very large. If you want to see a really big factory, you will find one in the next town over called the Bender Bakery. It's quite famous. Maybe we can go there too."

"The Bender factory is great," Kate said, wrinkling her nose. "But I like this one best. Two sisters run it. They're a lot of fun. I can't wait to introduce you."

"Are they Amish?" Alex asked, reaching for her video camera.

"No." Kate's mom shook her head. "But they do a lot of business with the Amish community, and they are respected because they still hand-twist their pretzels. And the pretzels are the family's original recipe, I understand."

"Besides, the sisters are so much fun to be around," Kate added. "I met them the last time I was here, and we've been emailing back and forth ever since I invented the Turbo Heat-Freeze. They're interested in it."

"Wow, Kate." Alex gave her an admiring look. "That's really cool." She paused for a moment. "But why is the factory called Twisted Twins?"

"Twisted. . .like pretzels. Get it?" Kate giggled.

"Oh, okay." Alex grinned. "Got it. But what about the twins part? Are they twin sisters?"

Kate nodded. "Yep. And guess what? They don't just look alike. . .they dress alike too. And wait till you see what they wear!"

"Wow." Alex grinned. "Can't wait."

"And this is really cool," Kate added. "They want to test-market my Turbo Heat-Freeze while I'm here. In fact, they promised to come by my booth at the Young Inventors' Festival to look at it. They even said they might hire me to work for them someday."

"Wow," Alex whispered. "Think about it, Kate. You're not even a teenager yet and already two different companies want you to work for them—Hershey, and now the Twisted Twins pretzel factory!"

Kate giggled. "They both sound like fun. I would have a hard time choosing."

"Not me." Alex laughed. "What can compare with chocolate, after all?"

"True." Kate responded with a little giggle. "At least you had salad for lunch! I had the chocolate-covered chicken!" Kate began to list all of the different chocolate-covered items she'd seen on the menu, and Alex just laughed.

They entered the building and Kate smiled as she saw both of the sisters working behind the counter. Each had pulled her bleach-blond hair into a hair net. They wore bright pink uniforms with the Twisted Twins logo on the front pocket and an embroidered pretzel below. Their earrings looked like silver pretzels and so did their necklaces. In fact, their charm bracelets were filled with little pretzels too.

Kate smiled as soon as she saw them, then glanced Alex's way and whispered, "See! I told you!"

"They're *definitely* twins," Alex said. "And they do look just alike! But do they always wear pink?"

"Yes. And just wait till you see the inside of the factory!" Kate's mom explained. "Everything is pink, even some of the machines. And everything has the Twisted Twins logo on it."

"Wow," Alex's mom laughed. "Very girly."

Kate giggled. What fun! And to think the sisters were older than her parents and still liked bright pink!

Kate's mother made the introductions. "This is Penny," she said, pointing to the first sister. "And this is Candy." She turned to the other one.

"Get it?" The first sister asked, the soft wrinkles around her eyes showing even more when she smiled. When Alex shrugged she said, "Penny candy."

"Penny candy?" Alex looked confused.

"Back when we were little girls, you could buy candy for a penny," the second sister explained, her rosy cheeks growing even rosier as she got excited. "And our mom loved sweets. So when she found out she was having twins, she decided to name us Penny and Candy."

"Ooo." Alex nodded. "I see. Very clever."

"Yes, we come from a long line of clever people. Our family is. . ." Penny's smile quickly vanished. Just as quickly, it returned. "Well, never mind all that. Now, what can we do for you today? We've got some of our large cinnamon-sugar pretzels, still warm from the oven. They're soft and chewy. . .and you never tasted anything so sweet."

"Yum!" Kate's mouth began to water.

"Cinnamon-sugar pretzels are my favorite!" Dexter said. "Next to the cheesy ones, I mean. And the pepperoni ones. And the chocolate chip ones."

He went on an an, listing all of his favorites, which amused everyone. Before long both families were laughing and talking about the flavors of the pretzels.

"We'll buy some after the tour," their mother explained. "Right now we'd like to show our friends your factory."

"You're just in time," Candy said. "The three o'clock tour begins in ten minutes. I'm leading it, so you'll get the best tour guide of all!"

Penny groaned, but didn't say anything. Kate laughed. She loved these two sisters. They were so much fun!

"Oh, just wait till you see how awesome the pretzel factory is, Alex," she said. "Then you'll know why I'm so excited."

"I'm crazy about all kinds of pretzels," Alex said with a nod. "The crunchy kind from bags and the soft, chewy kind you buy at ball games."

"The Twisted Twins make both kinds," Kate explained. "And they're so yummy!" She leaned over to whisper in Alex's ear. "And here's a little secret. . .at the end of the tour, they always give away samples in different flavors. I love the cinnamon sugar ones, but the garlic and butter ones are great too."

"Kate, stop! You're tempting me!" Alex giggled.

Dexter pouted and muttered something about not wanting to wait for a pretzel, but Penny's voice rang out, interrupting him.

"It's almost time for the tour," she said, clasping her hands together. "But before we do that, I want to tell Kate something," Penny looked her way. "Candy and I have decided we want to sponsor you in the Young Inventors' Festival. What do you think of that idea? Brilliant, right?"

"Sponsor me?" Kate repeated, not quite believing it. "Really?"

"What does that mean?" Alex asked.

"It means we cover any fees to enter the competition, and we put our company's logo on your booth and encourage our customers to visit you," Penny explained. "It's really good for our business. . .and for Kate—especially if she wins."

"You *are* going to win, aren't you?" Candy asked, her brow wrinkling more than ever.

Kate laughed. "Well, I can't be sure, of course, but my invention is getting great reviews. And one of the officials from Hershey liked it a lot. He stopped at my booth this morning and told me so in person."

"I think he's going to hire her someday," Alex said.

"Humph. We'll see about that." Candy folded her arms and narrowed her eyes. "We might have to fight him for you!"

Kate giggled.

Penny clapped her hands. "But don't you see, sister! Our instincts were right. We have a winner here. And who knows. . .one day maybe Kate *will* work for us. We need a whipper-snapper to tell us what the young people like to eat. She can help us come up with more pretzel ideas."

"What do you think, Kate?" Candy asked.

"Sounds great." She smiled. "But promise you won't be too disappointed if I don't win. I hope it doesn't hurt your business or anything."

"No. It couldn't possibly hurt our business," Penny said. "Why, we're the best in the county."

"Yes, we might not be the biggest, but we *are* the best," Candy added, looking more confident than ever.

"Some people say that bigger is better," Dexter commented.

Penny shook her head.

"Just because a company is huge doesn't mean it's the best," she said. "Quality has nothing to do with size. I wish all of the pretzel eaters of the world would understand that."

"They will soon enough, sister," Candy said, patting her hand. "We'll show them."

"Kate's mom told me about another pretzel factory in the next town," Alex said. "A really big one. With a funny name."

At once, Candy's smile vanished. "Do you mean the Bender factory?"

"Um, yes." Alex looked nervous. "Why? Do you know them?"

Penny nodded. "I supposed you could say we know them. Very well, in fact." She opened her mouth and started to say something but then stopped.

Kate could tell from the look on Candy's face that something was wrong, but didn't ask what. Thankfully, Alex didn't ask any more questions.

Just then a bell rang and Penny reached for a microphone. "Ladies and gentlemen, the tour is about to begin. Please line up behind Candy, your tour guide."

Dexter rushed to be at the front of the line and motioned for the girls to join him. Kate and Alex stood directly behind him. Before long, more than twenty people were ready to take the tour.

"Follow me, please," Candy said. "Our facility isn't very big, so the tour won't take long, but I will stop along the way and explain the pretzel-making process. You may take photos and videos, but please don't give away any of our Twisted Twins secrets."

Alex turned on her video camera and held it up as they walked together.

Candy led them down a long hallway where the main offices were housed. Then came the exciting part. They walked into the factory, and Kate looked down on a production room, filled with large ovens and conveyor belts.

"Wow, I thought you guys said the company was small," Alex said, looking through the glass to the workroom below. She turned the video camera to capture the action.

"Well, small in comparison to their competitors, maybe," Kate's mother said. "But still a nice-sized company, don't you think?"

"Definitely." Alex nodded. "I'm impressed."

"Me too," her mother said. "And look at those pink machines! They're so colorful and bright."

Candy began to explain the process of pretzel making and Kate and Alex stood together, watching through the glass. Kate gazed at the large machines below and watched an older man with white hair twist each pretzel and put it on the conveyor belt.

"We still hand twist our pretzels here at Twisted Twins," Candy explained. "Unlike other larger factories." She cleared her throat. "We still believe in the hands-on approach. If we want the pretzels to look just right, we have to work hard to make it so."

"Wow, the man twisting the pretzels is really fast!" Dexter began to move his hands, imitating the man, but couldn't keep up.

Candy laughed. "That's Mr. Whipple. He's been working for us for more than twenty years. He's the best pretzel-twister in the county."

She muttered something under her breath about how the Bender factory didn't have anyone to compare, but Kate wasn't paying much attention. Instead, she was focusing on Mr. Whipple, who seemed to move at the speed of lightning.

Unfortunately, the elderly man seemed to grow weary after just a few minutes. He stopped to yawn. . .and then stretch. Kate couldn't help but wonder how he kept going under such circumstances. Must be hard to stand there all day and twist, twist, twist!

As they continued to watch, the machine halted. All of the workers looked around with alarm, especially Mr. Whipple.

"Something's gone wrong down there," Candy said, pointing to the large machine. "They never stop production unless there's a problem. That's only happened a couple of times since the factory opened twenty-five years ago."

Kate and the others continued to watch as several workers ran over to the machine. Mr. Whipple worked on the machine a few minutes and finally got it going again. He stood near the conveyor belt as pretzels came through and reached to pick one up, examining it closely.

"Something must be wrong with the pretzels," Kate said. "They're stopping the machine again."

"I wonder what it is," Alex said, reaching for her video camera again.

Just then Candy received a call on her cell phone. Kate overheard some of the conversation. "Yes, I'll end the tour now."

Candy hung up the phone and looked at the group and sighed. "I, um, have to stop the tour. The problem is bigger than we thought."

"What's wrong?" Alex asked.

The wrinkles around Candy's eyes grew deeper. "The pretzels are going flat."

"Going flat?" Kate looked back down through the glass. From here, it was hard to tell what the pretzels looked like.

"Yes." Candy looked more concerned than ever. "Pretzels are supposed to rise before baking and for whatever reason, they're not rising. They're as flat as pancakes."

"Strange," Kate said as Candy led the group back to the front of the factory. "Soft pretzels are supposed to be warm and puffy. What good would they be if they didn't puff?"

"Exactly." Alex shrugged. "Very odd."

Candy looked more concerned than ever. "I'll lead the tour group back to the store at the front of the factory, then I'll go down to the factory floor to check on the machine. Sorry for the interruption, folks."

"No problem," Kate's mother said. "We're just sorry for your troubles."

They followed Candy to the store in front of the factory. Kate watched Candy race to Penny's side and whisper something in her ear. Penny picked up the telephone and made a call. Seconds later, she hung up and shrugged. "Bud. . .er, Mr. Whipple, says the pretzels aren't rising. Very odd. Very odd, indeed."

At once Kate grew suspicious. She turned to Alex and whispered, "It sounds like sabotage!"

Alex nodded, her eyes wide with excitement.

"But who would want to sabotage a pretzel factory?" she asked. "It doesn't make sense."

Kate pulled her to the side. "The obvious choice would be a competitor. You saw the look on Candy's face when you mentioned the other pretzel factory. . .that Bender place. I knew right away that something was wrong, didn't you?"

"Yes." Alex nodded. "But I never thought about sabotage."

"Good thing I brought my gadgets and gizmos," Kate whispered. "Looks like we'll need them if there's a mystery to solve, especially if we have to go to the other factory to get some answers."

"Right." Alex shrugged. "But I wonder if we're off track, Kate."

"What do you mean?"

"Maybe it's not a competitor at all. Maybe someone has a grudge against the owner. Someone is mad about something."

"Good point." Kate nodded. "Maybe it's an unhappy customer. Maybe the pretzels made someone sick."

"Oh wow. We'll have to let the Camp Club Girls do some research."

Off in the distance, something distracted her. Mr. Whipple walked through the room. His shoulders slumped forward and his thin white hair stood up all over his head. As soon as he saw Penny and Candy, he ducked his head and looked at the floor. He passed with his shoulders slumped forward.

"He looks exhausted," Alex whispered.

"Do you blame him?" Kate whispered back. "The poor guy twists pretzels around the clock. I never saw anyone work so fast."

"Still, I think he's acting strange," Alex said. "Did you notice he wouldn't look Penny or Candy in the eye? That's usually a sign of guilt."

"Maybe, but what's he guilty of?" Kate didn't want to accuse the exhausted old man of anything when they had no proof. Just because he was acting odd around his bosses didn't mean he was trying to sabotage the factory.

On the other hand. . .

Kate watched as he turned to look at Penny strangely then shuffled back to the hallway, his gaze on the floor.

Kate snapped back to attention when she heard her brother's voice. "Are we going to stand here all day talking about broken machines, or are we going to eat pretzels?"

Dexter pointed at rows and rows of pretzels behind the glass case, his eyes wide as saucers.

"Thank goodness these pretzels were already baked before the machine broke down!" Kate drooled as she stared at the assortment of pretzels.

Alex drew near, pointing at a tray of yummy-looking pretzels. "Look Kate. Garlic flavored."

"Yes." Kate nodded. "And look at this one: Pepperoni Pizzazz!" On and on they went, discussing the different flavors. "Yum! There's Sour Cream 'n Onion, Sugar & Spice, and even Blazin' Raizin."

"Our top seller is still the Salty Pretzel," Penny explained. "But we're trying some new things too, especially with our soft mini pretzels."

"Oh?" Kate looked at her, more curious than ever. "Like what?"

"Well, let's see. . ." Candy's eyes sparkled with excitement. "We've got birthday cake flavored ones, as well as cinnamon roll."

"Cinnamon roll. . .yum!" Dexter licked his lips.

"Yes." Candy nodded. "I agree. It's one of my favorites. I also love our spinach-flavored pretzel bites."

Dexter made a face.

"But my all-time favorite is the grilled cheese," Candy said. "There's just something about that melted cheese on the inside that gets me every time." She grinned and for a moment looked much younger than her sixty-something years.

"Grilled cheese sounds fantabulous," Kate agreed, her stomach rumbling at the very idea.

"Oh, if you think that's good, you should try our cookies and cream pretzel bites," Candy said. "And the toffee crunch is great too."

"Oh wow," Kate said with a nod. "I'll have to try some of these in my Turbo Heat-Freeze. I never thought of toffee crunch before."

"It's great," Candy said. "And you just haven't lived till you've had one of our pretzel dogs."

"How will we ever decide what to order right now?" Alex asked, gazing through the glass case at all of the pretzels inside.

"We'll just have to try several different kinds!" Kate's mom said. "Are you kids okay with that?"

"Are we ever!" Dexter practically shouted.

Kate's mom ordered several pretzels for the group, and before long all of the girls' questions about the faulty machinery were behind them. As they nibbled on warm sweet pretzels, Kate had only one thing on her mind—asking for more.

Before long, as they climbed back in the family's large van, Kate began to again ponder the mystery of the flat pretzels.

"If we're going to figure this out, we'll need the Camp Club Girls to help us," she whispered to Alex. "That means I have to send them an email."

She reached for her wristwatch. "I can send an email on my smart-watch," she said. "And if any of the girls are near their computers, we can do an internet chat right away."

"I think it's so cool that you can get on the internet on your watch," Alex said, giving her an admiring look.

"Yes, it's great for sending short messages," Kate said with a nod.

"One of my robotics students invented it," Kate's father added. "Hopefully it will be on the market soon and everyone can own one!"

"Very cool." Alex nodded.

Kate quickly sent a note to the Camp Club Girls and within minutes all of them had responded.

"Okay, we're good to go," Kate said. "They can meet us in five minutes in the chat room." She glanced up to the front of the car. "Dad, is it okay if we use your new laptop?"

"Sure." He nodded. "It's right there in the backseat."

"But how can we get on the internet out here, in the middle of nowhere?" Alex asked.

"No problem," her father said. "It's got a built-in card that picks up internet signals no matter where you are. Just handle the computer carefully, please."

"I will. Thanks, Dad." Kate pulled his tiny new laptop out of its case and showed it to everyone.

"Wow. That's a laptop?" Alex's dad asked.

"Sure is."

"It's no bigger than a CD case," Alex said, reaching to hold it for a moment. "How do you type on it?"

"Easy." Kate unfolded the keyboard and it popped into place.

"Oh wow," Alex said. "That's so cool."

Kate looked out of the window of the van and again noticed the beautiful Amish farms they were passing. She watched an Amish buggy rolling down the road. Then she turned her attention to a grassy field with a dozen grazing dairy cows. Kate wondered what it would be like to live without electricity, internet, or phones. Could she learn to live like that if she had to?

"Hmm." Shaking her head, she decided it would definitely be a challenge!

Kate quickly signed online. Within minutes all of the Camp Club Girls met her in their chat room. *K8 here,* she typed. *Everyone else here?*

Bailey: *I'm here! Ready for adventure!*
Elizabeth: *I really want to help. How can I pray? Just tell me what I can do.*

Kate smiled as she thought of how all of the girls depended on this fourteen-year-old to remind them of the spiritual perspective of their adventures.

Sydney: *I'm here. What's up, Inspector Gadget?*

Kate grinned as she read Sydney's familiar, yet humorous, nickname for her. By now, all of the Camp Club Girls knew how much she loved using her gadgets and gizmos to help solve mysteries.

McKenzie: *Kate, can you tell us more about what's going on? Your email didn't have much information.*
Sydney: *Yes, just something about flat pretzels. Didn't make much sense to me.*
Elizabeth: *Right. How are we supposed to puff up pretzels from halfway across the country?*

Kate laughed as she realized how funny the email must have sounded.

Kate: *Yes, this is a twisted-up mystery about pretzels. Something has gone wrong at the Twisted Twins pretzel factory in Lancaster County, Pennsylvania. Suddenly their pretzels aren't puffing up like they should.*
Elizabeth: *Very odd. Are you saying someone is sabotaging the factory?*
Sydney: *That's strange, don't you think? Why would someone do that?*

Bailey: *Doesn't make any sense to me.*

Kate: *I can think of dozens of reasons. But let's start with the obvious. Someone is angry.*

McKenzie: *But. . .WHY? Angry WITH who? Someone who works there?*

Kate: *Maybe. I know I'm usually the one doing the internet research, but I'm so busy with the festival. Do me a favor and check the internet to see if anyone has ever filed a complaint against the pretzel factory. Like maybe an unhappy customer.*

"Yes, and ask them to check the Better Business Bureau's records too," Alex said. "Maybe someone has filed a complaint against the owners or something. Let's keep checking until we figure this out."

Kate typed Alex's comments into the box and waited.

Elizabeth: *I'll check on that. But maybe we're looking at this the wrong way. What if it's not sabotage at all? Then what?*

Kate: *Then we look at other possibilities. Faulty machinery or something like that.*

McKenzie: *Ooo, maybe it's an inside job. An unhappy worker. Maybe he—or she—has done something to the machinery to mess it up to get even with the owner for not paying him enough, or for making him work extra-long hours or something.*

"There was one guy there who looked really tired," Alex said, her eyes growing large. "Remember? The man who was twisting the pretzels was yawning the whole time. Mr. Whipple. He looked exhausted. Did you notice?"

"Yes." Kate nodded.

Kate: *Great. Now you've given us another possibility!"*

The girls continued to chatter and the time passed quickly. Before long, Kate's father pulled the van up to the hotel.

"We're here," he said. "You'll have to tell your friends goodbye, Kate. Don't you have to be in your booth from six to eight this evening?"

"Oh, that's right!" She looked up from the computer with a grin. "I almost forgot. The public is invited to see our inventions this evening.

The exhibition hall is supposed to be filled with people from all over the country."

"No time to solve a crime right now," Alex said with a nod. "Figuring out the pretzel problem is going to have to wait. Right now the Turbo Heat-Freeze comes first!"

Kate signed off with the words *Supersleuths Forever*! Then she giggled as she shut down the computer and pressed it back into its bag. "You're right. Only one project at a time. . .and right now the Turbo Heat-Freeze is the project that's most important."

She saw her father smiling in the rearview mirror and gave him a happy grin. He understood what it was like to be an inventor, after all. And she wanted to make him proud. So staying on track was, by far, the most important thing she could do!

A Hoppy Night

After a quick dinner, Kate and Alexis hurried to the exhibition hall. Kate spent the next couple of hours talking to people as they stopped by her booth. Most were very excited about her invention. A few looked doubtful but loved the candy-covered pretzel samples once they tasted them.

"Wow, that's amazing!" one woman said, nibbling a candy-coated pretzel from the Turbo Heat-Freeze.

"How do you do that?" a little boy in a blue shirt asked. "It's like a miracle!"

"No, I'm no miracle worker, trust me. But it is a lot of fun." Kate grinned as she explained the process.

Off in the distance, she watched out of the corner of her eye as Phillip stood at his booth talking to people about his Weather-Cast Watch. Every now and again she would look his way and smile, but he only glared back. Kate wondered if they would ever get along, or if this friction between the two of them would go on forever. She hoped it would end soon. In the meantime, staying busy was a nice distraction. And besides, she loved talking to people. Kate had the time of her life chatting about her inventions.

I wonder if this is how Dad feels whenever he invents something? She smiled, thinking about how much like her father she had become. Maybe one day she would teach robotics at Penn State too. Or work at the Twisted Twins factory. Or work for the Hershey Company. The possibilities were endless when you enjoyed creating gadgets and gizmos as much as she did!

A few minutes before eight, Kate began to have a few problems with her machine.

"Strange," she said, as the chocolate came out too soft. "That's never happened before."

"Maybe you've overused it," Alex said. "We could take a break for a while and look around at the other booths."

Kate glanced to her right, noticing several other competitors were wandering around looking at the other competitors. She shrugged. "Okay. Sounds good to me." She stretched her arms and groaned. "I'm tired, anyway. And stiff." She quickly scribbled the words BE BACK SOON on a piece of paper and left it on her table.

"We won't be gone long," she said, giving Alex a smile.

"It will be fun to walk around. There's so much to see!" Alex looked excited by that prospect. "Just let me ask my mom if it's okay first." She walked over to a nearby booth to chat with her mother, who waved at Kate.

"You girls have fun," Alex's mom said. "We'll probably run into you at one of the other booths."

"Yes, have a good time," Kate's mom added. "There's a lot to see!"

Kate wandered past Phillip's booth. He didn't look up, so she just kept walking. She wanted to stop and talk to him, to tell him how much she liked his invention. . .but didn't. Maybe next time.

A couple of booths past Phillip's, she saw something very interesting.

"What is that?" she asked Alex, pointing at an unusual invention.

"Hmm. Looks like some sort of cage with little trap doors. I've never seen anything like it."

They drew near to have a closer look. She noticed the girl in the dark blue Amish dress and white cap near it—the same girl she had seen earlier.

"Hi, I'm Emma." The girl nodded and smiled, so Kate did the same.

"I'm Kate," she said. "And this is my friend Alex."

"Thanks for stopping by my booth," Emma said. "I'm afraid my cousin is bored to tears with all of this." She pointed to another little girl in Amish dress who looked up with an impish smile.

"Hi!" The girl gave them a bright smile. "My name is Rachel. Rachel Yoder."

"Rachel Yoder." *Cool name*, Kate thought.

Rachel leaned forward and began to play with the frogs through the bars of the cage, talking to one of them.

Kate turned her attention to Emma. "Tell me about your invention," she said, pointing to the cage. "I'd love to hear about it, if you have the time."

"Oh, I have the time." Emma blushed. "But in our community, we don't like to brag about our accomplishments. *Daadi* calls it 'singing your own praises' and he frowns on that."

"*Daadi?*" Alex looked confused.

"*Daadi* is what I call my father," Emma explained.

"Oh, I get it! Like *Dad*," Alex said.

Emma and Rachel nodded and giggled. "Yes."

Kate glanced through the bars of the cage at the frogs inside. "I'm curious about your cage, that's all. Are these trap doors?"

"Yes." Emma pointed to one and began to explain how the cage worked.

Afterwards, Rachel looked at Kate and grinned.

"So, what do you think of my cousin's invention?" she asked. "Pretty clever, isn't it?"

"Very."

Emma turned to Rachel with a scolding look on her face. "Rachel! Don't brag! You know that's wrong."

Rachel hung her head, and Kate giggled.

"She's not really bragging," Kate said. "She's just happy for you, I'm sure."

"That's right." Rachel looked up with a crooked grin. "I'm happy. There's nothing wrong with being happy, after all! The Bible says we are to be joyful. You can't argue with that, Emma!"

"No, I can't." Emma smiled. "Not that I would argue with you anyway. Who could argue with someone as sweet as you?"

Before long, all of the girls were giggling. Kate and Alex started talking to them about their trip to the pretzel factory, telling them about the flattened pretzels.

"That's quite a mystery," Emma said when she finished.

"Very odd," Rachel added. "We see a lot of pretzels in Amish country, but I've never seen a flat one before."

"We've seen all sorts of unusual things since coming here," Alex said.

Kate's gaze shifted to the table as she saw something green and slimy start to hop, hop, hop across the tablecloth. "Um, Emma. . ." She pointed. "Is that frog supposed to be out of the cage?"

"Out of the cage?" Emma's face paled. "No!"

Kate glanced at the table and squealed as she saw not one, but two frogs hopping around. "Oh no!" Before long two turned into three and three turned into four. Within seconds, half a dozen slippery green frogs were hop, hop, hopping all over the table. One took a giant leap through the air and landed on the floor. Kate squealed. A second frog leaped from the table to the floor. Then a third. Before long, all of the frogs were loose, creating chaos underneath the booth.

Emma dove under the table and came out with one, which she quickly put back inside the cage. "One down, five to go!"

Rachel leaned down and grabbed another one, now giggling merrily. "Two down, four to go!"

"We each need to grab one," Alex said, racing toward one of the frogs. "Hurry up, Kate! We've got to help."

"Ugh." Kate didn't move. She didn't like frogs. Still, she couldn't stay frozen in place forever! Not with four frogs going crazy at her feet!

"Let's work together!" Emma said, racing past Kate. Just as she reached the table, the frog jumped down and began to hop toward the next table. Seconds later, he disappeared underneath it.

"Oh no! Now what are we supposed to do?" Kate asked.

Rachel giggled as she came up with one of the frogs in her hand. "Never fear. I've been through this before, actually. Frogs are slippery little creatures, but they can't outrun me!"

She put the frog in the cage, hollering, "Three down, three to go!" then dropped to her knees and began to crawl under the table. Seconds later, Emma joined her. She came out with another frog seconds later.

"Four down, two to go!" She put the frog in the cage then dove back under the table at a nearby booth, almost causing it to tumble.

"Watch out!" Alex shouted. "You caught the edge of the tablecloth—" She never got to say the rest because Phillip's tablecloth—the one with the larger version of the Weather-Cast Watch on it—came sliding off.

Phillip let out a yelp and reached for his invention, grabbing it just before it toppled off the edge.

"Watch what you're doing!" he yelled.

"Sorry, Phillip," Kate said. "But Emma's frogs got loose."

He shook his head and rearranged his table.

"I don't care anything about goofy frogs," he said, glaring at Kate. "I only care about winning."

"Wow." She tried not to stare, but the angry look on his face made it difficult. "Sorry."

"You're sorry all right," he muttered. "And I know what you're doing, Kate Oliver. You're trying to sabotage me."

"Sabotage you?" She could hardly think of how to respond to such a silly suggestion. How could he think such a thing?

"Two more frogs to find!" Emma's voice rang out. "C'mon, girls! We need your help."

All four girls dropped to their knees and began to crawl under the tables, one after the other. Kate did her best to put Phillip's angry words out of her mind, but found it difficult.

"I've got one!" Alex hollered, coming up with a slippery green frog in her hand. "You girls keep looking for the last one."

Kate squeezed her eyes shut, praying she wouldn't be the one to find the last frog. So far she hadn't had to touch one. Hopefully it would stay that way.

"Do you see him yet?" Emma asked, looking around.

"He's so small!" Rachel said. "I hope we find him."

"What if he doesn't turn up?" Emma asked, suddenly looking worried. "Then what?"

"Then we're in big trouble!" Rachel said. "He's got to be here. . . somewhere!"

They continued to search. Kate decided to keep her eyes open. Something caught her attention, and she looked to her right to discover a hopping green frog.

"Get him, Kate!" Alex cried.

"I–I can't."

"Yes you can," the other girls echoed.

She reached out her hand, squeezing her eyes shut. Maybe this would be easier if she couldn't see him. Seconds later, she felt something slippery and slimy in her palm. She closed her hand tight, praying he wouldn't get away. Scooting out from under the table, she came up with the last frog.

"Quick, let's get him back in the cage," Emma said, joining her.

They all raced back to Emma's table, where Kate pressed the frog back into the cage. She sighed with relief as the cage door closed.

"Awesome!" Alex hollered. "You're the best frog catcher in the world, Kate!" A shiver ran down her spine. She'd rather be good at a thousand things, just not frog catching!

She stared at her hands, realizing they still felt slimy. "I think I'd better go wash my hands," she said. "Alex, are you coming with me?"

"Sure." Alex giggled, then waved goodbye to Emma and Rachel. "It was fun meeting you! Maybe we can catch up later."

"I would love that!" Rachel said, her smile widening.

As Kate and Alex walked toward the restroom together, they began to talk about what had just happened. Within seconds, they were both laughing. In fact, Kate laughed so hard that tears flowed out of her eyes.

"I wish you could have seen the look on your face when you grabbed that frog, Kate," Alex said, pushing open the restroom door. "It was priceless."

Kate shivered. "No thanks. I hope I never ever have to touch another frog."

"Still, you see what happened when we all worked together, right?" Alex said. "We accomplished our goal because we were all on the same team."

"Yes, teamwork is great," Kate agreed.

As she washed her hands, she thought about Alex's words. Life really was easier when you worked together on projects. Her thoughts shifted at once to Phillip and she sighed.

"Everything okay?" Alex asked, giving her a funny look in the mirror.

"I guess." She leaned against the sink and sighed again. "It's just that sometimes I get a little competitive."

"Well, you're at a competition, silly," Alex said. "Of course you want to beat others."

"Yes." Kate shrugged. "But I'm starting to wonder if being competitive is a good thing. I mean, a little bit can be good, but when you're always trying to beat someone, it's hard to get a lot done. And did you hear what Phillip said to me? He thinks I would actually sabotage him! Isn't that crazy?"

"It is crazy," Alex said. "And he obviously doesn't know you very well, or he would know better." She paused a moment. "But if you're concerned that you've become too competitive, just pray about it, Kate. God knows your heart."

"That's true." Kate smiled. "He does."

The girls made their way through the crowd until they found their parents. Kate yawned and her mother smiled.

"Tired, honey?

"Mm-hmm. Is it time to go back to the hotel? I'm wiped out."

"Yes, it's time."

A short time later they arrived at the hotel room, where Kate plopped down onto the bed, completely exhausted. "It's hard to keep my eyes open."

"You have a long day ahead of you tomorrow," her mother said. "So get some rest."

As Kate crawled into bed a few minutes later, she thought about everything that had happened that day—how she and Alex had visited the pretzel factory together. About how Mr. Whipple twisted the pretzels, one after the other. How the pretzels were flat, like pancakes, instead of fluffy and chewy.

She sat up in the bed.

"Is everything alright, Kate?" her mother asked.

"I'm just thinking about that man we saw today at the factory. . .Mr. Whipple. Something about him seemed a little suspicious."

Her mother laughed. "Kate, to you *everyone* looks suspicious."

Kate giggled as she leaned back against the pillows. "I guess you're right. Maybe I'm letting my imagination run away with me." She thought about that for a few moments, but eventually her eyes grew heavy. Kate drifted off to sleep

A Suspect!

Early the next morning, Kate's cell phone rang. She reached for it, groaning because she was still so sleepy. Who could possibly call at such an early hour? She recognized Alex's number and answered with a shaky, "H–hello?"

"Hello, Kate? It's Alex."

"You sound wide awake."

"I am." Alex giggled. "I checked my email when I got in last night and found one from McKenzie. She sent me a link to a website."

"Oh?"

"I think you're going to be very interested in this because it involves an employee from the Twisted Twins factory. Remember that man, Mr. Whipple—the pretzel twister?"

"Sure." Kate yawned and stretched, then sat up in the bed, trying to come awake.

"Remember how Penny and Candy said he'd been working for them for over twenty years? Well, he must work for the Bender brothers too."

"No way."

"Yes, I stumbled across a photo of him from some online article. It was taken about a week ago at the Bender pretzel factory in front of one of their machines. The picture was a little fuzzy, but I'm sure it's the same man."

"Can you send me a link to the article?" Kate asked, now fully awake. "I want to read it. And I'd love to see the picture."

"Of course," Alex responded. "Better yet, get dressed and come to my hotel room. I'll show you on our computer. I'm really sure it's the same man. And tell your parents that my mom and dad want to meet for breakfast at eight o'clock in the restaurant downstairs."

"Okay." Kate ended the call. She bolted from the bed and opened her suitcase, tearing through it to find an outfit to wear.

"Is everything okay, Kate?" her mom asked, then yawned. "It's pretty early."

"Yes, everything's fine. Sorry to wake you up. But Alex invited me to go to her room for a few minutes. And her parents want to meet us for breakfast at eight o'clock."

"Sounds good to me." Her mother yawned again. "Just call me on my cell phone, and we'll meet you down there."

"Okay." Kate took a fast shower, then slipped into her clothes. All the while, she thought about what Alex had said. So, Mr. Whipple worked for both companies. Either that, or he was a spy!

"Hmm." She sighed, realizing that right now he just seemed like an ordinary older man who worked two jobs.

A few minutes later, she arrived at the room Alex shared with her parents. She stood next to her friend as they looked over the website.

"I'm pretty sure that's him," Kate agreed, staring at the photo.

"Yes. And do you notice that he's shaking hands with the man in the Bender Bakery shirt?" Kate asked. "Very odd."

"Definitely. They must be friends or something."

"So, do you think Candy and Penny suspect him?" Alex asked. "I think they really trust him. Remember how Candy talked about how long he'd been at their company?"

"Yes, I'm pretty sure they think he's a faithful employee," Kate said. She sighed. "Or maybe we're just letting our imaginations run away with us. Maybe there's a logical explanation for this. . .and for what happened at the factory."

"True." Alex shrugged. She turned off the computer and stared at Kate. "But how will we know for sure?"

"There's only one way," Kate said. "We have to go back."

Alex looked shocked at this idea.

"But the first round of judging is at noon today," she said. "You don't want to miss that, Kate. You've waited a long time for this day. You don't need anything to spoil it."

"We'll get back in time." Kate looked at her watch. "I hope."

"Kate, it's too risky. It takes an hour to get there."

"We won't miss anything. I'm sure my dad will take us. He gets excited when I'm on a case. And this time we'll take Biscuit with us. He's good at snooping out the scene of a crime."

"It will be just like Scooby Doo," Alex said. "He can help us solve the crime!"

"He's great at it," Kate said.

"Of course we don't even know for sure that a crime has been committed," Alex added. "But if you're sure we'll be back in time, I guess it will be okay."

A few minutes later the two families met in the restaurant for breakfast. As they settled in at the table, Kate explained their predicament, telling her father everything they suspected.

"There's only one way to know for sure if the Twisted Twins are being sabotaged, Dad," she said. "We have to go back. . .right after breakfast."

He gave her a curious look.

"You're sure you want to leave the competition long enough to do this, Kate? This is your big day."

"Yes. We'll come back by noon. That's when they announce the finalists in the competition."

"What if you don't find out anything while you're there?" Kate's mom asked. "Then you've wasted a trip."

Kate shrugged. "I don't know. I guess we'll cross that bridge when we come to it. I only know that we have to try. I have the strangest feeling that there's more to this story than meets the eye. And we want to figure it out."

"But we also want to be back in time to watch Kate win the big prize," Alex said with a sparkle in her eye.

Kate felt her cheeks turn warm with embarrassment.

"We don't know if I'm going to win anything or not," she said. "And besides, today is only the first round of judging. They're narrowing the list. They won't name the actual winner till tomorrow's luncheon."

"True." Alex nodded. "But it's still more important to be here today for the first round of judging than at a pretzel factory, mystery or no mystery!"

Kate nodded. She didn't want to let anyone down, but she knew in her heart she needed to go back to the pretzel factory. Surely they would get back in time.

Kate talked her father into driving them back to the Twisted Twins factory, promising they would only stay for half an hour. He reluctantly agreed and before long, the three of them were on the road with Biscuit.

This time, Kate paid more attention to the Amish farms in the distance, pondering how different her life was from the children she saw playing here. She thought about Emma and Rachel and wondered if one of the houses they passed belonged to the girls' families. What were their lives like when they weren't at Hershey for a competition?

Kate didn't have much time to think about all of this. Before long, they arrived at the pretzel factory.

"Where would you like to go first?" her father asked.

In the distance, Kate saw Mr. Whipple walking toward the back of the building in the drizzling rain. He was carrying something small.

"Dad, if you don't mind, I'm going to follow him and see what he's up to."

She grabbed her digital camera and reached for Biscuit's leash. "Come, boy."

"Do you need his special digital collar?" her father asked.

"Yes, please." She reached into her backpack and came out with the special collar and snapped it on Biscuit. At once his tail began to wag. "I think he must realize we're trying to solve a mystery. See how excited he is?"

Kate grinned, then scratched Biscuit behind the ears. "Good boy!"

"You're switching out his collar?" Alex looked confused.

"Yes," Kate explained, "but it's not what you think. It's no ordinary collar. It has a tiny built-in microphone that transmits to this receiver." She held up the tiny black receiver and smiled. "So, if I want to hear something a suspect is saying, I send Biscuit to him or her and I can hear every word through the microphone."

"Very cool." Alex nodded. "Maybe his collar will record something we need to hear!"

"That's what I'm hoping."

When Kate had the collar in place she attached Biscuit's leash and put her mirrored sunglasses on. They might come in handy. Then she and Alex headed off on their way.

"Be careful honey, and keep your cell phone with you," her father called out. "I'll be right here watching."

"Thanks, Dad!"

She and Alex got out of the van and slipped across the front of the parking lot, following Mr. Whipple. When he approached the side of the building, Kate tiptoed a bit closer, finally deciding to hide behind the dumpster. Biscuit let out a little growl and she shushed him.

Small drops of rain fell on Kate's head and she wished she'd brought her umbrella. Still, it was hard to hide with a big umbrella in your hand!

Alex elbowed her. "Kate, look at him. He's acting really weird. He's hiding on the side of the building to make a phone call."

"Yes, that is strange." Kate squinted to get a better look. "I wonder who he's calling."

Alex's face lit up with excitement. "Maybe he's calling the Bender factory. Maybe he's sharing secrets or something. I saw something like this in a movie once." She started describing what she'd seen, but Kate found it hard to concentrate because she was so busy watching Mr. Whipple.

Kate's imagination began to run wild. "Maybe they're telling him how to sabotage the machines to keep the pretzels flat so they can put Candy and Penny out of business for good."

Alex put her finger over her lips as Mr. Whipple walked back by, still talking to the person on the other end of the phone. Kate heard him mutter something about having a secret, but couldn't make sense of it. The raindrops began to fall a bit harder now and Mr. Whipple moved to the side door of the factory then disappeared inside.

Kate and Alex tiptoed to the window. Thankfully, an awning covered them and they were safe from the rain here. However, the window was very high, which presented a real problem. Biscuit tried to jump up, but didn't make it.

"It's too tall," Alex said. "I can't see inside."

"Hmm." Kate looked around, finally discovering a large wooden crate next to the dumpster. She dragged it over to the window and then climbed on it. "Okay, I can see now." Rubbing at the dirty window, she tried to make out the shape of the man inside.

Alex joined her on the crate. "Is that Mr. Whipple?" she asked, rubbing the dirt away. "It's hard to tell."

"I think that's him. Don't you think it's a little weird that no one else is in the room while he's working?" Kate asked. "And he's messing with the machine that was broken yesterday."

She turned backwards and looked into the mirrored sunglasses, which were slightly magnified. "Yep! It's him!"

"Very odd," Alex said. "And very suspicious."

"Especially when you think about what he just said on the phone about a secret." A shiver ran down Kate's spine. She hadn't come to Amish country to wind up solving another mystery! She'd come to enter the Young Inventors' Festival. Yet here she stood, up to her eyeballs in clues and feeling that usual tug on her heart to figure things out.

Why, oh why, was her life never easy?

"What do we do next?" Alex asked with a puzzled look on her face.

"Hmm." Kate paused and pulled off her sunglasses. "Well, I guess we'd better get inside out of the rain. Let's go in the shop. I want to ask Penny and Candy some questions. And maybe. . ." She grinned. "Maybe I can talk them into giving us another tour."

"Like the one we took yesterday?" Alex asked.

"No, a private tour to places that others don't get to go." Kate nodded.

Yes, if only they could get inside the factory. . .maybe, just maybe, they could figure this out. In the meantime, they'd better get out of the rain before they ended up soaking wet!

A Private Tour

Kate's heart was still racing as she and Alex walked to the door of the pretzel shop.

"Want me to wait out here with Biscuit?" Alex asked, looking at the No Pets Allowed sign.

Kate shrugged. "Sure. I'll ask Penny if we can look around inside." She entered the busy shop and paused to shake off the rain. In the distance, she saw Penny and Candy, who both looked a little tired. Still, the sisters smiled when they saw her. Kate waved as she drew near.

"Welcome back, honey," Penny said, after waiting on the other customers, "What brings you back so soon? Hungry for more pretzels?"

"Just wondering how things are going today," Kate said. "Couldn't stop thinking about the pretzel problem last night so we decided to come back."

"We?" Penny looked around.

"Alex is waiting outside with Biscuit, my dog," Kate said.

"Ah, I see." Candy's brow wrinkled.

"So, what did you find out about the machine?" Kate asked. "Is it broken?"

"No, it's the strangest thing," Penny said. "Bud. . .er, Mr. Whipple, tested the machine and said it's working perfectly. The temperatures are just right and the oven is working fine too. We're so puzzled. Don't have a clue why the pretzels are going flat. And as you can see. . ." she pointed to the near-empty glass case. "We're almost out of the pretzels that were made before this fiasco hit."

She sighed. "This has created quite a problem for our business. If this goes on much longer, we'll lose a lot of customers." She looked at her sister and shrugged.

"And if we lose business, you know what that means. . ." A sad look passed over Candy's face. "It will mean folks will be going to Bender

Bakery to buy their pretzels."

"Don't get worked up, sister," Penny said, forcing a smile. "Hopefully it won't come to that."

"I sure hope not," Candy said. "We don't want Bender Bakery getting any of our customers, now do we?"

"We want to help you figure this out," Kate said. "But it might require a little snooping."

"Snooping?" Candy gave her a curious look. "What do you mean?"

"Alex and I would like to look around," Alex said. "See if we notice anything suspicious."

"No children allowed in the factory," Penny said as she shook her head. "Company policy."

"Oh, we don't want to go into the factory," Kate explained. "Just wanted to look around in the offices and down the hallway here." She pointed to their left. "Would that be okay?"

Candy shrugged. "I suppose so. I'm headed back into the factory because we have someone coming to check it out. You girls be careful."

"Okay. Is it all right to bring my dog inside?"

"Just don't bring him in the shop where we sell pretzels," Candy said. "Or any of the places where pretzels are made. That would violate the health code."

"I won't," Kate promised. She went outside and gestured to Alex. "They said it's okay to look around. Let's go in the side door, though. We can't bring Biscuit into the shop."

"Okay." Alex nodded and clutched Biscuit's leash, following Kate.

Kate led the way back into the building, avoiding the shop at the front.

"Where are we going, again?" Alex asked.

"I just want to check out the offices," Kate said. "I have a strange feeling about something. . ."

She and Alex walked down a long, narrow hallway with Biscuit sniffing the whole way. Kate snapped a few pictures with her tiny digital camera.

"Maybe he's hot on the trail of something," Kate said as the dog paused to play with a few cobwebs in the corner. He snatched up a piece of an old pretzel and chewed on it.

"Or maybe he's just hungry." Alex laughed. "Bringing Biscuit might not have been the best idea we've ever had. He likes to eat everything in sight!"

"Nah. He's going to help us solve this case. . .just watch and see." Kate nodded, then reached down to pat the dog on the head.

The girls tiptoed down the ever-darkening hallway until they came to a door with no sign on the outside.

"What's on the other side of that door?" Alex whispered.

"Hmm. I'm not sure. I've never been down here before." Kate eased the door open. It made a loud creaking sound. As soon as the door was open, a mop fell out and whacked her on the head.

"Ouch!"

Biscuit let out a little whimper, thinking she was hurt.

"I'm okay, boy," she told him. "Just a little bump on the head." She turned to face Alex as she pointed inside the closet. "Looks like this is where they keep the cleaning supplies."

"What about this one?" Alex pointed to another door.

Kate tapped on the door. When no one answered, she gently pushed the door open and they both stepped inside.

"Hmm. It's really dark in here, but it looks like a storeroom of some sort." She squinted. "Look, Alex. Bags and bags of flour. This is where they store the supplies used to make the pretzels."

Biscuit began to sniff, then let out a loud puppy sneeze.

"Not now, boy!" Kate said. "This isn't a good time to be allergic!"

Off in the distance, she heard footsteps. Kate peeked out of the door then whispered, "It's Mr. Whipple! He's coming this way."

"Quick. Hide behind the boxes." Alex rushed behind a large stack of boxes and Kate followed her, keeping a tight hold on Biscuit's leash.

Kate tried to steady her breathing and prayed her eyes would adjust to the dark. A couple of seconds later, the door creaked open and a sliver of light from the hallway flowed into the room. Biscuit began to make a soft growling sound and she shushed him right away. Thankfully, he quieted down.

Kate held her breath and looked at Alex. She could hear Mr. Whipple muttering something about flour. Then he said something else she couldn't quite understand. She squeezed her eyes shut and prayed the high-powered microphone on Biscuit's collar was picking it up.

He grabbed a bag from the top of the stack and Kate lowered her position, praying he wouldn't see them. She reached for Alex's arm and pulled her down a bit lower too. All the while she kept a close eye on Biscuit, praying he wouldn't bark. Or sneeze. Or growl.

Why, oh why, did I ever think bringing a dog would be a good idea?

Just as Mr. Whipple took a couple of steps toward the door, Kate's cell phone rang. Her heart began to race. She reached inside her pocket and pushed the SILENCE button.

"Who's in here?" Mr. Whipple called out.

The whites of Alex's eyes stood out against the darkness of the room and Kate mouthed the word *"Yikes!"*

"Who's in here?" Mr. Whipple called out.

When the girls didn't respond, he muttered something about needing to get his hearing aid checked. He stepped into the hallway, closing the door behind him.

"That was close!" Kate said, dropping to the floor in a heap. Her hands began to tremble. She reached into her pocket and pulled out the phone. "It was Sydney calling. She must have some information about the case."

"We'll have to talk to her later. Let's get out of here!" Alex took Kate by the hand and they eased their way through the darkness to the door. As she gripped it, the creaking sound rang out.

"Shh!" Kate whispered.

The two girls tiptoed out into the hall, and for a minute they thought it was empty. However, a few seconds later, they heard footsteps again. Biscuit began to growl once more. Kate shushed him, hoping he wouldn't bark and give them away.

"Kate, look!" Alex whispered. "It's Mr. Whipple. . .again!"

Kate grabbed her friend's hand and pulled her into the cleaning supply closet, pulling Biscuit behind them. She shut the door, but the smell of bleach and other cleaning supplies nearly made her sick at her stomach. Besides, they barely fit in the closet with the mop bucket and other supplies, especially with Biscuit panting and whimpering.

"Where is he going, do you suppose?" Alex whispered.

"Not sure, but I'll check." Kate opened the door just an inch or so and peered down the hallway.

"He's up to something," she whispered. After a moment of watching, she said, "Oh, it looks like he's going into Penny's office."

Kate snapped a picture with her digital camera in case they needed the proof. She turned back to Alex. "What do you suppose he's doing in there?"

"Sneaking around, for sure!" Alex whispered in response. "But why would he want to sneak into Penny's office? Don't you find that strange?"

"Yes." Kate nodded. "I can't help thinking about that picture of him in the paper with the Bender brothers. Maybe they're paying him to work here and spy on the sisters. Could be he's doing that right now, sneaking around in there, trying to figure out the Twisted Twins' secrets!"

"I'll bet you're right."

Just then a text message came through on Kate's phone. "Sydney again. She says to call her later."

"If we weren't hiding in a broom closet, we could do it now," Alex responded. "But right now we have more important things."

Kate poked her nose out of the door once more. She watched as Mr. Whipple snuck back out of Penny's office, picked up the bag of flour then headed off down the hall, whistling. "Very strange," she said. "He had a smile on his face."

She snapped another photo.

"Maybe his spying paid off," Alex said. "Maybe he found something to help the Benders in their case against the Twisted Twins. Maybe he's not going to give up until he stops them from making pretzels altogether!"

Kate shrugged. "I don't know. I just know that I'm tired of sneaking around! And Biscuit is slobbering all over me."

She opened the closet door and stepped into the hallway. She and Alex ran back up to the front of the factory, relief flooding her as they reached the parking lot. Unfortunately, the rain was really coming down hard, so they rushed to get inside the van.

"Wow, that was quite an adventure," Alex said, settling into a seat.

"Did you find anything?" Kate's father asked.

"Maybe!" Kate said, getting Biscuit settled onto the floor. "We need to talk to Candy and Penny, but there just isn't time. Maybe I can call them later."

"Oh? What's up?" her father asked.

"We're more suspicious of Mr. Whipple than ever!" Kate removed Biscuit's collar and pressed the rewind button. Straining, she heard the sound of footsteps, and then heard Mr. Whipple muttering something about keeping a secret. Finally, she heard him say something else: "Crazy woman. What I wouldn't do to get her."

Alex's eyes grew wide. "He's out to get her?"

"Sounds like it," Kate's father said. "And it sounds like he's not going to stop until the deed is done."

"But. . .what deed?" Kate asked. "What do you suppose he's up to?"

Alarm filled Alex's eyes.

"It's just like that game. . .Clue," she said. "Mr. Whipple did it in the factory with a. . ." She paused. "I haven't decided yet how he did it. I guess we'll figure that out later."

"Maybe." Kate sighed. "Right now I'm just confused."

Her father glanced at his watch. "We've spent a lot of time here when we should be getting back to the festival."

"Candy and Penny aren't going to be happy to hear that Mr. Whipple is sneaking around. Oh, I wish we had time to go back in there!" Kate said.

"Not today, honey," her father said. "We barely have enough time to get back to Hershey. I want to be there when the judge announces that my daughter is a finalist in the Young Inventors' Festival."

Kate giggled. "Dad, we don't even know that I'm going to be a finalist. Did you see how many other inventors there are?"

"Yes, but I've also seen the Turbo Heat-Freeze, and it's by far the best invention on the exhibition floor," he said, looking very proud. "So I have no doubt that you'll be a finalist."

Kate flashed a smile. She looked at Alex. "Now you see why I keep trying new things. My parents are like cheerleaders. They're always telling me I can do anything I put my mind to."

"Well, you know what the Bible says," her father reminded her as he turned the van on. "'I can do all things through Christ who strengthens me.'"

"I believe it!" Alex said. "And I agree with your father. You *are* going to be a finalist, Kate."

"Whatever you say." Kate leaned back against the seat and tried to think about the competition. Unfortunately, all she could think about was Mr. Whipple. He was up to something. She could feel it in her bones.

And she would prove it. . .if the week would just slow down long enough!

CHAPTER 8

Camp Club Girls on Call!

The drive back to Hershey went smoothly, though the rain slowed them down a bit. All the way there, Kate thought about Mr. Whipple and what he'd said when he didn't think anyone was listening. She wondered what he meant and how it might affect Penny and Candy. Would he really sabotage the two people who'd been so good to him through the years? All because of competition between the two companies?

Hmm. Speaking of competition. . .

Kate glanced at her watch, realizing they would barely make it back in time for the big announcement. She wondered what Phillip was doing. Was he wondering where she was? Bragging about how he was going to beat her?

That familiar bad feeling came over her as she thought about him. Why couldn't she and Phillip just get along?

Thankfully, Kate's father got them to Hershey just in time. She and Alex sprinted from the van to the exhibition hall with her father following closely. By the time she reached the stage at the center of the hall, Kate was tired. . .but excited.

She watched as Mr. Carmichael walked to the podium. Off in the distance she saw Phillip, standing with his parents. Alex pulled out her video camera just as Kate's mother and Dexter joined them.

"I was worried you might not make it back in time," her mom said. "Glad to see you."

"Can we just get this part over with and go ride the sooperdooper-Looper?" Dexter whined. "This is *so* boring."

Kate laughed. "Might be boring to you, but this is the best part to me. And besides, we're not going to the amusement park till tomorrow, remember?"

He groaned and crossed his arms at his chest, looking upset.

"It's not like we could go in the rain, anyway," Kate said. "The rides aren't even running when the weather is bad."

"I know. This whole trip is such a waste." Dexter rolled his eyes. "Well, except for the part where you're going to win the competition. That's pretty cool."

"I wish everyone would stop saying I'm going to win," Kate said. "You're all going to be disappointed if I don't!"

Dexter shrugged.

Mr. Carmichael's voice caught Kate's attention.

"We're so excited about our participants this year," he said. "We've seen some real winners in this group!"

Alex turned her video camera toward him, filming the whole thing.

Phillip looked over at Kate and raised his eyebrows as if to say, *"He's talking about me!"*

Kate just smiled and turned her attention back to Mr. Carmichael.

"One of the reasons we feel so strongly about the Young Inventors' Festival is because it helps students with issues like problem solving and research," he said. "We find that it also enhances their organizational and creative thinking skills. Best of all, it helps boys and girls learn how to communicate effectively and give a nice presentation based on what they've learned."

Kate thought about all he said. She had learned a lot by building the Turbo Heat-Freeze, and not just about pretzels and chocolate. She'd learned a lot about herself too.

She knew now that she took after her father. . .and that made her very proud.

She also knew that she wasn't afraid to stand up in front of people and make a presentation like she used to be back in grade school. Now she could stand before a crowd and tell them all about her invention. . . and not even be scared.

Well, not very scared, anyway. She still had to pray that the Lord would calm her down sometimes, especially in moments like this when she didn't know if she would be a finalist or not!

"We've narrowed our list of contenders from one hundred to twenty," Mr. Carmichael said. "The following young inventors have made our short list and will all receive college scholarships in different amounts. However, only one will be named tomorrow night as the Inventor of the Year."

He began to list names. Kate heard a squeal of glee as he called out one name after another. Out of the corner of her eye, she saw Phillip and his family. He looked nervous. For the first time, she felt a little sorry for him.

Mr. Carmichael continued to list names. When he spoke Kate's name, she squealed. Alex hugged her before putting the video camera in her face and starting to ask questions.

"Whoa, whoa!" Kate said. "Not so fast!"

"Well, I just knew you would be on the list!" Alex snapped off the video camera. "Your invention is the best one here."

"I don't know about that," Kate whispered back. "There are so many good ones." Still she was happy that she was one of the finalists. Her father grinned and gave her the thumbs-up signal. She smiled in response.

At that moment, she heard Mr. Carmichael called Phillip's name. Kate breathed a sigh of relief. She felt better, knowing he had made the short list too.

Glancing his way, she smiled. She hoped he would give her some sign that they were friends. Instead, he looked away with a sour expression.

Kate heard Mr. Carmichael announce the last name on the list—Emma. The Amish girl with all of the slippery frogs. Directly to her left, Kate heard a happy cry. She smiled as she saw Emma and Rachel standing there with their parents.

After Emma's name was announced, the crowd applauded and then everyone began to congratulate the kids who'd made it into the finals. Kate was about to congratulate Emma and Phillip when her family swept in around her.

"Kate, I'm so proud of you!" Her mother wrapped her in a loving embrace.

"That's my girl!" her father added, squeezing her. "I knew your Turbo Heat-Freeze would make it. I just knew it!"

Kate beamed with joy. She loved hearing her parents' comments and was so glad they were happy with her achievement.

She noticed Phillip's parents congratulating him. Well, sort of. They didn't really seem real excited, and she thought she heard Phillip's father say something about how his son needed to work harder to be the best. Wow. Well, that explained a lot, didn't it? Maybe Phillip had to work extra hard to get his father's respect and love. How sad.

She didn't have long to think about it. Her mother and father were saying they should all go out to eat a late lunch to celebrate. Kate stepped through the crowd with Alex at her side, chatting non-stop about how proud she was. Somehow all of this was a little embarrassing. Kate liked the idea of doing well in the competition, but getting this attention made her feel kind of. . .well, funny. Self-focused.

They walked out of the exhibition hall and toward the hotel's restaurant. After they received their meals, Kate got another text message from Sydney. She read it, and then looked at Alex, who was eating a plate of spaghetti.

"Sydney wants to know if we can do a conference call in an hour," Kate said. "She says one of the girls has some interesting news. That's why she was trying to reach us earlier."

Alex's eyes widened. "I wonder what it is."

"I don't know, but I'm sure it's about the case," Kate said. She picked up her fork and stuck it into the last piece of lasagna on her plate. Then she shoveled it into her mouth.

"Yum!" she said. "Good to the last bite!"

After eating lunch, the two families walked back to the hotel. Kate invited Alex to her room and they sat on the bed to call Sydney and the others.

Sydney answered right away. Within a couple of minutes, the other girls were on the phone too.

"Okay, Inspector Gadget, here's what I've learned," Sydney said, chiming in right away with her news. "I checked with the Better Business Bureau, and there have never been any complaints filed against the Twisted Twins factory. Not ever."

"Interesting," Kate responded. "I guess I figured maybe someone was mad at them. But if no complaints have ever been filed, maybe I was wrong."

"Well, don't rule that out," Sydney said. "I also found out that Penny and Candy once worked for another pretzel company in a nearby town, a much larger factory."

"Really?" Kate asked, perking up. "What company?"

"The Bender Brothers' Bakery," Sydney said. "From what I read, it sounds like Penny and Candy might be related to the people who run that place."

"No way! The Bender Brothers' Bakery?" Kate whispered, not quite believing it. Was it really possible that Penny and Candy were connected to their competitors? If so, then this case just got even more exciting! But why hadn't the sisters mentioned that?

Bailey started giggling and couldn't seem to stop.

"The Bender Brothers' Bakery?" she said between giggles. "Try saying that three times really fast!"

All of the girls did just that. . .at the same time. Before long, they were all laughing.

"So, what happened?" Alex asked finally. "What's the story?"

"The factory started in the early 1930s during the Great Depression," Sydney explained. "But in 1985 the brothers and sisters who had inherited the factory from their parents and ran it had a major falling out."

"Falling out?" Kate clarified. "You mean, an argument?"

"Yes," Sydney said. "The two brothers—Donald and Steve Bender— kept the original family company, and the two sisters started their own business, the Twisted Twins. They are chief competitors. Have been, for nearly twenty-five years."

"And now Twisted Twins is the second-best-selling company in the state," Kate said. "Wow."

"I'm sure the brothers aren't very happy about that," Sydney said. "They've always been number one. It looks like their sisters are gaining on them, especially in the last couple of years."

"I've done a little research too," McKenzie said. "And here's what I've learned. The sisters use a similar recipe for their pretzels, so the brothers are mad about that. Very mad. The Bender brothers have written about it in a couple of newspaper articles. They feel the recipe was stolen."

"Sounds like these brothers and sisters are a little twisted," Alex said.

"Twisted! Get it?" Bailey laughed again. "Pretzels are twisted, just like the brothers and sisters."

"Yeah, the boys are 'bended' and the girls are 'twisted,'" Alex said. "Funny!"

"Very." Kate giggled. Still, after a moment or two, she didn't feel much like laughing. In fact, every time she thought about Penny and Candy not getting along with their brothers, she had to wonder what had happened to cause it. And then she wondered what it would be like if she got into such a big argument with Dexter that they never spoke again. That would be awful.

Elizabeth remained quiet for a moment. "I'm not saying that all competition is bad," she said at last. "But whenever you start thinking you have to be better than the next person, something's wrong. God wants all of us to excel at what we do, not cut each other down so we can be the best."

Ouch. Kate thought about that in light of what was happening with Phillip. Who cared who had the better project or who got the better score on a test? As long as they were both doing their best, that's all that mattered, right?

"It's so funny you should say that," she said after a brief pause. "I just read a scripture that said we're not supposed to think more highly of ourselves than others."

"True," Elizabeth said. "Sometimes that's a hard lesson to learn, though."

"Sounds like the brothers are really mad at their sisters too," Sydney said. "Otherwise, why would they make such a big deal about the recipe?"

"Who knows?" Kate thought about that for a moment. "Penny and Candy used to work in the family business too, right? So they *always* had the recipe. And it came down from their parents, anyway. How can you steal something that your parents gave you? And why would brothers and sisters work for two different companies instead of just sticking together and working things out?"

She paused and sighed. The girls went on talking, but she couldn't stop thinking about her problems with Phillip, especially his comment about sabotage.

"Kate. . .are you still with us?" Sydney's voice rang out, snapping Kate out of her daydreams.

"Y–yes, I'm here," she stammered. "Sorry about that. I just have a lot on my mind right now."

"I'll bet you do!" Bailey said. "Tell us about the festival. How are things going?"

Before Kate could say a word, Alex dove in, telling all of the other girls about how Kate was a finalist in the competition. As they all celebrated this news, her heart sank. Hearing them sing her praises suddenly felt wrong, especially in light of the news about the quarrel between the Bender brothers and sisters.

"Kate's going to win the whole thing!" Alex exclaimed. "I just know it. Her invention is the best. You girls should see the video footage I got when they announced her name today. It was priceless. I can't wait to post it for my viewers."

"I. . .well, I don't care if I win or not," Kate said at last. "Honestly, I'm just happy to be here. And I'm especially glad, now that I know we have another mystery to solve." After a pause, she spoke her mind. "So, are we all on the same page? Do we think Mr. Whipple is the one sabotaging the Twisted Twins? Maybe the Bender brothers are paying him to do this?"

"Could be," Sydney said. "Though we can't be sure without more proof."

Kate sighed, trying to figure out how—and when—they would solve the case. After all, she had to spend this afternoon and evening in the convention hall. Tomorrow afternoon the winner would be announced at a big banquet and then all of the competitors were going to get to go to the amusement park together.

If it ever stopped raining.

Right now she wondered if it ever would.

CHAPTER 9

The Competition

Kate barely had time to rest after calling the Camp Club Girls because she had to be back on the exhibition floor for the rest of the afternoon. Alex's parents decided to spend the day shopping, but Alex offered to hang out with Kate at her booth.

"Sounds like fun," Kate said. "You can help me with the demonstrations!"

"I would love that!" Alex said. "And maybe I can get a little more video footage for my show."

When Kate arrived at her booth, she checked her supplies. Thankfully, she found the pretzels, jelly beans, and chocolate just where she'd left them. Before long, people were coming to her booth, asking for a demonstration.

The grown-ups loved the Turbo Heat-Freeze and so did the kids. Kate found herself making more and more candy-covered pretzel bites. After awhile, she felt a little dizzy! When would this crowd of people move on to another booth? Probably never, as long as she kept offering them free sweets!

Out of the corner of her eye, she watched as Phillip demonstrated his Weather-Caster Watch. When the crowd thinned, she noticed that Emma and Rachel were talking to Phillip, so she decided to join him. Surely he wouldn't say anything mean to her with them standing right there. She hoped.

Kate walked over to his booth with Alex behind her. "Hi, everyone," she said. "Taking a break?"

"Mm-hmm!" Emma's face lit up. "I'm so tired! Wish I could take a nap."

"Me too." Kate tried to hold back a yawn, but it came out anyway. "It's been a long day."

Emma smiled warmly. "Still, I've had the time of my life here. And I was just telling Phillip about another one of my inventions."

"What is it?" Kate asked.

"I've been working on a hydroponic garden back at our farm," Emma said. "I wish I could have brought it with me, but it's almost as big as a room in our house!"

"Wow," Kate said. "What gave you the idea to do a hydroponic garden?"

"My father is a farmer," Emma said. "He farms all sorts of things—corn and beans, potatoes and lettuce. He grows all of the food that we eat on our farm. Some seasons we have a great harvest, and other seasons the vegetables don't get enough rain. One year we lost our crop because of snow and ice."

"We could stand a little snow and ice right now," Alex grumbled. "It's so hot and sticky outside this week."

"I know." Emma's brow wrinkled. "Anyway, I got to thinking that I could create an environment in the barn where vegetables could grow in water. I used horse troughs to create the garden."

"Very cool idea," Alex said.

Kate thought about Emma's words for a moment. "You mean you don't go grocery shopping like we do? You grow all of your own vegetables?"

"Well, we get a few things at the market sometimes," she said. "But all of our vegetables come from our garden, and the meat we eat comes from butchering our cows and chickens."

"Oh wow." Alex looked shocked. "That's what life on a farm is like, I guess."

"Yes." Emma smiled. "I love it. The fields are so pretty in the springtime. It's so much greener than living in the city."

"Tell me more about your hydroponic garden," Kate said. "I saw one at a science museum once, but I've never seen one in a barn before!"

"We've been growing vegetables for years anyway," Emma said. "And my *daadi* and I have been working on a hydroponics greenhouse. It's a little different from what you're used to because, like I said, we started with an old horse trough."

"Very interesting," Alex said.

"Oh yes, but the vegetables are growing like crazy!" Emma said with a twinkle in her eye. "You should see the heads of cabbage. They're very large—bigger than any you'll find in the grocery store, and you've never tasted anything so good."

Kate wrinkled her nose. She wasn't sure she liked cabbage at all!

"And our corn on the cob is the sweetest you ever tasted," Emma said. "It's almost like eating candy. I wish you could taste my *mamm's* corn chowder. It's my favorite. Well, that and the shoo-fly pie."

"Shoo-fly pie?" Alex looked confused. "You have flies in your pie?"

Rachel giggled. "No, not at all! It's just the name of the pie. It's very tasty."

"I would love to have a bite and find out for myself," Kate said.

"I will ask my *mamm* to bring some back with her tomorrow," Emma said with a twinkle in her eye. "I think you will like it."

"Life is very different where you come from," Kate said, looking at Rachel and Emma. "But in some ways they're just the same."

Phillip shook his head. "Sorry, but I can't figure out how you manage without electricity. I don't think I could do that."

Emma shrugged. "When you've never had it, you don't miss it."

An elderly man approached Phillip's booth and began to ask questions about the Weather-Caster Watch, so the girls moved their conversation to Kate's table.

"Can I ask you a question?" Emma whispered.

"Sure." Kate nodded.

"We tried to talk to Phillip because he seems like such a loner, but he wouldn't say much to us. Is he always like that?"

Kate sighed. "Yes. He is. I've tried to be his friend for ages now, but he doesn't seem to like me. I think he sees me as a competitor most of the time."

"Oh, I see." Emma's brow wrinkled.

"Is he mean to you?" Rachel asked.

"Sometimes. . .a little." Kate shrugged.

"Once a boy in our community was mean to me," Emma explained. "*Mamm* told me what to do to stop his meanness, and it worked!"

"What's that?" Kate asked.

"She said to turn the other cheek. When he treated me badly, to be extra nice to him."

"Yes, that's what the Bible says," Kate agreed. "And I've been extra nice to Phillip. I even wrote him a note once, asking if we could work together and be friends. But it seems no matter how nice I am, he still doesn't like me."

"There has to be some reason why he feels this way," Rachel said, glancing at Phillip.

"If I had to guess, I'd say he's jealous of you, Kate," Alex said. "You're so smart."

Kate felt her cheeks warm with embarrassment.

"No point in hiding it," Alex said. "You know you are. And now that you're actually competing against him at a real event, he can't take the pressure. That's my guess, anyway."

Kate shrugged. She thought about her friend's words, knowing in her heart they were true. As much as she didn't like to admit it, from the time she and Phillip were in elementary school, they had bickered over who was the better student. Seemed like every year the competition between them grew stronger. And now it had grown into a big mess, just the sort of mess Elizabeth had been talking about.

Her thoughts then shifted to Penny and Candy. . .and to their brothers at the Bender factory. What could Kate do to help bring a broken family back together again?

A familiar voice rang out and Kate looked up, surprised to see Penny and Candy approaching with their arms full of posters and banners. Looked like God was giving her the perfect opportunity to do something to help.

She offered a quick prayer, and then turned to the ladies with a smile. She could hardly wait to see what they had up their sleeves!

CHAPTER 10

Dog-Eat-Dog World

Kate grinned as she looked at the Twisted Twins.

"I'm so glad you're here!" she said, looking back and forth between Penny and Candy. "What have you brought?"

"Oh, all sorts of things!" Candy showed her a large banner with the words TWISTED TWINS on it, along with a couple of posters. The cutest one was a picture of Kate's face peering through a large pretzel.

"How did you do that?" she asked.

Penny shrugged. "We took the picture from your blog and placed it into our logo. Very cool, right?"

"Very!"

"We want to put these on your booth, since we're sponsoring you," Penny said, lifting the banner. "Hope that's okay."

"Of course! I'd be honored!" Kate nodded and thanked them. Then she helped put up the banner. Afterwards, she stepped back, grinning at how the pretzel theme changed the look of her booth. "I love it!" she said, clasping her hands together. "Thank you so much for doing this."

"Well, of course," Penny said, giving her a hug. Her voice grew even louder as she said, "We think you're the greatest, Kate, and we want people to know it."

Kate's excitement suddenly disappeared, as Phillip looked her way with a sour expression. He must've heard Penny's words.

"I don't really think I'm the greatest at anything," Kate said softly. "I'm learning that God wants *all* of His kids to be successful, not just a few."

She thought again of Elizabeth's words and whispered up a prayer, thanking the Lord for teaching her this lesson.

Candy's brow wrinkled. "Well, I suppose that's true." She shrugged. "I never thought about it before. In our business, it's a dog-eat-dog world."

"Dog-eat-dog?" Alex—who had been putting up one of the posters—looked over, confused.

"Candy just means that we have to fight for recognition and only the one on top really gets noticed," Penny explained. "We want to be the top dog, the one to win the prize."

Kate glanced at Phillip once again before sharing her thoughts on the matter.

"Being noticed isn't a bad thing, and I suppose it's necessary when you have your own business. I just don't know. . ." She looked at the ground, unsure of what to say next. To be quite honest, she was tired of living a dog-eat-dog life. She just wanted her simple, noncompetitive life back, the one where she didn't have to worry what others thought. Where she could just relax and be herself.

"You'll see one day, Kate," Candy said with a nod. "Being number one is a good thing, a very good thing."

Kate just shrugged.

"Now, show us this Turbo Heat-Freeze," Penny said, looking at Kate's invention. "We've certainly waited long enough to see it."

Kate started demonstrating the machine at once, though she noticed the chocolate wasn't hardening like it usually did.

"That's so odd," she said. "I'm not sure what's going on."

"Well, it's still a great idea," Candy said. "And I can just imagine how much better it would be on a larger scale." She turned to face Penny. "Can you imagine, sister? We could use our longer pretzel rods. The crunchy ones. We could cover them in everything from chocolate and sprinkles to caramel and pecans.

"Yum. Caramel and pecans! That's sounds awesome!" Alex said.

Kate tried to think about yummy pretzels, but she had other things on her mind right now. Her troubling thoughts wouldn't leave her alone. She decided to change gears, to talk about something else that had been bothering her.

"Before we do anything else, I need to talk to you ladies about something," she said at last. "I'm still thinking about the flat pretzels at your factory."

The expression on Candy's face changed to sadness. "What about them, honey?" she asked.

"I have a couple of theories about what might have happened."

"What are you thinking, Kate?" Penny asked. "Tell us."

"Well. . ." She fidgeted with a jellybean, as she worked up the courage to speak her mind. Looking Candy in the eye, she decided to go for it.

"Okay, well, I'm wondering about your connection to the Bender brothers."

At once Penny's smile turned into a frown.

"Our connection?" She began to pace in front of the table then glanced at Candy. "She wants to know about our connection, sister."

"Oh dear, oh dear," Candy muttered, gazing down at the ground.

"Do we tell her?" Penny asked.

Candy shrugged. "I don't suppose it would hurt anything." She looked at Kate. "The Bender brothers are *our* brothers. Their names are Donald and Steve."

Kate nodded. So, it was true. The Camp Club Girls had been right all along. Penny and Candy were, indeed, part of the Bender family. Now to get to the heart of the matter. She had just opened her mouth to ask the next question when Alex interrupted.

"Did you have a fight with them?" Alex asked. "We're wondering because, well, someone we know told us about it."

"Yes." Candy's cheeks flushed pink and she started to fan herself. "It's not something we're proud of, but we did have a falling out with our brothers years ago." She shook her head. "It was all their fault, trust me."

"And you've been competing with them ever since?" Kate asked.

Penny sighed. "I guess you could put it like that. Our two businesses compete."

"Did it ever occur to you that your brothers might be sabotaging you in some way?" Kate looked Penny in the eye.

"The thought has occurred to me," Penny said, her eyes filling with tears. "Though I hate to think our own brothers would do something like that."

"I agree." Candy wiped away a tear from her wrinkled cheek. "I've been concerned all along that our brothers are out to get us. They've been angry since we left the company, and now they want to put us out of business." Her eyes narrowed even more. "I think you're right, Kate. Those brothers of ours would do anything to shut us down. Ever since. . ."

She started to say more, but stopped when she realized the girls were watching her. "Oh, sorry. Too much information. Besides, it's all water under the bridge, anyway."

"Water under the bridge?" Alex asked.

"She means it's all in the past," Penny said. "We had a. . .well, a quarrel with our brothers many years ago and we parted ways. Got really angry with them, in fact. But it's in the past. Over."

"Do you still see them?" Kate asked.

"No!" Both of the sisters spoke in unison.

"They can stay on their side of Lancaster County, and we'll stay on our side," Candy said, folding her arms at her chest. "Good riddance!"

"You mean, you don't even see them at Christmas or Thanksgiving or anything?" Alex looked confused.

Candy shook her head. "We haven't seen our brothers in twenty-five years."

"Wow." Kate shook her head, trying to imagine what that would be like. She couldn't imagine going more than a few days without seeing her brother, let alone twenty-five years! Who could hold onto their anger for that long? It seemed impossible!

"That's not completely true, sister," Penny said. "I saw Donald and his wife at the grocery store a couple of years ago." Her eyes filled with tears. "They were shopping with their granddaughter. She sure is cute. I wish I could. . ."

Brushing aside her tears, she said, "Well, never mind. It would never work out."

"Don't you miss family time?" Alex asked. "Can't you put your differences behind you and forgive one another?"

Penny stiffened at once. "They were the ones in the wrong, not us. If they want to ask for our forgiveness, they know where they can find us."

"Yes, but the Bible says. . ." Kate wanted to finish, to tell them that the Bible said they should forgive, even if their brothers didn't ask for forgiveness. But she didn't. She bit her tongue to keep from interrupting. She didn't want to stop the conversation, after all. Might as well learn as much as she could from them.

"If you don't mind my asking. . ." Alex looked at Penny. "What caused the fight? You don't have to tell us if you don't want to. I'm just curious."

"Humph." Penny began to pace, her fists now tightly clenched. "I'll tell you what started it. Candy and I are strong, independent women, but we still like to do things the old-fashioned way. That never settled well with Donald."

"He was all about progress," Candy said. "That's where the trouble began. He wanted to make some major changes to our grandfather's original recipe, and he wanted to spend money on new machinery."

Kate couldn't see why this should cause a problem, but didn't say so. It wasn't her place to interrupt.

"One thing led to another, and we eventually broke away from the family business and started our own company," Penny said. "We wanted to do things more like our parents and grandparents had done."

Candy dabbed at her eyes. "Unfortunately, our brothers' business really took off after we left. They became the largest pretzel-making factory in the state. And they rubbed it in every time we were together that first year. So, after a while we just stopped spending time with them."

"I have missed them at times," Penny said, wiping a tear from her eye. "But they're so. . .dishonest."

"Dishonest?" Kate looked at her, confused. "How so?"

Penny wrung her hands together. "Even though they're using the latest technology, they still claim to do things the old-fashioned way. It's just not right. They're not being honest with the customers."

"They'll do anything they can to stay on top," Penny said. "Anything."

"Hmm." Kate drew in a breath, wondering if she should respond. In some ways, the Bender brothers seemed just like the sisters. . .they wanted to win. They wanted to be the top dog.

Kate thought about that scripture on her text reader: *Don't think you are better than you really are. . .*

Hmm. At once her thoughts went to her situation with Phillip. She wondered if they would be like this in twenty-five years, still fighting over who was the best. Not if she had anything to do with it!

Candy kept talking, her voice growing more animated. "In some ways, our story is just like that biblical story of David and Goliath," she said. "Our brothers are like Goliath, and we're like little David. But remember who won in the end!" She raised her hand in the air and squeezed it shut for a triumphant shout. Then she added, "With just five little stones, David took the giant down!"

Kate watched this, feeling a little confused. Why did it matter so much whether the brothers or the sisters had the most customers? Who cared about all of their problems in the past? Why couldn't they just forgive each other and make up? Wouldn't that be for the best?

Kate decided to change gears once again, to tell the ladies about her other suspicions. She looked at Candy as she spoke.

"I don't want to have to be the one to tell you this," Kate said, "but I believe Mr. Whipple might be involved in all of this."

"W—what?" Penny stumbled over the word. "W—what makes you think that?"

"We caught him in your office, snooping around," Alex said.

"It's true." Kate nodded. "We watched him with our own eyes. I've got the picture to prove it."

She reached for her camera and showed Penny the photos.

"Oh my!" Penny's face turned pale. "I wonder what Bud was up to."

"I don't know," Kate said at last. "I just know he was in there for a couple of minutes and he said something about, well. . ."

"Go ahead. Spit it out." Penny's brow wrinkled as she waited on Kate to respond.

"He said something about crazy women."

Her eyes widened. "Did he now. He said crazy?"

"Well, I'm pretty sure he said crazy," Alex said. "But that's not all. He also said he was going to get you."

"*Get* me?" Penny looked stunned. "What does that mean?"

"I think it means he's trying to sabotage you," Kate whispered. "So you'd better be careful around him, Penny. He's a spy. I just know it."

"Hmm." Penny shook her head. "I don't like to think he's been snooping around. Why Bud Whipple has worked for us for years. He's a faithful employee."

She went on and on, talking about what a great man he was and how he had helped the factory grow, but Kate knew there was more to the story.

"Hmm, well. . ." Kate swallowed hard, then continued. "There's more to it than that."

"Ooh?" Penny turned pale.

"Yes. Mr. Whipple was recently photographed at your brothers' factory."

"No!" Penny began to fan herself. "Are you sure about that, Kate? It's one thing to suspect our brothers, another thing altogether to suspect Bud. . .er, Mr. Whipple. Why, he's worked for us for years and is our best employee!"

"It's true," Alex said. "I found the photograph online. He was shaking hands with your brother Donald in the photo."

"I can't believe we never saw the picture in the paper," Candy said, shaking her head.

"Well, we're so busy," Penny responded. "Who has time to read the paper?" She looked even more upset. "Still, I can't believe Bud would do anything to hurt us. He's been so loyal, so faithful."

"Do you suppose he's been working for Donald and Steve all along?" Candy asked. "As a spy?"

Penny's eyes grew wide. "Impossible!"

"It's more than possible, sister," Candy said, putting her hands on her hips. "And to think he knows everything about our business—from the type of machinery we use to the recipes for the pretzels. Why, he's the most logical suspect of all. I can't believe we didn't think of it before."

"Well, we thought of it," Kate said. "And he's the reason we came back to your factory this morning. We wanted to find out if our suspicions about him were right."

"We don't have any proof," Alex added. "But he said. . .and did. . . some suspicious things."

"If there's nothing wrong with the machinery, then maybe he has altered the recipe in some way," Kate suggested. "Perhaps he's deliberately left out the yeast."

"Maybe." Candy shook her head. "There's only one way to know. Let's get him out of the factory by sending him on some sort of errand over the next couple of days and see if this problem continues, even when he's not around."

Kate sighed. "I'll be going home tomorrow after the festival ends, so I guess I won't be able to help you figure this out. That's a bummer."

"Yes." Candy shrugged. "But honey, you don't need this distraction right now, anyway. Didn't you come to Hershey to win this competition? You should be focusing on that, not on our problem."

Kate nodded. "I suppose. But I always like to help."

Through the crowd, she saw a familiar face. He came nearer, nearer. . .

"Um, ladies. . ." Kate whispered. "We might have a bit of a problem on our hands."

"Oh?" Penny looked confused.

Kate pointed in Mr. Whipple's direction. "It looks like our number one suspect is headed right for us!"

Mr. Whipple's Secret!

Kate turned to Candy and Penny, her hands trembling. "Quick! You need to hide!"

"But where?" Candy asked, looking around. "And he's supposed to be working at the factory now."

"Behind the booth," Alex suggested.

The two sisters did just that, slipping behind Kate's booth just as Mr. Whipple approached. Thankfully, he only paused long enough to look at the TWISTED TWINS sign. Kate was grateful he didn't ask about the women. Instead, he just nodded and kept on walking.

"I think it's safe," Kate whispered. "You ladies can come out now."

Candy stepped out first, running her fingers through her now-messy hair. "Whew! That was a close one."

Penny came next with a sad look on her face.

"Are you okay, sister?" Candy asked.

Penny shrugged. "I guess. I'm just really disappointed to think that Bud might be involved in this. I've always, well. . ." She shook her head. "I always thought he was such a nice man."

"Me too," Candy said. "And maybe we're wrong about all of this. I hope so, anyway."

"I hope so too," Kate added.

"We could use a distraction," Candy said. "I'd like to look around at the other entries. Would you like that, sister?"

"Sure." Penny shrugged. "Looking around the exhibition hall will be just the thing to get my mind off of my problems."

The sisters gave Kate and Alex a little wave, then went off on their way.

For a while Kate tried to talk to people as they stopped by, but her heart wasn't really in it. Besides, the Turbo Heat-Freeze still wasn't working properly. She couldn't figure out why the chocolate wasn't hardening like it should. After a few minutes, Kate gave up trying. She decided to clean up her area and pack up the candies.

"Are you okay?" Alex asked, giving her a concerned look. "What's on your mind?"

"I don't know." Kate shrugged. "This trip is just turning out to be so complicated. And not much fun."

Alex nodded. "I know what you mean. I can't stop thinking about what happened at the pretzel factory. Do you think Mr. Whipple is to blame?"

Kate sighed. "I don't know." She paused, deep in thought. "The law says a person is innocent until proven guilty, and we don't have any proof. Not yet, anyway. So we have to assume he's innocent."

"I guess so." Alex sighed.

"If he's innocent, then there must be some logical explanation for why the pretzels are flat," Kate said. "Maybe it's something simple." She paused, thinking of the problems she'd had with her Turbo Heat-Freeze today. *Hmm.* An interesting idea occurred. One she hadn't thought of before. She was just about to share it when Penny and Candy came running back into the booth, breathless.

"He. . .he. . .he saw us!" Candy's eyes were wide in fear. She ducked behind the booth.

"I thought we lost him on that last aisle, but I'm pretty sure he noticed us!" Penny said as she dove under the table.

"What? Who?" Kate looked down the aisle, shocked to find Mr. Whipple headed their way in a hurry!

From underneath the table, she felt Penny moving around. In fact, the whole table began to shake.

Mr. Whipple arrived looking a little winded. "Girls. . .have you seen Penny and Candy?"

"Oh, well, I. . ." Kate felt Penny's fingernails in her leg. She couldn't help but let out a little cry of "Ouch!"

The table continued to jiggle. Mr. Whipple stared at it, his eyes narrowing into slits. "Hmm." He looked down at the table, then up at Kate and Alex. "What's going on here?"

"Oh, well, to be honest. . ." Kate didn't know what to say next.

At that very moment, Penny let out a loud sneeze. Make that two loud sneezes. No, three.

"Aha." Mr. Whipple dropped to his knees then lifted the edge of the tablecloth, peering underneath the table. "Penny Bender! What are you doing under there?"

She crawled out, covered in dust bunnies, which she brushed off with her palms. "I was just, well, checking under the table to see if Kate had dropped anything."

"Sure you were." He shook his head. "If I didn't know any better, I would think you and your sister were avoiding me."

At this point, Candy stuck her head out from behind the booth.

"Who me?" she said.

"Yes, you." He gave them both puzzled looks. "What's going on here?"

Candy came out from behind the booth and stood next to her sister. Both had worried looks on their faces.

"Bud, I need to ask you a question," Penny said at last. "What in the world were you doing in my office this morning?"

"Your office?" His face turned a rosy shade. "Who, um, who told you I was in your office?"

"Never mind that." She crossed her arms at her chest and stared him down. "We can talk about that later. Right now I just need to know what you were doing in there. Were you snooping around?"

"Snooping around?" He shook his head. "Now, why would I want to be doing that, Penny? After all these years of working for you?"

"That's what I want to know," she countered. "So, fess up, Bud. What's up here? You're up to something."

His gaze shifted to the ground. "Well, you're right about that."

As he spoke, Kate's heart began to thump madly. Maybe he would confess right here and now! He would tell them what they all suspected. . . that he worked for the Benders and had been spying on the twins.

"Here's the truth, Penny," Mr. Whipple said. "I snuck into your office to leave a little present on your desk."

"A present?" She shook her head, the suddenly her eyes lit with recognition. "Oh, wait! Did you leave a little note on my desk? Something about having a happy day?"

His cheeks turned redder than before. "I did."

For a second he looked into her eyes, then his gaze shifted again and Kate could sense his embarrassment. "If you want the truth of it, Penny, I had another note I wanted to leave, but I chickened out, so I left that one instead."

"Another note?" She looked confused.

He nodded, then reached into his pocket and came out with a folded piece of paper. "This is it."

"Oh?" She reached out her hand and Kate watched as he placed the paper in her open palm. She noticed the trembling in his hand and wondered what the note said. Not that it was really any of her business, after all.

Penny unfolded the note, her mouth falling open as she read. Her eyes filled with tears, and she looked over at Mr. Whipple with the strangest expression.

"Bud. . ." Her voice cracked. "Did you really write this. . .for me?"

Now his eyes filled with tears. "I did, Penny. And it's long overdue. I should've written it years ago."

A smile as bright as the midafternoon sunshine lit Penny's face. She pressed the note to her chest and gazed at him with a hopeful expression. "And you really mean what you said here?"

"I do."

"Well then, I have something to say to you too!" She raced across the room and flung her arms around his neck, giving him a kiss on each cheek. "I love you too, Bud Whipple! I always have, and I always will!"

Kate's mouth flew open at this revelation. Mr. Whipple had left a *love* note in Penny's office? She started giggling and couldn't stop. Before long, Alex joined her. Then Penny and Bud followed.

Candy looked back and forth between them and then grinned. "Well, it's about time you two came to your senses. I've been telling you both for years that you were meant for each other. What took you so long?"

"I'm just old and foolish, I guess," Mr. Whipple said, raking his fingers through his thinning hair. "Don't know what took me so long, to be honest."

"I'm just set in my ways," Penny added. "Change has never been easy for me. I guess I thought that falling in love would change my life."

"Oh, it will." Mr. Whipple winked and she blushed. "But I hope you'll like the changes."

"Well, forever more." Candy leaned against the table, looking back and forth between Kate and Alex. "So, this explains what he was doing in Penny's office. Bud is officially off your list as a suspect, girls."

"A suspect?" He looked at them with wide eyes. "Has a crime been committed? Something I don't know about?"

"Well, we thought maybe you had something to do with the pretzels going flat," Alex explained.

"What makes you think that?"

"Oh, well, I. . ." Kate paused, wondering if the time had finally come to share what they knew. She finally worked up the courage. "Mr. Whipple, we found a picture of you in the newspaper, taken with the Bender brothers."

Penny gave him a concerned look. "Yes, you have some explaining to do, Bud. What's up with that? What are you doing conspiring with the enemy?"

"No, no, no. It's not like that at all. Let me explain. . ." His eyes filled with tears. "Ladies, I've known you both since we were kids. Known your brothers too. We all played together as children. Why, it breaks my heart that you aren't speaking to one another. It's just not right."

"So, you've been talking to our brothers?" Candy put her hands on her hips.

"And working for them behind our backs?" Penny glared at him.

He shook his head, looking more tired than ever. "If you want the truth of the matter, I've just been running interference. I've been praying about a way to see your family come back together again—to forget about the arguments of the past and start over."

"Start over?" Candy began to pace the room. "After what they did to us?"

Mr. Whipple shook his head. "Ladies, you might remember that I lost my sister a few months ago. She passed away after a long battle with cancer. I miss her so much. I'd do anything to have her back so we could have one more chat. . .one more hug." His eyes filled with tears. "Sometimes you don't realize how much you love someone until you don't have them anymore."

"Well, the door works both ways. If the boys wanted to talk to us, they would come here," Candy announced.

"That's why I've been going over there," Mr. Whipple said, gazing down. "I've been trying to convince them to make the first move. To come to you."

For a moment, Penny had a hopeful look in her eye. Just for a moment. It faded quickly as Mr. Whipple added, "But they're as stubborn as you two are."

"Well, how do you like that." Candy began to pace the room. "Now one of our employees calls us stubborn."

Kate wanted to chime in, but didn't. It wasn't her place. If the Lord wanted to teach the Twisted Twins a lesson about stubbornness, He could do it without her help! And it seemed like Mr. Whipple was doing a fine job on his own.

"I'm just asking that the two of you pray about this," he said. "Go ahead and fire me if you like. I'm old. I'd planned to retire soon, anyway."

"R—retire?" Penny looked shocked. "A—are you serious?"

"Well, of course." He nodded. "I'm sixty-five. My hands are stiff and sore after years of working. I've worked hard for you."

"He has, hasn't he?" Penny gazed at Mr. Whipple lovingly. "We have no complaints about your work, Bud. You've made our company what it is today."

"Thank you." He shook his head. "But it's hard to go on working under such tough circumstances, especially when I still love your brothers so much. They're my friends. Always have been, always will be."

At this point, Penny erupted. "I might as well tell you the whole truth."

"What is it, sister?" Candy asked.

"I'm just so tired of all of this," Penny said through her tears. "It's been years. Why can't we just put the past in the past where it belongs and get on with our lives?" She sniffled. "Will we ever be a family again or will we always be divided like this?"

"I don't know," Mr. Whipple said, drawing her into his arms. "But one thing is for sure. I don't want to start off our new life together with all of these problems hovering over us."

"Our new life together?" She gave him a hopeful look.

He gently brushed her cheek with the tip of his finger. "Yes. If you'll have me, Penny. I want you to be my wife." He looked around the exhibition hall and then turned back to her with a shrug. "Not a very romantic proposal, I suppose. And I don't even have a ring yet. But I'd be the happiest man on the planet if you would agree to marry me."

At this point Penny let out a whoop that was so loud it scared several people in nearby booths. Seconds later Candy joined in and then the girls added their squeals of celebration. Before long, people were gathered round, trying to figure out what had happened.

Kate watched it all in great amusement. Not only had she been wrong about Mr. Whipple's involvement with the flat pretzels. . .she had totally missed the obvious. He and Penny were in love. With a sigh, she looked at Alex and shrugged. "I don't mind telling you I'm glad we were wrong this time."

"No kidding." Alex's cheeks turned pink as Mr. Whipple gave Penny a kiss, right there in front of everyone in the place. "Being wrong isn't always bad."

Just then, Penny looked at Mr. Whipple sternly. "Just one more thing," she said, pointing her finger at him. "What did you mean when you said you were going to 'get' me?"

"What?"

"The girls said they overheard you in my office, saying you were going to 'get' me."

He laughed. "I meant I was going to win your heart, Penny. That's all."

Kate sighed with relief. She was happy she had misunderstood.

Everyone began to talk at once. Kate started to join in but found herself distracted. In the back of her mind she still had to wonder about those flat pretzels. Something. . .or someone. . .had caused them to go flat. And Kate only had one day left to figure it out! Looked like she'd better get busy!

Mending Fences

On the final morning of the competition, Kate awoke to discover the rain had finally stopped. She could hardly believe her eyes when she saw the sun streaming through the window.

"Awesome!" She sprang from the bed and looked out the window at the amusement park. "We'll get to ride the rides after all!"

Her heart raced with anticipation, especially as she looked at the big roller coaster. Oh, what fun she and Alex and Dexter would have. Finally!

Her mother laughed as Kate went on and on about the amusement park.

"I would think you would be more excited about the fact that they're going to announce the winner today," she said. "Isn't that why we came to Hershey, after all? So you and your invention could be showcased?"

Kate shrugged. "Honestly, mom. I don't really care about that. As long as God is happy with me and I've done my best, I already feel like a winner."

"Good for you," Her mother said, giving her a tight hug. "That's my girl. Now, let's get dressed and meet the others for breakfast."

Kate stood at the window another moment or so, noticing it had fogged up. Probably from all of the moisture and heat over the past few days. She took her finger and ran it across the glass, making a little smiley face. As she did, she thought about those flat pretzels once again.

"Hmm." Maybe the Twisted Twins hadn't been sabotaged at all. Maybe the answer was as simple as the smiley face now staring back at her.

"Kate, are you coming?" her mom called out.

"Y–yes." She wanted to sign onto the internet to do some research. If only she had the time! Then she could prove that her theory was right.

"We need to hurry up and get ready," her mother called out.

"Coming!" she hollered. She would simply have to do her research later. Hopefully she would have time before leaving the festival.

After getting dressed, Kate and her family met Alex and her parents in the dining room for a quick breakfast. While there, Kate tried to sign onto the internet on her watch, but couldn't get a signal.

"Everything okay?" Alex asked.

Kate sighed. "I'm just working on a theory, but I can't get technology to work with me. I'm having internet troubles."

"That's funny," Alex said. "You know more about technology than any of us!"

Kate just shrugged. They finished their breakfast and headed back to the exhibition hall for the final morning of the festival.

When they arrived at the booth, Alex lifted her video camera and pointed it at Kate.

"Just two more hours and they'll announce the winner," she said. "Are you nervous?"

"Nah." Kate shrugged. "Not really. I prayed about it last night, and I definitely believe God is in control. We don't always have to be winners to win His approval."

"Oh, I know," Alex said. "And I agree. But winning can be fun too." She gave Kate a little wink, then stopped recording.

Kate started pulling out the candies and pans, and then got busy making candy-covered pretzels. She didn't have any trouble with the chocolate today. . .none at all. This definitely confirmed her earlier suspicions. Yes, that smiley face was definitely a clue as to why the pretzels had gone flat over the past couple of days. But how—and when—would she prove it?

Her cell phone rang, and she smiled as she saw Elizabeth's number. Kate answered the phone with a cheerful, "Hello!"

"Hi, Kate," Elizabeth said. "I just wanted to let you know that I'm praying for you today."

"Thank you."

"How are things going over there?" Elizabeth asked. "Any more clues?"

"Maybe!" She told Elizabeth everything that had happened with Mr. Whipple. Then she talked about her most recent theory about what might have happened to make the pretzels flat.

"Oh Kate, that's probably it!" Elizabeth said.

"I wanted to sign onto the internet and do some research," Kate said with a sigh, "but I can't get a signal on my watch and using the laptop is out of the question because I'm at my booth in the exhibition hall. I need to pay attention to the people stopping by."

"Would you like me to research it?" Elizabeth asked. "I can call you back in a few minutes."

"That would be awesome," Kate said.

"You know, it's funny. . ." Elizabeth said, and then paused. "When we first met at camp, I didn't know much about the internet. You were the one! Just goes to show you how much we've learned from each other since we met."

"Yes, and you've always been the mother of our group, caring for all of us and praying," Kate said. "You've taught me that prayer is far more important than anything else I do." After hesitating a moment, she added, "I'm so glad you're my friend, Elizabeth."

"Same here."

They ended the call and Kate went back to work, making candy-covered pretzels for everyone who stopped by her booth.

About an hour before the big announcement, Candy and Penny returned to the exhibition hall wearing their pink uniforms. Mr. Whipple walked beside them. He couldn't seem to stop smiling. Kate didn't blame him. He had a lot to smile about! They stopped at Kate's booth, chattering a mile a minute.

"How are things going today, Kate?" Penny asked. "Better, I hope."

"Yes, it's been an awesome morning so far," Kate said. "The candy-covered pretzels are turning out fine."

She started to explain her theory about why their pretzels had gone flat, but the funny smile on Bud's face distracted her. Kate turned to face him, wondering what he was up to. Seconds later, Penny looked his way too.

"Are you smiling because you're happy?" Penny asked at last. "Or are you smiling because you're up to something?"

"Maybe a little of both." He grinned. "I have a surprise for you girls." He paused. "I hope you find it a pleasant surprise. I've brought someone to see you."

He gestured to the right and the crowd parted to reveal two men with silver hair.

Candy gasped and she whispered, "Donald! And Steve."

"We've come to see you, sisters," the taller one said with a hint of a smile. "At last."

Kate could hardly believe it. These must be the Bender brothers. They drew near and Penny flung her arms around their necks. "Oh brothers!"

Donald's eyes filled with tears. "This visit is about twenty years overdue. Can you ever forgive us for waiting so long?"

"Forgive you?" Candy shook her head. "We are just as much to blame.

I. . .I can't believe we let this silly competition between us go on for so long. Can you forgive two silly, stubborn old women?"

"Of course." Donald nodded and then Steve joined him.

Kate looked at the first brother, then the second one. Then she looked back at the ladies. Yes, she could definitely see a family resemblance. They all had green eyes and fair skin, and each one had matching smiles.

The brothers and sisters began to talk at once, making it difficult to follow the conversation. After a while, Kate stopped trying and just enjoyed their friendly chatter.

After a few moments, both of the Bender brothers looked her way. She waved.

"Who do we have here?" Donald asked. "One of the young inventors?"

"Oh yes," Candy said. "You won't believe how talented she is. Penny and I are sponsoring her in the competition."

"But you still haven't told me who she is." Donald extended his hand and Kate took it, giving it a warm shake. Oh, did it ever feel good to finally meet these two, especially now that she'd figured out they hadn't really sabotaged the pretzel factory!

Candy quickly introduced them. The taller of the men was Donald. The one with the crooked smile was Steve. Both looked like nice men. Kate especially liked Steve's long silver mustache and twinkling green eyes. He looked like a lot of fun.

The reunion between the brothers and sisters lasted for several minutes. Kate tried to keep an eye on the time. After all, the winner of the festival would be announced at noon. She wanted to chat with several passersby, but that was impossible with the Bender family directly in front of her table! She continued to make candy-covered pretzels, handing them to Donald and Steve as she went. At one point, Donald looked her way with an admiring smile.

"Wow. You made these?"

She nodded. "Yes, sir. I love using my Turbo Heat-Freeze."

He drew near to look at it more closely.

Kate spent the next few minutes telling him all about it. He looked impressed, especially when she got to the part where she was sharing about how fast it worked.

"That's amazing," he said when she finished. "Truly amazing. Our large machines take quite a long time to cook and then we always have to add time at the end of the process for the chocolate covering to cool down. People could get burned, otherwise."

"Yes, this is really interesting, Kate," Steve said. "We love seeing new technology at work."

Candy sighed as he said this. "I guess you boys still think Penny and I are old fuddy-duddies for wanting to do things the old-fashioned way."

"Not exactly," Donald said. "We know you care about quality and want to keep the pretzels just like they did when Pop was alive."

"He was always so much fun," Steve said. "What a great businessman he was too."

"Yes, he was always so willing to look at new ways to do things," Donald agreed.

Kate pursed her lips and stared at Donald suspiciously. "Old-fashioned is nice too," she said.

"Of course." He shook his head. "Listen, we're not going to try to argue with you about. . .well, about anything. We're tired of bickering. Very tired."

"Same here," Penny said. "It's exhausting."

"Remember what things were like when our parents ran the business?" Steve asked. "Remember the stories they told about losing the farm during the Depression? Remember how Pop started the pretzel factory on a wing and a prayer?"

"A wing and a prayer?" Alex asked. "What does that mean?"

"It means they had very little money in the bank," Candy explained. "Almost none. But Pop had a good idea." She paused as tears filled her eyes. "A great idea. And even though he didn't have much money, he took that great idea and turned it into a great business."

"A business that his children argued over," Steve said with a sad look on his face.

"And we've missed out on so much in each other's lives," Penny said, tears rolling down her wrinkled cheeks. "I don't know my brothers at all. . .or your wives and children."

"And grandchildren," Steve said, sitting behind her and pulling out his wallet. He began to show off pictures of his grandchildren. "This pretty little girl with the blond hair is Maddy. I always said she looked like you girls when you were little. Same blond hair and everything."

"Oh, what a little doll!" Penny sighed. "I can't believe I've let my anger and bitterness keep me from getting to know her. That's so sad."

"Sad for all of us," Steve said. "We're all to blame."

"I have grandchildren too," Candy said, reaching for her wallet to show off the photos. "You never really got to know my daughters and granddaughters, boys," she said. "But I think you would love them!"

"I'm sure we would," Steve said.

She started showing off her photos and before long everyone in the booth was laughing and having a wonderful time. Kate's parents arrived at the table with Alex's mom and dad. They looked on, smiling.

"Wow, they really have forgiven each other," Alex whispered. "It's. . . it's like a miracle, isn't it?"

"It's always a miracle when relationships are restored," Kate's mother said. "And God's heart is very happy when we put our differences behind us and mend fences."

Kate's heart began to pound as she looked at Phillip. She looked at her mom. "I, um, well, I guess I have a few fences in my own life that need mending."

Her mom smiled. "Ah, I see. Working things out with Phillip, right?"

Kate nodded. "Was it that obvious that we haven't been getting along?"

Her mother gave a little shrug. "A little obvious, I guess. But I've been paying attention because I could tell you both want to win the prize so badly."

"I don't care about winning anymore," Kate said. "Honestly, I just want things to be okay between us. Is that silly?"

"Of course not." Her mother pointed at the Bender brothers and sisters. "Do you think what's happening here is silly?"

"No way." Kate shook her head.

God always loves it when we reconcile with people, Kate."

"Reconcile?"

"You know. Make up. Get over our differences. God loves that."

Kate smiled. "I see."

Her mother reached to give her a hug. "You know, my mama used to have an old saying: 'Doesn't matter who started it. You be the one to end it.'"

Kate thought about that as Penny and Candy continued to chatter with their brothers. She looked up in time to hear Steve share something important.

"I've been walking with the Lord for a while now," Steve said, his gaze shifting to the ground. "And I know that I'm supposed to forgive others and move on. The Lord's been working with me on this."

"And me as well," Penny said. "I'm just a stubborn old woman."

"It's one thing to know what's right and another thing to actually do it," Candy said. "I guess we're all guilty of knowing but not doing."

"That happens, no matter how old you are," Kate's mother added. "I once quarreled with my best friend, and we didn't speak to each other for days."

"Same here," Alex's mother said. "Only, in my case, it was my mother. We argued over something silly and didn't talk for weeks. In fact, I can't even remember what it was, now that I think of it." She laughed. "Just goes to show you, in the long run the only thing that matters is forgiving and moving on."

Steve pursed his lips. "Sisters, we once argued about technology. Donald and I wanted to use newer, modern technology and you two girls wanted to stick with the old way of doing things."

Penny sighed. "That does lead to one little problem, something we haven't discussed."

"What's that?" Donald asked.

"For the past couple of days, our pretzels have been turning out flat. We can't figure out why."

"Oh, I know! I know what's been causing it!" Kate raised her hand, as if answering a teacher's question in school. She cried out, "It's the humidity!"

CHAPTER 13

The Pretzel Pickle

Penny stared at Kate, her mouth half-open. "The humidity has been causing our pretzels to fall flat? Are you sure, Kate?" She did not look convinced.

Kate nodded and started to say something. At that very moment, however, a text message came through on her phone. She had to laugh when she read Elizabeth's words: YOU WERE RIGHT! IT'S THE HUMIDITY!

"I've suspected as much all along," Mr. Whipple said. "Those machines are so old and outdated and they don't handle the changes in weather very well. I've been afraid to tell you because of the cost involved in getting new machines."

Penny sighed. "I'm so sorry, Bud. So, you're agreeing with our brothers that we need newer and bigger equipment?"

Bud nodded. "I'm afraid so."

"Well, I'm ready to admit that you are all right," Candy said with a grin. "What's the point of arguing?" She glanced at Penny. "Looks like we need to move into the twenty-first century, sister."

"Amen to that," Penny said. "Sounds good to me."

"The Bible says there's strength in numbers," Kate's mom said.

"I guess we *could* accomplish more working together," Candy said.

Steve gave Penny a sympathetic look. "We're not spring chickens anymore, are we?"

Penny and Candy shook their heads.

"Spring chickens?" Dexter asked. "What does that mean?"

"He means they're not as young as they once were," Kate said. "He's trying to say they're getting older."

"That would explain their white hair and wrinkles," Dex whispered back.

Kate stifled a snicker.

"My sons have been working at our factory for years now," Donald said. "I've been thinking about retiring soon."

"Funny you should say that," Candy said. "I've been giving some thought to retiring, myself."

"Same here," Penny admitted. "Especially now that Bud and I are getting married."

"Getting married?" Donald looked stunned.

Everyone began to talk at once, congratulating Bud and Penny on their engagement.

"We're going to want to go on a long honeymoon," Bud said. "And Candy can't run the factory by herself when we're gone."

Steve began to pace back and forth in front of the booth.

"I have an idea," he said. "What if we struck a business deal?"

"Business deal?" A look of curiosity passed over Candy's face. "What do you mean?"

"What if we merged our family businesses and let our grown children take over running them?"

"Really?" Candy's eyes misted over.

"Sure," Steve said. "My wife has been begging me to take her on a cruise."

"I'm sure my wife would love it too," Donald said. "She's been after me for years to travel, but I've been too busy."

"But. . .how would this work?" Candy asked. "Which factory would remain open and which would we close?"

"Why not leave both open?" Steve said. "Your daughters can run one, and our boys can run the other. But they'll be one big happy family, and the business will be a joint venture." He gave her a hopeful look. "What do you think, sis? Agreed?"

Candy and Penny looked at each other, then back at their brothers with a smile. "Agreed."

"If we're merging our two businesses, we'll need a new name," Candy said. "What do you suggest?"

"I guess we'll have to think about that," Steve said. "We don't need to decide everything today."

"True." Penny nodded. "We have all the time in the world, now that we're. . ." Tears filled her eyes. "Now that we're getting along."

They began to talk about the ins and outs of the pretzel-making business, and before long Kate was distracted.

Kate looked over at Phillip, who stood alone in his booth. "Do you mind if I leave for a minute, Mom?"

"Of course not. You go right on over there and talk to him, honey."

Kate put a few candy-covered pretzels on a plate then drew in a deep breath as she took a few steps toward Phillip. He stiffened and looked the other way.

Kate didn't let that stop her. "Phillip, would you like a pretzel?"

"No."

She sighed and put the plate down on his table. "Well, can we talk for a minute?"

He turned with a sour look on his face. "About what?"

"I think it's time we put the past in the past," she said. "I know you're mad at me for winning the science fair at school."

"Who cares about a dumb science fair? That's nothing. I am going to beat you this time, Kate Oliver," Phillip said, his eyes narrowing into slits. "Just watch and see."

For a minute she felt like arguing, but just as quickly felt the gentle voice of the Holy Spirit whisper, *"Stop."*

She suddenly found herself feeling very calm and confident.

"Why is it always so important, Phillip?' she asked. "I mean, really. Why do we keep doing this?"

His expression softened for a moment and she half-expected him to say, "I don't know." Instead, he just shrugged and said, "I like to win. I want to be the one to come out on top, that's why."

Kate thought about what Penny and Candy had said about living in a dog-eat-dog world and almost giggled. So, Phillip wanted to be top dog. But she knew the Lord had a better plan.

"We've always competed against each other to see who would be the best student each semester at school," Kate said. "We've been doing that for years."

He shrugged again. "So what?"

She sighed. "So, I'm tired of competing. I'm a good student and you're a good student. Instead of always trying to outdo each other, we could be working together."

Phillip looked like he didn't quite believe her. "What do you mean by that?"

"I mean, instead of working against each other, trying to prove who's best, we could work together. After all, we both want the same things—to make our parents proud. To go to a great college someday. To get good jobs when we grow up."

"Right." He didn't look convinced.

"So, instead of fighting all the time over who's better, why don't we start studying together?"

"Studying together?"

"Sure, why not. I'm sure you have a lot to teach me." She grinned. "And who knows. Maybe I have a few things to teach you too."

He smiled for just a moment then shrugged. "Maybe. Who knows."

Kate stuck out her hand, hoping he would shake it. "So, is it a deal? Can we get over this crazy competition stuff and just work together?"

For a second, Phillip hesitated. Then, finally, he stuck out his hand and grabbed hers, firmly shaking it. "Deal."

Kate's heart grew so happy, she wanted to sing and dance right there on the exhibition floor. She reached for the plate and offered him a candy-covered pretzel, which he popped into his mouth.

"Yum."

"Yeah, they're good, aren't they?" She laughed. "I've been eating pretzels for days. You would think I'd be sick of them, but I'm not."

He reached for another. "They're great, Kate."

She giggled at his rhyme. Off in the distance, Kate saw Emma and Rachel looking her way with a smile. On the other side, she saw her mom nodding and grinning. Looked like everyone was happy that she and Phillip were finally going to be friends.

Just then a booming voice came over the loudspeaker. "Ladies and gentlemen!" the voice said. "The big moment has arrived. Would everyone please gather in the banquet hall for the announcement of our Young Inventors' Festival winner!"

Kate looked at Phillip and he looked back. For a moment, she saw a flicker of competition in his eyes. Then just as quickly, he relaxed and grinned.

"Let's get this over with," he said with a crooked smile. "I want to go to the amusement park. What about you?"

"You bet!" she practically shouted.

Clear Skies Ahead!

As soon as the luncheon ended, Kate sat at the table, waiting for the big announcement. She remembered the dream she'd had and couldn't help but smile. Though it might've seemed fun to win in the dream, in real life she had to admit that it seemed. . .well, impossible!

Finally the moment came. As Mr. Carmichael walked to the podium, Kate looked at Emma and waved. Then she glanced at Phillip who smiled shyly. Finally!

Mr. Carmichael tapped the microphone with his finger and the people in the room stopped talking.

"The time has come at last," he said with a nod. "We are ready to announce this year's winner of the Young Inventors' Festival." He paused to grin at the contestants. "Let me start by saying how proud we are of each and every one of you. Your inventions are amazing. I can only imagine how creative you will be when you're grown up!"

Kate smiled at her dad, who winked.

"Without further ado. . ." Mr. Carmichael opened a large envelope and paused as he looked at its contents. At once his face lit into a smile.

"Well, this has never happened before." He glanced out at the audience. "Ladies and gentlemen, apparently we have a tie."

A gasp went up from the crowd.

"For the first time in the history of our competition, the judges could not decide between these top two competitors." He lifted the paper and read the two names aloud. "Phillip Johnson, for his invention of the Weather-Cast Watch!"

Kate began to clap so loudly, she almost didn't hear the next name. "And Kate Oliver, for her invention, the Turbo Heat-Freeze!"

"W–what?" She looked over at Alex, stunned.

"He called your name, silly!" Alex said. "Go to the stage and get your trophy, Kate!"

She rose and took a few shaky steps forward, smiling as she reached Phillip's side.

"Can you believe it?" he whispered as they walked toward the stage. "We tied."

She laughed. "It's the perfect ending to years of competition, wouldn't you say?"

He nodded and gestured for her to enter the stage first. As she did, she heard Dexter call out her name: "Kate! Kate Oliver!" She led the way to the center of the stage where Mr. Carmichael waited with her trophy in hand.

"Job well done, Kate!" he said, as he passed the trophy to her.

"T–thank you, sir."

"Fine job, son," he said, giving the second trophy to Phillip.

"T–thanks," Phillip responded.

For a second, Kate stood on the huge stage with an overhead spotlight nearly blinding her. She waved at her parents, her heart soaring with excitement as her dad's thunderous applause rang out.

"Kate and Phillip, we would like you both to say a few words," Mr. Carmichael said.

She tiptoed to reach the microphone behind the podium, then spoke, her voice quivering.

"T–thank you so much for giving me this award." She held up the huge trophy with the words BEST YOUNG INVENTOR engraved on it and the audience members cheered once again.

"I. . .I'm so grateful," she continued. "I accept it on behalf of all of the young inventors around the globe!"

She turned to Mr. Carmichael and smiled. "And thanks to the committee for giving me this honor, which I share with my good friend, Phillip Johnson. I pray the Turbo Heat-Freeze is the first of many more inventions to come!"

As she stepped back, Mr. Carmichael gestured for Phillip to speak.

"I am honored to tie for first place with my friend, Kate Oliver, and I'm so grateful to the committee for allowing me the privilege of competing."

As soon as Kate heard the word "competing," she thought of the Twisted Twins. Thank goodness their story had ended well. So had hers. She could hardly wait to see what was next!

Mr. Carmichael stepped to the microphone and faced the crowd. "One more round of applause for Kate Oliver and Phillip Johnson, our young inventors of the year!"

The crowd members rose as their applause grew louder. Kate felt her cheeks turn warm with embarrassment. Never in her wildest dreams had she ever imagined standing here, in front of so many people! And what an honor. . .to win the award of inventor of the year!

"Three cheers for Kate! Three cheers for Kate!" rang out from the front row of the audience. She smiled at her parents, who sat with her little brother, Dexter, at their side. She waved back, nearly tripping as she turned to walk to the edge of the stage. As she did, cameras flashed, people taking her picture all at once. She walked down the steps, nearly dropping her large trophy.

"Careful, Kate," she whispered to herself. "You don't want to fall in front of thousands of people!"

Hmm. Hadn't she dreamed all of this? It seemed so real now, especially as she stumbled on the bottom stair! Thankfully, Phillip caught her before she fell. My, how things had changed!

People swarmed around her as she walked back to her seat, and as the event ended, people surrounded her, offering congratulations. Still, in spite of their kind words, she just had one thing on her mind.

"Mom, can we go to the amusement park now?"

Her mother glanced down at her and grinned. "I guess you have waited awhile for this moment, haven't you? And you did tell me just this morning how much you were looking forward to it."

"Mm-hmm." Kate nodded, then looked at Alex and Dexter. "Are you two ready for the sooperdooperLooper?"

"Am I ever!" Dexter hollered, then turned and sprinted toward the door. He turned back to grin at Kate.

"You won your prize," he said, pointing at the trophy. "Now I get mine!"

"Your prize?"

"The roller coaster! Woo-hoo!" He took off running again.

Kate looked back at Phillip, who stood alongside his parents, talking. She walked his way.

"Phillip?"

He looked at her with a smile. "Hey, Kate."

"Hey. We're going to the amusement park. What about you?"

He looked at his parents, who nodded.

"Sure." Phillip grinned. "What are you riding first?"

"The roller coaster, of course!" She laughed. "My brother's probably halfway there by now. He's waited for days for this!"

"Me too," Phillip said. "To be honest. . ." He leaned down to whisper the rest, "I've been more excited about going to Hersheypark than being in the competition."

"Me too!" Kate said. "And my brother feels the same way."

A short time later, all three families arrived at the amusement park. The kids headed straight for the roller coaster. As they drew near, Kate paused.

"Great technology," her father said, looking up at the monstrosity of a roller coaster. "Look at how smooth it is. Not jerky at all."

"Great design," Phillip added. "Very impressive."

"You know, for someone so young, you know a lot about how things work," Kate's father said, giving Phillip an admiring look. "Why some of my robotics students haven't even figured out the dynamics of roller coasters yet."

"Really?" Phillip looked pleased. "You teach robotics, Mr. Oliver?"

"I can't believe I didn't tell you!" Kate said. "I'm always bragging on my dad. He teaches at Penn State."

"No way." Phillip's mouth opened in stunned silence. "My parents graduated from Penn State, and they've got their hearts set on me going there someday." He gave Kate's father a happy look. "Who knows. Maybe someday you'll be my professor."

"He's the best one in the world," Kate said.

"How would you know that?" Her father reached over to give her a hug. "You've never been in my class."

Kate paused and shook her head, knowing better. "Dad, I've been in your class every day of my life." She giggled. "You're teaching, whether you're at work or at home. You're the smartest man I know and it shows in everything you do."

"Apparently a lot of that spilled over onto Kate," Phillip said. "She's the smartest girl in our school."

Kate felt her cheeks warm in embarrassment. This was the first time she'd ever heard Phillip compliment her and it felt funny. Good, but funny. She whispered a shy, "Thanks," then added, "and Phillip is the smartest boy."

"Well, if you're both so smart, why are you standing around talking when you could be riding the roller coaster?" Dexter asked with a groan. "Let's go!"

"Okay, okay!" Kate took him by the hand and, with Alex and Phillip on their heels, headed straight for the prize.

CHAPTER 15

Lessons Learned

Later that afternoon, Kate said goodbye to Alex. As they hugged goodbye, she whispered, "I'm going to miss you so much!" into her friends ear.

"Same here," Alex said. "I always have so much fun when I'm with one of the Camp Club Girls."

"Me too." Kate sighed. "Next time we'll invite the others to come to Hershey with us. Can you imagine how much Bailey would love the chocolate?"

"No kidding! And Sydney would be running laps around the park. You know how energetic she is." Alex giggled.

"Yes, and Elizabeth would be keeping an eye on all of us to make sure we were safe," Kate added.

They went on talking until Kate's mom drew near. "We really have to go now, honey. It's quite a long ride home, and Alex and her parents have to get to the airport to catch their flight back home."

"Okay." Kate sighed. After a few more giggles and grins, she and Alex finally parted ways, agreeing to text each other when they got home.

By the time Kate, Biscuit, and Dexter got into the van with their parents, it was almost five o'clock in the evening. Thankfully the sun was still out. She sent a quick email from her watch to the Camp Club Girls, thanking them for their help. Within minutes, all had responded. It was the perfect ending to a great day.

As they drove along, Kate looked out the window. Pretty soon, they passed through Amish country and she thought about something.

"Oh no!"

"What is it?" her mother asked.

"I forgot to say goodbye to Emma and Rachel."

"You can always send them an email," her mother said.

"No, you don't understand," Kate explained. "Emma and Rachel are Amish. They don't use email."

"Oh, I see." Her mother smiled. "Well, the competitors' addresses were on a list we received the first day. I have it in my bag. Maybe you can write them an old-fashioned letter."

"An old-fashioned letter?" Kate grinned. "That sounds like fun."

Her mom chuckled. "Yes, that's how we used to do it. . .back in the old days. We didn't have email when I was your age, you know. In fact, we didn't even have the internet."

Kate shook her head. She could hardly believe it! What did people do without the internet?

Up ahead of their car, a black Amish buggy plodded along. This time Kate took a close look inside. The man wore a dark suit and hat. He looked their way with a nod.

"You know," Kate said, "I've been thinking about something, Mom. At our house we have all sorts of technology. Computers. Cell phones. GPS tracking systems. A robotic vacuum cleaner. All of my gadgets and gizmos. You name it, we have it. But here in the Amish community, they don't have any of those things and they are as happy as can be."

Her mother smiled. "You're right about that."

"Here's a project for you kids," her father said. "Today, as we drive home, close the computer and pay attention to your surroundings. Don't use the phone. Don't text your friends. Just look around you and see what you notice."

Kate wasn't sure she could do it! She thought about Sydney's nickname for her: Inspector Gadget. Could she really do without her stuff for a little while?

"I'll try," she said at last. Kate looked out the window, noticing the green fields to her right. "Oh wow. That's really pretty."

"Yes, of all the things that man has invented—and they are many—they can't even compare to the beauty of God's creation." Her mother smiled. "All of your gadgets and gizmos are great, honey. And so is your Turbo Heat-Freeze. But the greatest inventions of all aren't the ones we've made. . .they're the ones *God* has made."

Kate looked out the car window, suddenly realizing just how green the fields were and how blue the sky was.

"Wow," she whispered. "I never noticed it before. And look at that barn, Mom. It's so white. She pointed at a tall round thing she didn't recognize. "And what is that?"

"That's a silo," her father explained. "Grain is stored there."

"I wonder what it would be like to be Amish for a day," Kate said. "Just one day without television or the internet."

"Or cars or cell phones," her mother added.

"Or video games," her father added.

Dexter looked shocked at that one! "Really? No video games? What do they do for fun?"

Their mother laughed. "They talk to each other, silly. And play games. Real games. In other words, they enjoy each other's company."

Dexter looked out the window, shrugging as he saw several dairy cows. "It would be hard to live without video games."

"What about electricity?" Kate asked. That would be even harder! Can you imagine?" She wrinkled her nose. "How would you blow-dry your hair?"

"If you were Amish for a day, you wouldn't pay much attention to your hair," her mother said. "In fact, the Amish care very little about trying to outdo one another with their clothes or hair styles. They're not competitive people at all."

"They don't believe in comparing one person to another," her father said.

"Is that why they dress alike?" Kate said.

"Yes." Her mother nodded. "You know, being competitive isn't all bad. It's fun to be involved in sports and competitions. But when you get to the point where you're always competing with others—to look better, to get better grades, to get into better schools—then something is wrong. It's especially wrong for Christians to act that way. We're all one body, the body of Christ. We should be building each other up, not trying to outdo each other."

"I've definitely learned that lesson this week!" Kate said.

She started to reach for her bag so that she could read that scripture on her text reader, but suddenly remembered she wasn't using any of her gadgets for the rest of the day. *Hmm.* She would have to work hard to remember it. Or. . . Suddenly she had a great idea.

"Mom, can I borrow your Bible?"

"Sure, honey." Her mother passed the Bible back to Kate and she looked up the verse. Kate couldn't help but smile as she read Romans 12:3: *"Because of the privilege and authority God has given me, I give each of you this warning: Don't think you are better than you really are. Be honest in your evaluation of yourselves, measuring yourselves by the faith God has given us."*

Yes, she had certainly learned that lesson.

Leaning back against the seat, she whispered a prayer of thanks to God for showing her that, in His eyes, all of His children are equal.

Working Together!

About three months after the Young Inventors' Festival, Kate received a letter—the old-fashioned kind—from Emma. She grinned as she read the words.

> *Dear Kate,*
> *Rachel and I had so much fun with you! It was great to meet you. Thank you for being so nice to us. I'm so glad you and Phillip won the competition. I forgot to ask my mamm to bring you a slice of shoo-fly pie on the last day of the competition, so I thought you might like the recipe. You will find it at the end of this letter. I am so happy to be your friend.*
>
> *Emma*

"Wow." Kate glanced at the bottom of the letter and read the recipe for the shoo-fly pie. She could hardly wait to show it to her mother. Maybe she would make it soon!

Right now, she needed to write back! Kate scribbled out a quick letter and put it in an envelope. "Mom, do you have a stamp?"

"I think so." Her mother looked in the drawer and came out with a stamp. "Are you writing to your friends?"

"Yes." Kate nodded. "And I need to write to Penny and Candy too. It's been ages since I heard from them!"

She went to the computer and signed online. Ironically, she found a note from the Twisted Twins in her email box! Kate opened it and smiled when she read it.

> *Dear Kate,*
> *We've retired! Candy and I are writing this email from*